The Way We WIN

USA TODAY BESTSELLING AUTHOR

TIA LOUISE

Dedication

"Find someone who grows flowers in the
darkest parts of you." —ZB

For everyone waiting for Jack & Allie's romance,
I hope you love them as much as I do 🩶

THE BRADFORD FAMILY

Arthur Sage Bradford & Lucille (née Knox)

Jack & Allie

Zane & Rachel

Garrett & Liv

Hendrix & Raven

Dylan & Logan

Edward Wells
Sage Bradford

Hayden "Haddy"
Bradford

Gina "Gigi" Bradford

Austin Sinclair
Kimmie Joy Bradford
Knox Bradford

Maverick Murphy

Playlist

"Why Not Me" - The Judds
"Fire Woman" - The Cult
"Great Balls of Fire" - Jerry Lee Lewis
"Strawberry Wine" - Deana Carter
"II MOST WANTED" - Beyoncé, Miley Cyrus
"Something To Talk About" - Bonnie Rait
"Burning Down the House" - Talking Heads
"Cowboy Take Me Away" - The Chicks
"monsters" - Ella Langley
"You Put a Spell on Me" - Austin Giorgio
"Lips On You" - Maroon 5
"Ride" - Chase Race, Macy Maloy
"Caution" - The Killers
"Ring of Fire" - Johnny Cash
"Soulmate" - Chanin
"Eternal Flame" - The Bangles

Prologue

Jack

GRAY SKIES SPREAD OVER THE BAY ALL THE WAY PAST DAUPHIN ISLAND as we look southwest. Thomas stands in front of us holding a large blue envelope. It's made of heavy, biodegradable paper, and a white sea turtle sits on top of it.

It's Dad.

The thought hits me like a fist in the chest, but I swallow that sob. With a blink, I look down and hold it together. My four siblings stand in a line beside me. We're all in suits and ties except for Dylan. She's wearing a navy dress that hangs to her calves and blows in the wind.

Her dark hair is pulled away from her face in one of those skinny bows, and she rests her head on Miss Gina's shoulder as she openly weeps.

Miss Gina slides her hand up and down my little sister's arm, and I realize it's the first time I've seen that old lady cry. Her blind eyes are typically glittering with joy when we're around, but today they shine with empathetic tears as she holds my sister.

We're in a line from oldest to youngest with me at the top. Zane is beside me, his dark hair moving in the nonstop breeze. He's not smiling, but he's not crying. His eyes follow Thomas as he walks slowly to the water's edge.

Zane never talks about how he feels. He's the quiet brother, who wears his dark hair long over his eyes and who prefers to drift down to the stables south of town and care for the horses. But he doesn't have to tell me. I know.

Garrett stands a head taller at Zane's side. His expression is stoic, but his girlfriend Liv is beside him touching her eyes with a tissue every few minutes. The wind pushes her long, strawberry-blonde hair behind her shoulders, and her dark red dress clings to her legs. She'll take care of him.

My youngest brother Hendrix is doing his best to stand up straight and not cry. He almost breaks me when he drops his chin and shoves a fist across his cheek. He tries real hard to be as big as the three of us elders, but at thirteen going on fourteen, he's just a kid.

We didn't talk as I helped him tie his necktie this morning, as I helped him fix his collar at the back of his blazer. We just lost Mom less than a year ago, and now this.

That leaves our "baby" sister Dylan, eighteen months younger than Hendrix. She's sassy and spoiled by all of us—always bright, always shining and optimistic. I can't even look at her or I'll lose it, and they need me to keep it together.

They're all looking up to me now.

People want to say our dad died of a broken heart, that he couldn't keep going after losing the love of his life, but I'm not so sure.

Dad would've stuck around for us. He wouldn't have wanted to leave the five of us orphans. The truth is, after Mom's sudden diagnosis and rapid decline, we all saw the extent of our dad's illness as well.

She covered for him, but the effects of his long career as a legendary quarterback during a time in the industry when safety wasn't a priority and players pushed through things like concussions and traumatic brain injuries had taken a toll.

Losing Mom was a hit he couldn't push through.

Which brings us here, on this gray day, to grant his last wish to be put to rest in the beloved ocean down the hill from our sprawling family home and restaurant.

Thomas holds the envelope with the turtles on top. It's a fitting vessel to send our dad on his journey.

He knew Dad better than any of us. The two of them were teammates for the Texas Mustangs their entire careers. They were the dream team until Dad retired. Then when Thomas stopped playing, Dad brought him here to our small, south-Alabama community to be the head chef at Cooters & Shooters, our family restaurant on the coast.

He's been with us since Dylan was a baby, and now, with me not quite twenty-one, he's stepped up to get us through the gap.

Miss Gina greased a few palms as well to keep the state from taking Hendrix and Dylan away—or sending them to live with relatives in Birmingham. Nobody wanted to be the jerk who broke up the family of Art Bradford, football legend and small-town hero.

Thing is, I was just drafted by the Texas Mustangs to be their new starting quarterback. I'm graduating a year early, and the contract is burning a hole in my pocket.

Dad would be so proud, but I'm not sure what happens now.

"We'll never forget Art's sense of humor…" Thomas's deep voice draws our attention.

He's also wearing a dark suit, and his large, brown hands hold the thick envelope with the care of a dear friend. *Best running back in the game,* Dad would say. *I'd trust Tommy with my life.*

It was only right for him to hold him in death.

"He loved you kids more than anything." Thomas slides his light brown eyes down the line of my siblings. "Jack, he knew you could step into his shoes, or he would've held on longer. You got this."

My jaw tightens, and I swallow the thickness in my throat,

giving him a brief nod. Stepping into his shoes is exactly what I'm doing, in more ways than one.

"Zane, you're going to help your brother Jack take the lead, and Garrett, you keep protecting the little ones."

The muscle in Garrett's square jaw moves. He's got his game face on as he nods briefly.

"Your dad loved football, and he'll always be remembered for his accomplishments. But his proudest accomplishment was you five. He'll be watching you from above, standing at your mama's side. Don't let him down."

Hendrix inhales sharply, and Dylan and Liv simultaneously reach for his hands.

"His spirit lives on in you." Thomas looks into my eyes. "We'll always remember the good times, and we'll think of him now, reunited with the ones who went before."

He's at the water's edge, and he bends a knee to place the blue packet on the waves. "Ashes to ashes, and dust to dust. We release you to the beautiful waters you loved."

Standing on the edge of the bay, my eyes lock on that white sea turtle as it drifts farther out, where it will swirl into the tide and continue to eternity.

I realize every muscle in my body is tight when Dylan's arms go around my waist. Releasing the death-grip of my arms crossed over my chest, I wrap them around her.

Another pair of arms wraps around my side, and I realize Hendrix has come to me as well. Garrett follows, putting a hand on my shoulder, and Zane turns his head to give me a sad smile.

He's staying close, at least, attending a small private college not far from Newhope. Garrett has one more year of high school before he moves to Tuscaloosa. Holding my family, I inhale a shaky, fortifying breath.

Thomas returns to where we're standing, takes one look at our huddle, and gives me a satisfied smile.

I'm the oldest. I'm the leader. When we were kids, and we'd

have chores or we'd play scrimmage in the park, Dad would say I was team captain.

I wonder if he knew then what he was preparing me to be.

Either way, I know who I am. I know what's expected of me, and I'll carry us through this. Protection, family, leadership… it's what I do.

Chapter 1

Allie

Present day

"WHERE DO YOU TAKE A BOOK ON A DATE?" KIMMIE JOY BRADFORD wrinkles her nose as she lifts a paperback wrapped in brown paper and tied with an elaborate red bow off the shelf.

We're well into teacher prep days, getting ready for the new school year to start, and she and Edward Wells are helping me set up the library.

It's become our tradition since my son Austin started high school and joined the football team three years ago.

Jack Bradford is head coach of the Newhope High Captains, and as we're both single parents working at the high school, we've developed this little trade-off situation. His daughter Kimmie stays with me while Austin attends summer football camp with him.

It's Austin's senior year, and his first year as starting quarterback. He's been working toward this goal since he went out for the team as a freshman. I can't believe three years have already passed so quickly.

Jack took him under his wing, training with him on the weekends, working with him every summer and fall. I've done my best not to fawn all over him for being so good to my only child, but it certainly doesn't help that while he's quiet and stern, he's also kind and attentive.

Jack's a former quarterback himself, a football superstar in Texas, and sex on wheels. At six-two with a square jaw, dark hair, and sapphire-blue eyes, my breath catches sometimes when he looks at me.

His little sister Dylan befriended us when we moved here from New Orleans. I'd landed the job as high school librarian, and Austin was a quiet middle schooler.

We had little money and no family to speak of, so she asked if I could be head waiter at their family's restaurant on the bay, Cooters & Shooters.

She claimed they needed more help in the summer, and since I'd waited tables in the French Quarter to pay my way through college, a sprawling family restaurant in a small, south Alabama town was a piece of cake.

Dylan also recruited Austin to babysit Kimmie, who was still in preschool at the time, and we were both grateful for the extra income.

Working in the library, sharing my favorite books with the students, helping them find new authors to love, and all the things library-related make me so happy. The job has great benefits, great hours, great holidays… and very little pay.

It's hard to afford rent, a car payment, groceries, and save for college—or anything else—on a high school librarian's salary, so working at the restaurant helps a lot. It also introduced us to a whole family of new friends.

I picked up Edward a few years ago when his sister Rachel moved here to be the new nurse for Miss Gina Rosario. Miss

Gina is this rich old blind lady who lives north of town in a gor-geous, Italian-style villa overlooking the bay.

She's sort of everyone's honorary grandmother, and I think she might be a little psychic—or maybe that's just the New Orleans in me. Wise old ladies always seem to know things be-fore they happen.

Edward is mildly neurodivergent, and Rachel had been so worried about him starting at a new high school and not know-ing anybody.

Jack's brother Zane thought helping me would be a good way for him to establish a familiar, quiet place if he needed it, and after how good they've always been to me, I said yes so fast…

That bit of kindness (along with some pretty intense chem-istry) is why Zane is now Rachel's husband.

It's a win for me, too, because Edward is one of my best li-brary aides. I'm pretty sure he's read every book on the shelves.

"You take the book from the library, but the book actually takes you on the date." I try to explain the concept in a way a second-grader will understand.

Kimmie's little face only squints harder. "But how does it do that? Books can't drive."

"When you read the book, the story takes you on a journey in your mind." I boop her button nose, channeling my inner el-ementary-school teacher.

It's been years since I worked with her age group, but it all comes back.

"It's a metaphor." Edward's logical voice joins our conver-sation. "It could even qualify as *anthropomorphism*, since you're attributing human behavior to an inanimate object."

Pressing my lips together, I watch Kimmie's amber eyes widen. She nods, pretending very hard to understand all the big words he just said.

Ever since Edward called her *Kim*, she acts very mature whenever he explains anything. It's hilariously cute.

"Here, sweetie." I hand her a stack of die-cut cards with the words *Romance*, *Adventure*, and *Sci-Fi* printed on them. "Put the red labels on the top shelves, the yellow on the middle, and the blue on the bottom."

I got this idea from social media—where I get all my ideas. The students pick a book and get points for reading that add up to prizes like a Starbucks gift card or a free car wash or whatever else I can get local businesses to donate.

Yes, it's bribery, and I've done my best to choose old and new titles in different genres. Our school library serves grades 7-12, which is a tough mix, but as a certified bookworm myself, I enjoy the challenge of trying to hook even the most reluctant readers.

"I can't believe you're already in second grade," I say as Kimmie takes the labels off my fingers, ready to march them over to the shelves. "It seems like last year you were starting kindergarten."

"That was three years ago, Miss Allie," she says, still acting like a small grown-up. "I never take a nap at school now, and we won't even drop sticks this year."

"What does it mean to drop sticks?" It's Edward's turn to be confused.

"If you don't walk in the line straight or if you forget to take your tray to the window after lunch or if you talk during reading circle…" Kimmie counts on her fingers. "You have to drop a stick. First grade was hard, but now that I'm in second grade, I do everything right."

"What happens if you don't?" He's completely serious, not a hint of a tease.

She hesitates at his question, then shrugs. "I just will!"

Again, I fight a laugh at these two.

I really love everything about my job, and lately, it's the one thing distracting my brain from the very real fear pressing against my temples any time I'm alone with my thoughts.

Less than a month ago, I got the text alert on my phone

I've been dreading since we fled New Orleans: my ex-husband, Austin's father, is out on parole in Louisiana.

Rip Sinclair is the worst mistake I've ever made.

I was so young and stupid when he pulled up to the Sister's Court restaurant in his leather jacket and motorcycle and tattoos and glittering green eyes.

I had no sense of self-preservation, and like a child, I believed when I got pregnant, we were supposed to get married.

Rip believed once we got married, Austin and I became his property. No matter how many laws he broke or how dangerous his life dealing drugs became, in his mind, we belonged to him.

One night, I got him drunk enough to sign the divorce papers, which was the only reason the state was able to make me testify against him in court.

I wanted to wash my hands of the whole situation and walk away clean. Instead, the last words he said to me when they took him away were "This isn't over."

So I set up the alert on my phone, and I can't help looking over my shoulder. Still, I've tried to act like everything is normal… And I had a house alarm installed.

My chest is tense and my shoulders ache. I know that asshole better than anyone, and if he said it, he'll do it. I don't know when or how, but I know he's looking for us.

I hope by moving here and staying off social media, we're hidden. At least we're out of state.

I chose Newhope because friends would talk about it like it was the best place in the world. It's a beautiful small town on the coast with flower boxes on every window and trees that light up with twinkle lights every night like a promise, a hope of a better life.

Then Dylan became my friend, and now we're practically part of the family. Still, it's not a guarantee of safety.

Stepping back, I cross my arms, evaluating the library. "I think we're ready for prime time."

"Prime time is typically between the hours of 8 and 10 p.m.," Edward notes.

Smiling, I carefully place my hand on the top of his shoulder, doing my best not to crowd him. "You're right. We're ready for *school* time."

The serious expression on his face relaxes. "It's a very nice display."

"Thank you, Edward."

"Thank me, too!" Kimmie skips up, having neatly placed the cards I gave her on the shelves. "I helped!"

"Thank you, too, Miss Kim!" I give her a squeeze, and she lifts her chin with a proud smile. "Now, who's ready for lunch?"

They both light up, and I grab my bag. We'll lock up and head to Cooters & Shooters for lunch and to check in with everybody.

"Raven wants to bring Haddy home for Halloween." Dylan is in the kitchen reading the face of her iPad Pro when we arrive.

Her brother Hendrix is a tight end for the Los Angeles Tigers, and he and his wife Raven and their two-year-old daughter Haddy all live in LA.

"Hey, baby Haddy!" Kimmie runs to the counter, bouncing on her toes and waving at the screen.

"It's a group chat, Peanut, not FaceTime." Dylan leans down to kiss the top of her niece's head.

Kimmie's shoulders drop, and she frowns up at her. "How long until Halloween?"

"October thirty-first," her aunt replies.

Kimmie looks like a mini-Dylan with their matching amber eyes and curly, dark brown hair.

"She wants to know all our favorite movies so she can put together a girls' movie night," Dylan continues.

"That sounds fun!" I take lunch fixings out of the industrial-sized refrigerator. "How about grilled cheese sandwiches with grapes and apple slices for lunch?"

"Not with Aunt Deedee's spicy cheese." Kimmie's face scrunches.

"Got it." I put the pepper jack back in the fridge. "Only sharp cheddar—sound good, Edward?"

He enters the room through the screen door at the back of the kitchen. A gray cat is against his chest, and he pets it slowly.

"Yes, ma'am, although Miss Gina asked if I'd help her with her new batch of kittens after I helped you in the library."

"More kittens?!" Kimmie squeals. "Aunt Deedee, we need another kitten to play with Smokey—then he can have a friend!"

Dylan holds up a finger. "One. Tell her we'll take one more kitten, but that's it."

"She's got to get those cats fixed." Craig breezes into the room carrying a tray of ketchup bottles and salt and pepper shakers to be refilled.

Like me, Craig's a close friend of the family. He was once Dylan's ballet partner and now co-manages the restaurant.

He's also head DJ and choreographer of her weekly "Dare Nights," when Dylan makes a special ultra-spicy pepper dish for daring customers to try.

Sometime back, it turned into a raucous dance party with *Coyote Ugly*-style bar dancing and fire-themed music—all selected by Craig.

He sets the tray on the large, stainless-steel work table in the center of the room, and I automatically start turning the ketchup bottles upside down. "I'm thinking about trying this new sugar-free diet I read about…"

"Diet!" Dylan's voice goes high. "What in the world, Al? You don't need to lose weight!"

"It's more about being healthy." I look down at my medium-sized figure. "Do you know how much sugar is added to everything we eat? And I mean *everything*. It's pretty shocking once you start reading the labels. There's sugar in ketchup, pasta sauce—even peanut butter!"

"Not this again," Thomas grumbles as he passes me on his way to the grill in the back of the room.

Thomas is head chef, and he makes the best hamburgers I've ever tasted—using a secret recipe, of course. Now I wonder if it contains sugar.

"Don't you want our customers to be healthy?" I call after him.

He lets out another grumble, and Craig walks over, leaning close. "Remember when I tried to reduce the amount of french fries we were serving? Don't be healthy. Customers don't like it."

"I didn't mean the *customers* couldn't have sugar. They can have whatever they want."

"Give me the sugar!" Kimmie twirls around in front of Edward, doing some kind of modified cheerleader kick. "Cookies, cake, candy!"

"How much sugar have you had today?" Craig bumps her with his hip.

"None," I laugh. "That's her baseline."

"Kimmie Joy, your daddy doesn't let you eat all that junk food, and you know it." Dylan fusses.

"Austin used to make me pancakes on Fridays," she argues. "He said it's for T-G-I-F."

"It's okay in moderation," I try to explain. "But too much is bad for your pancreas, it can cause heart disease, Type 2 diabetes…"

"My sister has hypoglycemia," Edward notes.

He's standing with his back against the wall petting the cat, which has gone completely limp in his arms. Kimmie dances over to him, reaching up to pet the long animal.

"In that case, Rachel needs sugar." I take six slices of bread out of the bag and butter one side of each before arranging them on a metal baking sheet. "I'm really just talking about adding it to things."

"Yo, D, what's for lunch?" Garrett Bradford enters through the back door, dressed in his thick khaki sheriff's uniform. "I could eat a horse!"

"Uncle Grizz-lay!" Kimmie spins on her toes, running to greet her giant uncle by jumping on his back.

He's pretty intimidating at six-foot-four with a black gun belt at his waist, but he's also a gentle giant, now carrying his niece piggyback.

"Miss Allie said we can't eat any more sugar!" Kimmie's head tilts to the side, and she practically yells in his ear.

Garrett lifts a finger to shake in his ear. "Dang, Allie, what's that about?"

"That's not what I said." I take out four more slices of bread for Garrett and butter them. "And I was only talking about me— *I'm* trying to cut back on my sugar intake."

I know it's a cliché, but if I can't control anything else in my life, at least I can control what I eat.

"She said it's bad for your pancakes." Kimmie continues.

"Pancreas," Edward corrects her.

"What's that?" Kimmie frowns.

"Particle Man." Garrett holds out a fist for Edward to bump. "I'm supposed to give you a ride to Miss Gina's. I heard she has more kittens."

"I want to help with Miss Gina's kittens, too!" Kimmie cries, and her uncle gooses her with his elbow.

"You're breaking my eardrum, Peanut." Reaching around, he pulls her off his back and sits her on the metal work table.

She hops off the table at once, following Edward to put the cat outside. "Uncle Grizz said I can help you with the kittens!"

They continue out the back door, and Garrett leans closer to me, lowering his voice. "Heard anything new?"

"Not a peep." I shake my head, pressing my lips together.

We're doing our best to keep the situation with Rip under wraps around the kids. I don't want to scare the littles, and I don't want to get in Austin's head right now, in the middle of summer camp with Jack picking his starting lineup.

"Like I said, he's breaking parole if he leaves the state." Garrett watches as I finish preparing the sandwiches and pop them into the broiler. "If he shows up here, I'll be glad to arrest him and ship him right back to Angola."

"Liv can help you get a restraining order," Dylan adds.

Garrett's wife Liv is a lawyer.

"You could get a restraining order all by yourself," Garrett notes, "but it might alert him to your location."

"I've done everything I can to stay off social media and keep a low profile. I'm praying if we do that, he won't know where we are." Hugging my arms over my body, I lean against the refrigerator. "The few friends I have in New Orleans know not to say anything, and we didn't leave a forwarding address."

"You should move into the house with Logan and me." Dylan walks over to wrap her arms around my waist, over my arms. "You could have the entire upstairs floor, and Logan will be there if anything happens."

I give her a squeeze. "What would I tell Austin?" Shaking my head, I step out of her embrace. "It's better if we stay where we are. We're not too far from everyone, and I have a house alarm."

Dylan's lips twist, but she doesn't pressure me. Instead, she taps my arm with her finger. "You haven't told me your favorite movie for girls' night yet."

"*Party Girl*, of course."

My friend's brow furrows. "Why of course?"

"Because she wants to be a librarian, she spends all night learning the Dewey Decimal System… Although, we're not really using that anymore—Melville Dewey was kind of a jerk."

"Gah, weren't they all?" Dylan laughs. "What are you using now?"

"Library of Congress system. It has more categories."

"Have you ordered your glasses yet?" She leans on her forearms on the table, waggling her eyebrows.

"You're wearing glasses?" Garrett returns from chatting with Thomas, munching on a handful of french fries.

"No." I cut my eyes at her.

"I'm confused." Garrett frowns at his sister.

"I was just saying, as a librarian, Allie should wear glasses." She gives him a wink.

Garrett picks up on what she's saying at once. "Riiight… so you can take them off." He gives me a teasing grin. "And let your hair down. I know someone who'd be into that."

"We just have to figure out a way to lure Coach Jack to the library after hours," Dylan adds, and I'm on my way to the back door.

"Flip the grilled cheeses. If you're taking Kimmie with you, I'm headed home—see you tomorrow."

"Allieee," Dylan cries after me. "Don't leave. I'm only teasing!"

She is definitely *not* teasing, and I'm not standing around turning bright red in front of Sheriff Grizz.

I might think Jack Bradford is the best-looking thing I've ever seen and the kindest and the best mentor to my son, but I'm not having the entire Bradford clan meddling in my love life—or ruining any chance I might have with him, which up to now seems like none.

"Call me if you need anything," Garrett yells after me, and I wave a hand over my head.

When I get to my car, my eyes slide to the plastic bag on my passenger's seat. Inside it is a pair of prescription glasses.

They're pretty mild, but Dylan has a point. It couldn't hurt to have a pair on hand, and I've been experimenting with messy, updo hairstyles.

A laugh huffs through my lips, and I shake my head at my own self for getting sucked into their silly, match-making conspiracies.

As if I even know what Jack Bradford likes.

Chapter 2

Jack

"I WANT TO SEE YOU HUSTLE OUT THERE." MY TONE IS SHARP AS THE boys line up facing each other. "The Dolphins will be ready for you. Show me you're ready for them."

In the entire school district it's the Crystal Shores Dolphins and us, and every year, the rivalry gets more intense.

We've been out here for a week, and I've just about got the starting lineup set. We've got several freshmen on the defensive line this year, but our offensive line is full of seniors. I'd rather have a strong defense, but we'll get there.

Offense scores points. Defense wins games.

I stand on the sidelines with my arms crossed and my cap lowered to help me focus. Buddy Outlaw, my assistant coach, is with my brother Zane drilling the D-line boys. I could use Garrett out here working with them, but he's riding around in his truck keeping Newhope safe from jaywalkers and litter bugs.

Lord knows we don't have any real criminals around here.

The brief thought tightens my throat, and I study Austin Sinclair calling plays and leading the team like he's been doing it all his life.

My protective instincts rise, knowing he has no idea his dad is out of jail, that his mother is on guard, and that basically the entire Bradford clan is on low-key alert watching over them.

The idea of some ex-con drug dealer roaming the highways, possibly searching for her has me sleeping poorly at night and on edge during the day.

Allie's a hard worker like her son. She's good and honest. She takes pride in her work at the library, and she's a great help to Dylan at the restaurant.

She has a sweet smile, and her pretty blue eyes are framed with thick, dark lashes. Her shoulder-length brown hair has a slight wave, and when she stands in the sun, it shines auburn.

In the summer, she wears cutoff jeans that hug her round ass and show off her muscular legs, and the way the Cooters & Shooters logo stretches across her full breasts…

Clearing my throat, I grab the reins on my wandering mind. Jesus, I'm out here sweating my ass off at training camp. Last thing I need is to get hotter.

Still, I can't deny whenever I see her, my chest muscles tense. She always walks over to speak or to make a joke or to offer me a drink, or to thank me for helping with her son, and I always do my best not to touch her or put my arm around her or pull her close.

Austin's a good kid, and even though he's a teenage boy, he has plans. He wants to get into a good school and have a good career. He wants to take care of his mom, and I'm proud of him for that. His dad might be a shithead, but Austin shows no signs of following in those footsteps.

They came to Newhope to escape a bad situation, and when the time comes, Austin will move on to something better. Allie should move with him, and I should keep my mind and my hands to myself.

Allie's too strong and too sweet, and as much as she appeals to me, she's too close to my family. I know from personal experience my private tastes aren't for everyone, and I won't take that chance with her.

These thoughts make me restless and frustrated and angry, and I've got a crowd of parents in the stands behind me analyzing every decision I make. I don't have time to wrestle with my feelings—my horniness, more like.

I need to keep my head in the game.

These boys come here to play for the son of legendary hometown hero Art Bradford. They hang on my decisions to help them rise above difficult circumstances or to help them land scholarships.

I take it very seriously—and all their dads, uncles, and grandparents are ready to bend my ear if I don't put their son in the game. Not to mention the moms who constantly hound me about safety.

Safety is my priority in all things. I'm as cautious with my boys as I can be. Still, football is a contact sport, and if they come out for the team, they're going to take some hits.

"Looks like a killer starting line." Dylan's husband Logan steps up beside me.

As a former professional wide receiver, he helps me field the offensive line every year. I appreciate his help, and the boys all know him.

When he retired from pro ball, he moved here and started a local sports-radio talk show, so he's a bit of a celebrity as well.

"If he keeps going at this rate, Austin's going to have his pick of colleges," Logan continues. "Not sure if you noticed, but there are a few logo caps in the bleachers today."

I haven't looked behind me all week, but I've heard the boys talking about college scouts coming out to watch them play.

"We need to stay focused," is all I say.

Austin crouches down, and the snap happens. Tyreek Johnson charges forward to hold the line while Austin falls back, scanning the field.

I see two options. Noah Redford cuts a path around our cornerback, Flynn Barnes.

"Rich Hightower is wide open in the middle," Logan muses.

Austin pulls back and fires a pass straight to Rich, our tight end, who spins away from the one defensive lineman near him and runs thirty yards for a touchdown.

My throat is hot, and I exhale a low growl. "That D-line is not working. They shouldn't be letting anybody through that easily."

"We need Garrett," Logan agrees. "He could whip those boys into shape in a day. Two tops."

My biggest younger brother was a killer lineman when he and Logan played together in New York, and he has a way of delivering constructive criticism that still manages to keep the boys motivated.

My expertise is offense, but the buck stops here if our D-line is weak.

"I'll talk to Buddy." The boys circle around Rich, slapping his shoulder pads and celebrating his score, and I call to them. "Take ten, hydrate."

Logan walks over to join them near a cooler of Gatorade. He'll give them pointers while I head over to where my assistant coach is talking to my brother Zane.

Zane was a professional kicker before an injury forced him to retire. Now he works with Logan on the radio show. Their audience grows every year, and it really spikes when my brothers and I join them to talk shop. They discuss the pro teams, while I talk about the high school and college up-and-comers.

Rome Allen is our kicker, and he's showing improvement this year as a junior. Still, he isn't consistent. All these weaknesses have me tense.

"Rich was wide open just now, Bud." Even I can hear the sharpness in my tone, and Zane pats Rome on the shoulder. "Take a break. Get something to drink."

The boy jogs away, to where the rest of his teammates are

gathered on the sidelines. Buddy crosses his arms to mirror my stance, his brow lowered.

"We've got a lot of new guys on defense. It's taking them a minute to come together as a team."

"We're running out of minutes." I don't like excuses.

"They need to communicate better post-snap." Zane's low tone is more measured. "They'll get better the more they play."

"We've been at it a week, and I'm still not seeing a starting line." I'm not even going to look at the bleachers.

The last thing I need is input from the peanut gallery.

Buddy uncrosses his arms. "What are the chances Garrett might come out one afternoon? He's pretty good at spotting weaknesses."

I struggle not to get cross with him for depending on my brother to do his job. Buddy's too focused on his nephew Lucas these days and getting him ready to take over when Austin graduates.

"I bet Garrett will come out next week," Zane says. "He said something about going to Miss Gina's this afternoon. I'll text and see if he'll swing by and see what he thinks."

Squinting up at the sky, I exhale. The sun beats down on the field, and it's hot as hell. The humidity is high, and if it weren't for the nonstop breeze, it would be unbearable.

"I don't know how much these kids have left in them today." We've been working hard all week, and it's almost 3 p.m.

I start camp early so we can end it before the heat gets too intense. Some coaches don't mind if players vomit and get overheated, but it's not my style. Dad never treated us that way.

"I'll give him a call and get his ETA." Zane takes out his phone, walking away from us.

"Did you see Lucas out there today?" Buddy's eyes dance with excitement, and I swallow my annoyance. "We'll be sitting pretty next year when Sinclair graduates."

"He's a talented kid." I nod, ignoring the twist of loss in my stomach.

I've been coaching high school boys for seven years now. I've seen many good players graduate and move on to college. It's a good thing; the way it should be.

There's no reason for me to grieve as if my own son were leaving the nest. It's not even my nest, dammit.

"Garrett said he can be here in ten. Rachel's got the kids, and they're just tracking down kittens."

Miss Gina and her kittens. "She needs to get those cats fixed."

"I think she loves her yearly batch of babies," Zane says with a chuckle. "Or she loves having all the kids over to play with them."

We walk over to join the team, and I hold up my hand to get the boys' attention. "Take ten more. My brother Garrett's on his way over, and we'll run a few more plays so he can get a feel for D-line. I need you boys to show me some teamwork. Offense, you're looking good. Keep it up."

The boys are sweaty, but I see some of them getting excited at the prospect of Garrett Bradford watching them play. He's a favorite, and I'd wanted him to join my coaching staff when he retired from professional ball.

Looks like I'll be stuck with Buddy a while longer.

"You've got the makings of a championship team out there, Bro." Garrett leans against the bar, sharing a beer with Logan, Zane, and me at Cooters & Shooters. "I saw some real talent on defense. They're just green."

"They'd better mature quick." I take a sip of my beer. "I need twenty-two players ready to go in two weeks, and right now I only have eleven."

"You've got more than that," Garrett laughs, gripping my shoulder. "Take a breath. We got this."

"O-line is top tier," Logan announces. "Austin has really turned into a leader, and the boys like him. He has a good attitude, and he keeps calm under pressure. If he does well in college, he could go all the way to the pros."

I take a drink, doing my best not to beam with pride. It's bad enough I get accused of favoritism by some of the parents. I don't even respond to them. They need to wake up. Like I wouldn't put my best player at the top of the roster.

Nostalgia warms my chest when I remember his first camp three years ago. He was hungry and as clumsy as some of the boys out there today, but he was determined.

I could see he was a hard worker. Dylan said he'd been practicing every day leading up to camp, and when he made that first catch, the way Allie almost cried…

Clearing my throat, I distract my thoughts from her shining blue eyes, the way she looked at me like I was her hero. "Lucas Outlaw's coming along. I expect he'll be QB-1 next year."

Logan nods. "He doesn't have the natural talent that Austin has, but he's enthusiastic."

"They're all green at this stage, but they'll be ready to play by the end of next week." Zane is always there to provide calm logic.

He's come a long way from the broody, wounded loner who returned from Baltimore on crutches after a shocking injury forced him into retirement. He was hobbled and in a dark place for a while. We were all worried.

If it weren't for Rachel and Edward, I'm not sure he would've seen the light. Edward's special needs and interest in horses were the first step, then Rachel's sunny disposition and healing hands broke through his anger.

Now they're married, and he even smiles occasionally.

I glance over at him. "How are you feeling about Rome?"

"I'll get him there." Zane tilts his beer to the side, but he's not smiling now.

Dad always said a good kicker can save a game, and he was

never wrong. Not only that, I've been in games where the extra point cinched the win.

"Hey, Coach." I recognize Austin's voice. "I'm surprised you're still standing. I'm about to pass out."

He's with Edward, and I'm sure they're going to play pool.

"Austin, Edward." I smile at the boys. "I won't be long."

They continue walking, and the petite woman following quietly behind them sparks a low hum of electricity beneath my skin.

"Hey, Coach." Allie's voice carries a cute tease, and she pauses where I'm standing with my brothers. "Is this a Bradford Boys official meeting?"

"Hey, Al." Garrett straightens, going to where she stands blinking up at us."You working tonight?"

As I expected, she's wearing those cutoff jeans that show off her legs and a red Cooters & Shooters tee that hugs her breasts, which are small but look like nice handfuls.

She's doing something different with her hair, piling it all on top of her head in one of those messy buns, and she's wearing glasses. I didn't know she needed glasses. *Interesting*.

Her legs are tanned, and her bright red toenails peep out from her black flip-flops. She's the picture of a south Alabama beach girl, and it doesn't just make me want her, it feels like she's mine. I'd like to put her on her knees, and...

"No, sir, I'm only here Thursday nights during the school year." She lifts her chin, smiling up at him. "I'm just dropping off the boys, and I have a special delivery for Coach Jack."

My dick jumps when she says it that way. I imagine her saying it as I tell her how pretty she looks taking my dick. *Shit*.

Turning away, I take a sip of cold beer.

"Look, Daddy!" My daughter prances up behind Allie clutching a small, orange kitten to her chest. "Aunt Deedee said we could get one more kitten, but *that's it!*"

Her imitation of my sister's cross voice is a good distraction, shutting down my unbidden thoughts of Allie.

Kimmie is so much like my sister was at that age, it makes me smile. This little girl and I've been through a lot since her mom left us in Texas.

I found out quickly that relationship was a mistake. She didn't understand me, and she didn't want to. She pushed me away and said I was a misogynist, and when she turned up pregnant, I put all my needs away.

I was ready to be whoever I needed to be for my daughter. I wanted to be a good dad and husband, but Danielle didn't want to settle down.

I'd never badmouth Kimmie's mom, but her dreams came first. She left me alone in that penthouse apartment hundreds of miles from any help.

My contract was up for renewal, but I was at the top of my game. I was a star, on my way to being a legend like my dad. None of it mattered.

The first time my baby girl looked up at me with her big brown eyes, exactly like my mother's and my sister's, that was it. I retired and came home.

"Let me see this guy." I take the prickly critter from my daughter's hands.

"It's a girl, Daddy. Her name is Apricot, and Miss Gina said she's a born mouser!"

"She'll have her work cut out for her around here in a few months."

Cold weather doesn't last long this far south, but when the temperatures drop, we usually get a few field mice. Heck, when the temperatures drop, a lot of unusual things seem to happen.

"Can we keep her at our house til she gets a little bigger?" Kimmie blinks up at me, but I'm immune to her charms.

Most of the time.

"Not this time, Peanut." Squatting down to her level, I pass the kitten to her again. "She needs to stay here with Smokey and establish her territory."

And I know if we bring Apricot to our house, she'll never leave.

Kimmie's bottom lip pokes out, and she makes a pouty noise.

Straightening, I put my hand on her shoulder. "You'll be starting school in another week. Who'll play with Apricot then?"

Her pout twists into a half-frown as she thinks about it. Also like my sister, her little Type-A logic is the one saving grace in all her enthusiastic impulsivity.

Exhaling a resigned breath, she shakes her head. "I do have to go to school, I guess."

"I guess you do." I hold back a chuckle, but she's pretty cute doing her best to act as grown-up as the adults surrounding her.

She turns, slowly walking to the kitchen as the small orange cat claws its way onto her shoulder.

"Jack Bradford?" A deep male voice approaches from the door, and a man about my height with light brown hair and a clean-shaven face leads a boy even taller to where we're standing.

The man's dressed in khakis and a light blue golf shirt that stretches over his thick middle. I don't recognize them, but I can see the boy is high school-aged.

The man gives me that smile I know well. It means he's about to give me an order—but in a friendly way. I get that a lot in this job.

Only, I don't take orders. I give them.

I square my stance, facing them. "That's me."

The man sticks out a hand. "Name's George Powell, and this here's my son Levi."

Reaching out, I give him a firm shake. "Nice to meet you, Mr. Powell. Levi."

"Call me George." He smiles, but again, it's only conditionally friendly.

"George," I say easily. "Something I can do for you?"

"More like what I can do for you." He grins like a salesman. "We just moved here from Gainesville. That's in Florida."

"I'm familiar with it."

"Levi was starting quarterback at his old high school, and when I heard *the* Jack Bradford was head coach at Newhope High, I said my son had to join the team."

It's a line I've heard before.

My eyes move to his son, and I meet his gaze head-on, trying to get a read on this young man. Levi is slightly taller than I am. He has well-defined muscles, which means he's been training. His light brown hair is a bit too long and shaggy, but his brown eyes are serious, if a bit loose.

"What grade are you in, Levi?"

"I'm a senior, sir."

"This isn't the military. You can call me coach."

"Yes, sir, Coach."

My lips press, but I let it go. We're in the south, where saying *ma'am* and *sir* are just part of the culture.

"How do you feel about playing football?"

"It's the best thing in the world, Coach. It's the only thing that matters to me."

"Your grades will need to matter to you if you play for Newhope. You'll be off the team if they fall below a 3.0 average."

Levi nods, and I glance at his father, wondering what kind of parent moves a kid one state away from home at the start of senior year just for me.

I'm good, but there's more to getting into college than a coach.

Maybe they came here so Levi could play a year with me, or maybe they came here for some other reason. Whatever it is, all of it will impact the way he behaves and performs on the field, which is my business.

"How do you feel about joining a new team as a senior?"

Meaning, the team has already been established, the boys all know each other, and the starting lineup is set as far as they know.

Hell, everyone's been watching Austin for the past two years. These guys aren't ignorant if they know high school ball.

Levi hesitates, glancing at his father before returning his eyes to mine.

His chin lifts, and a cocky expression crosses his young face. "I'll be the best player you've ever had, Coach. Just put me in the game."

It didn't answer my question, but my face remains neutral. I feel a shift in the group of brothers behind me, and I know they're all eavesdropping.

"Is Levi enrolled at the high school?" Never hurts to be sure.

"We got him signed up this week," his father answers.

Inhaling slowly, I think about what this means, how it will impact the offensive line I've built. It's good to have a backup quarterback. It'll bump Lucas down to third string, but it's only for a year.

Shifting my stance, I nod, exhaling slowly. "We're halfway through training camp. I need you to suit up and be on the field Monday at 7 am sharp so I can see what you've got."

"He'll be there." George puts a hand on his son's shoulder, smiling.

So many parents are over-involved in their kids' lives. I know it's because earning a scholarship is a big assist, but these two don't look like they need money.

Looks can be deceiving, I suppose.

"Nice to meet you both." I leave it at that, returning to my brothers.

Chapter 3

Allie

WHEN HE RETURNS TO WHERE WE'RE ALL WATCHING HIM FROM beside the smaller bar near the pool tables, Jack has that look on his face. It's the same one he wears when he's watching his brother Hendrix play a tight game. *Intense.*

Garrett is the first to speak. "Good-looking kid."

Logan adds, "Tough-looking kid."

The muscle in Jack's square jaw moves attractively. He's not a big talker like Garrett or Hendrix or Logan—when Logan's in the mood.

Zane is also quiet, and he's watching his oldest brother like I am.

"Did I hear him say they moved here from Gainesville?" Zane's voice is quiet. "That's a tough district. A lot of good players come out of there."

My chest tightens, because I also heard the man say his son is a starting quarterback. Jack's been working so closely with Austin for so long, and I know he's as proud of my son as I am.

At the same time, I know he's under a lot of pressure to win every season. Parents want headlines, because headlines draw scouts, which in turn draws scholarships.

Lord knows, Austin has to get a scholarship if he's going to attend college—or get a loan, which I hate. But there's no way I can pay for tuition on a waitress-slash-school librarian's salary.

Logan leans against his elbow on the bar. "How do you think the boys will respond?"

"I don't know." Jack's blue eyes flicker to mine, and they soften ever so slightly. "We'll make it work."

I take a sip of my beer, doing my best not to let the heat burning in my chest move up to my cheeks. I have no reason to respond to him the way I do. Jack Bradford has only ever treated Austin and me with respect and courtesy... much to my disappointment.

Despite what certain parents might think, he doesn't show favoritism. If there's a better player than Austin on the team, he'll put that boy in the best spot. It's part of the reason I have a knot in my throat at the thought of Levi Powell.

"My goodness, did I walk into a stable?" Liv's laughing voice joins us, and she walks up with her daughter Gigi on her hip. "Why all the long faces?"

As soon as Garrett's daughter sees her daddy, she starts fussing and reaching for him.

"There's my little princess." Garrett lifts the two-year-old from his wife's arms, then he kisses Liv's cheek. "And my queen."

"Bruh," Logan teases, and it almost breaks the tension.

"Jack just got a surprise new player," Garrett tells her, ignoring his bestie. "He's a good-looking kid from Florida, who has his eye on the QB-1 position."

"But that's Austin's spot." Liv's brow furrows, and her hazel eyes cut to me. "You okay, Allie?"

"Yeah... Yes!" I try not to sound as flustered as I feel. "Of course."

I take another sip of beer, wishing I could figure out a way to slowly drift away from this conversation. The expression on

Jack's face is close to a wince, and we all know it's because of me and my son.

He might not show favoritism, but he's been very quick to promote Austin.

"I'd better check on Dylan." I take a step back. "I'm not really on the clock anymore, but Friday nights can get busy."

"I'll go with you." Liv takes my arm, and I'm thankful for her support.

The guys smile and nod, but none of them say a word. We turn, and the first person I see is Lucas Outlaw's mother Marilyn. She's sitting with her husband at a booth not too far from where we were all talking, and they're watching everything closely as we are.

With the noise in the bar, I can't tell if they were able to hear what was said. Still, I'm pretty sure they saw the new man and his son talking to Jack. Coach Bradford doesn't do too much this time of year that the parents don't notice, and Lucas will be affected as much as Austin if a new quarterback joins the team. He'll go from backup to third string.

Warmth swirls at my back, and a strong hand grips my shoulder, stopping me in my tracks.

"Hey, Allie?" My heart jumps to my throat at the sound of Jack's voice.

I turn to see him frowning down at me.

"Hey." My heart beats faster, but I force a smile. "What's up, Coach?"

"Don't worry about all that." His brow is furrowed and his jaw set. He almost seems angry. "Austin's going to be fine. He's going to have a good year."

The urgency in his tone squeezes my chest. It doesn't help my secret crush when he's so over-the-top protective of us and so obviously concerned about my feelings. *What am I going to do with you, Jack Bradford?*

I nod, keeping my voice quiet. "Okay."

"And ah, I like your glasses."

Reaching up, I realize I'm still wearing them... *and he likes them*. "Thanks."

His blue eyes hold mine a tantalizing moment longer, and his lips press like he might say more. Breathless seconds tick past, but he releases me and takes a step away.

"Okay." His expression is tight, but he turns, going to the booth where Lucas's family is having burgers and fries.

I want to linger and see what he'll say to them, if he'll tell them not to worry like he told me, or if he'll simply make small talk and tell them Lucas is doing well.

He's good with words of encouragement, even with the overbearing parents. He's a good coach. He's an even better man. *Fuck me, I'm so gone for him.*

I force my feet to move, to follow Liv into the kitchen, feeling the weight of all the eyes in the restaurant on everything that's happening.

Liv stops to hold the door for me, and as I pass she mutters under her breath, "I swear, you two."

"Allie!" Dylan's loud yell interrupts, and I hurry over to where she's sitting on the large metal workplace holding her iPad Pro.

Craig is standing near, and I guess they're planning next week's Dare Night.

"Are you looking at recipes?" I ask, stepping closer. "Show me what you've got."

"You know me so well." She tilts her head, fluttering her lashes at me and laughing. "I'm going to miss you so much when school starts. I miss you already! Are you sure you don't want to work here full time?"

"But I really like working in the library." I move her curly hair off her shoulder.

"I know," she frowns. "Why does Liv look like she's annoyed with you?"

"Not with her." Liv walks up, crossing her arms over her chest. "With your big brother."

Liv and Garrett started dating when they were in high school, which means she's basically been part of this family all her life.

"Which one?" Dylan laughs. "They're all pretty pig-headed in their own special ways."

"Jack." She glances from Dylan to me. "He walked all the way across the room to tell Allie not to worry about her son's football career. Then he just walked away."

Dylan's lips twist, and she looks at me curiously. "What did you say to that, Ms. Sinclair?"

"Stop." I hold up a hand, shaking my head. "Your brother has a lot on his plate dealing with this team and his daughter and all those parents… Not to mention all of you. I thought it was nice of him to even care that I was worried."

"I don't understand. Why would you be worried?" Dylan frowns. "Austin is so talented, and he's being recruited like crazy."

"There's a new kid in town." Liv's eyebrow arches. "Levi Powell. All the way from Gainesville, and his dad is clearly over-involved and expecting him to be QB-1."

"Oh." Dylan blows a laugh through her lips. "That won't work with Jack. He's impervious to pushy parents."

"Still, wasn't it nice of your big brother to make sure our favorite sexy librarian wasn't spooked?" Liv cuts her eyes at me, and my throat tightens.

I'm ready to argue when Kimmie Joy marches into the room clutching the squirming orange kitten to her chest. "Apricot doesn't want to stay outside by herself, Miss Allie, and Daddy said we have to leave her here so she can establish her territory. But how can she do that if Smokey won't play with her?"

Bending my knees, I squat in front of her, petting the struggling kitten. I don't know if it's because she looks so much like my best friend Dylan, who threw us a lifeline when we needed it most, or if it's because her dad has been so kind to my son.

All I know is this little girl has a special place in my heart, and I do like spending time with her. I like that she comes to me for help.

Placing my hand on her back, I smile. "You know, cats are really self-sufficient."

Kimmie's bottom lip pouts. "But it's dark outside, and she's used to being with her mama cat and all her brothers and sisters. She doesn't have anybody to cuddle with."

"Want to know a secret?" I lean closer.

Kimmie's eyes light, and she nods.

"Cats are nocturnal." Her little chin pulls back, but I continue. "That means they like to stay up all night. You know how her eyes shine in the light? That means she has night vision. Apricot will figure out her territory if you let her."

The little girl still seems worried, but I take her hand, rising slowly and leading her to the back door. "She'll have so much fun playing tonight. You'll see, then we can come back and see her tomorrow."

Kimmie hesitates, looking through the screen into the pitch-black yard. "But what if there's something out there she doesn't like? Edward said 'possums eat kittens, and he knows everything!"

"He is pretty smart," I concede. "But Apricot will stay away from 'possums. She knows what to do, and she can climb trees and hide." I rub my hand over her little shoulder. "She'll be fine. She's smart."

It takes a minute, but she finally relents. She bends down and puts the kitten on the top step, and as soon as she lets her go, Apricot scampers under the building.

"Oh!" Kimmie takes a step down. "What if she doesn't know how to get out?"

Reaching for her hand, I give her another encouraging smile. "She'll come back for the good food and pets and lots of love."

Kimmie's on the fence, but she takes my hand, letting me lead her into the restaurant again. A frown tugs at the side of her mouth, and a sliver of anxiety is in my chest. I'm pretty sure I'm right about all of this, but I hope nothing happens to that little cat.

Be okay, Apricot, I silently pray.

"You are so good with her." Dylan shakes her head as I walk back to where they're standing. "I'm way too much of a pushover."

Kimmie's hand is in mine, and she frowns up at me. "Are you really never going to eat sugar ever again, Miss Allie?"

It's such a little kid thing to worry about, I almost laugh. Only, Garrett is in the room now along with most of his brothers, including Jack, which has my senses on high alert.

"It's probably better to stay back here," Zane tells him. "It's filling up with parents out there."

Jack takes off his ball cap, scrubbing a hand through his soft, dark hair. "Yeah, I'm beat, and Kimmie needs to get to bed."

Ocean blue eyes roam the room until he finds his daughter holding my hand, then he looks up at me, and it's like a mini-explosion.

I blink quickly and manage a smile before looking away, my neck all hot.

"I agree with Kimmie," Garrett announces loudly. "Diets are not allowed at the Coot-Shoot."

"What's that?" Liv frowns at me, taking her sleepy baby from Garrett's arms. "Why are you dieting, Allie?"

I literally want to die. On the spot.

"I'm not." I do my best to speak quietly, not wanting to discuss this in front of Jack. "I'm just monitoring my sugar intake and not adding more to my food."

"Oh." Liv nods, patting Gigi. "Diets never work. The minute you go off one, you go right back to what you were doing before."

Jack has moved closer to where I'm standing with his daughter, his blue eyes holding mine in a way that has my stomach squirming.

"Are you sick?" Concern laces his tone.

"No," I answer quickly, wishing I'd never said a word. "It's just this nutrition study I read."

"You don't need to lose weight, Allie." His brow lowers, and the gruff way he says it is hot as hell. "You look good."

I swallow air, and it doesn't matter that he might be fussing at me without raising his voice. I'm hot all over because he just said my body looks good.

I want to thank him and say *right back atcha, big boy*. Jack Bradford's body looks *so* good.

Instead, I feel six pairs of eyes locked on us, and these meddlers have enough ammunition as it is.

"Okay." I huff a laugh, turning to open the refrigerator door and hoping the cool air will calm my blushing. "I'm sorry I even brought it up. I didn't know it would turn into a federal case."

"Trust me when I say this..." Craig leans closer. "*Healthy* is not a word people like at the Coot-Shoot. I've been trying it for years."

"You make it sound like I serve unhealthy food," Dylan argues. "Peppers are very good for you!"

"I know, I know." Craig waves her away. "Keep your shirt on, Pepper Spice."

"It's all about portion size," she continues.

"And you saw what happened when I tried to cut back on the portion sizes for French fries."

"Well, you can't skimp on the fries." She returns to her iPad screen. "People get mad."

"Buddy Outlaw gets mad," Craig gripes.

Jack takes Kimmie's hand. "Bedtime."

"Goodnight, Aunt Deedee!" Kimmie calls. "Goodnight, Miss Allie! Goodnight, Uncle Cray-cray, Goodnight, Uncle Grizz, Goodnight, Major Tom—"

"Okay, okay," Jack grins, interrupting her.

Peeking over my shoulder, I love the way he handles her. I love that dimple in his cheek. My lip goes between my teeth, and I wonder what it would be like to take his hand and go home with him. I'd eat all the sugar he wants. I'd cover him in chocolate syrup and lick it off.

Hell, I'd do anything for him.

"Night, guys," he says, leading his daughter away.

All the eyes fly to me, and I lift my chin, closing the fridge.

"You're right," I say, ignoring all the pointed stares. "It was a silly idea."

"What's a silly idea?" Rachel's bright voice enters the room, and I almost groan.

"Allie wants to cut sugar out of her diet," Liv says, *almost* getting it right.

Rachel's eyes light up, and she smiles. "That's a *great* idea, Al! Y'all wouldn't believe how much sugar is in our food—even in things that don't really need it—and sugar is linked to so many health problems, obesity, diabetes…"

"Here we go again." Craig snorts a laugh. "Spoken like a true wellness guru."

"You think I could be a wellness guru?" Rachel lights up even more. "I talked to Zane about recording my yoga classes and putting them on YouTube. He said their producer could help me, and there's a real market out there!"

Craig narrows his eyes at her. "Just don't get weird and start a cult."

"Craig!" Dylan shoves him with her foot. "I think that's a fun idea, Rach. I love your yoga classes."

"I think that's a cool idea, too." I walk over to her. "I should do more of them. Lord knows when school starts, I don't get nearly enough exercise."

"Speaking of school starting, Mrs. Laverne's at it again." Dylan grins at Liv.

"The principal?" My brow arches. "What did she do?"

Liv shakes her head. "Mrs. Laverne will have us all working at that high school before she retires."

"She's the best," Rachel sighs. "She was so kind and welcoming to Edward. I never worry about him when he's at school."

"He's one of the smartest students we have," I tell her. "He just doesn't like assemblies. Or fire drills. Or pep rallies…"

"And she *never* makes him feel bad or weird for it." Rachel's green eyes shine as she smiles at Dylan. "She's a great lady."

"She's definitely a great recruiter," Liv grumbles.

"What if you did it for one year?" Dylan hops off to the table, taking Liv's hand. "Remember how much fun we always had on game days? It'll be like old times."

"Yes, game days are fun, and the rest of the time, it's all work work work." Liv slides her hair behind her shoulder so Gigi can rest her head. "I have a baby now, Dee, I'm trying to establish my law practice…"

"Okay, somebody has to catch me up." I look from Dylan to Liv. "Mrs. Laverne wants to hire Liv?"

"The drill team coach had to retire suddenly to take care of a sick relative," Dylan explains. "And since Liv was the drill team captain in high school, Mrs. Laverne thinks it's meant to be."

"It's *not* meant to be." Liv's tone is firm.

"But we need you!" Dylan gives her sister-in-law a look that's pure guilt-trip. "You know everything about the team, the school—"

"What Dylan's not saying is if I don't do it, *she'll* have to do it."

My brows rise, and I press my lips together. "Oh."

"That is *not* why!" Our friend cries. "I'd be glad to do it, but ballet is completely different from precision dance."

"If I remember correctly, you helped me prepare my audition tape for college." Liv does a gentle rocking motion, patting her daughter's back.

"I helped you with the switch arabesque and the pirouettes. You did all the rest."

Garrett walks up, placing a hand on his wife's shoulder. "Want me to take Gigi home? She's falling asleep."

"No, I'll go with you."

"Garrett, tell Liv she needs to coach the drill team." Dylan grabs her brother's arm.

"Oh, no." He hugs his little sister, lifting her off her feet. "You're not roping me into this one. Liv does what she wants."

Dylan's bottom lip goes out, and I can't help a snort. "You really are the original Kimmie Joy."

"Right?" Garrett gives me a wink. "I've been saying that since Jack brought her home."

He puts an arm around his sister, and she blinks her brown eyes dramatically at Liv, causing her to laugh.

"It's time you and Logan had a baby," Liv says. "Then you'd see how much work it is."

"Gigi can come with you! We'll get her a little dance costume, and she can be our mascot…" Dylan reaches for my hand. "Allie can help us, since it's Austin's senior year. Wouldn't it be fun to cheer for Jack and Austin and the team?"

She arches her eyebrow at me, and I confess, "It does sound fun. I don't know squat about dance teams, but I'll already be at school, and I love the pep rallies."

"Yay, Allie!" Dylan bounces on her toes. "That's the spirit."

"Traitor," Liv quips at me. "Now I look like the bad guy."

"Just think about it." Dylan holds out a hand. "Don't say no so fast."

"I'll think about it," Liv grumbles, going to where Garrett is walking out with Zane and Rachel.

"While you're thinking, can I catch a ride home? Austin's staying with the guys."

"Of course." Liv slides a hand in the crook of my arm, leaning into my ear. "Too bad Coach Jack already left."

I don't answer—mostly because I'm thinking the same thing. Although, after everything that happened this evening, I'd probably be as awkward and obvious as hell.

As it is, I follow them out, hopping into the backseat of Garrett's big ole truck and helping Liv get Gigi settled in her car seat.

Country music plays softly on the short drive, and when we stop in my driveway, Garrett gets out to walk me to the door.

"Want me to come in and check the place with you?"

My heart beats a little faster, and I look at the kitchen light I left on when I went to work this morning. "I've been using my security alarm." My tone is tentative. "But… if you don't mind?"

He smiles, gesturing to the front door. "It'll only take a second."

Tapping in the code, we enter my small house. I hate this new feeling of fear creeping up my shoulders every night. I've always felt so safe and at home in Newhope, and I hate Rip Sinclair for taking that from me.

"I'm pretty sure he has no idea where I am." My voice is quiet.

I lead Garrett down the hall, and he looks in Austin's room, opening his closet door and checking under the bed. We repeat the process in my room and in the bathroom, looking behind the shower curtain.

When we're satisfied it's all clear, he returns to the door. "I'd be on everybody's shit list if I didn't check. I'd deserve it, too, if something happened."

"Thanks, Garrett." I hold the door, giving him a grateful smile.

I wave to Liv then close it again, turning the lock and re-arming the security system.

Chapter 4

Jack

"HE'S GOOD." LOGAN'S VOICE IS LOW, AND MY CHEST IS TIGHT. We're standing on the sidelines with our arms crossed, and it's another hot as hell August day in the south.

"There's more to being QB-1 than being a talented player," I answer equally low.

The crowd of onlookers in the stands behind us is bigger today, and the word about a new player on the team has spread through town like wildfire. Everybody's curious to see what he looks like and how he'll play—and what I'll do.

We watch Levi complete pass after pass, even pivoting quickly and running it up the middle when he spots an opening.

Garrett is on his second afternoon working with Buddy on the defensive line, and I'm seeing improvements. Still, they have lapses like this where a hole will open for Levi to charge straight through and look like a superstar.

"Your brother should be on the coaching staff," Logan says under his breath. "Even when we were just players, he was a great motivator. He talked a lot of shit, but he also helped a lot of our teammates improve their game."

"He got it from our dad." My arms are crossed, and I hold my expression steady.

I don't want to give anyone in the bleachers any ideas.

"Even Zane has that little Allen kid looking better this week." Logan lowers his arms, putting his hands on his hips. "You're a family of coaches."

Garrett puts his hand on the shoulder of a teenage boy who's as tall as he is. He gives him a playful shake, pointing to another big boy and telling them what to do. I can hear him saying they have to work together, read each other's minds.

"But he wants to be sheriff." It's as much as I can say.

I can't say I'd hoped he'd take Buddy's place when he retired.

"Maybe he'll outgrow it." A tease is in Logan's tone, but I don't smile.

"I doubt it. You know my brother loves being in the community, talking to people, and knowing everybody's business."

Logan huffs a laugh, and we look up to see Levi barely escape a sack by stepping out of a big lineman's grasp. He pitches the ball to Austin, who's in the running back spot for now.

My jaw clenches as I watch Allie's son take it all the way down the field, stiff-arming a cornerback and almost crossing the goal line.

"Damn," Logan exhales. "That was a sweet play. Those two work well together."

"Yeah." I nod, a low growl in my throat. "Austin's a team player."

We've come a long way in the three years we've been working together. I've trained him to be my star quarterback. I'd envisioned his senior year, having all the scouts recruiting him, and him landing a deal that takes care of him and his mother.

Now we have two wildcards in the mix—Rip Sinclair and Levi Powell.

"Let's call it. They've done enough for one day."

Giving his whistle a sharp tweet, Logan waves for the boys to come off the field. They all go straight to the cooler, ripping off helmets and drinking Gatorade or pouring it over their sweaty heads.

Garrett walks over to where Logan is with them on the sidelines, and I walk over as well. The boys straighten, facing me, and I take off my cap.

"Good practice today." I nod, meeting their eyes, one by one. "I saw a lot of good hustle out there. D-line, you're coming together. Week two is starting off strong."

They know I'm right, and I like seeing the satisfaction in their eyes. Football is as much a head game as a physical one. I notice Levi standing a little bit apart, and I make a mental note to work on this.

Even if he is throwing a wrench into my plans, my boys need to come together as a team.

"Thanks to Sheriff Bradford for assisting Coach Outlaw." The boys clap, and a few of them make cheer noises. "Thanks, bro."

"Glad to help." Garrett nods. "You've got some good talent out here. It won't be long before nobody's getting through that line."

"Get some rest, and I'll see you all out here tomorrow, bright and early."

They turn, walking off the field in the direction of the parking lot. Hanging back, I look over at the rest of my coaching staff, and we're all a mix of optimistic and concerned.

"Told you he's a good boy." George Powell walks up to my side. "He's your QB-1."

"I have a QB-1." My tone is even.

I don't like being told how to run my team, and the minute I start letting parents call the shots, it's all over.

George's eyes narrow, but he smiles. "Not trying to tell you how to do your job, Coach. Just proud of my boy."

I don't answer, and my expression is neutral. A crowd of

onlookers watches us from the stands, and I'm not about to open those floodgates.

"See y'all tomorrow."

Having two great quarterbacks is stressful, but in this last week of camp, it's a good problem. On my mind today are the kids who won't make the cut, and I dread this time of year as much as I look forward to it.

Newhope is a 7A school, which means we're one of the biggest in the state. We draw a lot of boys from all over the county, and for many of them, it's their one shot at getting into college.

It's on my mind every day of camp, and I relate to it on a personal level. After our parents died, it was my family's situation as well.

But I'm expected to win games, and I can't field a team of charity cases. It doesn't matter how good of a coach I am or how strong the rest of the players are. They all have to be good for us to win games, especially against the other big, local schools.

Then, if we advance to the state championships, we'll face teams from Birmingham, Montgomery, and Huntsville. I've got some hard conversations coming up, and I don't relish the thought.

At least I have my brothers with me.

"Kimmie's upstairs in the bathtub." My little sister meets me at the house. "Allie had her at the library most of the day, and she had a Thomas burger for dinner."

"Thanks, Dee." I open the refrigerator, taking out a beer. "I appreciate it."

Dylan has helped me with Kimmie since we moved back to Newhope when my little girl was only a year old. For a few years, Austin helped in the summers, when he was in middle school and not old enough for the team.

It's when we got to know each other, and I saw how interested he was in learning the game. I'd be tired from camp, but I'd walk out with him to throw a few passes before he went home.

He'd never played tackle, but he had a good arm and could throw a straight spiral. We started playing on the weekends and in the summers, and he soaked up my instruction like a sponge.

These thoughts press against my temples when I turn to see my little sister with her arms crossed, studying me.

"I know that look." Her voice is gentle. "What's worrying you, big brother?"

I twist the top off my beer with a wince. "Levi Powell is a strong player."

Her full lips tighten, and she nods. "I had a feeling he might be. You're worried about Austin?"

"He's worked hard. He earned his place as starting quarterback." Leaning my elbow against the side of the appliance, I rub my fingers over my eyes.

"And you've taken a personal interest in Austin. Something you never do." My sister's voice is measured. "Does Levi have more natural talent?"

"No." I shake my head. "But he's quicker. His instincts are good, and it's clear he's had more experience in the position than Austin has."

She leans against the counter watching me. "What can you do about that?"

"Not much. Austin's only been playing three years. He's only played in Newhope against the other teams in the county. Levi plays like he's been doing it all his life."

I think about my early conversations with Allie, how she told me he played some flag football in elementary school, but she didn't let him play peewee tackle. She protected him, and I don't blame her. Knowing what we do now about brain trauma and early childhood development, I think she made the right call.

Levi, on the other hand…

Dylan's brow furrows. "Can't you have two starting quarterbacks?"

"Yeah." I nod, thinking how in the past it was pretty common with high school teams. "But a good coach would figure out how to make best use of both players. Austin's a good running back. Hell, he's a good team player. Whatever I tell him to do, he gives 110 percent."

And it fucking breaks my heart, because I know his dreams.

She steps forward to give me a hug. "In that case, I'm not worried. You're the best coach in the world."

Exhaling through a smile, I return her hug. "Thanks, sis."

"Don't forget your little raisin upstairs." She nods, heading for the door. "See you in the morning."

I return my beer to the fridge and jog up the stairs to where I hear Kimmie in the tub singing some girl song I sort-of recognize. It's something Dylan would've listened to at her age, about learning to drive or driving around a neighborhood.

"Hey, Peanut," I call, putting my hand on the door to open it.

"Daddy!" She screams so loudly, my heart flies to my throat.

"Kimmie!" Bolting for the door, I stop in my tracks when she shouts.

"Don't come in here, Daddy—I'm *naked*!" Horror is in her tone, like how dare I try to see her without clothes on?

Standing in the hallway, I put both hands on the door jamb. How the hell do I navigate this new development? Hell, just last night she was dancing around the house with no clothes on, and when I finally made her get in the tub, she wanted me to hold the towel so she could jump into it.

That was less than twenty-four hours ago.

I glance out the window at the top of the stairs, but Dylan is gone.

"Okay…" I exhale, trying to think. "Can you get out of the tub on your own and dry off?"

"I'm seven years old, Daddy." She's already getting pretty good at that teenager tone.

Leaning against the wall, exhaustion rolls over me. "Don't make a big mess, okay? Let me know when you're done, and I'll tuck you into bed."

I hear splashing on the other side of the door, and I envision water covering everything. Holding back, I go to my room to change out of the clothes I've had on all day. I need a shower myself, but I'll do it in the morning. I don't have anyone to impress tonight.

The thought tugs at my chest, and my mind flickers to Allie. I wonder what she's doing right now. I imagine Austin getting home, tired and hungry. I imagine she'll fix him something to eat. Do they watch TV shows? Does he go straight to bed?

"I'm ready, Daddy!" Kimmie yells to me from down the hall.

I pull a T-shirt over my head and walk to her bedroom to tuck her in and kiss her goodnight.

"You're still wet, Peanut." Her cotton gown sticks to her skin, and her dark hair is damp on the ends.

"I rubbed the towel on me." She looks at her little body, and my lips twist.

If it were winter, I'd probably insist she do it again. I'm going to have to talk to Dylan about this before it gets too cold.

Mom was still around when my sister was small, and I didn't pay a bit of attention to what they did.

Now I'm alone with a sassy little girl as stubborn as every member of my family.

"Let me at least dry your hair." I pick up the heavy towel, and my brow lowers. "Why is this towel so wet?"

Her brows rise over her amber eyes and she shakes her head, looking to the side. "You told me not to make a big mess, so I had to clean up the water."

"Did you clean it up before or after you dried your body?"

"Before, Daddy!" She laughs like I'm the crazy one.

Scrubbing my hand over my mouth, I have to let this go

tonight. I'm too exhausted to deal with it, and I've got another long day of practice starting at 7 a.m.

"Next time, dry your body first." I carry the wet towel to the door and drop it in a heap. "You're cleaner than the bathroom floor."

At least, I hope she is.

She's busy arranging her pillows into their usual formation for our bedtime routine. I take the book from her small bookshelf, and when she has everything situated, I sit on the bed beside her, with my back to the headboard.

Lifting my arm, she scoots closer to my side, and I open her current favorite book, *Dogzilla* by Dav Pilkey.

"E.G.," I read aloud. "This book has been rated Extremely Goofy. Some material might be too goofy for grownups."

She giggles, cuddling closer, and I smile. It's a book I used to read to Hendrix when he was a kid, and he got a kick out of it as much as my daughter does.

It feels good when she laughs at the same parts he did, like it's a link to a time before my life went sideways.

A time when I was still innocent, too. Before the world came down on my shoulders.

I start to turn the page, but Kimmie stops me. "Don't forget the cast list, Daddy!"

"Right." I clear my throat. "Starring Flash as The Big Cheese, Rabies as Professor Scarlett O'Hairy…"

I continue reading the book about a colossal canine menacing the city of Mousopoulis. It's not a long book, but it's just enough to have my daughter's eyes closing as I get to the part where the brave mice are chasing the hot dog with all the relish they can muster.

When we get to the final page, Kimmie shouts *Puppies!* with me, and I exhale a chuckle. I realize *Dogzilla* is as much a part of my bedtime routine as it is hers.

My eyes linger on the little bundle of energy curled up at my side. My daughter.

Leaning down, I kiss the top of her head. I can't imagine her being left alone the way we all were that year that never seemed to end, the way Dylan was at her age.

I only ever want Kimmie to have the things we lost—family, love, security. Her mother left before she knew her, but Dylan and I've worked hard to fill that gap.

Although, one day Dylan will have her own babies…

My mind drifts to a pretty brunette with bright blue eyes. A petite beauty who's a protective mother of her only son and who looks up at me like I'm her hero. The way she looks at me stirs a need so deep in my soul. It's a need I've tried so hard to deny.

Closing the thin paperback, I set it on the bedside table, pushing those thoughts away. I can't start something with her now. I'm not the man they all think I am, and when the mask falls, I've seen what happens.

Clearing my mind, I nudge my little girl. "Prayers."

She nods, lifting her small hands and clasping them together in front of her nose. She starts with the "Now I lay me down to sleep" part, but when she gets to the end, she starts to freestyle.

"Bless Aunt Deedee, and help her have a baby with Uncle Logan for me to play with. Bless Uncle Grizz and Aunt Liv and Baby Gigi. Bless Uncle Zane and Aunt Rachel, and help them have a baby for me to play with. Bless Uncle Craig and Uncle Clint, and help them have a baby for me to play with." Her little brow furrows, and she looks up at me. "Can they have a baby, Daddy?"

"Sure." I pat her little back, leaving the conversation about adoption and surrogacy for another night when I'm not exhausted.

"Yay!" She grins, then promptly closes her eyes again. "Bless Eddie and Aussie and Major Tom and Miss Allie… and help Daddy not be blind so he can see how much Miss Allie loves him like everybody says."

My chin jerks, and I study her tightly closed eyes, wondering if she understands what she just said. If she does, I wonder how she feels about it.

"And bless all the kittens, and don't let Apricot get eaten by a 'possum." She finishes with an *Amen*, and her eyes pop open. "Was that a good prayer?"

I slide to my knees beside her bed and lean closer to kiss her forehead. "Yep, I'm pretty sure you got everybody."

When I'm not getting up at 7 a.m. to stand around baking in the hot sun all day, I'll follow up with her about a few of these items—or specifically, the part about Allie.

A few years ago, I chatted with one of the school guidance counselors about divorce and dating and small children. The counselor said she wasn't a real therapist, so she wouldn't go on the record with any of her advice.

Still, she suggested I let Kimmie tell me how she understood things, then figure out the best, age-appropriate explanation. Or let her go with her own interpretation, depending on what it was.

The more we talked, the more I realized the counselor was leaning closer, smiling up at me and blinking, saying what a good dad I was. Then when she suggested helping me test the dating waters, I made a quick retreat.

Since my disastrous marriage, I haven't been interested in going down that path again with anybody. Until Dylan insisted I meet her new friend Allie.

I remember the day she walked into the restaurant holding her son's hand and looking up at me, cautiously but with so much strength.

She came to Newhope for that very reason—hope, and I felt something shift at her very first smile. It triggered something primal in me. I wanted to put my hands on her and tell her she'd been brave for so long, but she didn't have to do it alone anymore.

Even when I'm asleep, I can see her blue eyes and sweet smile. I imagine threading my fingers in both sides of her hair.

I imagine curling them and pulling her head back so I can cover her mouth with mine. I imagine bending her over and...

"Do you want to read another book, Daddy?" Kimmie sits up in her bed, blinking at me.

"Ah, no." I pat her shoulder, holding the blankets so she can slide down again. "Let's get some sleep."

I turn off her lamp, and the base of it glows like a pale moon.

Kimmie rolls onto her side, cuddling her stuffed turtles to her chest. "Tell Snappy, Happy, and Earl goodnight!"

"Night, boys." I give the stuffed cooters pats on the head. "Night, baby. Sweet dreams."

Going to the door, I leave it open a crack before continuing to my bedroom.

I'm in my bare feet, a T-shirt, and joggers, and I only manage to put one knee on the bed before I let go and fall onto my stomach. I don't even get under the blankets before I'm sound asleep.

Chapter 5

Allie

MY ALARM GOES OFF JUST AS I HEAR THE DOOR CLOSE BEHIND Austin. With a groan, I pick up my phone to see it's 6:45 a.m. I'd meant to get up in time to make him breakfast, but he leaves so dang early during camp.

Rolling out of bed, I grab my thick terry cloth robe off the chair before running to the door. He's in my small car when I open the door, waving frantically.

"What?" Austin frowns when he sees me, sticking his head out of the open window.

A laugh huffs through my nose, and I tiptoe on bare feet to the car. "Just wanted to tell you bye, I love you, have a good day. Did you get any breakfast?"

"Coach Outlaw always brings Krispy Kreme."

My lips twist. "Will that hold you?"

Krispy Kremes are fried yeast donuts dipped in sugar glaze. They're incredibly delicious, but I know how hard they work on the field. Donuts have zero protein.

He exhales, leaning his head against the seat. "I'll get a hamburger for lunch. I gotta go, Mom. I'm going to be late."

"Okay." Reaching out, I give his forearm a squeeze, wondering when my little boy turned into this grumpy, muscled teenager. "I love you."

His hazel eyes soften, and he nods, giving me the tiniest flash of how he used to be three short years ago. "Love you."

"I'll be in the library all day, but maybe I'll walk over and watch you practice this afternoon?"

He nods, but his face tightens. "Okay."

That response bothers me. Austin is usually excited for me to watch him play, and I'm worried this is about Levi Powell.

I don't want to make him late, so I let it go for now, stepping away from the car so he can back out of the driveway.

Dylan will pick me up in an hour or so after she picks up Kimmie from Jack's house. Then my little helper and I will go on to the library.

No maybes about it, I'm going to see what's up this afternoon.

"How do you feel about poetry, Edward?" I stand behind the circulation desk examining the contents of a box of books donated from an estate sale.

He walks over and takes a thin volume from the stack of new books and reads the cover. *"The Collected Works of Mary Oliver."*

"Oh, let me see that one!" He hands it to me, and I open the cover, quickly scanning the table of contents. "They have it! Tell me what you think of this."

I quickly flip the pages, and Kimmie climbs onto a chair beside me, standing and putting her hand on my shoulder so she can see.

"I like poetry!" she says.

"You do?" I glance at her. "What poetry do you like?"

"*Horton Hears a Who* and the Grinch and *Green Eggs and Ham*..."

"Dr. Seuss is narrative poetry," Edward says flatly.

"You still said *poetry*," Kimmie argues.

My lips twist, and I tilt my head side to side. "I think that counts." I hand the small book to Edward. "Read this and tell me what you think—it's called 'Wild Geese.'"

Kimmie hops out of the chair beside me and goes over to the one beside him, climbing up and scanning the page as he reads silently.

Her little brow lowers, and she looks up at me. "Daddy says I have to be good. He says I have to do what you and Aunt Deedee say and not talk back."

She's referencing the first line of the poem, which is, *You do not have to be good.*

"It means *perceived* goodness," Edward says. "Not doing what you're told."

"That's right, Edward." My smile is warm. "I'm surprised you picked up on that. It's a sophisticated concept."

"I like it." He hands the book to me again. "I like how she describes the animals."

"I have a place in my family!" Kimmie blinks up at me earnestly.

It's the last line of the poem, the wild geese *over and over announcing your place in the family of things...*

"Yes, you do." I walk over to put my arm around her. "You both have very important places in your family, and Mary Oliver says you also have a place in the world."

Kimmie's eyes go to the book again, and she nods. "So you shouldn't be lonely."

"That's the hope." I give her a squeeze, and she smiles proudly. "Now, let's go check on your dad and the boys playing football. We'll finish sorting these books tomorrow."

My strategic brain is working hard on this new box of books. I've found high school kids to be surprisingly open to poetry. Or maybe it's not so surprising, considering how emotional and fiery the age can be.

"Maybe we can have a favorite verse contest," I think aloud. "Or maybe we can combine it with art or music."

Edward and Kimmie continue into the hall, and I turn to survey the large media center once more before locking the doors. School could start tomorrow, and we'd be ready.

The "blind date with a book" shelves are in the left corner, and large, flatscreen computers are arranged on tables down the center of the room. Perhaps the right wall can be our poetry area.

A smile curls my lips, and I think Edward is right. It's a welcoming space, and students like to hang out in the media center during lunch and after school. It might be a low paycheck, but I get a lot of satisfaction from this job.

Kimmie takes my hand, skipping beside me as we walk out to the football field where the boys are practicing. It smells like fresh-mowed grass, it's so hot, but thankfully there's a breeze. Back home in New Orleans, the hot, wet air doesn't move.

"I'll tell Daddy about the wild geese," Kimmie says, skipping along beside me. "Maybe we can read it at bedtime after *Dogzilla.*"

"That sounds fun." I picture the two of them reading together at bedtime. *How adorably swoony is that?*

A sharp whistle draws our attention, and the noise of plastic pads crashing greets us as we approach the field.

My smile fades when I notice Austin isn't in the quarterback spot as they line up. The new boy Levi is there, and Austin's expression this morning makes sense to me now. My stomach sinks, and I hate to think Jack would demote him. *After all their hard work?*

"Uncle Grizzlaay!" Kimmie takes off running to her oversized uncle, and he bends down to scoop her onto his back. "Hey, Peanut. How's it going? Hey, Al. You good?"

He lifts his chin at me, and I do my best to hide my feelings.

"Yep, all good!" My voice sounds just the opposite, so I deflect. "Hey, what do you think about giving some lucky kid a ride in your patrol car?"

His dark brow lowers. "I don't drive a patrol car—just my truck. Why?"

That's a fail. "I'm looking for donations, and I thought it would be a fun prize."

"Prize for what?"

"Reading contests. I have a bunch of different activities going—it's to get the kids excited about reading. All the local businesses donate stuff."

"Dang, Allie, I wish you'd been the librarian when I was in school." He chuckles. "Although, it probably would've just made me mad when I never won anything."

Garrett recently found out he has dyslexia, but instead of being upset, he was relieved. He said it explained why he always struggled in school when it was so easy for his siblings.

"When you learned to read, did they teach you phonics?"

"That's when they sound out the letters?" I nod, and he shakes his head. "No."

"Keep that in mind if Gigi has trouble reading. It makes a huge difference."

The boys break, and we return to watching them practice.

Levi falls back, scanning the players as Austin runs straight down the field. The new boy fires a pass to my son. It's smooth and low, and Austin catches it easily, running it straight into the end zone.

"Phew." Garrett shakes his head, clapping. "It's hard to top that."

My chest is tight, and I look up at him. "Is Jack making Levi the starting quarterback now?"

Garrett's jaw flexes as he studies the field. "I don't know, but whatever he does, he won't make the decision lightly. It's a hard time of year."

A short, sharp whistle tweets, and my eyes go to Jack

standing on the sidelines. The brim of his cap is low, and his expression gives nothing away. He doesn't smile. He only waits as the two boys jog to where he's standing.

They have a brief chat, and the boys nod before returning to the field, this time with Austin in the quarterback position.

"What's he doing?" a male voice in the bleachers retorts loud enough for us to hear down here on the sidelines.

My shoulders tense, and I have a feeling I know whose voice it is. Garrett shifts his stance, crossing his arms, and when I glance up at him, he's making the same face as his brother—tight-lipped, jaw set, eyes on the boys.

It's a mask of focus, giving nothing away.

Sadie Duck walks up holding Kimmie's hand. She's a senior like Austin, and she's on the varsity cheerleading squad. Her cousin Salina works with me as a waitress at Cooters & Shooters, so I've met her a few times. She's a pretty girl with a bouncing blonde ponytail and big brown eyes.

"Hi, Ms. Allie." She smiles politely before turning her attention to the field.

"Go, Aussie, go!" Kimmie bounces on her toes beside us, kicking her leg up like I've seen the cheerleaders do.

Then she jumps up and down, pumping her arms over her head and screaming as loud as she can. Only, it's less like a cheerleader's yell and more like the kind of noise you'd make when someone is attacking you.

"Dang, Peanut," Garrett growls at her. "You hollered like you saw a gator."

Sadie leans forward with a laugh, taking a knee to hug Jack's daughter. "Good energy, KJ. You'll make the squad for sure when you get bigger."

"I'll be the best cheerleader." Kimmie nods like she already knows. "I've got the legs for it."

Sadie's brown eyes cut up to mine, and we both bite our lips to keep from laughing.

"Okay!" is all she says.

The boys break, and Levi rolls away from a lineman, running around the outside of the field and down, following a similar path to the one Austin cut earlier.

Clasping my hands, I hold them in front of my mouth as I watch him. He doesn't seem to be hustling as hard as Austin did to get clear, and when Austin scans the field, he doesn't have any passing options.

Two big guys surround my son, but they don't sack him. They put their hands on his shoulders, and Jack tweets the whistle.

"That's a sack," Garrett explains. "They're not going to nail him in practice. No point hurting our best player."

He gives me a wink, but my chest is tight as the man in the bleachers loudly complains again. "You call that leadership?"

My stomach tenses, and I glance up to see Levi's dad on his feet striding down to where we're standing beside the field. Levi and Austin are with Jack again, and he's talking quietly to them.

Levi's eyes cut from Jack to his dad fuming beside us, but he quickly turns, nodding before heading out to the field where Austin again is in the quarterback spot.

"He's not going to start him, is he?" George Powell glares at Garrett, and I'm impressed by his bravery.

Garrett Bradford is several inches taller than him and 250 pounds of pure muscle, not to mention he's Jack's brother.

Still, Garrett is pretty laid-back for a big guy. I've only seen him angry a few times, and both were when bullies tried to mess with Dylan and Liv. Although, I heard he stuffed a guy into a dumpster when they were in high school for bullying Craig for being gay.

"Jack puts the boys where they shine the brightest, where they benefit the team most." Garrett gives the man a tight smile, and there's a hint of warning in his tone. "He'll be watching them all week—and all season."

George crosses his arms, and I take a subtle step away from

them, closer to Sadie and Kimmie, who is still cheering for Austin like nothing happened.

The boys break, and again, Austin falls back scanning the field. This time Levi attempts to run up the middle and is immediately stopped by one of the boys on D-line.

Garrett nods and claps. "Good hustle, Darnell!"

I'm still watching my quarterback son, wondering what he'll do or if he'll get sacked again.

Just in time, Noah Redford appears downfield, and Austin pulls back to fire a high, wobbly pass in his direction. The ball just leaves his hands when another big boy grabs Austin around the waist, playfully lifting him off the ground instead of tackling him.

It's a momentary distraction from what's happening with the ball.

Noah doubles back, stretching hard to complete the pass. It almost bounces off his fingers, but he manages to hold onto it, getting the first down.

"That's what I'm talking about!" Garrett's growling yell sends a thrill to my toes.

It was an amazing catch, and Kimmie Joy erupts into more cheers and screaming, holding her hands over her head and jumping up and down, kicking her leg almost to her nose.

"Lucky break," George grumbles beside me, which ignites my Mama Bear instincts.

"Well, he's definitely not getting help from certain players." My eyes are laser-focused on George, and I'm ready to go at it.

He's coming for my son, and I'm ready to go twelve rounds to defend him. It's obvious Levi is only performing his best when he's in the quarterback spot unlike Austin, who gives 110 percent wherever he's placed.

"Way to hustle, D-line!" Garrett steps forward, breaking our contact almost like he knows.

He's smiling when Jack gives his whistle a short tweet and

tells the boys that's it for today. It's hot as hell, and they're all dripping with sweat.

They head straight for the big green cooler, but Jack walks over to where Logan is standing, and Garrett goes to them as well. They're only a few feet away, and I can hear their conversation.

"D-line's coming together." Logan holds up a hand, and Garrett grabs it in a clasp. "You sure you don't want to join the coaching staff?"

"Who would keep Newhope safe?" Garrett grins. "I'm building a rapport in the community."

"Looks like your decision is clear, Coach." George Powell doesn't miss a chance to walk straight up to where the three of them are talking.

Jack's jaw tightens, and I know that look. Jack Bradford doesn't like being told what to do with his team, which he takes very seriously—especially not by pushy parents.

"I'll see how he does this week." Jack's voice is even, and his blue eyes fix on George's.

"You can't deny what you see with your own eyes." George's voice rises. "Levi's the best quarterback on the field."

"I wouldn't say that." Jack's voice remains calm. "He's got a lot of talent, but I want to see him be more of a team player."

"A team player? He's a team leader." George isn't backing down. "He threw a touchdown before you took him out of the game. Is that how you run your team? You're supposed to be a legend."

"My dad was the legend." It sounds like a joke, but an edge is in Jack's tone. "I'm only the head coach, and I decide who plays where and when."

George turns to me. "This is Allie Sinclair? Austin's mother?"

My lips part, but my back straightens. "I am."

I might be small, but I'm not afraid of this man.

"Uh-huh." He nods like he knows something. "And that's Coach Bradford's daughter? The one you're always keeping?"

He points at Kimmie Joy, who is jumping around beside Sadie.

Jack walks over to stand between me and Levi's dad. "What's on your mind, Powell?"

"Nothing at all, Coach." A wicked grin curls his lips. "But she's a pretty lady. I don't blame you for giving her son preferential treatment. Maybe those favors go both ways."

Jack moves so fast, I can't believe Garrett catches him. He holds his brother's arms, looking over his shoulder at Powell.

"You'd better get going, George." Garrett gives a sharp order. "One more word, and you'll be lucky if Levi's on third string."

My heart hammers in my chest, and Jack's jaw is set. Zane walks over to stand beside his brothers, and I notice his fists are clenched.

Logan is with the boys on the sidelines, and they're all watching the scene. My face is hot, but Austin is frowning. Levi looks up at the sky, then he jogs onto the field, grabbing his father's arm.

"Come on, Dad." His voice is quiet, but I can still hear him. "Let it go."

"Don't tell me what to do, boy," George snaps, throwing his son's arm to the side.

Levi's eyes fall to the ground as if he's embarrassed, and I blink up at Jack.

Garrett's grip on his arms relaxes, and while he's still angry, the tension in his body relaxes a bit.

George is still seething, but Jack looks to where his team stands in a group, waiting for what happens next.

"Daddy!" Kimmie runs up to Jack, catching his hand. "Did you see me cheering? Sadie says I'm a good cheerleader. She says I'll be on the cheer squad when I'm big!"

He lifts her off the ground, putting her on his hip. She puts her arms around his neck smiling, and he turns, going to his boys.

Chapter 6

Jack

"WE'VE GOT A BIG YEAR COMING UP, AND I REALLY LIKE WHAT I'M seeing out here." My tone is even, no hint of what almost happened.

Garrett had me around the shoulders, and I'm not going to lie, I was pissed as hell. My brothers know me well, and they were right to gather around me.

But when I looked up and saw my team watching, the worry in their young eyes, I was right back in that room the night my father died.

I had to step back and remember my position here. It's easy to give in to anger. Control is much harder, but it's always the right choice.

The hardest part was catching a glimpse of Allie making a hasty retreat back to the school. I'm worried she was hurt or embarrassed. I hate that she was alone.

Instead, I'm standing in the huddle, making eye contact, one by one, with boys I've known since they were little guys, shouting at me from the park to *watch what they we do, Coach.*

"I was impressed with your hustle, D-line. I can tell you're working hard." I look from Darnell to Rome. "You're going to win us the game one of these times."

From there, I go down the row, Noah to Rich to Tyreek to Flynn, finishing up with my boy Austin. "It's your year, buddy."

He nods, and I give him a warm grin.

Only Levi stands at the edge, looking at the turf.

Reaching out, I pat his arm. "I'll see you tomorrow, and I want to see more teamwork."

The boy's lips press into a frown, but he nods. "Yes, sir, Coach."

"Go, Captains!" Kimmie pumps her little arms over her head from where she sits on my hip, and it breaks the tension.

All the boys exhale a smile, and with that, I leave them, going to my truck and driving home.

Kimmie's tucked in bed, and I'm exhausted. Walking through the house, I'm keyed up, and everything about the confrontation on the field burns in my memory.

It's been a minute since I was that pissed. It was the first time in a long time I'd wanted to punch a man square in his stupid face.

I didn't even want to be with my family at the restaurant tonight. I carried Kimmie to the truck, and we came home and had a dinner of frozen pizza and chicken nuggets, which she thought was special.

I sent her up to bathe, preparing myself to clean up a big mess. I was not prepared for her to yell for me to come catch her as she jumped out of the tub. Of course, I trudged up the stairs and held the towel for her to jump into my arms, then dried her off and helped her get ready for bed.

Reading *Dogzilla* helped my mood some, but even after prayers and my own shower, I'm still knotted up inside. Part of it is the confrontation, but a bigger part is I wish I'd talked to Allie before I left.

I should've made sure she was okay. She was right there in the middle of it listening to his accusations, hearing him say terrible things about her.

Levi's dad is an asshole, and the things he said were way out of line. Still, I've dealt with parents like him before. Hell, I've dealt with worse parents than him.

I've seen men trying to relive their glory days through their sons, and I've seen men with obvious addiction issues try to smack one of my players right in front of me.

Every time, I've handled them firmly and finally. The abusers I tell to stop hitting their kids or I'm calling child protective services. For the rest, I make it clear, if they want their sons on my team, they'll keep their shit at home.

Until today.

Seeing how he treated his own son is the one thing that helped me regain control. That, and my little girl walking right into the middle of the whole thing and holding up her hands to me. She and the boys help me remember what matters.

But I should've gone to Allie.

I should've made sure she wasn't embarrassed or hurt or anything. I should've made sure Austin didn't take what George said to heart.

I should've made sure the people who matter to me know I care.

Rubbing a hand over my face, I look up at the clock. It's almost eleven, and Kimmie's in bed asleep. I can't go over there now.

Picking up my phone, I see a string of texts on the screen.

Garrett: Bruh, where are you?

Logan: I can't believe I missed it all. I was talking to Rich.

Zane: I only caught the tail end—that guy was way out of line. Is Levi off the team?

Hendrix: Seriously, WTF?

Garrett: This is what you get for being in LA.

Hendrix: I swear, G...

Logan: New kid in town, goes out for QB1 today in camp. Jack alternates him and Austin, and the dad loses his shit. Says Jack is giving Austin the top spot because he's sleeping with Allie.

Hendrix: That's bullshit—Austin's clearly a talented player.

Zane: Levi's very good, too.

Garrett: If Jack doesn't kick him off the team.

Logan: I don't like punishing the kid for his dad, talking from personal experience.

Garrett: He was pretty embarrassed.

Logan: Hate that.

Hendrix: If he's that good, use them both. High schools do it all the time.

Logan: It gives them less time on the field, less opportunity to show what they can do if scouts are there.

Zane: Just waiting to hear from our coach.

Garrett: Where you at, bro? You okay?

Zane: Talk to us, Jack.

I study the screen a long time, considering a reply, but it's late. The chat ended a few hours ago. I'll talk to them tomorrow.

My thoughts are on Allie. I could call her. My thumb hovers over the button when a light tapping sounds on my door. Lifting my chin, I wait for it to sound again.

When it does, I walk over to see who's out there. I half-expect to see Dylan making sure we had dinner. I don't expect to see Austin.

"Hey, you're out late." I open the door, holding it so he can come inside. "Everything okay?"

"Hey, Coach." He walks into the kitchen, and I shut the door behind him. "I'm sorry for coming over like this, but I couldn't sleep."

All the thoughts I've been wrestling with press against my temples, and my throat tightens. "What's on your mind?"

He puts his hands on the bar, exhaling heavily. "I was thinking about Levi."

I cross my arms, leaning against the counter. Austin isn't the boy he was three years ago. He's grown up a lot since the days when he used to babysit Kimmie, when he got her hooked on penny cakes for Friday breakfast—*because it's T-G-I-F*, as she likes to say.

He's taller. His brown hair is a little shaggy on top, but it's neatly trimmed around his ears and collar. His shoulders are broad, and his muscles are well defined since he started working out with weights.

All of these things are what I told him to do to improve his game.

Austin does everything I tell him to do to be the best player he can be, and I think about the contrast between how I treat him and how George treats Levi.

Lifting my chin, I nudge him. "What about Levi?"

"He feels really bad about how his dad acted." Austin's hazel eyes cut up to mine. "He said it's the reason they had to leave Gainesville—and Kissimmee and Apalachicola."

I glance at the floor, shifting my stance. "I can't let his father's behavior pass. If I do, it'll turn into a real problem."

"I know." Austin nods, but I can tell he's worried.

"What are you thinking?"

The boy's expression tightens, and he clears his throat. "He made some really good plays out there today. He looked good. Real good."

"He did."

"I was just thinking…" Austin's jaw flexes. "We want to win state this year, and if we're going to do that, we need the best quarterback leading the team. Maybe it should be him."

Pride swells in my chest. I know how much starting quarterback means to Austin, and hearing him selflessly offer to give it up for the betterment of the team scores a lot of points with me.

"I'll make that decision."

"I know." He nods. "I'm just saying. I think he's kind of… better than me."

"No, he's not." Uncrossing my arms, I put my hands on the bar, gentling my approach. "There's a lot more to being QB-1 than completing passes. You're a leader, Austin. You've worked hard, and your teammates know you. They trust you. You care about them."

"I do." His jaw tightens, and he huffs a breath. "I guess I don't want him to be penalized for something he can't help." His voice goes quiet. "I have a bad dad, too."

It's a punch in the chest, and protective energy surges to fill the space.

"Do you trust me?"

His eyes flicker to mine. "Yeah?"

"I care a lot about you and your mom, but that doesn't mean I'd tell you something that wasn't true." His brow lowers, and I walk around the bar to put my hand on his shoulder. "You're not only a great player, Austin. You're a good kid. You have a good heart, and you care about your team. That's what makes you a leader."

His shoulders relax. "I don't think I've ever run plays like Levi did, though."

"Well, come on, then. Let's take a look and see if we're forgetting anything."

I lead him into the living room, and with a few taps, I pull up our private YouTube channel. We spend the next hour watching highlights from last year's games, when he was the backup quarterback.

We watch him throw the winning pass against the Pirates, thirty yards straight into Noah's waiting arms. A few clicks, and I show him looking around, not seeing an opening and running right up the middle for a twenty-yard first down.

After a little while of watching him being a real star, I see his confidence returning.

"What do you think?" I ask.

He nods. "Is it okay if I watch a little more?"

"Sure." I start for the kitchen, but he stops me.

"Oh, one more thing, Coach?"

"Yeah?"

He sits straighter. "Would it be okay… I mean, would you help me do something for my mom?"

My brow furrows, and I take a step closer. "What do you need?"

"You know Christmas gets here real quick once the season starts, and when I'm playing, I can't really make any money." I nod, and he continues. "I was thinking maybe I could make her something, but I'd need a place to do it where she won't see. I was thinking maybe I could do it here?"

"What did you have in mind?"

"Well, she likes to read, and she has her books kind of stacked all over her bedroom. I was thinking maybe a bookcase?"

I picture Allie's bedroom with books all over the place. *Sexy librarian.*

"I think that's a great idea. I've even got some tools you can use. I can show you how."

His face relaxes with a smile, and I'm glad he's lighter than when he arrived. "Thanks, Coach."

I continue to the kitchen, where I prepare Kimmie's and my lunches for tomorrow and put them in the refrigerator. When I return to the living room, Austin's eyes are closed, and he's sound asleep.

My lips press into a smile, and affection warms my chest. Austin's been a good kid as long as I've known him, since he rolled into town a scrawny thirteen-year-old lurking behind his mother.

They were the same height in those days. His bangs were long over his eyes, and he kept his chin down. He didn't say much, and awkward, early-teen insecurity clung to him like a coat.

I'd seen it so many times, but I also watched him grow out of it. As the years passed, as we worked together, he got stronger. He made friends and his confidence grew.

Then he made the team, and he stopped hanging his head, barely speaking above a mutter. He laughed and joked around, and like his mom, he fit right into our clan.

Hesitating, I glance up the hall in the direction of my bedroom. He can sleep on the couch no problem, but I wonder if Allie knows he's here.

I walk to the back door, but I don't see their car outside in the driveway. He must've walked over here.

Allie's house is less than half a mile away, and I don't like to think of her being there alone, especially with her ex-husband MIA.

As far as I know, Austin still doesn't know his dad's out of prison or I'm sure he wouldn't have walked over here.

Casting a glance back at the living room, I head out into the darkness.

Chapter 7

Allie

Dylan: Where are you? I've been waiting for you to come to the restaurant all afternoon!

Liv: Garrett told me what happened. You okay, hon?

Raven: What happened??? This is so not cool with me in LA. Is somebody hurt? 911!

Rachel: Your guess is as good as mine, Stormy Spice. I have no idea what's going on. I've been doing water aerobics with Miss Gina.

Dylan: Some new kid's dad yelled at Jack in front of everyone. He said Jack's giving Austin preferential treatment because Allie's giving him "favors."

Raven: Whoa… he's dead. I want his name, photo, address…

Liv: Take it easy, Stormy Spice. I'm sworn to uphold the law.

Dylan: I'm with Rave. You'll have to sit this one out, Liv. He's dead 😡

Rachel: You should slip him one of your lethal peppers. I read somewhere a kid died from drinking caffeinated lemonade. Surely, a pepper can go up against lemonade.

Dylan: If George Powell dares to show his face in Coolers & Shooters, he'll have more than a pepper to worry about.

Raven: Allie, where are you? Are you okay?

Hey, friends. I'm okay—I kind of have a headache.

Rachel: Sometimes cutting back on sugar causes headaches.

Dylan: Allie! 🤗 Come let us hug on you.

I would, but I'm already in bed. It's okay, really!

Liv: Slight change of subject, I said yes to coaching the drill team. Dylan, Allie, I expect you two to help me. Dylan, you promised!

Dylan: I'm there!!! It's going to be so much fun!

I'll be there 💙

Dylan: We'll have the team kick George Powell in the shins 👟

I put my phone aside. I don't feel like texting anymore.

My emotions have been all over the place since Levi's dad went after Jack and Austin on the field in front of God and everyone.

At first I was in full-on mamma-bear protective rage that he would try to push his son onto the team and then bully Jack into giving him the QB-1 spot after one day of practice.

I was furious that he tried to imply Austin wasn't good enough to lead the team, when everyone in sports media has been talking about the upcoming season and seeing him play.

Just as fast, I was embarrassed when he implied Jack was advancing my son because of "favors" I might be giving in exchange. I was ready to claw his eyes out. He basically called me a whore, and I wanted Jack to punch him in the face.

It seemed like Jack had the same reaction, but then he only picked up his daughter and walked away, leaving me standing there with Garrett and Zane.

A knot was in my throat when I glanced at the stands, wondering if everyone heard what George said, and even worse, if they were all thinking the same thing.

As if reading my mind, Garrett put his hand on my shoulder, giving it a squeeze. "Ignore that noise. If they can't see how talented Austin is on the field, they need glasses."

Blinking quickly, I smiled up at him, doing my best to play it off. Still, I was humiliated, and I wanted out of the public eye.

I rode back to the house with Austin and whipped up some dirty rice. My starving son wolfed it down, but I wasn't hungry. I told Austin I had a headache, and he didn't question it.

He's been pretty distracted ever since the showdown on the field as well. So I gave him a hug and told him I was going to bed early.

After a quick shower, I curled up under the covers with my new favorite sexy romance. This one's got a BDSM trope, and it's hot as fire. Every time the hero says *Good Girl*, I shiver.

People don't understand a librarian like me reading "trashy" romance novels, especially ones with domination in them. They say I'm messed up or I want to have bad relationships, and that's how I ended up with Rip.

First, rude. Second, romance is not trash. It's well-written and for many women it's healing and empowering. My brand of feminism says women deserve to have whatever type of sex turns them on—in a safe, consensual environment, of course.

Reading dark romance lets us explore sexual fantasies in a way we can control. It says more about *their* sexual hangups than ours that they can't understand it.

I must've fallen asleep, because when I lift my head off the pillow, it's dark outside. The house is quiet, and I wonder if Austin remembered to set the alarm. He doesn't understand why I'm using it, and I still haven't told him about his dad.

I'd planned to do it after fall camp, but maybe it's time—if only so he'll be more careful.

Rubbing a hand over my eyes, I walk to the living room to check the panel on the wall by the front door. The system is un-armed, and a sliver of fear trickles through my chest. My eyes drift up the short hall in the direction of my son's room.

It's dark, but I'll tell him in the morning.

Returning to the keypad, I'm about to enter the code when I glance out the window and nearly scream. A man stands in the shadows watching the house, and my heart flies to my throat.

My hands are shaking, and I'm about to run to my bedroom to call Garrett when the clouds move away from the moon.

The man's features grow clearer, painted in the silvery light, and with a hiccuped inhale, I know him. *Is it the moonlight? Is this a dream?*

It's Jack.

I'd recognize that gorgeous face anywhere.

My feet are bare, and I'm only wearing soft cotton shorts and a long-sleeved, cotton shirt. I don't care. He draws me to him without saying a word.

I fling the door open and run out to where he stands.

His hands open as I get closer, and he takes a step toward me. "Allie?"

"What are you doing here?" I'm breathless, my heart beating wildly in my chest.

He's so tall, I have to arch my neck to look up at him. His cap is gone, and his dark hair hangs messily over his forehead. He looks younger, more vulnerable because of it.

His bare arms are lined with muscles, and the T-shirt he's wearing stretches attractively over his chest. He's so handsome—even more in the twilight.

His dark brow lowers over his blue eyes, and he shakes his head, seeming as bewildered as I feel. "I started walking…"

I swallow my emotions. "What about Kimmie?"

"Austin's with her. He fell asleep on my couch, but I was worried about you. I didn't want you to be here alone."

"Austin's at your house?"

"He was upset about what happened and wanted to talk. Then when he fell asleep, I needed to see you."

A shiver moves through me. *Needed…* "Why?"

We're standing here in the moonlight facing each other, barely holding back.

He takes a step closer. "I'm sorry I couldn't go to you on the field today. I was angry, and I had to take care of the boys. But I hated what he said about you."

"It wasn't your fault. You're doing your job, being a great coach." My tongue touches my bottom lip. "I only wish…"

I can't say it.

He steps closer. "What?"

Soft wind moves around us, and I look up at his intense gaze. His beautiful blue eyes move over my face like it's a puzzle he's trying to solve. His arms are straight at his sides, but his hands flex, almost like he's fighting to hold them back.

The breath is tight in my chest, and my fingers tremble. I've never been in this place with him before, so close, so alone, so free.

I lift my hand, wanting to touch him. He's always distant, forbidden, yet here he is, right here…

Light as a whisper, my hand floats over his heart. The warmth of his skin heats my fingertips. "I wish I knew what you were thinking."

His lips part, but he hesitates. The muscles in my body tense as I wait, needing to know what he'll say.

He turns, taking a step to the side and looking down. "Every year, a new set of boys comes to me with dreams. Their parents come with dreams, and they all want me to make them come true."

"It's a lot of pressure."

"It's not that… I don't mind helping them do their best to achieve their goals."

My brows furrow, but I don't interrupt. He seems to be struggling with what he wants to say.

"It's different with you." Lifting his chin, he holds my gaze, and energy squeezes my heart. "I've always been able to control what I want."

He steps closer, and I swallow a whimper. I want so much for him to say the words, to break the tension.

"What do you want?" I whisper.

His hand moves as if he'll touch me, but he stops himself. "I want you to be safe. I don't want you to be afraid."

I blink up at him slowly. "I'm never afraid with you."

"Allie…" The ache in his low voice is warm liquid in my veins. "You don't know what those words do to me."

I can barely breathe. "Tell me."

His straight white teeth close as if stopping himself, as if he said too much. "I know what it's like to trust the wrong person, to wish someone could be different… could be what you need."

Inhaling a shaky breath, I want to be what he needs.

"I always knew Rip was bad. I guess I thought he would make my life more exciting. I was so stupid. I should've known he would only hurt me."

He shakes his head. "You never know." Stepping away, he rubs his hand over his forehead. "I just wanted to be sure you were safe."

He's shutting me out again, withdrawing, and I want to scream for him to stop, to come back to me.

I take a step closer. "Jack!"

"I can't..." He pauses. I think he'll leave, but instead he takes my hand roughly in his. "Come on."

He walks ahead of me, leading me to the house. I watch his broad shoulders stretching that shirt, so strong and imposing. He's moving fast, and I stumble behind him as we get closer to my door.

When we reach the still-open entrance to my house, he turns, pulling me in front of him. Need pulses through me on every rapid heartbeat.

"Go inside and set the alarm. I'll take care of Austin tonight."

"But Jack..." It's a pleading sound, but he practically lifts me off my feet and puts me through the open door.

"Do what I say, Allie." Reaching forward, he grabs the doorknob, pulling it shut with me inside. "Set the alarm."

Our eyes hold through the glass. Mine are begging, but his are firm.

He waits as I slowly go to the panel and enter the numbers. It's armed, and I look up at him through the locked door once more.

He's not smiling, and instead of goodnight, he simply says, "Good."

Lifting my hand, I press it against the cold barrier.

He only returns the way he came, walking fast until he disappears into the darkness.

Chapter 8

Jack

"Edward wants to join the team." Zane stands with his hands on his hips, looking out at the boys on the field.

My brow furrows, and I glance at my brother. "He does?"

"Apparently, he's been watching my old reels and reading about kicking techniques. Last night he told me he'd like to learn in case Rome can't play."

I take a beat to consider this. Zane wouldn't suggest Edward for the team if he didn't think he could do it, especially with Edward's situation.

"It's a lot of stress." I study my brother's face. "Will he be okay with that?"

Zane puts both hands in his back pockets, looking at Edward standing on the sidelines. "He taught himself to play pool, and he won the tournament. He taught himself to ride, and he's one of our best horsemen. We don't have a backup kicker, and I can work with him at home."

"Okay, then."

A hint of a smile crosses my brother's lips and for the first time since I left Allie last night, I feel like I got something right.

Walking over to the cooler, I think of her standing in front of me in her bare feet in the moonlight.

I left the house needing to see her. I needed to tell her I was sorry for walking away after what George said. I didn't expect the rush of feelings I had when she ran out to me in the darkness.

Her bright eyes were so blue. It was as if she were outlined in silver light. Her lips seemed fuller somehow, and when she said, *I wish…*

I realized I'd made a big mistake.

In the daylight with all the kids and their parents around us and my family watching and the boys and everything, I can put up a wall. I can control my emotions. I'm safe.

In the darkness, with only her and me, with her dressed in only a thin cotton shirt that allowed me to see the shape of her full breasts rising and falling with every pant…

The mouthwatering scent of her apple body wash or shampoo or whatever it was, taunted me like forbidden fruit. All the years alone, all the times I've wanted her, watched her, hit me hard.

Desire burned like fire in my chest. My dick was a rod in my jeans. I was so close to dragging her into my arms and kissing her.

I had to put her inside her house and close that door.

I wouldn't let George Powell have a foothold. I wouldn't let all the whispers of the parents, the accusations that I've only helped Austin to get to her be true.

Maybe she's the reason I noticed him, but Austin can stand on his own, and I won't create a scandal that could hurt his reputation.

I'm the head coach. The leader. I have to control myself.

I want Austin to have his dream, no questions asked.

Last night, when I got back to my house, he was still asleep on the couch, only Kimmie was curled up asleep at his feet like a little kitten.

Shaking my head, I lifted her carefully and carried her back to her bed. I tucked her in again and went back to put a blanket over Allie's son before putting myself to bed.

Then the alarm went off too early this morning.

I'd spent the night tossing and turning, wanting her and feeling like I'd only made everything so much worse.

Austin was gone when I dragged my ass to the kitchen, and Kimmie was still asleep. I was dressed and finishing my cup of coffee when Dylan arrived.

"You okay this morning?" Dylan caught my arm, giving it a squeeze. "Everybody was talking about what happened at Cooters & Shooters last night."

"That's why I came home." I put my mug in the sink. "Last thing I needed was to hang around all that gossip."

"If it makes any difference, we all know the truth." She filled her own mug of coffee. "Anyone with eyes can see how talented Austin is. George Powell is only making his situation worse. He runs the risk of making Levi an outcast."

My lungs tensed, and I thought about Austin coming here last night. Dylan's words were his fear, and to his credit, he didn't want that to happen.

"Are you going to kick him off the team?" She gazed up at me with those big brown eyes.

I thought about the brother's chat and what Logan said. Levi's a talented kid, and he shouldn't be punished for his father's lack of self-control.

"No."

Her shoulders relaxed, and she stepped forward to wrap her arms around my waist. "That's why you're the best coach and the best big brother in the world."

Putting my arms around her, I huffed a laugh, giving her a brief squeeze. "I don't know about all that, but I'll judge him on his own merits. Now I've got to get to school."

"We'll see you in a few hours," she called after me. "Liv's coaching the drill team, and they have their first meeting this afternoon. Allie and I are helping her."

I swallowed the knot in my throat, internally berating myself for the flush in my neck, the uptick of my pulse. It was an immature response. Of course, I'd see Allie again. She works at the school, she works at my family's restaurant, she's Austin's mom.

I'd deal with these feelings the way I always do.

"See you then." My tone was level, and I headed out the door.

Allie's pretty face was on my mind the entire short drive, and I pulled into the parking lot right before the rest of the team arrived, just in time to meet Zane on the field and give Edward the thumbs up.

Now I'm exhausted.

It's going to be a long day.

Logan's whistle blasts, and the offense lines up. Austin is in the quarterback position, and Levi is in the backfield across from Noah in a basic split-back formation.

It actually hasn't been as shitty of a day as I was bracing for it to be. George isn't in the stands, and the sky is overcast, bringing down the heat.

"Austin's playing better today than he has all camp." Logan stands beside me, watching him fake a pass, then charge up the center, cutting through the line and getting the first down.

"Where you at, Defense?" Buddy yells from the sidelines. "I could've driven a truck through that hole. You need to run more laps?"

Garrett's not here today, but he'll be back tomorrow and Friday afternoon. The short time he's been able to help has brought my starting lineup together, and once we get to play-ing, they'll really gel.

Logan tweets his whistle, and the boys huddle. I see Austin standing tall, nodding at his fellow teammates and telling them *Ace*. I'll have to tell him to use hand signals, because all eyes will be on him, reading his lips.

They go down for the snap, and my shoulders tense when I hear the sound of girls jogging out to join us on the sidelines.

I keep my eyes on the team.

Rich breaks off from the line, going downfield, and Levi finds another hole in the center. Austin quickly scans both boys, makes a decision, and fires a pass to our newest player.

This time Levi catches it easily, strong-arms a lineman and runs it twenty yards to first and goal. Offense breaks into celebration, surrounding Levi and slapping his back, lifting him off his feet.

My chest warms, and I'm gratified to see the smile on Levi's face.

Parents clap and cheer from the bleachers, and the new drill team now present on the sidelines jumps up and down, cheering for the boys.

For the first time in almost twenty-four hours, the tension in my chest breaks. They look like a team, and those rumblings of taking state are starting to feel real.

Then I see Allie.

As if drawn by an invisible force, my eyes go directly to hers. She's standing on the other side of the crowd of girls, almost like she's hiding behind Liv, but I find her.

Our eyes clash, and energy pops in my chest. My throat constricts, and I can't look away. I want to drink in the sight of her. I want to fantasize about all the things I could do to her.

Today, she's wearing a white skirt and a red tank top to match the colors of the team, red and white. The top is tight, clinging to her curves, her full breasts and narrow waist, and the skirt is short, showing off her cute ass and tanned legs.

Her short hair bounces around her shoulders, and her lips are also red. She's wearing white socks and chunky tennis shoes, and she looks better than any cheerleader. She's a fucking fantasy.

"Daddy!" My daughter runs up and grabs me around the legs, breaking my lusty thoughts. "Miss Allie is helping Aunt

Deedee and Auntie Liv coach the drill team! I think I could be on the drill team. I'm good at kicking!"

Kimmie bounces beside me, kicking her leg straight out, and I have to step back fast so she doesn't rack me in the nuts.

"Watch where you're kicking, Peanut!" Zane covers his mouth with his hand, snorting a laugh. "You almost made your dad a soprano."

Kimmie squints one eye, looking up at him. "What's that?"

He's still laughing. "It's a person with a very high voice."

I put my hand on my little girl's shoulder. "Let Aunt Liv do her job. Don't interrupt her, and stay out of the way."

Kimmie nods, watching the girls lining up in formation on the sidelines. Liv walks down, moving people around based on what appears to be height.

They're in two lines, staggered so each girl is visible from the field, and Dylan leans into Allie's ear to say something. My sister is also wearing a white skirt and red tank, and I realize all the girls are in either white shorts or tennis skirts and red tank tops.

I've only been looking at one person.

"This will be your spot for the year." I'm close enough to hear Liv's instructions. "Be spatially aware of each other."

Logan's whistle draws me back, and I remember I'm supposed to be watching the field, not Allie Sinclair.

"One more, Coach?" Logan looks at me, and I can't tell if he saw where my attention had drifted.

"It's a good day." I look up at the overcast sky. "I hate to waste it."

"We can take a break and then run a few more."

Liv's girls launch into a series of hand moves, swinging their hips in time to music coming from a small speaker.

Allie and Dylan stand back with their arms crossed as Liv leads them through the choreography, and every few minutes, Allie sneaks a glance in my direction.

It's a fresh little explosion every time our eyes meet, and I clear my throat, realizing Logan is waiting for my answer.

"You're right. The boys have been working hard. Let's go one more round and wrap it up."

"You sure?" A teasing grin lifts the corner of his mouth, and I know he busted me that time. "We could stay longer if you'd like."

"I'm sure. I've seen all I need for today."

Logan tweets the whistle then circles his finger above his head. "One more round, and that's a wrap."

The boys huddle quickly before lining up again. Another snap, and the girls get quiet watching them. Noah shoots down the field on the outside, but Flynn Barnes, our cornerback, is on him. Austin is under pressure, as two big guys barrel forward.

"Where's Tyreek?" My voice is low, but I see our offensive lineman is on the ground. "Shit."

Austin's on the verge of being sacked when his eyes light, and he pulls back, sending it easily into Levi's waiting hands in the end zone.

Again, the spectators go wild.

The drill team jumps up and down, shaking their small pom poms over their heads and kicking to their noses as the parents in the bleachers stomp their feet and cheer. Even Kimmie is jumping up and down, kicking her leg and yelling for Austin.

"Looks like we've got a winning pair." Zane glances at me, and I nod.

"We'll reverse it and see how they do tomorrow."

The boys all crowd around the cooler, and I can't stop myself. One more time, I look over at Allie standing with my sister. This time she looks right back at me, smiling broadly.

It's the best thing I've seen all afternoon.

Chapter 9

Allie

"**D**ON'T TELL LIV I ASKED YOU THIS, BUT HOW IS THE DRILL TEAM different from the cheerleading squad?" I'm standing in the kitchen at Cooters & Shooters watching Dylan finish up tonight's Dare Dish.

It's Pepper X pork chili with a coconut and sour cream base. Plastic gloves are on her hands, and she's wearing a plastic shield over her eyes as she carefully moves the pot of chili onto the rolling cart.

"Drill team is an all-girl precision dance line. The cheerleaders are co-ed, and they do cheers, chants, climbing formations, and tumbling."

"But the drill team cheers, too." I step back as a spicy pepper sensation in the air makes my nostrils tingle. "Dang, Dylan! What is that? It's burning my nose."

"Isn't it wild?" Her eyes are wide, and she slips off the plastic gloves and grabs several loaves of French bread. "Pepper X is currently considered the hottest pepper in the world." Her eyes widen behind the safety shield. "It's hotter than a Carolina Reaper."

I hold a towel over my mouth and nose for protection. "Who's going to eat that?"

"Oliver Duck," she snips. "And if I hear one more word out of him about how my Dare dishes have fallen off, I'm going to make him eat a whole one raw."

"Okay, Miss Feisty." I laugh, raising my eyebrows at Craig, who's just entered the room.

"She's still working on it?" He jumps back, going to the other side of the large table and holding a hand over his nose. "I thought you'd be finished by now. The crowd is lining up out there."

"I'm being careful. This one's a baddie." Dylan puts the lid on the pot and nods at the freezer. "We're going to need all the ice cream tonight, Al."

"What's our warning? Only try this one if you have a death wish?"

"Here, I wrote it down." She hands me the iPad, and I scan the note she has on the screen.

I've spent two days working with Liv on the drill team. Two days going out to the football field and watching Jack stand with his strong arms crossed, ball cap lowered over his eyes, that muscle moving in his square jaw.

For two days, I've tried *not* to act like a love-struck teenager every time I catch him looking at me. I can't take my eyes off him since he lifted me by the arms and practically shoved me into my house, closing the door like it was all he could do to put a barrier between us.

I was awake the rest of the night. My insides were soaring, and all I could see was the fire in his eyes. I repeated his words over and over in my mind, *I needed to see you… It's different with you…*

Then he took my hand and dragged me to the house like it took all his willpower to get away from me.

Now it's burning between us like a wildfire. Every day I go to the field, and I try to watch my son. I don't know what Jack said to him, but his confidence is restored. He's playing better than he's played all year.

Even when Jack switched up the positions yesterday, putting Levi in the quarterback spot, it wasn't the same. Levi couldn't match the energy Austin had, and even though all the running backs were doing their best, it was clear who the boys wanted as team captain.

Austin was back in the top spot this afternoon, and all everyone could talk about was the Captains going all the way to the state championships.

It feels more possible than ever before.

I wonder if Jack will come to the restaurant tonight. He's stayed away every night since Monday, from what I've heard. I came back Tuesday, ready to face him and get it over with, but he wasn't here.

He wasn't here last night, when Rachel told us Edward was joining the team as the second-string kicker.

We were all excited and encouraging, but Edward's expression never changed.

"Kicking requires more focused skill than brute strength," he explained in his usual, logical tone. "It's the only position I could have on the team, as kickers rarely get hurt."

Austin smiled, patting him on the shoulder. "I think it's pretty cool having you onboard. I hope Rome gives you a chance."

I've always been proud of my son, but the way he befriended Rachel's brother and always looks out for him at school and now on the team makes me feel like he didn't get any of his father's bad genes.

His father, who as of now, hasn't made a peep.

I watch the news every day, and I text with friends back home. They say he's in the city, but he's lying low. The thought of him roaming around our old neighborhood makes my stomach churn, but we've got a thousand eyes on him. I've got to believe at least one of them will warn me if anything changes.

"Are we doing this?" Craig hollers from where he's standing at the PA system in his blond Sandy-from-*Grease* wig.

Every Dare Night, he picks out a special fire-themed song to play while the brave customers line up to try Dylan's latest concoction.

"Yes!" I step up on a chair to give the warning. "Okay, people, this one's a baddie. Ready to be warned?"

A low roar moves through the line, and I start to read. "Pepper X is currently the hottest pepper in the world. It ranks higher than both the Carolina Reaper and the Komodo Dragon with a score of three million on the Scoville heat scale. Seriously, y'all, this one is experts only."

A few people step out of line, shaking their heads and laughing. I nod, pointing at them as I continue, finishing off the warning.

"Dylan has made a delicious Pepper X pork chili with a coconut and sour cream base. It's loaded with beans and cheese to help cut the heat, and as always, we have cups of vanilla ice cream, milk, and tomato juice for our lactose-intolerant friends. Water or beer will not soothe the burn, since it's an oil."

I'm about to put the iPad down when Dylan hisses at me. "You skipped the last part!"

"Oh, sorry!" I hold up a finger. "One last thing—this one's for you, Oliver Duck."

A chuckle ripples through the crowd as Dylan's teenage nemesis smirks and walks to the front of the line. He's a skinny, red-headed guy with wire-rimmed glasses, and he hasn't met a pepper he can't eat. He makes me believe in that old "redheads don't feel pain" myth.

Dylan hands him a serving, and he takes it, running his eyes over her hand before lifting the spoon and taking a bite.

He holds a minute, and we all watch him closely. I don't see a change, or maybe that's a slight flinch in his left eye?

Without a word, he turns and walks back to his table.

"That's what I thought," Dylan says to me.

"Did you get him?" I lean in to speak in her ear.

"Let's do this!" Craig hits the music, and we serve the rest of the line.

Tonight he starts off with "HandClap" by Fitz and the Tantrums, and three of the waitresses hop onto the small bar with him to dance, rolling their hips and clapping their hands.

"I love this song!" Rachel skips up to where I'm standing behind the table with Dylan handing out spoons and cups of vanilla ice cream.

"Get up there!" I nod to the bar. "Unless you're brave enough to try this chili from hell."

She shakes her head. "I'm getting some for Liv's mom, but I'm too scared."

"I don't blame you. I'm not sure my intestines can handle it."

The music slides into "Dangerous" by Kardinal Offshall, and my eye catches the outside double doors opening. Then my heart jumps to my throat when Jack enters the room with Garrett at his side.

Their brows are lowered, and they seem to be having a serious conversation. But as soon as Craig sees Garrett, he's on the mic. "Sheriff Grizz, we've got a 10-33 on the bar—immediate assistance needed."

Garrett breaks into a laugh, and he holds up a finger before disappearing into the kitchen. Jack is left alone at the door, and of course, he looks straight at me.

A hint of a smile lifts one corner of his mouth, and I can't move. I can barely breathe.

"Allie," Dylan bumps my hip. "You're holding up the line, girl."

Garrett dances into the room again in his own blond Sandra-Dee wig, shaking his ass and going straight to the small bar. Female whistles and catcalls ripple through the room, and an old Judas Priest song starts.

In a single move, Garrett hauls his six-foot-four frame onto the small bar with the dancers, and everyone cheers as they fill the makeshift dance floor in the cleared-out center of the dining room.

It breaks the spell Jack has on me, and I return to handing out spoons and cups of ice cream to the waiting line. They all slip a few dollars into the tip jar, but it's all volunteer. Dylan doesn't make anyone pay for Dare Night.

Liv walks in behind Jack with Gigi on her hip, and she gives him a nudge. He smiles in response, saying something so calmly, it makes me wonder if I'm the only one who felt that earthquake when our eyes met.

Gigi bounces her little arms up and down like she's trying to keep time with the music. The last daring client takes a bowl of Pepper X chili, and Dylan puts the lid on the pot.

"All done!" She crosses her arms, scanning the room. "Where did Oliver go? Did he finish his serving? Is he crying?"

We scan the crowd. Some people are attempting to eat the chili, but most are holding the small cups of vanilla ice cream directly onto their tongues. Others are blowing their noses or blotting their eyes.

"There he is!" I point to a table in the back near Miss Gina and Liv's mother's booth.

The cup is in front of him, and he gives Dylan a thumbs-up.

"That's right, you little curmudgeon." She shakes her head. "He's too young to act that old."

"You know he's got a crush on you." I help her load up the rest of the bowls and plastic utensils, and I grab the large plastic bin of ice cream cups to put what's left of them in the freezer. "Now that he's eighteen, he probably thinks he has a shot—if he can get Logan out of the picture."

"He can get over himself, because I'm a very happily married woman."

I laugh as I follow her to the kitchen, which leads us right past where Liv and Gigi are standing with Jack. Swallowing the knot in my throat, I force a smile.

Jack and I've never been awkward around each other, even if

I have been crushing on him hard since the day we met. He has always treated me like any other parent, much to my dismay…

Until he let the mask slip, and I got a peek behind that sexy curtain.

"There you are," Dylan yells over the music. "It's about time you came for dinner. Want some Pepper X chili?"

Jack holds up a hand. "No, thanks."

"Hi, Jack." My voice is weird, so I clear my throat. "Hey, Liv, and little Miss Gigi."

"Say 'Hey, Miss Allie,'" Liv waves her baby girl's arm, but Gigi is wiggling to get down.

Reaching into the tub, I take out a cup of vanilla ice cream and hold it out to Liv. "Need this?"

"Maybe." She takes it before chasing after her two-year-old, who's heading straight to the bar where her daddy is dancing.

A laugh puffs through my lips, and I turn to see Jack watching me. The intensity of his gaze makes the skin on my neck prickle.

"Let me help you." He takes the plastic bin from my hands, turning to follow his sister into the kitchen.

My arms fall to my sides, and I walk behind him to where Dylan stands at the large silver table, transferring the leftover chili into a plastic bowl.

"Chili for you, Thomas?" she calls to our old friend, who's grilling burgers while he watches sports on his small, black-and-white television set.

"No, ma'am," he answers in his low voice. "You know I stay away from all that foolishness."

"Smart man." Logan enters through the back screen door, patting Thomas's shoulder as he passes. "Got a burger for me?"

"Always do. One for Coach Jack, too."

Jack straightens from where he emptied the ice cream cups into the bin in the freezer, and he's so good-looking with that gray T-shirt stretching over his broad shoulders and those faded jeans hugging his tight ass just right.

It's the end of the week, and he seems more relaxed than before—when he's not looking at me with the intensity of a thousand suns.

"Ready for tomorrow?" Logan punches him lightly on the shoulder. "I expect you-know-who will be back, ready to hear your starting lineup."

"I'm ready." Jack adjusts his ball cap.

"George Powell had better watch his mouth." Dylan snaps the plastic lid onto the chili, then walks around the table to stretch up and kiss her husband. "We'll all be out there with the drill team, and if he so much as looks in Allie's direction—"

"He won't," Jack interrupts, a touch of flint in his tone.

Logan wraps his arms around his petite wife, hugging her close. "Did you set Oliver straight with your dish tonight?"

"He gave me a thumbs-up." She lifts her chin in defiance.

They're so sweet, I'm getting a toothache, and when I look at Jack, he blinks away from me, going to the door. "I'd better check on Kimmie."

"She's at the pool tables with Austin and Edward," I say as he approaches where I'm standing. "I'll go with you."

He stops to hold the door for me, and my bottom lip goes between my teeth. More heat prickles my skin as I pass close to his chest.

When we enter the large space, the lights are lowered, and a disco ball sends sparkles around the room. The music is more mellow, slower country, and the song is "Strawberry Wine" by Deana Carter.

Jack and I both pause, watching all the couples dancing together on the floor. I've never slow-danced on a Dare Night, mostly because I've always been too busy helping Dylan serve and then clean up, but tonight, I could be persuaded. If the right guy were asking.

We're standing side by side when Logan leads Dylan past us, out onto the floor.

"I love this song," she coos, putting her hands on her husband's broad shoulders. "Jack, dance with Allie!"

It's like a splash of water in my face, and a little "Oh!" jumps from my lips.

It's a silly response, considering we've walked down the aisle together in every one of his sibling's weddings, but after this week, what I used to believe was only friendship—with me dying on the inside every time he smiled—is now something a lot more serious and potentially more explosive.

"Screw what he said," Logan calls from the floor. "You two can't be the only ones not dancing."

I look around the room to see Liv and Garrett moving together like Johnny and Baby. Zane has Rachel hugged to his chest, and even Craig and Clint are dancing near the bar.

Jack turns to face me, holding out his hand. "I guess we're dancing."

It's not a question, and I put my hand in his, stepping closer. "Looks like it."

He leads me into the group, putting a large hand on my waist and holding my other hand in his as he surveys the room.

We're not hugged up like our married friends. We sway side to side like a couple of middle schoolers, with me chewing my bottom lip as I sneak a glance up at him.

He meets my eyes with a curious expression then leans closer, speaking in my ear. "Is this okay?"

Chills skate down my arms, and I answer in a high voice. "Of course!"

Then Garrett and Liv glide up next to us, and Garrett gives me a little push, sending me closer into Jack's chest.

"What is this, *The Mickey Mouse Club*?" he taunts. "Put your arm around her, man."

My cheeks burn red. My nose is in the center of Jack's chest, and I realize he went home and showered after practice. He smells delicious, like leather and sandalwood.

I sneak another glance up at him, and he wraps his arm around my waist, holding me close in a warm embrace.

He leans down to speak in my ear again, and again, it's a cascade of chills down my body. "Is *this* okay?"

I nod, lifting my chin. "I guess they'll all be talking about us now."

The song slowly drifts to an end, and Beyoncé's "Most Wanted" comes on.

Jack takes my hand, leading me off the floor. "If they're going to talk, we might as well make the most of it."

I'm not sure what he means, but he gives my hand a little pull. I follow him in the direction of the small playground out behind the restaurant.

A screen door in the middle of the dining room leads to the fenced-in, sandy lot, and I look back over my shoulder to see who might be watching us.

The room is so crowded with dancers, we're pretty much hidden from the people sitting at the tables and in booths, and the dancers are way more focused on their partners than on us.

So I follow him out into the night, my heart thumping like a rabbit in my chest.

Chapter 10

Jack

I T'S A WARM NIGHT, WITH THE FIRST HINTS OF FALL SLIPPING IN AROUND us on the breeze. It's a promise of change in the air, like the feel of Allie's hand in mine as I lead her down the sandy path to where the briny water laps softly against the shore.

The moon isn't as full as the night I walked to her house. Every night it gets a little smaller, but it's still big enough to highlight the path in front of us and to tip the waves in silver.

When we reach the edge of the surf, Allie slips her hand out of mine to take off her shoes. She tosses them to the side and stands facing the dark bay.

"I'll never get tired of this." She softly sighs, wrapping her arms around her waist.

I stand a little behind her, watching her love this place as much as I do. I think about growing up here, running along this stretch of beach with my brothers. Throwing the football and splashing in the water as we laughed and played.

It's my home.

"You'll have to come back and visit us." My voice is level, even as I hate the thought of her going away.

When she turns to look at me, her brow is furrowed. "What do you mean?"

"Austin wants to go to the University of Tennessee. He said you have family there."

"Oh." Her shoulders drop, and she shakes her head. "I have cousins in Cookeville, which isn't too far from Knoxville."

"He'll have his pick of schools." I look out at the water. "I figured you'd go with him."

She takes a step closer to where I'm standing, and my skin tingles at her proximity. "Why would I do that?"

Shrugging, I slide my hand into my pocket. "To be safer, to be closer to your family."

Looking down, she huffs a laugh. "Going to Tennessee might be exactly what Rip would expect me to do."

My jaw tightens, and I can't express how much I hate this guy I've never even met. "I hadn't thought of that."

"It's okay." Her pretty eyes blink up to mine, slightly hesitant. "I'm not planning to move to Tennessee."

"Are you planning to go back to New Orleans?"

She exhales a little laugh. "You sure are eager to get rid of me."

"I'm not." I say it too fast, and I'm concerned I've shown my hand. Clearing my throat, I step away from her, closer to the water. "There's nothing keeping you here with Austin gone."

"I wouldn't say that." She follows me down to the water's edge. "I've made a lot of good friends here. I like my job at the school, and maybe… I don't know."

Her voice trails off, and I look over at her. She's so close, right at my back, her head at my shoulder. "What?"

"Maybe I was hoping someone might give me a reason to stay." She blinks up at me, and I know she's holding the door wide open for me.

I should step right through it. Hell, I want to step right through it. The only problem is she doesn't really know me. No one does.

I cross my arms, looking out at the water. "I've decided to make Austin starting quarterback."

A few seconds pass, and she exhales softly, returning her attention to the rolling waves. "He'll be so happy."

"I'm also making Levi a starting quarterback." Lowering my arms, I put my hands on my hips. "It's not ideal, but we'll see how it goes for a few games. We're playing the Broncos next week followed by the Lions. They're both 7-A teams, so it'll be a good test."

"I trust you." Her voice is quiet, still open, and I hate this war inside me.

If I can't be the right man for her, I can at least be sure she's safe. I can at least make her son happy.

Allie's had enough disappointment, and Danielle's words still sting in my memory as she walked out the door. *Twisted pervert…*

Shoving the past into its box in my memory, I lighten my tone. "I've heard my daughter wants to be on the drill team now."

That makes her smile. "She's a very enthusiastic dancer."

I think of Kimmie almost kicking me in the nuts on the field, and I huff a laugh.

Her eyes hold mine again, warm and wanting. "Is that a laugh from serious Coach Bradford?"

"I'm not so serious." It's a lie. I'm seriously guarded as fuck.

She turns and faces me. "It must be hard to be alone all the time."

"Are you kidding?" I deflect. "I'm never, *ever* alone."

"You know what I mean. What about at night, after Kimmie goes to sleep?"

My stomach twists, and we should go back inside the restaurant now. "I'm usually pretty tired at night."

"And when you're not tired? What do you do then?"

"I watch highlight reels… I think about my parents." My honest answer slips out unbidden.

"Really?" A warm smile crosses her lips, and she steps closer to my side. "What about them?"

My shoulders tense, but somehow I can't stop answering her. "They did all this together. This restaurant, this family… but the only thing Dad cared about was her. When our mother died, it was over for him. I don't know what that's like."

But I want to know…

She touches my arm gently, her voice softer. "To love someone that much?"

A churn is in my stomach, but I can't stop myself. "To be loved by someone that much." My defenses start to rise, and I take a step away. "Sorry, I'm just… It's late, and I'm tired. I'm not trying to bring down the mood."

"Don't do that." Her fingers curl on my arm, holding me. "I want to know the things you think about. It doesn't bring me down."

My brow lowers, and I need to stop this. I've never talked to anyone this way. I'm always in control.

Except…

"My parents were like a fairytale, but they didn't have a happy ending."

Her slim brows pull together. "I wouldn't say that. Your parents made this big family they loved so much, and they left a legacy of good people who help each other and so many others. That's a beautiful ending. Everyone dies, but not everyone leaves so much love behind."

A gust of wind hits my face, and I turn my cap around. "I guess I'm too close to see it that way."

"You could have it." Another step closer. "You're too good a man to be alone."

The ache in my throat persists. "You don't know that."

"I know you deserve to be with someone who loves you that much, who dreams of you at night… who wants to take care of your needs."

It's that door again, wide open.

I should turn and walk away. I shouldn't go through it, but when she reaches up, my control slips.

It's a mistake, but I let her touch me. I don't pull away when her thumb lightly traces the line of my jaw. "Why not me?"

Reaching down, I do what I've wanted to do for so long. I put my hands on her soft cheeks, sliding her hair back from her face.

Her eyes are round and deep, and her full lips part. Desire races below my belt, and I lean down to seal my lips to hers.

A whimper slips from her throat, and her hands grip my wrists. Her mouth opens, and our tongues slide together, and oh, fuck. I tilt her head to the side, so I can kiss her deeper. She tastes like sweet vanilla ice cream, and I want to devour her.

Another little noise comes from her, and I'm so hard. If we were inside, I'd press her against a wall and lift her off her feet. Instead I move one hand to her back, drawing her soft body flush against mine.

"Oh, God," she gasps, and I know she feels my erection.

Sliding my hand lower, I cup her ass, moving my fingers between her thighs and lifting her to me.

"Jack…" Both her hands are on my chest, and her fingers curl in my shirt.

She pulls the thin cotton higher on my stomach, and her hands move lower. They pass over my stomach, and my muscles tense.

"I want this." She looks down to where she's touching me. It feels so good. "I've done this so many times in my mind."

She looks up at me again, but we can't do what I want to do here. "If anyone sees us, it'll make all the rumors true."

"They won't see us." Rising higher, she presses her lips to my throat.

My hands move to cup her breasts over her T-shirt. I feel her nipples hard through the fabric of her bra. Lifting and squeezing, I want to take them out and pull them into my mouth, between my teeth.

"It's only a few months until the season ends." My voice is hoarse. "We should wait."

"Can you do that?" It's a broken plea.

"It's the right thing to do." My mouth is on her cheek, moving to her ear, which I pull between my lips. "For Austin."

Her hand moves down, and she slides it up and down the front of my jeans, taunting my erection. I exhale a low groan. I want to lift her off her feet and fuck her right here.

"You're right." Her other hand rises higher under my shirt, spanning my bare back. "I have to think about my son. He always comes first."

My lips find hers again, and we're saying the right words. Only our actions aren't following.

"Allie…" By sheer force of will, I take a step away from her. "I won't let you be hurt again."

Blinking up at me, she's fucking gorgeous in the moonlight. Her lips are swollen from my kisses, and her eyes are dark with desire. Her breasts rise and fall with her rapid pants, and when she speaks, her voice is pure sex.

"I know." She stretches out her arm to me, and I take her hand, lifting it to kiss the back of her fingers before walking away fast.

Chapter 11

Allie

"**O**CTOBER WILL BE HERE BEFORE WE KNOW IT." DYLAN KNEELS beside me in front of the chain-link fence in her ballet uniform of black leotard and black nylon joggers.

We're on the field with the drill team, sticking red Solo cups between the links to spell out *Go Captains!*

The cheerleaders are on the other side of the fence, painting a giant paper banner the team will run through before the game, and Liv is a little ways down, supervising the girls filling red and white balloons with helium to release Friday night.

The guys are on the other side of the fence, finishing up practice, and as I hide behind the cups, I sneak peeks at sexy Coach Jack standing there as always in those jeans that hug his perfect ass with his muscled arms crossed and his cap pulled low over his eyes.

Every now and then, he'll look in our direction. My heart jumps to my throat, and I have to blink away before he burns me up with a single glance.

I've been floating on air for a week.

He kissed me.

More like he *devoured* me. I bite my bottom lip, forcing my attention to stay on my work.

I'm doing better than I was last Friday. I could barely breathe as we all stood on the sidelines waiting for him to announce the starting lineup.

Not even hulking, menacing George Powell could bring me down.

Jack quickly read through the names as parents and friends stood around hissing a *Yes!* or quietly high-fiving. I already knew what was coming when he moved from the defense to the offensive list.

As he said each name, the boys would run out and join the group on the field, and the girls would cheer and shake their small pom poms. When he read Levi as second starting quarterback, my skin prickled as all eyes landed on me.

Then he added, "First starting quarterback is Austin Sinclair," and I couldn't fight the smile breaking across my face.

The girls broke into cheers, kicking their legs, and even Kimmie was right there with them, cheering for Aussie and screaming at the top of her lungs.

To his credit, my son smiled humbly as he jogged onto the field to stand with his fellow teammates. They clapped hands, grabbed his shoulders, shook his arms, and hugged each other.

Even Levi congratulated him, before they all went back to pulling on their game faces for Coach Jack's final words of motivation going into the fall season.

George Powell didn't say a word, but his jaw was set, annoyance clear in his expression.

He could go straight to hell for all I cared. My boy worked his ass off for that spot, and the best coach in the world believes in him.

Pride expanded in my chest, and my stubborn eyes had to find Jack's.

Of course, he was looking at me, and the gleam of

satisfaction in his gaze launched a kaleidoscope of butterflies in my chest.

A nod was all the thanks I could give him without feeding the rumor mill, because everyone was watching us.

Then school started Monday, and we've been back at the grind, him on the field, me in the library. Still, the promise of more hums in the afternoon air.

"They asked me to get prize donations from local businesses." Dylan surveys the list on her phone. "You're so good at this, maybe you could help me?"

Her long hair is wrapped in a bun on the top of her head, and she's talking about the drill team's big fundraiser of the year.

It's actually a joint fundraiser with the cheerleading squad, and it's going to be a big Halloween fair, complete with an oversized hay maze—which sends a chill down my back.

I shiver. "I hate hay mazes."

"What? Hay mazes are so fun!" Dylan sits with her back against the fence beside me. "And this one's going to be *massive*. They're bringing in scaffolding so you can't see over the tops."

More shivers. "Haven't you seen *The Shining*?"

"That was a hedge—in a blizzard."

"Doesn't matter. All I can think about is running and running and not being able to see around the corners and Jack Nicholson chasing me with an axe."

Dylan's eyes light with her smile. "That was really scary. We need to tell Raven to put it on our list for Girls' Movie Night."

"I can't wait to see them again!" I sigh, popping my last cup into the fence.

I push off my knees to stand, and my friend hops up beside me.

"I like this look." She circles her finger around my head.

"You should." I slide the black-rimmed glasses higher on my nose. "You've been demanding it for months."

"They're really cute, and that messy updo makes you look very naughty."

"I don't know what you mean." I put a finger on my bottom lip, rolling it back and forth like some kind of cheesy old music video about being hot for teacher.

She snorts a laugh. "Where is my grumpy older brother? Coach Jack, you're needed at the cup fence, stat!"

"Shh!" I grab her arm, pulling her closer as we break into laughter. "They'll hear you."

"Who cares?" Dylan whines. "Kimmie loves you; we all love you. He needs to get his grumpy head out of his butt."

A sharp whistle tweets, and the guys run off the field. Sadie Duck skips up to where we're standing behind the fence.

"I talked to Coach Stef, and she said it would be okay if I moved from the cheer squad to the drill team!" Sadie's blonde ponytail flips around her shoulders as she bounces on her toes. "If that's still okay?"

I remember her holding Austin's arm on the field earlier, and I think I'd like to get to know her better, since it looks like he might ask her out.

"Liv said if she didn't mind…" I look at Dylan, unsure if I'm overstepping. "But I'm really only third-string here. I don't know how things like that work."

"Of course, you can!" Dylan puts her arm around the girl's waist, giving her a hug. "I'll email you the forms and where to get your uniforms. You can help us at the pep rally, but it's too late for you to be in the line for the first game."

My stomach jumps, and I imagine us under the lights, with the drama of the game surrounding us. Jack is always so good with the boys, and now I've got two men on the field to cheer for.

"I'll see you at Cooters & Shooters?" Dylan points at me, and I nod.

"It's Dare Night! Only, I might be a little late."

"What's up?"

"Nothing, I just want to have dinner with Austin. We've

been like two ships passing in the night lately, and we need to chat."

I haven't been able to tell him about his dad, and I'd like to feel him out about things like me dating and how he feels about it, specifically if I were to date someone like Coach Jack.

"Want me to ask Thomas to make something for you?"

"You know me so well."

I can't help a laugh. Hell, I haven't been able to stop smiling for a week—even with all the things going on and how indefinite we left them.

Maybe we're waiting. Maybe we're sneaking around. All I know is I haven't been this happy in a long time, and the first game is Friday.

"Thomas made a spicy dare burger for you." I dig through the bag of food Dylan had ready for us when I dropped off Kimmie. "He said it's your favorite? I didn't know that."

"Thanks." Austin breezes through, picking up the plastic container and starting for the door. "I'm meeting Edward and Sadie at the Coot-Shoot."

"Hey, slow down a minute!" I laugh, reaching for his sleeve. "I wanted to have dinner with you here."

He looks up at the clock over the sink, and his shoulders drop. "Tonight?"

"Yeah, tonight." I pull his sleeve in the direction of the table. "Come sit down with me."

"But it's Dare Night." He stands beside the table.

"Not until seven. I want to talk to you."

He puts his burger down and pulls out a chair, glancing at me from beneath his brow. "Am I in trouble?"

My eyes narrow. "Should you be?"

He doesn't answer right away, opening the cardboard box

and slowly taking out his burger. "I didn't know I had to read all three books this summer. I thought I just had to pick one, and Mrs. Easley said I could do a makeup quiz next week."

I sit straighter in my chair. "You didn't do your summer reading assignment?"

"I had football practice."

"Austin, I'm the school librarian!" I take the lid off my box to find grilled chicken on a bed of romaine and spinach, topped with beets, feta cheese, walnuts, and dried cranberries.

A handwritten note inside reads, *sugar-free*, and I shake my head.

"It was an honest mistake." He hulks forward, taking a big bite of hamburger, then leans back with a groan. "That's good."

"Always is." I pour the balsamic vinaigrette over the top. "But of all things, Austin, you didn't do your *reading* assignment? You're making me look bad."

He presses his lips into a near-smile. "Sorry, Mom."

"I'm not mad." I stab a big chunk of chicken with my fork and put it in my mouth. It's also delicious. "I guess if she's letting you make it up, it's okay."

"You look like a librarian with your hair all like that and your glasses." He bobs his head with a grin.

A blob of mustard is on his cheek, and I hand him a napkin. Sometimes I still catch glimpses of the little boy he used to be not so long ago and warmth filters through my chest.

"Thank you, I guess?"

"Nah, it's good. I was just saying."

"Are you excited about your first big game?"

He takes another big bite of burger, nodding. "Um-hm."

"You've been really cool about Levi. I heard his dad kind-of made a scene during camp."

My son's eyes are fixed on the french fries in his box, but he nods. "He does that a lot. Levi said they've had to move three times because of it."

"That sucks." I take another bite of my dinner. "He must be really embarrassed."

"More like pissed off." Austin takes his final bite of burger. "He's a good player, though."

"That's what I've heard. Although, I can't imagine anyone being as good as you."

That makes my son laugh, falling back in his chair and rolling his eyes. "I'm hardly the best player."

"Top ten."

He shakes his head, shoving a handful of fries into his mouth. I take a few more bites of salad, and we're quiet a moment. I have two big things to talk to him about, and I have no idea how on earth to ease us into either one.

"I heard Levi's dad said something about me." My voice is quiet, and I stab at my salad some more.

He frowns now, glancing up at me briefly. "He said a lot of stuff. I don't think anybody pays attention to him."

Putting my fork down, I'm not sure I can eat as I say this. "How did you feel about what he said about me?"

"He was just talking out his… behind." Austin stands, collecting his trash. "Everybody knows how it is with us."

A knot is in my throat, and I stir my plate, trying to think. He dumps his trash into the can and wipes his hands on another napkin.

He seems like he's about to bolt, and I clench my lips then just say it. "Would you care if I dated someone?"

He walks quickly past my chair, not seeming to pay attention. "Nah, that's cool."

"Austin, stop." I go to where he's already in the living room, waiting impatiently. "I'm serious."

His shoulders drop, and he shoves his hands in his pockets, looking off to the side. His brown hair hangs over his eyes, and he's so tall now. In my bare feet my head barely reaches the center of his chest. "Mom, I've got to go."

"Tell me the truth."

"It is the truth." He holds out a hand. "I don't want you to be alone, and I'm leaving in a year for college."

"Yeah, about that. Coach Jack said you want to go to UT? You didn't tell me you wanted to go there."

His shoulders relax, and he steps back, giving me a minute. "I was just saying maybe."

"I think that's a great idea. You'd be close to Aunt Myrtle Dale and her family."

His lips poke out, and he nods. "If I make the team, I won't have time to visit much. I'll be practicing and stuff. Traveling."

"I know." Turning to the side, my fingers clench, and I inhale deeply. "I've been meaning to talk to you about this for a while. It's just been so crazy with camp and all the things going on. I didn't want you to be distracted."

"About college?" He frowns at me, and I reconsider.

Maybe telling him about his dad before the first big game would also be too distracting?

Forcing a smile, I reach out and squeeze his arm. "It can wait. Let's make a date to chat this weekend—after you win the game."

The corner of his mouth lifts with a half smile, and I notice a framed picture on the shelf behind him. It was taken his freshman year, when Dylan had just started teaching ballet at the high school, and it's of him holding Mia Pine in a ballet pose.

"Remember this?" I point at it, and he huffs a laugh.

"How could I forget? Tyreek's always teasing Josh and me for taking Aunt Dylan's ballet class."

Aunt Dylan… I'm encouraged by the ease with which he says it.

"He's just jealous you got to hug all over Mia before she graduated."

"Mom!" He snorts, putting a hand over his nose.

"It was very sweet of you to help Dylan, and you were really good. I think she has a video of your performance somewhere."

"YouTube."

"What?" My brow lowers.

"It's on YouTube. Everybody's seen it." I want to know more, but he's at the door. "I gotta go, but I'll show it to you on our date."

"Speaking of dancers, Sadie's joining the drill team." I give him a little nudge. "She seems like a sweet person."

He smiles sheepishly, and I hold up my arms for a hug. Leaning down, he gives me a brief squeeze.

"I'm really proud of you." I tug the side of his hair. "Have fun tonight."

"You too." He straightens, going to the door. "And if you want to dance with Coach Jack again, that's okay with me."

"Oh, is it?"

"He seems like a sweet person." Our eyes meet for a second, and a sly smile crosses his lips.

Then he's out the door, leaving me shaking my head. That boy might look like he's not paying attention, but he doesn't miss a thing.

"After last week, we're going easy on you tonight, bringing back a spicy fave." I'm on the chair, reading Dylan's warning to the line of daring customers. "Spicy pepper refried beans with habañeros…"

A noise of approval ripples through the crowd, but Oliver Duck makes a face.

"That's three steps down from Pepper X, which we now know is the hottest pepper in the world." Sliding my finger up the screen, I continue Dylan's note. "We've got all the usual to ease the burn, and I have a special bottle of pure capsaicin for you to put on your serving, Oliver Duck. Oh…"

Blinking up, I see his frowning face and Dylan's crossed arms, and I snort a laugh. "Let's go!"

Craig immediately cues up "Hot Stuff" by Donna Summer, and we dish it out as fast as customers can take it.

The party is getting started, and I scan the room between each person looking for Jack. I don't see him anywhere, but if I ask Dylan, she'll nail me for it.

I know who'll tell me. "Is Kimmie watching the boys play pool?"

I hand out a cup of ice cream, smiling at the familiar local.

"I think so." Dylan scoops out another serving of spicy refried beans. "She's spending the night with me tonight, since Jack won't be here."

My stomach sinks at that information. "Is everything okay?"

"I think so." She nods, smiling at another familiar patron. "He said he had some stuff to take care of before tomorrow."

I hand out the last ice cream cup completely deflated. He's been avoiding me all week, and I'd hoped, maybe we might dance together again. Maybe we'd even walk outside, and who knows what else might happen. I was hoping we might do more than last time.

"That's it!" She covers the pot, and I help collect the serving utensils and the tip jar.

We walk to the kitchen, and I don't feel like partying. I don't feel like dancing.

"I might head on home now that we're done. I'm kind of tired myself."

"You sure?" She frowns at me, but Logan walks into the kitchen to wrap his hand around her long ponytail and pull, tilting her head back to kiss her. "Hey, honey."

Her face lights, and her entire demeanor changes. I think about Liv dancing with Garrett and the way they grind their hips. Hell, even Zane touches Rachel like she's made of the finest porcelain.

"Yeah, we've got a big night tomorrow," I finish. "I'm going to curl up with my book and get some sleep."

"A left-handed read?" Her eyes slant up at me, and my eyebrow arches.

"Perhaps."

"I'm digging the look here, Allie." Logan nods at my messy updo and glasses. "It's cute."

"Hmm…" I lean into Dylan's ear and softly repeat. "*Cute?*"

"Logan, puppies are cute." His wife fusses. "Allie's a sexy librarian."

"I'll leave that for Jack to say." He wraps his arms around Dylan, smiling at me with a teasing grin. "You know I prefer women who try to kill me."

She playfully slaps her husband's muscled forearms. "I didn't try to kill you! You did that all on your own."

"Set the record straight, Allie." Logan nods at me. "You were here. She left that ghost pepper out knowing I'd think it was salsa."

"I most certainly did not!"

"I gotta go." I wave a hand over my head. "See y'all tomorrow at the game."

Logan says something about being a wimp as I leave, but I don't pay attention to him. They'll be arguing about the first day they met for the rest of their lives.

Driving home, I sing along to the old Chicks song "Cowboy Take Me Away" at the top of my lungs. I don't have a polished, pageant-girl voice like Raven, but alone in my car, I'm Adele.

Walking up to the house, I disarm the security system and go into the empty house alone. My shoulders fall, and I have a moment.

I don't particularly like being alone, and with Austin leaving in a year, it's feeling closer than ever. I see myself ending up with one of Miss Gina's kittens, surrounded by nothing but romance novels.

As much as I love my spicy book boyfriends, they don't put their arms around me when I'm cold at night or tug my ponytail to kiss the top of my head.

My mind drifts to Jack, and I think about him standing on the field this afternoon, only casting me one fiery glance. I think about him on the beach kissing me. *Can he really wait so long?*

I walk over to the window, leaning my head against the curtain and looking out into the dark. My heart stops when I see him there, again. Only, tonight he's not hiding in the shadows. He looks both ways before jogging across the street and walking right up to my front door.

The security code is entered, and I open the door before he even has a chance to knock.

"You're here." My voice is breathless, and I blink up at him.

"I drove up to the restaurant, but your car wasn't there." His low voice floods my veins with heat.

"Dylan said you weren't going to be there tonight."

"Is it okay if I come in?"

"Yes…" I jump back, holding the door for him to enter.

He walks into my living room, filling the entire space with his presence. I close the door and press my back against it gazing at him standing there, looking back at me.

The ever-present cap isn't on his head. He's dressed in another light gray T-shirt and loose, faded jeans. Boat shoes are on his feet, and it almost looks like he left his house in a hurry.

"You were looking for me?" I could only dream he might be.

Lifting his hand, he rubs his fingers over his chin. "I was thinking about Austin. Tomorrow's going to be a big night for him."

My heart squeezes, and my lips press into a smile. "You were worried about my son?"

"I didn't want you to be worried." His blue eyes hold mine. "He's going to do well."

Pushing off the door, I take a step closer to him. He says we have to wait, then he comes here and says something like that to me.

I reach out my hand, and he takes it in both of his. "Tell me why you're really here."

Chapter 12

Jack

ALLIE STANDS IN FRONT OF ME IN THAT CUTE WHITE SKIRT AND RED Cooters & Shooters tee. She was helping my sister tonight, and I told myself I was going to stay away.

The last time I went to Dare Night, I took her outside and kissed her. Then I told her we had to wait.

I don't want to play games with her or send her mixed messages, so I decided the best way to deal with these *feelings* would be to stay away from situations where I'm tempted to touch her—like Dare Night with all my siblings insisting we dance together.

Then after only two hours of pacing my house in my bare feet, I realized nothing would kill my desire to touch her. I'd have to erase her from my mind if I wanted that to happen, and the only place I've seen that done is in movies.

Pressure was in my skull, and my head was hot, like I had a fever. I realized denial only made my craving for her more intense. At least if I went to Dare Night, I could see her, and my family and half the town would be there.

They'd keep me from going too far.

The way they did last time?

Still, I shoved my feet into a pair of boat shoes and grabbed the keys to my truck, driving into the night. The restaurant was lit and music poured from the windows when I pulled into the parking lot, but her car wasn't there.

I sat for a minute, wondering what to do as more and more people entered through those double doors. I decided it was a sign. She wasn't at the restaurant, and I should go home.

Then like the devil, another thought hit me—everyone is here… Everyone except the two of us.

I quickly turned the wheel and headed back the way I came. Parking in my driveway, I took off on foot, moving fast, not knowing how much time we had.

Sure enough, Allie's car was in her driveway.

Now I'm standing in front of her in her living room looking exactly like what I am, a man obsessed.

Not only that, Allie can see right through me. *Why are you really here?*

Lifting my hand, I scrub my fingers over my forehead. I can't say because I'm a horn-dog who can't stop fantasizing about seeing her naked.

I'm losing my mind, and I don't know why, after years of control, I can't stay away from her for one more second.

I'm a big liar. Allie Sinclair is the reason I wasn't at the restaurant tonight.

Her cool hand touches mine, and she steps closer, the apple scent of her hair juicy and fresh. "Tell me, Jack. Why are you here?"

Clearing my throat, I meet her bright blue eyes, and an invisible hand reaches in and squeezes my heart. "Everyone's at the restaurant."

"I know."

It's no use. I reach out to slide a glossy tendril off her cheek, behind her ear. "I like your hair like this. You looked really pretty this week."

Her cheeks turn a soft shade of pink, and she smiles up at me. "You like it?"

"Yeah, and I didn't know you wore glasses."

"They're new." She blinks up at me so expectantly.

I move my hand to the side of her head. Cupping her cheek, my thumb is on her full bottom lip.

"Can I kiss you?"

She nods, rising higher on her toes, putting her soft chest against my hard one. Lifting my other hand, I hold her face as I cover her mouth with mine.

Like before she opens to me readily, and our tongues slide together. It's a cascade of sparks through my veins. She's so soft and pliable in my grip. This need burns so strong in my chest. It beats like a drum in my brain.

Anxiety twists my chest, but I can't deny myself. She has to know, and I have to know what she will say. Before we go any further, I have to say it.

Moving my lips to her ear, I kiss the shell first. "How would you feel if I told you what to do?"

My hands still hold her cheeks, and I feel her frown. "What do you mean?"

She's whispering as well, like we're sharing a secret.

"I want to tell you what to do, give you orders, and I want you to follow them without question."

Her breath stutters, and she lifts a hand to hold my wrist.

The thunder of my heartbeat is in my ears, and I brace for her to push me away, to tell me she's a smart, intelligent woman, not an object to be ordered around.

"You want to…" she hesitates. "Dominate me?"

"I need to." My voice is quiet, neutral so I can be sure she understands.

She shivers in my arms, and my chest tightens.

"Jack…" It's a sigh akin to a moan.

Her body is turned so her shoulder is at my chest, and the

light casts a silhouette over her curves, the little points beneath her shirt, and heat surges below my belt.

Lifting my hand, I lightly graze my palm over her breasts, her hard nipples. "Does this mean you like the idea?"

She turns in my arms to face me, and I'm hanging off the edge of a cliff. Her expression is serious, and she swallows once.

Then she nods, speaking quietly. "Only with you."

"Because you trust me?"

She nods again, and my eyes slide closed. I pull her to me, wrapping one arm around her waist. I hold the back of her head in my hand, and I lift my chin, feeling the imprint of her body against mine.

Her slim arms are around my waist, and we breathe together. She feels so good. She feels made for me. *Could it be possible?*

"What do you want me to do?" she whispers.

"Get on your knees." My voice is low and strong.

Taking a step back, her eyes meet mine before she obeys.

She drops to her knees, sitting on her feet and placing her palms on the tops of her thighs. I don't question how she knew to do it exactly right.

I squat beside her, placing my finger under her chin and lifting her face so our eyes meet. Hers are open and deep and full of longing. It hits me hard.

"You're so beautiful when you look at me that way."

She blinks quickly, and a happy smile spreads across her cheeks. It feels so good to praise her and watch her bloom like a rose under my touch.

Standing straight, I turn away, walking to the door. "My ex didn't understand. She thought I was broken. Her actual words were *twisted pervert*." Shuffling noises meet my ears, and my tone sharpens. "I didn't tell you to get up."

Hesitating a moment, I look over my shoulder to see her on her knees again. This time when I walk over to lift her chin, anger and a touch of sadness is in her eyes.

Sliding my thumb along her tightened jaw, I tilt my head. "That makes you unhappy?"

"Yes," she answers flatly.

"Why?"

"She didn't know you."

"I'd say she did. She was the first person I'd ever been honest with about my needs. She was my wife."

"She wasn't your wife." Allie's pretty lips are a straight line of anger, and it does something to me.

Leaning down, I cover those lips with mine. Again they part, and I sweep my tongue to hers firmly, curling them together.

A soft whimper slips from her throat, and I hiss. "Those little noises…" I kiss her again, more forceful, more demanding. "They make me so hard."

Stepping back, I study her. Her head is waist-high to me. Her cheeks are flushed, she's breathing fast, and her eyes are dark with desire.

"You want to touch me?" I ask.

"Yes."

"You want to do whatever I say?"

"Yes."

I smile at her quick responses, sliding my fingers along her cheek. "You're so beautiful. I can't wait to play with you."

Her pink tongue slips out to wet her bottom lip, and it takes all my strength to hold back. "We have to lay some ground rules first."

"Okay."

Going to the door, I pause before leaving. "You can get up now—and arm the security system."

It's our first home game. The stands are packed with parents and friends. Rachel is at the 50-yard line with Miss Gina. My brothers are on the sidelines with me, arms crossed. Buddy is in the box, and I have a headset around my neck.

The cheerleaders hold a tall sign under a red-and-white balloon arch, and once the national anthem finishes, the players burst through it, running onto the field where a roar of cheers greets them.

We win the coin toss and give the Broncos first possession. A crash of helmets, and low grunts of boys running, pushing. A hole opens in our defensive line, and the Broncos quarterback runs straight through it for a thirty-yard first down.

The visitors' side goes wild.

"Come on, Darnell!" Garrett roars from the sideline. "Where you at?"

My jaw is tight, arms crossed. Bright lights blast onto the dark green field, and the cheerleaders drop one by one off the shoulders of their bases.

Allie is on her knees, looking up at me with blue eyes full of trust and desire. I push the memory away, but the girls chant on the sidelines, drawing my eyes to hers. It's a shot of pure adrenaline.

Josh dives to the side for a near-interception, and it's pandemonium in the stands. The home spectators stomp their feet to the beat of "We Will Rock You" by Queen as the boys line up again.

Flynn Barnes comes out of nowhere to sack the Broncos' quarterback, and the screams turn deafening.

Their kicker runs out to try for the field goal and makes it by a hair, putting the Broncos on the board.

It's our turn to lead, and the boys run out onto the field. Austin speaks quickly to the huddle, and they clap, heading to the line.

On the snap, he falls back searching for a receiver. My throat tightens as he searches, searches… then barely avoids the sack by firing a tight pass to Rich for the first down.

This is my world.

The boys line up for another go. Another ten, and we make our way down the field, closer and closer until it's ten and goal.

Austin's game is smooth. He's controlled and focused, looking for all the world like he's been doing this his whole life.

They make the snap, and he steps back, eyes focused on the end zone. He looks side to side, when out of nowhere he goes down, falling on his ass, his face twisted with pain.

"Austin!" I hear Allie cry, and I lunge forward as if I'll go to him on the field.

Before his butt hits the ground, he manages to pitch the ball to Levi, who spins and takes it to the outside. Austin doesn't get up, but Levi has caught the opposition off-guard. He jumps over a safety and runs it in for the score.

We jog out to check on Austin, who's sitting on the ground holding his ankle. *Fuck.*

"How's this?" Hal, the team trainer, kneels in front of him, holding his ankle in both hands and moving it side to side.

Austin winces, shaking his head. "Hurts."

"We could wrap it and let him keep playing." Hal looks up at me from where he's kneeling in front of Austin. "But it'd be better not to take a chance on further injury."

My chest is tight when I make the call. "Levi will finish out the game." Pointing at Austin, I give the order. "RICE."

He knows the old acronym—*rest, ice, compression, elevation.* Austin's jaw clenches, but he doesn't argue. Garrett bends down to help him limp off the field as the spectators clap, and when I turn, Allie's watching me with worry lining her pretty face.

I want to go to her and pull her close, tell her he's going to be okay. It's only the first game of the season. He'll be able to play more, but I don't want him sustaining an injury that won't heal. He needs to let this one go. We're just getting started.

But I can't do any of that. Instead, Garrett jogs over to talk to her while I huddle with the team.

It's infuriating.

The announcers say Levi Powell will finish the game, and Rome trots out onto the field for a quick extra point.

Following another near-score by the Broncos, Levi takes the field as quarterback. Noah takes his spot as running back.

He's smooth as silk, falling back on the snap, easily calculating until he finds a receiver, then making a clean pass. On the next, he rolls away from the sack and runs the ball down the outside for another first down.

We end up winning the game, but it's a bittersweet victory with Austin on the sidelines, his ankle elevated.

The buzzer sounds, and the players flood out onto the field to shake hands. I grip the outstretched hand of the opposing coach with a *Good game*, before heading to the locker room with the boys.

Austin is on crutches, but it doesn't dim his enthusiasm. He joins his teammates, yelling and clapping hands and running postmortems on which plays worked and which didn't.

Levi is right there with them, smiling and seeming lighter than he has since he arrived.

I hold up a hand, and all eyes are on me. "That was a great start. Way to pivot under pressure, offense, and bring it home. Defense, your second half was much better than the first. I like what I'm seeing out there. If we keep this up, we'll go all the way. Now have some fun."

A cheer rises, and they're pulling off their gear and changing out of their uniforms.

I pull Austin to the side on my way out. "Take it easy on that ankle. We'll have the doctor look at it and make a decision about next week's game."

He nods, looking down with his jaw tight. "Yes sir, Coach."

With a tight smile, I pat his shoulder. "We've got nine more games. You'll get plenty of time to shine."

In the past on Friday nights, I'd head to Cooters & Shooters after the game for drinks and to get Kimmie from my sister.

Tonight, when I exit the locker room, only one person is on my mind.

Allie is with Liv and Dylan on the sidelines with the drill team, talking to the girls. Kimmie is on her hip, and she sways side to side.

For a moment, I hesitate, watching this woman I can't get out of my head holding my daughter. It's like I'm seeing my future.

"Daddy!" Kimmie jumps when she sees me, and Allie lets her down at once.

My daughter runs to where I'm walking up to them, and I scoop her onto my hip.

"You won the game!" She pumps her little fist before putting it on my shoulder. "But Aussie got hurt."

"He's going to be okay." I continue walking to his mother, directing my answer to her. "It's a bad sprain, but I told him to rest it. We'll check him out and see if he can play next week."

"Okay." Her voice is quiet, and my chest squeezes.

I want to pull her to me and kiss that worried look off her face. Instead, I have to deal with a voice I don't want to hear.

"You made the right call, Coach." George Powell walks up to where we're standing. "Levi won that game for you tonight. You can't argue with the facts."

My eyes are still on Allie's, and a little smile lifts her lips before she turns away.

Logan is at my side, and I exhale, turning to confront this man. "He did a great job. He's a talented kid."

"He's your starting quarterback. Keep putting him in, and you'll win every game."

"We need to keep working on our D-line to win every game." I give him a firm smile. "The boys will play when and where I tell them."

George holds up both hands, stepping back. "You're the coach."

"Yes, he is." Logan's tone is sharper than I've ever heard it.

I'm not interested in fighting, and I'm not about to give this parent more oxygen than he deserves. "Thanks for coming out and supporting the team."

What I really want is to figure out a way to shake this crowd and find some alone time with my star player's mother—rumor mill be damned.

Chapter 13

Allie

THE FRIDAY NIGHT CROWD AT COOTERS & SHOOTERS ISN'T AS BIG as Dare Night, but it's crowded with the parents and friends of players, dropping by to have a drink, celebrate, and wind down after the first big win.

Austin's with his friends, and now that he's almost eighteen, I only ask him to be safe and not to do anything that will put Sheriff Grizz in the position of having to arrest him.

The truth is, he's a good kid—more responsible than I was at that age, considering I was pregnant with him at eighteen.

We've reached the point in our relationship where I try to give him advice and hope he follows it. And I do a lot of praying.

I also make sure he has all the supplies and knowledge he needs to practice safe sex.

Yes, that means I buy my son condoms.

Some parents might frown at that, but I've found it's better to be honest and proactive about these things than to pretend it doesn't happen. Not talking about sex is the best way I know to wind up with an unplanned, teenage pregnancy.

"The drill team sounded so exciting tonight!" Miss Gina

walks up to where I've just cracked open three Corona longnecks for Liv, Dylan, and me. "It was all I could do not to stand up and dance right along with them."

She's holding Rachel's arm as she does a little steppy-jig.

"We might have to put you on the team." Dylan laughs, giving the old lady a hug.

I reach for another beer. "Would you like a Corona, Miss G?"

"Oh!" She laughs, her blind eyes drifting over my head to the fans slowly spinning. "I can't remember the last time I had a beer."

"Sounds like a yes to me." I pop open another longneck. "Lime?"

"Do you think it's safe, Rachel?"

Rachel stage-whispers into her ear, giving me a teasing glance. "I've learned never to trust drinks from Allie, but if you're worried about driving home, Zane and I've got you covered."

Miss Gina smacks her hand on the edge of the bar as she laughs. "That does it, I'll have one. You girls keep me young! "

I hand everyone a beer, but Liv isn't smiling as she takes a sip.

"I haven't had enough time with them." She's a total perfectionist, and I can see why Mrs. Laverne wanted her to be the coach. "They need to be hitting those kicks, all the way to their noses in a straight line."

"But you want them to have fun, too, right?" Dylan tilts her dark head up at her sister-in-law.

"They're not babies, Dylan. If they want to get scholarships or join a college team, they have to be perfect. You think I got on the Golden Girls by being sloppy? Would you have gotten into the American Ballet Academy looking like that?"

"They were a lot of fun to watch," I carefully add. "The kicks were a little wobbly, but they didn't miss a single hip-flick."

"We're practicing every afternoon next week," Liv replies.

Rachel and I exchange a glance that says *yikes* as we sip our beers. I'm only the third-string coach, thank goodness. I suck at bringing down the hammer, but after this new venture, I'd love to see Liv in a courtroom handing some prosecutor his ass.

"Well, they sounded like perfection to me." Miss Gina's kind voice resonates, and she tries another sip of beer… and frowns. "I don't think I like beer."

"I'll take it, Miss G." Zane walks up, taking the beer from the old lady's hand. "I'll mix you up an old fashioned."

Miss Gina makes a relieved comment, and I sneak a peek past Zane to see if Jack is here. The brothers were all together when we left the stadium.

"Did you see me do my kicks, Aunt Deedee?" Kimmie runs up to our group. "I kicked real good, all the way to my nose like you said. Want to see?"

Now I know he's here, and my breath tightens in my chest.

"Tomorrow, outside." Dylan's tone is firm. "You almost knocked Uncle Lightning's family jewels out of commission, and we're trying to get pregnant."

"You are?" Rachel's voice goes high.

"You knew that, Rach." Dylan shakes her head. "Logan's been asking for a little wide receiver since Liv and Raven popped up with babies."

"Always wait a year to have babies." Liv's mom walks up to where we're standing. "You'll have plenty of time for babies, but you'll never have that first year of marriage again."

"Thanks, Mom," Liv carps.

"Obviously, I wasn't talking about you, Olivia. Hand me a beer please, Allie."

"Yes, ma'am." I reach into the cooler behind the small bar in the center of the room.

"I know what you mean, Miss Plum, but you know Logan and I've been married two years now."

"You have?" Her eyebrows rise as I hand her the cold bottle. "Time just keeps on flying, doesn't it?"

"Where were you tonight?" Liv puts a hand on her hip. "I

thought you were going to come to the game and watch the drill team."

Ms. Plum takes a long sip of her beer. "I had an emergency D&D meeting this afternoon at the senior center, and it ran long. I asked Garrett to tell you."

"I didn't know Dungeons & Dragons had emergency meetings," Dylan teases. "What happened? Did somebody get stuck in the third dimension?"

"You're thinking of Quantum Conundrum." Liv's mother isn't fazed one bit.

"Hey, Ms. Plum!" Garrett walks up, giving his mother-in-law a hug and lifting her off her feet. "What are you doing here? I thought you had to do some fire-breathing elf-bard thing or something."

"Lord have mercy, Garrett Bradford, I'm the elf bard who plays bagpipes and wields the bow and arrow." She shakes her head, finishing her beer. "I don't breathe fire. That would be ridiculous."

Garrett holds up both hands. "My bad."

"Anyway, I'm sorry I missed the game. I heard it was a nail-biter, and I heard Austin got hurt. Is he okay?" She looks right at me, but I don't have a chance to answer.

"He'll be fine." Jack's deep voice joins the conversation, and my entire body lights up. "He has a bad sprain, but if he rests it this week, he should be okay."

I quickly reach into the cooler and pull out a beer, opening it for him. He smiles as he takes it from me, and our fingers graze. It has me nearly melting to the floor.

"I'm glad to hear it." Liv's mother nods. "Well, I'll be heading home now. Is Gigi spending the night with me tonight?"

"She is." Liv steps forward to kiss her mother's cheek. "One of the Simpson girls is babysitting her at your house, and I've already paid her."

"Then I'll see you tomorrow. Night, kids."

"I suppose I ought to be getting home, too." Miss Gina

wraps her shawl tighter around her narrow shoulders. "It's past my bedtime."

"Okay, then." Rachel's eyebrows rise, her tone teasing. "I guess that means we're heading out since we're your ride."

"Oh, you don't have to leave on my account!"

Zane exhales a laugh, patting her shoulder. "See you all tomorrow. Good game, bro."

He nods at Jack, who sips his beer as he watches them leave.

"You ready to make the most of our night off?" Liv arches an eyebrow at Garrett, and he bends down to lift her over his shoulder.

"Let's go make a baby!" he shouts, slapping her on the butt.

"Garrett!" Liv smacks him on the back. "Put me down. My goodness."

He doesn't, and somebody lets out a taxi-whistle as he carries her out the door into the parking lot.

"He knows how to keep her down to earth." Dylan laughs, holding out her hand to Kimmie. "Are you spending the night with me tonight?"

"Yes! Yes! Yes!" Jack's daughter jumps up and down, pumping her hands over her head. Then she stops, seeming to remember. "Is that okay, Daddy?"

Jack smiles down at her with so much affection in his eyes. "I guess I can tuck myself in tonight."

Her brown eyes widen with worry, and she takes her father's hand. "Will you be sad and lonely?" She quickly grabs my hand. "Miss Allie can spend the night with you. She's all alone, too!"

I swallow air, and Dylan bursts out laughing. "Kimmie, that is a great idea!" She steps forward to kiss Jack's cheek. "Isn't it, big brother?"

His eyes narrow, but he doesn't respond.

"Speaking of making babies…" Logan catches his wife around the waist. "Let's get this little one to bed so we can practice."

"Keep my brother company tonight, Miss Allie!" My face is

on fire, and Dylan waves over her shoulder to me as she leads her skipping niece to the kitchen.

Chewing my lip, I glance up at him. "I do not want to make a baby."

"Good." He turns, facing me. "Still, they have a point. We are both alone tonight."

"You're not too tired for a sleepover?" Somehow I manage to tease.

Shifting his stance, he moves closer. "No."

"Hey, Allie!" A loud voice from behind me almost makes me throw my beer.

"Shit!" My palm flies to my chest, and I turn around to see Ronnie Freeman standing behind me smiling.

Ronnie teaches math at the high school, and he's about my height. A little chunky, but always nice and friendly.

"Did I scare you?" His dark brow furrows.

"Oh, no, I just nearly jumped out of my skin is all."

"I'm sorry!" He puts a hand on my elbow, and Jack shifts behind me.

I don't dare look at him.

"I saw you over here, and I figured I'd come over and say Hi." Ronnie's round cheeks remind me of an elf when he smiles. "You've been looking really pretty lately."

My eyes do flicker to Jack's this time, and his brow arches.

"That's so nice. Thank you, Ronnie."

"You can call me Ron. I was wondering if you might want to have dinner tomorrow night at Parky's." He leans closer and adds, "With me."

I'm completely caught off-guard, which isn't good for my lying skills.

"You were?" is the best I'm able to conjure.

"Yes, ma'am." He continues standing there, smiling.

"Well, I'll be… This is so unexpected." I lift wide eyes to Jack, who is not smiling.

"We've known each other a few years, and well, I'd like to get to know you better."

My lips press together, and I nod slowly. "I'll need to double-check my schedule, but that's such a nice invitation. Thank you, Ronnie... er, Ron."

"Don't think too long, now." He gives my elbow a gentle squeeze.

A soft growl comes from Jack, and the hair on my arms rises.

I cough a little laugh as Ronnie steps back. "I won't."

He tips his hat to Jack. "Good game, Coach."

"Thanks, Ronnie." It's a curt reply.

The man leaves, and I hold my expression completely neutral as I turn to Jack. His face is unreadable, but his eyes are hot. I can't tell if he's angry, but I'm very aware of my heart thumping hard in my chest.

"What were we saying?" I blink up at him, trying to keep it light. "Kimmie doesn't want you to be alone?"

He takes my beer and his and puts both in the trash. "My place, ten minutes, wear your sexy librarian dress."

It's an order, and my stomach flips. "Yes, sir..."

His nostrils flare, and he goes to the door. I fall against the bar to catch my breath.

Chapter 14

Jack

RONNIE FREEMAN IS A HARMLESS LITTLE MAN, A MATH TEACHER AT the high school. Allie is clearly not interested in dating him, but it's a testament to my state of mind how badly I wanted to rip his arms off and shove them up his ass for daring to touch her.

We haven't even discussed Rip Sinclair, and the pain I'm prepared to inflict on that man if he dares to show his ugly face in Newhope—or anywhere near my girl.

I'm not sure when the switch was flipped or how, but there's no going back for me. Allie is mine, and I won't let anyone hurt her or try to date her.

The soft tap on my door breaks my murderous thoughts, and my muscles tense in anticipation of seeing her again.

I quickly go over, open it, and pull her inside fast.

"I Icy—Oh!" She falls back against the door with a huff of exhale. "Good thing it was me, I guess."

To her credit, she always manages to make me smile.

I brace my hands above her head, leaning down. "Just making sure no one sees us."

Her cheeks flush attractively, and she straightens her back, stretching like a kitten to put our faces irresistibly close.

"Am I your dirty little secret, Coach Jack?" It's a sexy whisper that activates my dick.

Fuck. I lean down to trace my nose along the line of her hair. She smells like a juicy green apple. *Forbidden fruit.*

"Yes." My voice is rough.

Her hands touch my waist as she exhales a soft hum. Everything she does makes me hard.

Pushing off the door, I take a step back to look at her. She did exactly what I told her to do, changing into a tight purple sweater with a tantalizing V-neck, and a flowing gold skirt with white flowers. *Easy access.*

Her silky dark-brown hair is tied up in a messy bun on her head with small pieces escaping around her cheeks. Those black-rimmed glasses are perched on her nose, and the cherry on top are her deep red lips.

Crossing my arms, I almost smile. "You're perfect."

She takes a cautious step closer, lifting her chin. "Just following orders."

Relief exhales through my lungs, and I walk over to pour a scotch. I usually only have one beer at night, but I'm also usually on duty as a single dad.

Tonight is a scotch night.

Lifting the crystal tumbler, I turn to face her, arching my eyebrow. "Are you planning to tell Ronnie yes?"

Her chin pulls back, then her hand drops. "Ronnie *Freeman?*"

The way she says it almost makes me break character.

"You said you'd think about it." I sit in the chair, crossing my ankle over my knee as if I'm angry.

She exhales a short noise. "Well, that's because he's harmless. You're not really upset about that are you?" Her eyes blink quickly, and she's adorably flustered. "You know I'm only interested in you."

My veins simmer. "I'm going to need you to convince me."

Those velvet-red lips pout, and she comes to where I'm sitting. "Tell me what to do, Coach. I'm ready to get in the game."

Lifting my finger off the tumbler, I point to the arched entrance to the hallway leading to my bedroom.

"Stand there." My eyes run down her sexy breasts. "And strip."

Her pout turns to a naughty smile, and she walks to the hallway, swaying her ass as she goes. Then she turns to face me and starts to unbutton her sweater.

"Stop."

Her fingers freeze, and I uncross my legs, going to where she stands and flicking on the yellow overhead light behind her. From there, I walk to the kitchen and turn off the lights, leaving only the small lamp beside my chair still lit.

The effect casts her in a perfect silhouette, and I sit in the leather chair again, crossing my ankle. "Now begin."

She turns, leaning her back against the wall and lifting her breasts. Her body is outlined in light, and I watch as she unbuttons her top.

"Music would help." Her voice is soft, and she looks at me, lowering her glasses.

Taking out my phone, I tap a few times until the sultry beats of "You Put a Spell on Me" by Austin Giorgio filter through the room.

"Mmmm…" She smiles slowly. "That's good."

"Yes. It is."

She moves her hips in time, and she's fucking gorgeous. Her entire body rolls like a wave on the ocean, and I can't take my eyes off her.

She lowers her hands, and her top falls open to reveal a black lace bra underneath, pushing her tits up. Every time she twists her hips they bounce, and she slides her arms out of the sleeves before pushing the skirt to the floor.

She's wearing a matching black lace thong, and reaching

up, she lets her hair down with one tug. It sweeps down to her shoulders, and she turns her back, letting me see her round ass.

She rotates it, and my dick hardens.

Turning to face me again, her legs step apart. She slides her palms up her sides to lift her tits, and my hand instinctively moves over my erection. I want her to straddle my lap and grind. Then I want to bend her over the table and fuck her hard.

"Crawl to me." It's a low order, and I put my foot on the floor and lean forward to rest my forearms on my knees.

Her blue eyes widen, and she looks side to side before carefully lowering to her knees. Soft brown waves bounce around her cheeks with every move, and her tits sway as she carefully puts one hand in front of the other.

She's a work of art in motion. My mouth waters as I watch her get closer in only that sexy underwear and black-rimmed glasses.

When she reaches me, I open my hands. "Come up here."

She straightens, and I cup her cheeks in my hands, studying her pretty eyes. I take the glasses off and put them to the side. She's so open and pliable in my hands.

"You're beautiful." I kiss her lips softly before releasing her and leaning back. "Take out my cock."

Her pink tongue touches her cherry-red bottom lip, and heat fills her blue eyes. She reaches for the button on my jeans, unfastening it and lowering the zipper.

My dick strains against my boxer briefs, and she slides her fingernails over it, making me hiss.

I slide my finger along her jaw. "Tell me what you want to do."

Her eyes are on her hands rubbing me through the black fabric, and her breasts rise and fall with her pants. "Everything."

My jaw clenches, and my dick can't get any harder.

I hold back a groan. "Be specific, Allie."

She licks her lips, blinking up at me. "I want to put it in my mouth."

"Put what in your mouth?"

"Your cock."

"And…"

Her lips twist, and her eyes slide away.

The song changes to "Lips on You" by Maroon 5. I'm aching with need for her, but I cover her hands with mine, halting her movements and leaning forward.

"What are you thinking right now?"

She shakes her pretty head, eyes fluttering down. "I don't know why I feel shy around you now."

She's kneeling in front of me looking like my dream come true, and she's afraid?

"Look at me." I cup her cheek, lifting her pretty eyes to mine. "We've known each other for years. I've walked you down the aisle at all of my siblings' weddings. Sometimes you were more hungover than others, but you remember."

"Those bachelorette parties could get wild."

"Allie." I give her a gentle smile. "I haven't changed."

"But don't you see?" Her voice is quiet. "In those days, you were this gorgeous guy, Dylan's sexy big brother, an impossible dream I could never have." Her shoulder rises, and she exhales a little huff. "Now I have you. I just… don't want to fuck it up."

Her face is in my hand, and I smooth her hair back with my other one. "I'm more in danger of fucking this up than you are."

"I don't mind a little kink." She tilts her head to the side. "I'm from New Orleans."

"Right." I huff a laugh.

"Except… Can we talk about some of them?"

Releasing her cheek, I grow more serious. "Of course."

"I'm not really into ropes." She winces. "I mean, being restrained sounds like fun, but some of that tying up looks… painful."

"How do you feel about neckties or a silk scarf?"

"Better." Her lips press into a smile, and I imagine her tied to my bed, blindfolded, mouth open.

Fuck, that's hot.

"And no fisting… or peeing." She covers her eyes. "Or, oh my god, pooping."

Reaching for her wrists, I uncover her eyes, holding her hands in mine. "None of that will happen."

"I don't want to be hurt with weird implements, like nipple clamps or hooks."

"How do you know about these things?" I confess, I'm impressed by her knowledge, and wondering if it means she's hiding her own secret kinks—which I'd very much like to explore.

"I'm a librarian, Jack. I've read books."

"I didn't know you had books on BDSM in the high school library."

"I have my own romance novels."

I smile, exhaling a laugh. "Good to know."

Her chin drops, and she studies her hands in mine. I look down at them as well, slim and fair, soft in my rough grip.

"How many have there been?" Her voice is just above a whisper. "I won't judge. I just… I've never done this before, and I don't want to let you down. I don't want to be bad at it."

A new feeling surges in my chest, protection, acceptance. "You're my first."

"I am?" She peeks up at me. "Well, that's a relief."

At last I get a glimpse of the sassy Allie I've always known.

"The first person I shared this with called me a twisted pervert."

"So I've heard." Her eyes narrow. "You're not."

"Forget her." I kiss her cheek. "I have."

"I'll tell you what I want now."

"Okay…"

Her blue eyes darken, and she moves closer, her voice dropping to a whisper. "I want to suck your cock until you're thrusting it down my throat, moaning my name. Then I want to ride you until my pussy is raw."

"Shit." My dick springs fully to life, and I take her face in both hands.

Leaning down, I kiss her hard. My mouth seals over hers, and I push her lips apart. I take her tongue with mine, curling my fingers against her scalp, doing my best not to devour her whole.

She rises higher onto her knees to meet me, holding my face in her hands and returning my kiss with equal passion. We break apart with a gasp, hot eyes holding briefly before we're back together, lips chasing each other's, tracing down jaws and necks. Soft whimpers come from her throat, and I exhale a deep groan in response.

"I want to possess every part of your body." It's a low growl, hunger and desire mingling in my blood.

"You can do whatever you want to me. I want all of it. I want everything."

"We need a safe word."

"Anaïs."

"Anaïs…" I repeat it. "Any particular reason?"

"She's my favorite author. She loved to be dominated, but most of all she loved to fuck."

Resting my forehead against hers, I exhale slowly. It's possible I've found my perfect match. "Are you sure you're ready for this?"

"Yes." She blinks up at me. "So sure."

"Then open your mouth and swallow my cock like a good girl."

Chapter 15

Allie

My hands are on his hips, and I trace my lips from the base of his cock to the tip, flickering my tongue all over the edge before pulling him into my mouth.

His hands are in my hair, and he groans deeply as he lifts his hips, hitting the back of my throat. Lifting my gaze, I look up at him to keep from gagging.

My thong is soaked, and I want to show off for him. I want to give him everything he wants. I love it when he groans my name. I love that he's looking at me like he doesn't believe I'm here with his dick in my mouth.

I'm his first. He's my first. We're like twisted, perverted virgins, and two very willing parties.

Holding his waist I bob my head faster as I feel him thickening in my mouth. His head presses back, and he moans deeply. He threads his fingers in my hair, chanting my name like he can't get enough.

I'm on the edge myself. One touch and I'll come apart for him. This gorgeous man, this man I've watched be so stern with his arms crossed, his jaw set. This man who loves my son and treats him like his own. This man, who thinks I'm beautiful and praises me with so much affection.

I want to be his good girl. I want to make up for the shitty woman who didn't know what she had.

"Stop," he groans, lifting my face and moving to stand.

"What?" I gasp, my brow furrowing.

He lifts me to my feet then into his arms. "Come with me."

We're moving fast down the hall to his bedroom. He tosses me onto the bed, and I squirm to rise onto my elbows in time to see him standing there, wet cock fully erect, gorgeous muscles in his chest heaving, six-pack abs flexing with every breath as he looks down on me with hooded, hungry blue eyes.

Reaching for my waist, he quickly removes my thong. "Spread your legs."

My legs part at once, and he wraps muscled forearms around my thighs, dragging me to the edge of the mattress. At once, his mouth covers my pussy, and I fall back with a cry.

"Jack…" Thrusting my fingers in his thick hair, I can barely breathe his name for the energy surging through my pelvis.

He slides his tongue over me with a firm stroke before centering on my clit and circling. It only takes a few passes before all the pent-up desire explodes through my veins.

I scream his name as my thighs quiver madly. My stomach muscles pull, and I rise off the mattress with a moan. The intensity of pleasure surging through my body blanks my mind. I can't stop fluttering, and he smiles, still holding my legs in his hands.

"I'm going to fuck you now." His voice is ragged, and his lips shine with my come.

Reaching down with one hand, he lines himself up with my core before leaning forward to slam fully into me. A loud cry jumps from my throat, which he matches with a guttural moan.

"Fuck me, Allie, this feels so good." His face drops, and he presses warm kisses to my neck, my chest, and up to my lips again. "It's been so long."

"It has…" I've lost the ability to form sentences. "So long…"

"Oh, God, I can't stop." His hips move faster.

He's thrusting violently, and it's so good, I try to grab his ass to urge him on. I can't remember the last time I've been fucked, and I know it was never this good.

I want to feel him all the way to my soul. I want to feel him every time I move tomorrow. I scoot closer, squeezing my body to try and hold him.

I'm too wet. He's too feverish. We're lost in a deluge of need, finally set free.

"Jesus, you're like a glove." He groans, and he drives five, six more times before holding, bowing over me, pulsing deep in my clenching core.

My leg slips from his grasp, and his hand slaps the mattress beside me. Every muscle in his gorgeous body flexes, and he groans, coming hard and long. I reach for him, wanting his body next to mine.

Releasing my other leg, he wraps his arm around my waist, hauling me higher into the bed while never losing contact.

We shudder and breathe together, coming down from that monumental high. One large palm smooths my hair off my face. I'm cradled in his arms, firm against his body. Sweat is slick between us, and I can't believe it.

Did I manifest this? After years of dreaming and hoping and wishing, I'm holding Jack Bradford in my arms. He fucked me hard and fast, and it was more incredible and mind-blowing than I ever expected.

Our breathing slowly returns to normal. He kisses my neck, sliding his thumb over my cheekbone gently.

"You're perfect." His voice is so rich. "I'm a fool for waiting this long."

I only smile, cuddling closer into his chest, wondering how any woman could turn him away. At the same time, I'm so glad she did.

"Hang on." He kisses my shoulder before leaving the bed.

A few moments pass, and he returns with a warm washcloth, cleaning both of us before helping me beneath the covers.

"You don't need this." My bra is gone, and he slides a hand up to my bare breast, moving his thumb over my hardened nipple. "So beautiful."

Leaning down, he kisses and bites the soft mound. He gives it a hard suck before moving to the other one and doing the same.

"You're going to make me horny again," I tease.

His eyes never leave my breasts, and he lifts them in his hands, squeezing and kneading. "I fully plan to fuck you again tonight. Probably a few more times."

I exhale a happy noise. "I can't wait."

Dawn lights the edge of the horizon, and my body is completely relaxed and thoroughly used. The rich, bittersweet scent of coffee meets my nose, and I blink slowly as a warm hand smooths my hair off my cheek.

Soft lips touch my brow, and I'm surrounded by the scents of sandalwood and leather. It tingles in my stomach, and I can't stop the smile splitting across my cheeks.

Rolling onto my side, I cover my face with my hand, squeezing my eyes tighter. "Don't—I'm having the most amazing dream. The man I'm obsessed with just fucked my brains out all night." Parting my fingers, I grin at him. "Oh… it's you."

A deep chuckle curls my toes. "I have to get you home before everyone finds out you slept here."

Lowering my hand, I look up at him sitting beside me on the bed. His dark hair is pushed back from his face, and a light scruff is on his square jaw. Full lips part over straight white teeth, and heart-stopping blue eyes hold mine.

I push slowly to sitting, feeling the delicious ache of how

many times we fucked deep in my core. It was at least three more times after the first one. Back, front, back again…

Holding the linen sheet over my bare breasts, my eyes stay on the mug of coffee in his hand. "I still feel you inside me."

He reaches for my chin, leaning forward as if he'll kiss me, but I dodge. "Nooo—morning breath!"

"Allie." He slants his eyes at me, and I take the coffee from him, quickly sipping.

"It's all so perfect." I shake my head as I drink more of the warm, hot beverage. "Don't spoil it."

He laughs, taking the mug out of my hands and setting it on the nightstand. Then he grabs my waist and hauls me onto his lap.

"Look at me."

Pushing my hair back, I meet his playfully stern eyes, and my stomach flips. "Mm-hmm?"

I can't truly be expected to form sentences when he's so close and so gorgeous.

"Nothing could spoil what we shared." He leans forward to kiss the side of my neck, right under my ear. "We're only getting started."

Energy flows down my back, and I reach out to hold his cheek. Then I kiss him briefly on the mouth before leaning back again.

"Still, I'd like to keep some allure."

"You have no idea how alluring you are to me."

Crawling off his lap, I look around for my underwear. I find my bra, but my thong is nowhere to be seen.

"What happened to my thong?" I glance up, and a sheepish grin is on his lips. "Did you steal my underwear?"

He stands, going to the dresser and opening a drawer. "Wear this."

A light blue jersey is in his hands, and I hold it up to inspect the bright red number 18 on the back under *Bradford*. On the front, the word *Mustangs* is written in script above the number, and a small bucking horse is beside it.

I swallow the tiny squeal trying to escape my throat, clearing it away as I very calmly state the obvious. "It's your football jersey."

"Yep." He walks to the bathroom, and I study his narrow waist and tight ass in those faded jeans.

My bra is on, and I pull the soft cotton over my head so fast. "I hope you don't think you're ever getting it back."

He returns from the bathroom, and that dimple in his cheek deepens with his grin. "Who said I wanted it back? See if these fit."

I take a pair of maroon cotton boxers. "Where did these come from?"

I happen to know from last night he looks very sexy in his boxer briefs.

"I think I bought them by mistake when Kimmie was a baby. I was barely sleeping in those days."

I try to picture him as a single dad with a baby girl, doing his best to take care of her. I know from the stories he came back here soon after Danielle left, when Kimmie was still very small, and Dylan helped him with her.

"I'll just be keeping these as well."

"Be my guest. They've never been worn."

I'm pretty sure my feet don't touch the ground as I float beside him into the living room. My clothes are folded neatly on the back of a chair, and my shoes are beside it.

"Need these?" He holds up my glasses, and I take them, parking them on top of my head.

"Not too much. My prescription isn't very strong."

"I know. I checked."

"Did you try on my glasses?" I snort a laugh.

"I just held them up. Come with me." Clasping my hand, he walks me to the door, hesitating to peek out of the curtains. "It's still early enough. We should be okay."

Still holding my hand, we walk out to his truck. "If I'm your dirty little secret, you're not trying very hard to hide me."

He stops, pressing my back to the passenger's door. "Maybe I'm not."

Leaning forward, he seals his mouth over mine, but I stop short of full-on tongue-kissing him. "When I've brushed my teeth."

A hint of annoyance flashes in his eyes, and his voice lowers. "If I want to kiss you, I will."

My stomach jumps, and I exhale a nervous laugh. I won't lie, Bossy Jack is hot as fuck.

Licking my bottom lip, I nod, and he puts his hands on my face, both thumbs on my cheeks. The intensity in his gaze shallows my breath. If I were wearing panties, they'd be soaked.

He holds me, but as he studies my expression, he seems to soften. Lifting his chin, he kisses my forehead.

"Get in the truck." Releasing me, he walks around the front of the vehicle.

I try not to collapse on the spot—or drop all of my things. I open the door and hop inside. It takes less than five minutes to get to my house, and I hold his hand the entire way.

My entire body is lit with excitement, euphoria, elation… all the *E*-emotions I can summon. I spent all night with Jack Bradford. I'm smiling as I gaze at the brightening sky through the windshield.

"What are you singing?" He lifts my hand to his lips and kisses the back of my fingers as we pull into my driveway.

"Was I singing?" I try to think. "I have no idea… I didn't even realize."

"Fuck, Allie." He laughs, pulling me closer and kissing my neck. "You are so damn cute."

His words flood warmth through my entire body.

"Now get out of here before we're busted."

"Yes, sir!" A laugh hiccups on my breath, and he shakes his head.

The hint of a smile curling his lips has me floating all the way into my small house.

"What time did you get home last night?" I look up as Austin scuffles into the kitchen.

I'm sitting at the table holding a cup of coffee and reading the *Library Journal*'s newsletter on my phone. I've changed out of Jack's jersey and boxer shorts, and now I'm in black leggings and a long-sleeved T-shirt.

He exhales a grunt, holding the counter as he hops over to pull a Mountain Dew from the fridge.

"That late?" I tease, putting my foot down and hopping up to give him a hug before checking the oven. "I made Pillsbury cinnamon rolls. Want one?"

Another harumph, but he nods. "I want all of them."

Going to stand by my big boy, I muss the front of his long brown bangs. "You never were much of a morning person. But you still have to share."

An exhale huffs through his nose, and he lifts his chin. "What time did *you* get home last night?"

My brow rises, and I peek over at him from where I'm glazing the rolls.

He's watching me, and I force a laugh. "What do you mean?"

"When I got home, your bedroom door was open." He hops over to sit at the table and put his foot up on a chair. "You were not in bed."

"Ahh…" I scrub the front of my hair, trying to think. "What time was that?"

I feign confusion, but he's a smart guy. I'm not going to get away with anything if I'm not convincing.

"I don't know, I didn't look. One?"

"Austin! You were out past midnight?"

"Mom." His head tilts to the side, and he levels his eyes on me. "We just won our first game of the season. We were all together at the bonfire. You know that."

I do know that. It's a longstanding Newhope tradition—at least with the football team and the cheerleaders, and I guess the drill team? After every home game, they build a bonfire on the beach, listen to music, and do whatever teenagers do.

They don't get into trouble. At least, I hope they don't.

"I was a little restless last night, too." True. "I went for a walk at some point, I guess that must've been when you got home."

"Dang, Mom!" His voice is a hiss. "You'd let me have it if I did that. It's dangerous."

Twisting my lips, I can't decide if I'm incredibly proud of him or annoyed that my teenager is so damn responsible.

"You're right." I nod, carrying the plate of cinnamon rolls to the table. "I did not use good judgment, and I'm really lucky we live in such a safe place as Newhope. I'm sorry, I won't do it again."

I take a cinnamon roll off the plate, using a napkin to hold it.

"Okay." He shrugs, taking a small roll and stuffing the entire thing into his mouth.

My mind wanders to where I was last night, and a little smile curls my lips as I take a small nibble of my roll. I wonder what Jack is doing right now. I think about being his dirty little secret, and a thrill moves through my body.

"What's that face about?" He shoves another whole roll into his mouth.

I jump, schooling my features, when I see the pan. "Jeez, Austin! You've eaten four already!"

"They're small!" he argues through the mass of cinnamony dough in his mouth.

It's another reminder of what he was like not so long ago, and while I love him as an almost-man, I do miss my little guy sometimes.

"It's fine," I relent. "I'll probably only have this one."

If I'm going to be doing stripteases, I'll definitely need to be cutting back on the sugar for sure. Maybe add a little strength training to the mix, sculpt my muscle tone. Look better naked.

"What did you want to talk about before?" He shifts in his chair, taking the last roll from the plate.

Standing, I go to refill my coffee cup, a lead weight pressing down on my chest. I have so much shame around the choices I made as a young woman.

I know I wouldn't have Austin if it weren't for Rip, but at the same time, I wish I'd picked a better man to be his dad.

A man like Jack—a man who has actually been a better dad to him than his own father.

Walking back to the table, I watch him slowly unrolling the final cinnamon bun like a spool of ribbon.

Clearing my throat, I sit forward in my chair, cupping the mug in both hands. "Do you ever think about your dad?"

He shifts in his chair, his slim brows furrowing over his eyes. "No."

I bite the side of my lip, wondering if his anger is okay or if I should try to get him to talk about it more—if not to me, to someone.

"Well… you know how he's been in prison?" He gives me a faint nod, and I continue. "He's out now. On parole. It's very recent, less than a month ago."

"I hope he doesn't try to come here and bother us." His voice rises slightly, and I wince.

"I don't think he can leave the state." My voice remains low, and I hate this. "But it's important for you to know what's going on."

"Is that why you bought the house alarm?"

"Yes… And it's why we have to use it."

"You're worried he might come here." It's not a question.

Nodding, I study my plate. "He said he'd be back. I don't know what that means or what he thinks will happen."

Austin scoots around, closer to hug me. "Don't worry, Mom. I'll protect us."

My heart breaks a little. He shouldn't have to.

But I do what I always do—try to find a silver lining in this shit-cloud.

I trace his wavy bangs off his forehead. "We're in a good place, a safe place, where we're surrounded by friends and allies. Garrett knows what to do, and Liv is prepared to file a restraining order. I just don't want to give him an opening."

Austin shakes his head. "Why would he bother me?"

"He probably won't."

I don't want him to worry. I don't want him to think about this.

I want him to have the best senior year with his friends. I want him to play football and be QB-1 and make all the good memories he deserves.

"That's all." I lift my chin, doing my best to smile. "As far as I know, he doesn't even know where we live now, which means hopefully you won't even have to think about it."

His lips pull down on one side with a frown. "But you still think about it."

Leaning forward I pull him into another hug, my caring son. "The Bradfords were all there when I got the alert on my phone, so they know. I'm not worried about your dad. I've dealt with him before. Hell, I used to live with the guy."

"Before he went to prison."

It's a sentiment that makes my blood run cold, because it's true. Rip was a hard man, wild and unpredictable before he was busted for dealing large quantities of drugs. I can only imagine what he's like after seven years in Angola.

Sitting back in my chair, I level my gaze on my son. "Do something for me, will you?"

"Sure."

"Live your life. Have the best year, and don't let him steal anything from you. I'll let you know if something changes. Can you do that?"

He nods, holding the table as he stands. "I'll have a better year once this ankle heals."

"It will, and Jack said you'll have your time to shine. We're just getting started."

"Jack?" He cuts me a look, and I stand, carrying my mug to the sink.

"That's his name, isn't it?"

"Yeah. I just didn't know you knew it."

"Well, that's silly, as long as we've all known each other. I'm getting ready for yoga class. I told Rachel I'd meet her at Miss Gina's."

Chapter 16

Jack

"**A**PRICOT CAUGHT A CHIPMUNK, DADDY! AND SHE TORE ITS HEAD off, and she left the body part on the step for Aunt Deedee. There was blood everywhere!" Kimmie is wound up when I arrive at my family's old house up the hill from Cooters & Shooters.

Dylan and Logan live here now, and it's not far from my place.

"That's pretty gross, Peanut."

"I don't know if she's a mouser like Miss Gina said, but she can hunt!"

"I thought Apricot lived at the restaurant." I watch my bundle of energy, skipping around me as I enter the back door.

"It's just right there, Daddy!" She points out the door, shaking her dark curls. "She's going to wander around her territory. Cats are nocturnal. She can even see in the dark! Miss Allie told me."

Miss Allie. A smile curls my lips at the mention of her name, and an ache of longing twists my chest.

I wonder how to broach the subject of dating with a

seven-year-old. Could she possibly understand what it means? Is it better not to say anything and let her think what she wants?

"I'm taking her outside to see if she'll catch another one for me!" Kimmie pushes through the screen door, letting it slam behind her.

"Hey, big brother." Dylan meets me in the kitchen, holding out a mug of coffee. "Did you get a good night's sleep?"

Nope. Not at all.

"Sure." I deflect. "Thanks for taking care of my little firecracker."

Dylan's nose wrinkles with her smile. "You know I love that little girl like my own."

"Speaking of your own…" I take a sip of coffee, watching her move around the kitchen. I know she and Logan have been trying to get pregnant, and when her cheeks flush, I grin. "Are you planning to tell everybody?"

"We only just found out two days ago. I took a home pregnancy test, then I went to see Dr. Pierce yesterday to confirm it."

I place my coffee mug on the counter and walk over to pull my little sister into a hug. "Congratulations."

Her shoulders drop, and she exhales a laugh, wiping her eyes. "I don't know why I'm crying. I've never been so happy!"

Releasing her, I go back to lean against the counter. "From what I've heard, pregnancy hormones are pretty crazy."

"Well, so far, so good—other than being dead tired." She stares at the coffee pot like she's trying to make a decision. "Dr. Pierce said I'm ten weeks along. I should probably wait three more weeks to tell everybody."

"That's the second trimester?"

She makes a little grimace and nods. "Supposedly you're out of the woods by then."

"My lips are sealed."

"I wonder if mine are." She laughs, ducking her head. "You know I suck at keeping secrets."

"Hey, bro." Logan walks into the kitchen, going straight

to the coffee pot, cutting me a glance. "Did you and Allie have that sleepover last night?"

My expression remains neutral as I glide right past his question. "I heard congratulations are in order."

His face breaks into a big smile, and he turns to Dylan. "I thought we weren't telling anybody yet?"

"He guessed!" Dylan's tone is so much like Kimmie's. "Anyway, he's my big brother. I had to tell Jack."

Holding out my hands, I shrug. "She had to tell me."

Logan exhales a laugh, walking over to my pint-sized sister, who's leaning against the bar in shorts and a T-shirt and bare feet.

"What am I going to do with you?" His voice is low, and he pulls her into a hug, kissing the top of her head.

I turn to get a refill on my coffee, ignoring the pinch in my chest.

I'm happy for my little sister. She has something I never did, as much as I wanted it. A loving partner, excitement for a new life.

Danielle had already soured on our marriage when she turned up pregnant with Kimmie. I'm just thankful she told me and didn't do anything unforgivable.

I wonder how Allie feels about having another baby. As if we've even gotten anywhere close to such questions. I've got to get a handle on my fantasies.

"I can't keep a secret!" Dylan's laugh draws my attention. "Jack will tell you—I always ruined Christmas."

"You never ruined it." I put cream in my mug before taking a sip. "We learned pretty fast what not to tell you."

"See?" She gestures to me while looking up at her husband.

"Does this mean I can tell the guys now?"

She inhales slowly. "We really should wait before we tell everybody."

Logan looks at me, shaking his head. "The girls will all know by the end of the week. Bet me."

"Nope." I hold up a hand, polishing off my coffee.

"Just have my back when the dogpile begins."

"I got you." I put the mug in the sink and head for the door. "I'll grab Kimmie, if I can get her away from that cat."

"You should let her keep Apricot," Dylan calls after me. "She's a great mouser."

"Don't start. Let me know if you need anything. I'll be at Garrett's. I need to get him back out to practice."

"I'd like to have you on the show soon, if you're available."

Pausing at the back door, I think about appearing on Logan's radio show. He always wants me to talk about the seniors to watch, and from what I hear, a lot of scouts—as well as parents and fans—tune in to what I say.

"Let's wait until Austin is able to get some time on the field. He should be back in the game next week."

"I'm ready when you are."

I give him a wave as I head out to find my daughter.

"I hope you made the most of last night." Garrett meets me at the door of his cottage on the bay. "Allie was looking fine in those glasses, and that thing she's doing with her hair now."

I'm about to punch him on the shoulder when my daughter pushes past us.

"Where's baby Gigi?" Kimmie runs into the house. "I want to hold her!"

"Wow," Garrett gripes. "I remember when she used to be excited to see me."

"Gigi's cuter."

"Aunt Liv's picking Gigi up from her grandma's."

"Aw!" Kimmie stomps back to where we stand, her little shoulders slumped. "What am I gonna do now?"

My brother pats her shoulder. "You'll just have to hang out with us for a few minutes."

Kimmie's bottom lip pokes out, and Garrett bends down to swoop her off her feet.

"Uncle Grizzlay!" she squeals.

He puts her on his back. "I know what you like."

I shake my head following them to the kitchen.

When I get there, my child is sitting on the bar in the middle of the room, and my brother is holding a can of whipped cream. "Ready?"

"What are you—" I don't finish the sentence before he sprays a blob into her mouth, then does the same for himself.

"It's Redi-Whip!" She cheers with her muffled voice. "More! More!"

Garrett's all teed up to give her another squirt, but I take the can out of his hand. "That's enough of that."

"Da-*day!*" Kimmie complains.

"Don't be a pooper, Jack." Garrett joins the chorus.

"I came over to talk football, not put my daughter into a sugar coma."

"Don't tell me you're doing the no-sugar diet, too." His eyes brighten. "So you did hook up with Allie."

"I like Miss Allie." Kimmie's head tilts to the side. "Why would Daddy hook her?"

"Well, you see—" my brother starts, but I catch his arm in a firm grip.

"Stop." My tone is level, and he holds up both hands.

"It's a game." He shifts gears, holding up his index and pinky fingers. "Like in Texas, they say 'Hook 'em, Horns.'"

"Can I play?" Kimmie's little brows rise.

"Hi, guys!" Liv thankfully interrupts the conversation.

"Gigi!" Kimmie hops off the bar and runs to where her little cousin is on her feet now.

My daughter tries to hold the toddler's hand, but Gigi only squeals, waving her arm around and trying to get away from her.

Gigi's wearing a ruffled red onesie, and her hair is a pink halo of curls around her head. She's a chunky little thing, and since she started walking, she's gotten very independent. Not that Kimmie doesn't still try nonstop to hold her or play with her or lead her around.

"Are you here because of the news?" Liv's expression is serious as she joins us in the kitchen.

I hesitate before answering. She might be talking about Dylan being pregnant, but she might not.

"Nope." Garrett saves me. "What's up?"

"It's all over the paper how Levi Powell dominated on the field last night." Annoyance is in her tone, and she glances from my brother to me. "Everybody's saying how he's a rising star and not a word about Austin."

Her eyes are worried, and my throat tightens. My mind is on Allie, and I don't want her to be concerned.

"Levi played a good game." I keep my tone calm, sticking to the facts. "We knew he was talented. It's why he's the second starting quarterback."

"These guys were making it sound like he should be first." Her voice is low.

"Those guys aren't the coach." Garrett straightens, tugging on the waist of his jeans. "Jack decides who plays and when, and they can deal with it."

Liv glances at me. "What do you think?"

"I think Austin's ankle needs to heal, and when he's back in the game, they'll say the same things about him."

Her brow furrows. "You don't think sitting out will kill his momentum?"

"Nah, we'll ease him back into training, and after the way he played second week of camp, he'll snap back." I put the can of whipped cream on the counter. "He's not losing anything."

"Buncha Monday-morning quarterbacking," Garrett grumbles.

"I wanted to talk to you about our defensive line. We got lucky last week, but we're facing some big teams. Can you come to practice this week?"

"I'll be there." Garrett holds out a hand, and I clasp it. "You know I will."

Baby squeals come from Gigi's room, and Kimmie stomps into the living room with her arms crossed. "Gigi won't do anything I tell her to do. She keeps saying *dog*."

"I told you." Garrett grins at Liv. "She came out for that lady's dog. We gotta get her a puppy."

"I am not having a puppy and a toddler at the same time." Liv holds up a hand. "When she's bigger, we'll get her a dog."

Garrett makes a move like he'll grab her, and Liv hops around behind me.

"You'd better hide behind Jack. You know I'll throw you over my shoulder if you start sassing me."

"Garrett Bradford!" Her voice goes high, but she's trying not to laugh.

It's another twist in my stomach, and I'm again frustrated at my siblings and their damn happy families.

"We're taking off. See you next week." I grab Kimmie's hand, and Liv squeals as my brother takes off after her.

"Uncle Garrett's got Aunt Liv over his shoulder." My daughter watches behind me. "Is that how you get a puppy, Daddy?"

"It's how you get something."

Holding the door to my old red pickup, I help her into the passenger's side and buckle her into her car seat.

My phone vibrates, and I pull it out of my pocket. On the screen is a single sentence from Allie, a.k.a., my *dirty little secret*.

DLS: I told Ronnie no.

Chapter 17

Allie

ANOTHER WEEK GOES BY, AND AUSTIN STILL ISN'T IN THE GAME. The doctors examined his ankle and said he ought to wait one more week, and Jack didn't even question it.

Still, when I see the frustration on my son's face as he leans on crutches on the side of the field, it takes all my strength not to go to Jack and talk to him.

He hates when parents interfere, and I do trust him. But it's really hard.

I stay on the sidelines with the drill team doing my best to assist Liv, but my eyes are fixed on Jack as he walks over to Austin to talk to him.

"L-E-V-I! Levi, Levi, he's our guy!" The cheerleaders work out a new chant behind me, and my teeth clench when I see them jumping up and down shaking their pom poms.

Then, Levi jogs past them onto the field and gives a little wave, and they fall together in giggles. Rolling my eyes, I exhale a soft growl.

Austin stands on crutches beside the cooler, and his jaw is tight as he watches, too.

"It'll turn around when he's back in the game." Liv is at my side, putting her arm around my shoulder. "Try to keep him encouraged."

"It's hard when everybody's obsessed with the new kid in town."

My phone buzzes in my pocket, and I reach for it absently. I almost drop it when I see a text from "Sir" on the screen. *Sir* is how I saved Jack's number in my phone.

Liv gives it a glance, but she walks back to where the drill team is lining up with their hands on each other's waists.

"I want to see those kicks all the way to the nose!" She shouts out orders, while I turn away to see what Jack has sent me.

> Sir: I know this is hard, but trust me. I've got this.

> It's very hard, but I do trust you.

> Sir: I'll see you tonight, but I won't stay long. Busy day tomorrow.

> Game day.

> Sir: I think about you. All the time.

Happiness sparkles in my stomach, and I try to hold back the grin splitting my cheeks.

It won't make sense for me to be smiling like I won the boyfriend lottery when my son is on the sidelines feeling forgotten.

> Same.

> Sir: Bring me a beer tonight, so I can touch you.

Another thrilling zip shoots through my middle.

I'll bring more than one.

A whistle blasts, and Garrett yells at the defensive line. My eyes lift, and I see Jack watching me from across the field. Adrenaline surges in my muscles, leaving me weak.

I want to wave. I want to skip over to where he is and throw my arms around him. But I can't do any of that.

All I can do is give him a little smile and return to the drill team. Just a few more hours, and I'll bring him all the beer I can carry.

"What are you doing with these guys?" I enter the kitchen at Cooters & Shooters and walk over to where Dylan is all suited up in her mask and plastic gloves.

"I'm using them for tonight's Dare dish. Cubanelles stuffed with salsa and cheese."

Pulling my chin back, I frown at her. "And what else?"

"What do you mean?" She grabs another large green pepper, slicing it down the center.

"I mean, like, is there another pepper in there? What's the warning?"

"Cubanelles are hot! I bit into one this morning, and I had to eat two cups of vanilla ice cream to stop the burning. I almost stuck my tongue in the coconut oil!"

Her eyes are wide, and she carefully scrapes the seeds from the thick, fleshy fruit.

"Okay, gross, but I feel like I'm missing something here."

Craig sashays into the room, jumping to the side when he sees me holding up one of the green peppers.

"What's that?" He grabs a towel, holding it up like a shield. "Why are you touching it with your bare hands?"

"It's a *cubanelle*." I tilt my head at him. "It's the Dare Dish tonight."

"Why are you saying it all weird like that?" Dylan fusses, waving a hand. "Cubanelles are spicy!"

Craig's eyes meet mine, and we both frown for a half second then we say it at the same time. "You're pregnant."

"What!" Dylan's voice goes high. "Why would you say something like that?"

We both close in on her at the table, and she takes a step back, holding the half pepper she's preparing to stuff.

"Cubanelles are at the bottom of the Scoville scale." Craig sounds like a cop questioning a suspect. "It's the first pepper that has a heat index above bell peppers."

"You've dropped like three hundred thousand on the scale!" I made that up, but it's close to true.

Dylan blinks fast, looking from us to the pepper and back again. "Logan's baby hates peppers!" Her tone is horrified.

"You're pregnant!" I throw my arms around her, jumping up and down.

"You're going to have a little pepper-hating baby just like me!" Craig throws his arms around my arms, and we're both jumping up and down.

"I thought this pepper was so hot." Dylan's voice is dejected from the middle of our cuddle dogpile.

"It's okay, little mamma." Craig pets her head, stepping back. "You can return to eating Satan's fruit in nine months."

Her eyes widen, and she grabs his arm. "Don't tell anybody. I'm supposed to be keeping it a secret. Logan's going to kill me."

I give her another hug. "He must be so happy!"

"What are we going to do about this dish?" Craig frowns, pointing to the rows of sweet peppers waiting to be baked. "It is not daring at all."

"We'll tell them you made it." I grab two pans, sliding them into the oven. "We're taking a break from the off-the-charts heat of Pepper X and habañeros."

"Nobody's going to like that," he grumbles, thumbing through his playlist. "What should I play to make it up to them?"

My lips twist, and I can't resist. "What about 'Lips on You' by Maroon 5?"

"An oldie but a goodie." Craig taps on the front of his phone. "I'll follow it with 'Ride' by Chase Rice. That should make them happy."

"So no warning? Just dig in?" I look at Dylan as she pulls off her plastic gloves and eye shield.

"I guess not. Unless the warning is for Logan." She snorts a laugh. "His wimpy tongue would probably be burned by this one."

"Hardly." Craig shakes his head. "Even Kimmie Joy can eat this dish."

We put the final pans in the double oven and set the timer. I dig through the cabinets for paper plates and napkins. No need for ice cream tonight.

The buzzer sounds, and we pull out the sheet pans, arranging the mild offering on serving trays.

"That's a strange scent." Craig frowns. "What is it? I can almost place it."

"It's making me think of breakfast…" I look up at him, tilting my head.

Stomping noises come from out front, and I glance at the clock. "Nevermind. Let's get out there. It's already going to be a tough sell."

"It shouldn't be!" Dylan argues. "Everyone can eat this one, I guess."

Craig grabs his blond wig and the three of us march out carrying two trays each. Cheers and clapping fill the large dining room, and we go to the picnic tables arranged in the corner near the small bar.

Jack leans on the bar beside Zane and Garrett, and my stomach tingles. Craig puts his trays down, going to the PA system to link his phone to the Bluetooth. I can hardly breathe, waiting to see how Jack will respond when the song plays.

"Tonight we've got something for everyone!" I announce as the crowd waits. "Craig has prepared a special family recipe for us, stuffed Cubanelle peppers that should be safe for all to enjoy!" A grumble moves through the crowd, but I push on. "Come on up and help yourselves, but please only take one at a time."

I nod at Craig, who's behind the small bar ready to put on the music, and I slowly make my way around the crowd to where the brothers are standing.

The kids have come in from the pool table area, which is separate from the rest of the dining area. I'm not paying attention to them as I quickly grab three Coronas out of the cooler and pop the caps.

Dylan is at the serving table smiling like everything is normal, and Logan walks over to put his arms around her waist and kiss the side of her neck.

The first strains of the song begin as I approach Zane and Jack holding the beers, as the girls hop onto the small bar and start popping their hips. Our eyes lock, and his gaze darkens.

Heat flows down my arms like syrup, and I hand a beer to Zane.

"Hey, thanks, Allie." He smiles, but my eyes are on his brother's.

I don't even care if I'm being so obvious. Holding out the bottle, he looks down at me, blue eyes moving around my face, down my neck, before returning to mine.

He remembers the last time we played this song. He remembers what I look like in only my black lace bra and thong. On my knees.

He knows what I'll do for him.

Everything...

Lifting his hand, he takes the bottle, and our fingers slide together. My breath burns in my chest, and I almost shudder from the contact.

Turning, I walk away from him, in the direction of the screen door against the back wall. The crowd closes in behind me, and non-pepper eaters are grinding and dancing. Kids are jumping up and down with their hands over their heads.

I step outside into the cooling air, but nothing can cool the fire raging beneath my skin. The song continues, and I wait, my mind counting down the seconds. I don't even know if he'll come to me. I came out here on impulse.

Seconds slip past, and the song is past the midpoint. He hasn't touched me or spoken to me or appeared outside my house since that night. I'm not the one in charge here, he is. What makes me think I have any control over him or this situation or even how he feels?

My heart sinks in my chest, and I'm so stupid. I have no reason to cry.

Reaching for the door, I gasp when it opens in my hand. His tall frame passes quickly through the space, and he takes me by the wrist, pulling me away from the building.

A laugh whispers from my throat, and I quickly push the silly tears away. He pulls up quickly, turning me so my back is against the big live oak tree at the edge of the play area.

He steps closer, surrounding me in his distinctive scent of rich leather, warm woods. Before I can speak, he cups my cheeks in his hands, covering my mouth with his.

I moan on a breath, opening my mouth to meet his. His tongue invades, taking mine and curling it with his. He turns my head like he always does, devouring me, kissing every part of me, pulling my lips with his, raking his teeth across my jaw.

"You came," I gasp, doing my best to hold his arms, his waist, as he kisses me like a starving man finding food.

"I couldn't stay away." He groans, moving his mouth to mine again in another consuming kiss. "It hurts." Another kiss. "Physical pain…" Another pull of my lips, another swipe of his tongue. "My sexy little secret."

My eyes roll back, and I gasp at the heat pooling between my thighs. "Why are we a secret again?"

"For Austin."

"Oh, right." I'm trying to remember why Austin would care. I'm sure he wouldn't. "For how long?"

Warm lips trace the top of my cheek, and he lifts his face to meet my eyes. His are so full of affection. "Eight more weeks."

"Fuck."

He smiles. Lifting his chin, he looks out at the water, and he actually exhales a chuckle.

I hiccup a breath, ordering myself not to weep with joy.

His gaze returns to me, and I grip his wrists to keep from melting into a puddle on the spot. "It'll get better. He'll be back in the game next week, and everyone will see how good he is. Maybe we won't have to wait that long."

"I'm ready when you are."

One more kiss, one more hit of pure bliss, and he releases me. "I've got to go, but I'll see you tomorrow. Wear that white pleated skirt to the game."

"Okay." I watch him slowly backing away in the direction of the restaurant, where the sounds of Maroon 5 pour from the open windows. "And I'll sleep in your jersey."

"I'd like to see a picture of that."

"Maybe you will."

Shaking his head, he bites his bottom lip, and I exhale a soft whimper. *Damn, he's so fine.*

Then he pulls the door open and disappears.

Chapter 18

Jack

WALKING AWAY FROM ALLIE WAS LIKE PULLING MY INSIDES OUT AND leaving them on the ground at her feet.

She makes me want things I'm in no position to have right now. I'm not a young man. I'm not a free man. I have a family of siblings who look up to me, a whole team of boys needing me to be a strong leader, and a school that trades on my reputation as fair and unbiased.

I'd sacrifice it all to spend tonight in her arms.

Fuck who knows. Let them say what they want, call me compromised, thinking with my dick. Fuck it all. I want her.

I hear her voice, and my body catches fire. I see her pretty eyes, and my muscles tense. I touch her, and desires dormant for so long in my body come raging to life.

Walking back to the restaurant, I think about all the times we walked down the aisle together. My head lifted a little higher with her by my side. I've always been a proud man, but she completes the circle.

Our first night showed me just how much she completes me.

She fits me like a glove.

Eight more weeks.

My phone hums in my pocket, and I take it out, hoping it's her. We don't text each other much, just a word now and then, a beacon to let her know she's always on my mind.

If she texted me to come back to her, I'd do it.

Instead, it's my brother.

Zane: Remember when I was home and healing from my injury and Rachel kept reaching out to me?

How could I forget? You were stubborn as a damn mule.

Zane and I are the closest in age, and as the two oldest, we're pretty practiced at giving each other shit.

Zane: And you told me to get my head out of my ass.

Actually, I told you to try CBT.

Zane: You said I had happiness right in front of me, and not to be afraid to take it.

That's good advice.

Zane: Then follow it. You gave up a lot when Dad died, taking care of all of us, making sure we were all okay.

You helped.

Zane: Still, everyone looked to you, and you did a great job.

Thanks, bro.

Lifting my chin, I exhale deeply. How many times have I thought this?

Levi plays like he's going straight to the pros, completing passes, evading sacks, making first downs on every turnover. It's clear the other teams haven't had a chance to study him, and he's taking full advantage of it.

Garrett's work with the D-line pays off, and between Levi's performance and their ability to hold the line, we beat the Lions 21-7. It's the biggest win we've had against that monster team, and I'm sure we'll pass them again on the road to the championships.

Our next game is on the road, and I brace for the shit I'll catch putting Austin in the starting spot.

He's ready. He's been on the bench grinding his jaw and looking like a sad puppy for two weeks. Still, he's been a good sport, cheering on his team and supporting them as he watched Levi make play after play, listening to George in the stands loudly proclaiming his son a star.

It's been hard on him, but he's shown his character. He's a leader, and I'm not letting anybody pressure me to keep him on the bench.

I've struggled with my own particular torture, watching Allie on the sidelines with my sister and Liv. She must've bought a few more of those little cheerleader skirts, because it's all she wears now, and the heat in my blood is a low simmer at all times.

As ordered, she sent me a picture of her in my jersey. Only it wasn't just a picture. She was on her stomach in her bed. Her silky brown hair was styled half up and half down, and those glasses were perched on her nose.

Her head was tilted to the side, red lips curled in a naughty smile, and the best part? Her ass was completely bare, the jersey was bunched high around her back, and the way she laid gave me a healthy view of the side of her round breasts.

It's possible I've jerked off to that photo more than a few times. It's possible I've closed my eyes in the shower and jerked off to the sight of her on all fours swallowing my cock more than a few times.

Now, riding the bus to our first out-of-town game, she's all I can think about. Not the stress of parents who might be pissed at me for starting Austin. Not the stress of how he'll play, getting back in the game for the first time in weeks.

It's only Allie.

I like your skirt.

I hit send, huffing a laugh through my nose.

The boys cut up in the back of the bus, teasing and giving each other shit. They're amped up to play, but I'm amped up to see her again. I want to see her smile when I put Austin in the game, and I want to see her smile when our eyes meet.

DLS: Thank you, Coach.

I'd like it on the floor of my bedroom.

DLS: Along with my underwear.

My dick jumps, and I shift in my seat, pushing it down with my hand.

Even better.

DLS: Seven more weeks.

The Trojans win the toss, and Austin comes off the line on fire. Noah is ready for him, and he fires a tight spiral right down the line into the running back's arms. They don't waste time.

Moving like they've been playing together all season, they get in formation without a word. It seems he took my short warning about lip readers to heart.

Another snap, another ten yards for the first down. The plays come swift and strong, and we're all the way at the goal line when the home team seems to realize what's happening.

Austin attempts to run up the center, and he loses a yard. George Powell is quick to growl complaints from the bleachers. I'm not calling a timeout this early in the game.

Instead, I'm standing on the sidelines, arms crossed, jaw tight as I trust Austin to follow his instincts. He goes for the center run again, and again, they're pushed back.

We're at fourth and goal, and Austin looks at the sideline where Levi is watching. They exchange a nod, and Austin turns to call the play. He's got this, and I'm proud there's no animosity between the boys.

The snap happens, and Austin falls back. Scanning the end zone from left to right, he hops on one foot as the rushers close in on him. My throat tightens, my mind on that ankle.

His face lights at once, and in a blink he fires off a pass to Rich, who's waiting just past the goal line. It's a little high with a slight wobble, but Rich runs back, doing a little hop and easily plucking it from the air for the score.

The visitor's side erupts into screaming. The cheerleaders go up on their partners' shoulders, and my gaze finds Allie.

Her smile is so big. She's clapping and jumping up and down with my daughter right beside her, kicking her little leg and yelling for Austin.

Our eyes meet, and she stills, holding her hands in front of her mouth. With a subtle move, she presses her fingers to her lips and blows me a kiss. It's the simplest thing, but it hits me right in the chest. A punch of pure joy.

It's not an easy game, and every time the home team makes a touchdown or nearly intercepts a pass, I hear George growling from the stands. It almost becomes a joke, until we're all the way to the end, with the score showing 20-21, the Trojans ahead.

My back is tight, and we have possession. As hard as Austin's tried in the final moments, they've held him, leaving us with twenty-five yards to the goal and a fourth down.

He signals for the timeout, and I nod. It's our last time out, but we don't have time to waste. Jogging to me, he pulls off his helmet.

"Put Eddie in the game, Coach." Austin's tone is confident.

My chin pulls back, and I look over to where Rome is pacing, chewing his thumb and looking nervous. Edward is calm as always. He actually seems to be doing math in his head as we talk.

"Are you sure?" I meet my favorite quarterback's eyes, and he nods.

He's sure as sunrise, and I exhale, looking down at the turf.

Zane is in the box tonight, and Buddy is on the sidelines with Garrett.

I look at Austin one more time. "Think he's ready?"

"I've been watching him practice, and he's good. Coach Zane would tell you. He can do this."

If we're going to do it, now's the time. I wave to Edward, and he jogs to where I'm standing with Austin.

Reaching out, I put my hand on the top of his shoulder pad. "Austin thinks you can make the field goal. Want to try it?"

Edward's brow lowers, and he looks from the 25-yard line to the uprights. "I've been practicing from the thirty at home."

"Get out there and win this thing."

Edward nods, pulling on his helmet. The announcers explain what's happening, and a hush falls over the visitors' side as he runs onto the field with Tyreek serving as holder.

Keeping my expression neutral, I cross my arms. Austin is by my side, helmet off and swaying from one foot to the next.

"You got this, Edward!" he shouts in his low, teenage voice.

The boys line up, and the home defense gets in position. I glance at the sidelines, and every student's face is worried. I'm glad they all care, but I confess, I'm nervous.

If something happens to Rachel's little brother, I'm going to feel like shit. Not to mention the shit I'll catch.

The home team is jumping up and down and yelling, doing all they can to create a distraction. Edward seems to zone out, stepping side to side then doing a little trot forward and practice kick.

The boys line up. My stomach knots. Tyreek catches the football and brings it down after the snap. Edward's expression is straight focus as he does a little jog forward and a practice kick.

Our side of the field erupts into screaming. It's a straight line, directly through the center of the uprights, and we won it. Edward backs away, watching the win, and Tyreek is on his feet, jogging to him.

The boys know not to grab him, but they're jumping on

each other's backs, holding out their fists for Edward to bump them. He looks down at the turf, blinking fast, and I jog onto the field to where he's walking, shoulders squared.

"Evan Noel, St. Stanislaus, made a 61-yard field goal in 2024 to set the state record in Mississippi. Peyton Houstin made a…"

"You did good, Eddie." I put my hand on his shoulder gently, bending down to speak near his face mask. "You won us the game. That's better than any record."

Zane is at my side, hustling over to Edward. "Your backswing and contact were perfect." He walks beside his young brother-in-law. "That follow-through was the best I've seen from you yet."

Edward's expression relaxes, and he gets as close to a smile as I've ever seen him. "It felt good. I had a feeling it was right."

Pride swells in my chest, and I look over at Allie. She's in a group hug with Dylan, Liv, and Rachel, and tears are streaming down their faces.

"Austin Sinclair looked like a pro on the field these last two weekends." Logan is behind the mic with his headphones on.

It's noon on a school day, and I'm spending my lunch hour as a guest on his radio show with Zane. Garrett is also with us to talk shop. It's our usual thing, with me dropping in to discuss the high school players.

Our game against the Bulls was another victory, and Austin is playing as I predicted. Instead of being intimidated by Levi's performance, this time it lit a fire in him. He's played better than he has all year.

"I know you were under a lot of pressure after the way Levi Powell started the season," he continues. "You've got two great quarterbacks, Coach."

"It's true." I shift in my chair. "You don't always get such good talent all at once. I'm trying to be sure both boys have their chance to shine."

"Looks like it's Newhope's year to go all the way." Zane's voice is calm and polished after two years of broadcasting with Logan.

"It looks like it," I say.

Logan and Zane's talk show is broadcast weekly, focusing on the professional teams. Garrett stops by more frequently than I do, since he's recently retired, and our youngest brother Hendrix joins them when his schedule permits. He's still a tight end for the LA Tigers.

Every quarter, they drag me into the booth, and it's the first year we've had such a focus on Newhope.

"You've always fielded a great team." Logan glances at me. "What do you think made the difference this year?"

"I've got a lot of seniors." My answer sends a ripple of laughter through our group.

"You know what that means." Garrett shifts in his chair.

"Next year might be a rebuilding year, but not necessarily." I lean on my forearm on the round table between us all. "Our defensive line has a lot of freshmen this year. You've been a big help getting those guys up to speed, and a strong D-line wins games."

"Speaking of freshmen, talk to us about that field goal against the Trojans." Logan grins at me, and Zane leans back in his chair.

"Zane can speak to this as well as I can. He's been working with Edward Wells since summer camp, and it looks like it's paying off."

"I've been working with both the boys," Zane replies. "Rome Allen is a strong kicker as well."

"Yet you didn't put him in the game at that critical moment." Logan has a degree in broadcasting, so I know he's trained to ask the follow-up question, even when it's sticky. "How do you answer parents who might say you show favoritism?"

"I don't."

Logan laughs. "You don't answer them, or you don't show favoritism?"

The show is recorded and rebroadcast on YouTube, so I do my best to keep my expression neutral as I answer. "Austin was confident Edward could do it. The team wanted him in there, so I made the call. I don't play favorites. I give every player a chance."

So far, no one's complained about my decision to put an unknown freshman in over our more experienced kicker. Probably because it won the game, and Rome has been unpredictable since Day 1.

"It was a stunning move, that's for sure," Garrett jumps in, lightening the tone. "I think it's safe to say Eddie's got a bright career ahead of him."

"Speaking of bright careers, some of these plays are getting regional attention." Zane shifts us away from his young brother-in-law. "Austin's on all the highlight reels from Tampa to New Orleans…"

We continue discussing plays and upcoming games, and after an hour, Logan brings it to a close. The lights change, and our mics turn off.

"Damn, Logan, you trying to get Jack in trouble?" Garrett stands up from his chair, hiking up his khaki uniform pants.

"What do you mean?" Logan frowns.

"People don't need your help getting the wrong idea in their heads." Garrett pats his shoulder.

"I thought it would be a good way for Jack to tackle it head-on. Edward made a great kick, and Austin's on fire." Logan turns to me. "Sorry, bro. I was trying to help."

I shake my head, chuckling. "Don't worry about it. I'm glad you did. Now I've got to get back to school. See y'all tomorrow."

It's just after lunch, and I'm energized and a little amped. A cool breeze winds through town, and that crisp splash of autumn has the kids talking about sweaters and letterman jackets and bonfires on the beach.

The scent of cinnamon and spice floats in the air, and large cranes pile bales of hay in the city park for the Halloween fundraiser and hay maze. It's only a few weeks away, and everyone's excited.

Hendrix will be in town with his little family, and I haven't been able to keep my mind off of Allie and pulling her close, snuggling around a fire, maybe slipping my hands under her sweater.

I'm not thinking about parents or favoritism. I'm thinking about one thing as I head in the direction of the library.

Chapter 19

Allie

Rachel: Jack Bradford is my hero. I haven't stopped crying all week.

Liv: He said it was Austin's idea to put him in the game.

Rachel: Austin is my hero as well. But Jack didn't have to do it.

Dylan: I have the best big brothers in the whole world. You're all welcome 🌀

True—and Logan's pretty great, too!

Raven: Hey—just finished the noon report. What'd I miss?

Hey, Stormy Spice! What's the weather like in LA?

Raven: Sunny with a high of 79 today.

Dylan: That's the same as us!

Raven: Would you like to hear about the traffic on the 405 or will somebody please tell me why Jack made everybody cry???

Rachel: He put Edward in the game, and he scored the winning field goal!!! I'll send you the video. It's kind of hard to see, because I was not prepared AT ALL…

Raven: Your Edward? When did he join the football team???? Y'all aren't telling me the important stuff!!!

I'm sorry, but to be honest, we didn't think he'd play! He's just a freshman, and Jack's very protective of him.

Raven: Just got the video—hold pls…

Dylan: What am I going to do about Dare Night?

Liv: What's wrong with Dare Night?

Dylan: Oh…

You might as well tell. Craig can't keep taking the heat for those dishes.

Rachel: OMG, what? Is it…

Dylan: I'm pregnant

Liv: DYLAN!!!!

Rachel: DYLAN!!!

Raven: I said hold, and now I'm crying!!! First, that kick—Edward is so poised! Like he never doubted for a moment it was good. Second… DYLAN!!!!

Dylan: I know! And Logan's baby hates peppers 🐤

I think your baby hates food. Last week's dish was inedible. I think I saw someone actually spit up in the trash.

Dylan: That's just mean.

Liv: It was pretty nasty. What did you do?

She put cloves in the pepper salsa! Then she tried to blame poor Craig.

Liv: That's the sign of a true friend. He took the blame and everything.

Raven: Oh no! 🐤 cloves in salsa sounds… interesting?

Rachel: It was bad.

Dylan: My taste buds are all wrecked. I can't tolerate heat. Foods taste different.

Liv: This is what happens when you burn your taste buds off.

Raven: Sounds like you need some backup—I can spot you when we get to town, Pepper Spice

Dylan: Raven—of course you can!!! What a perfect idea!

Raven: In the meantime… good luck 😬

We'll figure it out, but we've got to announce it this week, otherwise, we're losing business

We all sign off, and I slide my phone into the pocket of my dress. Today I'm wearing a forest green-and-navy-plaid dress, and my hair is up in space buns. It might not be classic librarian, but with my glasses and red lipstick, I'm feeling sassy.

I notice Sadie and two of her friends from the cheer squad surveying the poetry graffiti wall. I hung a large sheet over the bulletin board across from the *blind date with a book* shelves. Then I added Sharpies on strings, and I have poetry prompts all over it.

I've been happily surprised by all the additions to the "wall." Most are variations on well-known verses mixed with Taylor Swift lyrics and some nursery rhymes. I don't judge. I know they have to feel free to be silly if they're going to open up and be deep.

"Hey, ladies!" I walk over, smiling. "Looking for something in particular?"

"Oh, Hi, Miss Allie!" Sadie turns to me, smiling. "We need a poem about love."

Lifting my chin, I try to think. None of the English teachers alerted me they're starting poetry units. Usually they give me the heads up.

"Senior-level poetry?" I walk to the donated books I arranged on the shelves near the wall. "I've got Langston Hughes, Nikki Giovanni… Or the classic Shakespeare's Sonnet 18, 'Shall I compare thee to a summer's day?'"

The girls' noses all wrinkle at once—as if on cue.

"Shakespeare is…" Sadie shakes her head. "No."

"I can't understand any of it," her brunette friend adds.

"How about Nikki Giovanni?" the other girl asks. "What did he write?"

"Nikki Giovanni is a woman, and she's famous for the phrase 'We love because it's the only true adventure.'"

"I like that!" Sadie brightens, and I hand her the slim volume.

"You should reconsider Shakespeare." We walk to the front center of the room where the circulation desk is located. "It's easier than you think."

"Can I ask you something?" Sadie leans on the desk as I scan her card.

"Of course!" I smile. "That's what I'm here for."

"You had Austin when you were sixteen?"

My back straightens, and I hand her the book. "I was eighteen, which isn't much better."

"It's better than sixteen," she laughs. "At least you'd finished high school."

The three girls stand around my desk, and my brow furrows. "Is there a particular reason you're asking about this?"

My heart is in my throat. Sadie and Austin have been spending time together, and I've worked so hard to help him be safe and careful.

"You're like Lorelei Gilmore!" She smiles, but I'm not sure if I should be relieved.

"I never watched that show."

"She got pregnant at sixteen, and she moved to this small town to raise her daughter, and it's all quirky and fun. Just like you!"

"First of all, that was a fictional show, and second, looks can be deceiving."

"I think you look great, and you're so young and cool." Sadie smiles, lifting her chin. "I'd like to be like you."

"I'm no role model." I look down, reconsidering my sexy librarian attire. "You're not... pregnant, are you?"

"No!" She bursts out laughing, and I almost collapse with relief. "But I want to be a young mom."

"Just finish your education first. Having a baby is a lot harder than it looks. I got lucky landing in Newhope, but it wasn't always easy."

"If you say so!" She twirls around, and I decide to have another chat with Austin.

I need to be sure he's got everything he needs to be safe—and that he's using it.

"Hi, Coach!" Her chipper greeting stops my heart.

"Hi, Sadie, Lana." It's Jack.

I turn around to see him standing there, looking like a dream.

"Coach Bradford..." I'm breathless.

"Hello, Miss Sinclair." His gaze levels on me, and electricity flashes in my veins. "What do you have here?"

He looks at the makeshift poetry wall, and I do my best to get control. We're standing right in front of the girls, for heaven's sake.

"It's a graffiti wall, where students can leave poems for others to read and comment on or write their own."

"It's very romantic, Coach." Sadie's eyes slide from him to me, and I hold my expression steady, not giving anything away. "The guys are leaving love poems, and the girls are supposed to write poems back."

"They are?" My lips part, and it all makes sense now.

"Well, yeah," Sadie laughs. "Why did you think I was asking? Only, some of them are originals... I'm not that good."

"Wow, okay... in that case, add 'Love's Philosophy' by Shelley or 'Wild Nights' by Emily Dickinson to your list."

Her eyes light up with her smile. "Thanks, Miss A!"

"No problem." She dances away, and my eyes drift up to the wall where I see a few new couplets have been added.

I can't help a smile. *It's working...*

"Hi, Coach." Edward sits at one of the long tables and takes out a textbook.

"Hi, Edward." Jack smiles at the school's newest star athlete before turning that naughty grin back on me. "Can I see you in your office?"

Heat is in his tone, and I look around to be sure all the students are focused on their studies.

"I don't... have an office," I answer quietly.

"Is there somewhere private I could speak to you?" His tongue wets his bottom lip, and I lose the ability to breathe properly.

Is he really doing this here? I know what's on his mind, and there's no way in hell I'm saying no. I just can't believe it.

"I have a, um… supply closet. This way."

Walking quickly, I lead him through the tall rows of books to the back of the room where a metal door is situated in a corner.

My body vibrates with anticipation, and every brush of my thighs against each other stokes my arousal hotter. My underwear is already damp.

Glancing all around, I don't see any students in this part of the library.

My hands fumble with the lock, and I quickly open it, hitting the first switch, which illuminates a row of pale green lights in the rear of the room.

The metal door slams, and he turns me, pushing my back against it.

"Oh!" The word escapes on a gasp right before his hand grips my chin and his mouth covers mine.

Full lips open mine, and I'm breathing fast, doing my best to keep up. His hard body is firm against me, and he reaches down, clasping both my wrists in his hands before raising them over my head.

"Jack," I gasp as his lips move to my ear.

"This week has been torture." It's a low growl, and his hand is between my thighs. "I can't concentrate on the game. I can't focus on the plays."

His fingers jerk my panties aside, and he rubs my bare clit firmly, up and down, around and around as I whimper with need.

"All I can think about is how you sound when you come on my cock."

His hand moves faster, and I'm on my toes with my back arched, rocketing higher with every firm stroke of his hand.

"Oh, God, yes." I gasp as he slides two fingers into my slick core.

Warm breath flows down my neck as he bites the side of my ear, speaking directly, softly into my brain.

"Every time I jerk off, every time I have my dick in my hand, I picture driving it into you. Every place, every hole, from your pretty little mouth to your round sexy ass. My dirty little secret."

He kisses me again, and I'm right on the edge. Energy floods my veins, rising higher in my thighs. My orgasm twists tighter in my belly, and I'm whimpering, writhing against his body.

"You're so wet." He looks at me. "Spread your legs."

"Jack..." My sigh turns into a moan as he quickly unfastens his pants.

Anticipation floods my lungs when I feel his hard cock against my thigh. I want to touch him, but my hands are bound in his firm grip.

"I'm going to fuck you now. Don't make a sound."

"I can't..." I moan, his fingers still circling my clit. "I'm going to come."

"Allie." It's a stern order, and I whimper, nodding.

Releasing my hands, he grips my outer thighs, lifting me off my feet as he spreads me wide. Then, with a firm thrust, he fills me.

I bite my lip, snorting with a groan at his thickness, his hard invasion, his delicious possession. It's so good.

He's fucking me hard and fast. His drives are relentless as he grunts low words of need, desire, praise. My back arches as my orgasm rises on every thrust. My legs spread wider as he holds me against the door, owning me like he's possessed.

I'm surrounded by his rich leather scent. His fingers tighten on my ass, and I cup his cheeks, kissing him hungrily, as violently as his movements.

Salt covers my tongue, filling my mouth as we consume each other. It's been so long. We're both feverish with need.

The orgasm teased to life by his fingers erupts into a blaze against his cock. It rockets through my pelvis, and my head leans back. My eyes roll shut.

His mouth covers mine again, and I realize I'm moaning as he swallows the sounds.

My core clenches tighter, irresistibly tight, then my orgasm breaks. My muscles shudder. My core muscles flutter, spasming as repeated waves of mind-blanking pleasure control me.

His head turns, and he groans, finishing with two more thrusts, two low grunts, pressing his forehead against my sternum. His cock pulses deep in my body.

"Allie," he moans, and my eyes slowly open.

We're both gasping. I'm trembling, weak from adrenaline and spent from so much need fulfilled at once. His large hands squeeze my ass, and he thrusts once more, drawing out his orgasm with a deep groan.

Dropping my head forward, I kiss his ear. "You needed to see me?"

A laugh rumbles in his throat, and happiness soars through my chest. My arms tighten around him, hugging him closer.

"You're so perfect. Everything you do makes me happy." He kisses the side of my neck, and I glow under his sweet words.

Carefully pulling out, he lowers me to my feet. I'm in front of him, and he strokes my hair away from my face, gazing deep into my eyes with so much affection.

His thumbs trace my cheeks, and I blink quickly. I startle myself as I almost start to cry.

Dropping my chin forward, I swallow that back. *Holy shit, talk about too much too fast.*

Yes, I've been dying for him for at least three years, but just because he's mine right now doesn't mean I can say it.

"Hey." His voice is quiet, and he gives me a nudge.

Clearing my throat, I manage a smile as I look up at him. "Yep?"

"Me too." Leaning forward once more, he kisses my forehead, the tip of my nose, my lips, slowly, gently. "Me too, sweet Allie."

Stepping back, I look down at my bare legs. "I'm a mess."

He looks around the room filled with books and boxes and tape and pens and Post-its. "Is there anything?"

"Oh!" I step around a corner to where several unopened boxes of tissues are stacked.

"Yes." He takes a box from me, opening it quickly and pulling out several.

Then he drops to his knees, carefully cleaning my thighs. Emotion clogs my throat again, but I quickly swallow it away. He leans forward to kiss the side of my hip, pressing his face against my stomach and inhaling deeply.

My fingers thread in his thick, dark hair. Strong arms go around my legs, and he holds me several quiet moments. I never want to leave this place, but I've lost all track of time.

Bending down, I kiss the top of his ear. "I hate this, but I have to get back to the library."

He releases me and rises slowly, tracing his fingers over my ear. A hint of a smile curls his full lips, and his pretty blue eyes hold mine.

"Soon, my sweet Allie."

"Not your dirty little secret?" My eyebrow arches, and I'm feeling a little more in control.

"Maybe it won't be a secret." He kisses my lips once more. "But we'll always be dirty."

A laugh hiccups in my throat, and I nod. "I can do that."

Holding my hand, he opens the door, peeking out. "Coast is clear."

"Go ahead." I nod. "I've got to repair my hair and check my lipstick.

He looks back at me, reaching out to slide his thumb over my chin, under my bottom lip. "Perfect."

Another wash of happiness fills my stomach, and I hold his hand briefly before he disappears, leaving me glowing and so satisfied.

"Is it straight?" Rachel is on a step stool on one side of the room with Liv on the other.

I'm standing at the back of the room, watching as they raise a sign that reads *Congratulations, Dylan & Logan!*

"Up a little on the right." I motion to Liv's side, and she raises it. "Perfect!"

Two thumbs up, and I scurry to the kitchen again where Craig is running interference with Dylan while we throw together decorations for the big night.

I've been floating on a cloud the past two weeks, starting with Austin back on the field winning games and looking so good, followed by my sexy encounters with Coach Jack.

"I don't know why you even want me to make anything since I'm so off my game." Dylan stands in front of the industrial-sized blender pouting.

"What do you have in there for tonight?" I step forward, peering into the plastic bin.

An odd aroma rises to meet me, and my eyes slide to Craig's. He shakes his head slowly.

"It's Peter Peppers with figs and barley."

My chin jerks. "Figs and barley?"

"At least the peppers are hot this time—if you consider jalapeños hot." Craig lifts a red pepper by the stem. "Check out this guy."

A laugh snorts through my nose. "It looks like a penis!"

"Isn't that crazy?" Dylan leans forward with a laugh. "I want to put some out around the dish."

"As in, 'This dish tastes like a dick'?" I pour the oddly scented mixture into a large serving bowl.

"No, ma'am, dick tastes much better than this culinary disaster." Craig sniffs, and I fall onto Dylan, giggling.

"Y'all are being so mean. I'm not cooking another thing." Dylan pulls her gloves off and goes to the sink to wash her hands.

"Nooo, come on now!" I move the bowl onto the rolling cart. "Trust me, it's going to be a fun game!"

"It's time." Craig pulls on his blond wig. "I'm not sure what to play with this dish. 'Caution' by The Killers?"

"Mean!" Dylan fusses.

"Just play 'Sally.'" I wrap an arm around my friend, giving her a squeeze before we head out to the dining area.

The crowd has picked up since last week. We put out the word we'd have a special treat tonight, and people are slowly ambling in.

"We hope you brought your sense of humor tonight." I stand on the step-stool like I usually do for the warning. "Tonight's pepper is named after a certain part of the male anatomy, and we have a few up here for you to see. The Peter pepper is a little hotter than a jalapeño, but I'm not going to vouch for the flavor of this dish…" A rumble moves through the group. "The best news is our very own Pepper Spice, Dylan Bradford-Murphy, is expecting her very first baby! And it seems to be impacting her taste buds."

Cheers break out, and I see our extended "family" at the back table, Miss Gina, Liv's mom, Gloria, and Sandra, all clapping and hugging each other. Logan joins us behind the serving table to wrap his arms around his little wife.

A few taxi whistles rip through the noise, and I wave my hand.

"It looks like we'll have to suffer through a few more months of crazy dishes, but we're turning it into a game. Up here in the tip jar, you're welcome to rank Dylan's worst pregnancy Dare dish on a scale of one to five, with five being worst…"

"Rude!" Dylan cries, and more people laugh.

"Tonight's dish is Peter peppers with figs and barley…" I shrug. "The dare is if you can get through it without barfing, and we're offering half-price Budweiser to help wash it down."

Craig hits the music, and "Sally, When the Wine Runs Out" gets folks out on the dance floor. A line forms, and I hand out little trays of tortilla chips as Dylan scoops out the salsa.

A few people comment on the pornographic peppers, and even Oliver Duck gives her a begrudging congratulations.

Jack is nowhere to be seen in the dining hall, and it's my turn to be a little pouty. I finish the last serving, dance with the girls for a few minutes, then make an excuse to duck out early.

My phone buzzes in my pocket as I head out the door, and when I pull it out, I see a text from a blocked number. I'm about to tap it when another text from Jack appears on top of it.

Sir: Couldn't make it tonight, but thinking about your sexy body.

A smile curls my lips, and I glance behind me to where everyone is dancing and having a good time. Austin is with his friends, and I expect he won't be home for at least another hour.

I get in my car and quickly reply.

Leaving now. Maybe I'll take a walk when I get home.

Sir: Kimmie is here.

Maybe I won't 😞

Sir: Have you ever tried anal?

I duck forward, covering my mouth with my hand before replying.

No, but I would for you.

Sir: 

Sir:

Snorting a laugh, I drive my car home. I've showered, and I'm in bed reading my spicy romance novel when Austin arrives. He calls goodnight to me and says he's setting the house alarm.

I pick up my phone to check the time, and remember the text I didn't read earlier from the blocked number. It's just a short sentence, and my breath stills.

I see you.

Chapter 20

Jack

"I'M NOT TRYING TO TELL YOU HOW TO DO YOUR JOB. IT'S ABOUT MY son's chance of getting a scholarship." George Powell is in my office, and to his credit, he's keeping his cool. "Levi's not getting the same amount of time on the field."

It's true, and I can't argue with him.

I've been playing Austin more, because when Austin's in the game, Allie is so happy. When Allie's happy, I'm happy, and I like seeing Austin play. It's the definition of favoritism, and I don't have a leg to stand on.

My jaw is tight, and I nod, looking down at my desk. "You're right. I'll start him in tonight's game against Crystal Shores."

They're our longstanding rival team. They're big and tough, and we have the added disadvantage of playing them on the road. Still, it'll get Powell off my back and free up Austin to play in next week's homecoming game.

Homecoming coincides with the Halloween fundraiser and the return of Hendrix and his crew. They'll be wanting to see him play, and I'm looking forward to having the family all together again.

We give Dylan a hard time about wanting us all in Newhope again, but I wouldn't mind that scenario either. It's been a difficult journey, but our family is strong in love and support.

George stands, holding out his hand to shake. "I heard you were an easy man to work with. I see those rumors were correct."

I stand slowly, taking his hand and shaking it. "I want all the boys to succeed."

He nods and turns to leave my office. I'm thinking about going to the library to see what Allie's doing. After last night's brief text exchange and my last visit, my blood heats thinking about her. I also have a little something in mind…

Then I see her sitting on the edge of a chair in the lobby.

She's so pretty in a maroon dress with little white flowers on it that hugs her shape in a way that should be sinful. Her dark hair is twisted up on the back of her head, and her lips are a beautiful wine color.

But she's not wearing her glasses, and when our eyes meet, hers are wide with fear.

It's a punch to the chest, and I don't care if George is standing at the receptionist's desk. I go straight to her.

"Are you okay?" My voice is urgent.

She stands quickly, walking straight past George Powell and into my office without a word. I follow her inside and close the door before going to put my arm around her.

"What's wrong?"

"This appeared on my phone last night." She hands me the device, and my brow lowers.

A text from a blocked number is on the screen.

I see you.

Anger burns in my throat, and my eyes snap to hers. "Is it him?"

"I don't know." Her arms wrap around her waist, and she steps out of my embrace. "I messaged a few friends in New Orleans, and they haven't seen him lately. They can't remember how long it's been. I mean, it could be an accident. It could've been meant for someone else..."

"But the number is hidden." I shake my head. "We're not taking a chance."

Her eyes lift to mine, and she's so frightened standing in front of me, protection surges in my veins.

"Come here." I pull her to me again, and she melts into my arms with a little huff.

Her head is against my chest, and a shiver moves through her body.

Leaning down, I kiss her temple, sliding my hand up and down her back.

"You're not alone in this." Holding my lips against her head, I inhale deeply her apple scent. "I'll take care of you."

She nods against my chest, but when she lifts her chin, her brow is lined. "How?"

Gazing into her pretty face fills me with calm assurance. "You'll move in with me until we've located him."

"I can't do that." She exhales a scoff. "What about Austin?"

"I'll stay at your place, then."

"And Kimmie?"

"Dylan will help me with her." Reaching up, I slide a lock of hair behind her ear. "I won't leave your side."

"I have a house alarm. We should be good with that."

"I don't like *should*." She has no idea the lengths I'm willing to go to guarantee her safety. "Have you shown this to Garrett?"

"No, I came straight to you."

I like that she came to me. I want her to come to me always. "We'll loop him in on this, and he can have his guys watching. He can find out the last time Rip checked in with his parole officer, and that will give us an idea of what we're working with."

"I hate this so much." Allie's jaw tightens, and she starts to pace again. "I hate that he has this power over us. I hate being afraid. It makes me so angry."

"He doesn't have power over us." My tone is final. "If he's

stupid enough to come here, he'll find out just how big of a mistake he's making. We take care of our own, and nobody is going to touch you or Austin."

Her brow is still furrowed, and I touch her cheek. "Look at me." Her face lifts, and I hold her gaze. "Do you trust me?"

"You know I do."

"Then don't be afraid."

She blinks a few times, and the mist in her blue eyes twists my chest painfully.

"Allie," I whisper, taking her hand. "We've got you."

At last she relents, looking down, but managing a smile. "Okay."

"Let's talk to Garrett."

"He last checked in two days ago." Garrett types on his desktop computer as we sit across from him in his sheriff's office. "He hasn't been granted permission to leave the state, but he requested it."

"Can he do that?" The panic in Allie's tone has me reaching for her hand.

All thoughts of keeping our feelings a secret are gone. I'm not letting a dangerous criminal threaten her or her son, and everyone can deal with it.

Garrett doesn't even seem to notice. "He can request it. Doesn't mean he's going to get it. In fact, I expect he'll be denied. He hasn't been out long enough, and he's got some heavy charges on his record. Law enforcement doesn't want to lose track of him."

"What can we do?" My tone is sharp, and my brother stands, adjusting the holster on his waist.

When Garrett told me he wanted to be sheriff, I only thought how it would affect my plans for him to join my coaching staff.

Now that I see him at six-four in his official uniform, I feel a lot better about his decision to keep the town safe.

"I didn't find any record that he'd bought a vehicle."

"You don't really need a car in New Orleans." Allie's voice is quiet.

"That'll slow him down some. I'll ask highway patrol to keep a lookout for any out of state plates headed this way, and I'll have Sam add your street to his rounds at night."

"Sam Allen?" I frown up at him. "I thought he was in Animal Control."

"Hey, don't knock Animal Control. Some of our best officers got their start there." My brother grins, and I know he's talking about himself. "He moved over a few months back. He got tired of getting alligators out of the road, but he's a good officer."

My brother's upbeat nature goes a long way towards easing the tension in the small room.

He puts a hand on Allie's shoulder. "I know it doesn't seem like it, but one of the best things he could do is show up here. We'll nail his ass, and he'll be back in Angola."

Allie scrubs her fingers across her forehead. "I'm sure you're right. I just don't know what to expect."

"It's tough, but I'll talk to the guys now. Best thing you can do is try to go about your business. Don't let him win."

She looks up at me. "We have the game tonight. I'll be with all the girls, then when we get back…"

"I'll see if Dylan can keep Kimmie, and I'll spend the night at your place."

"What do I tell Austin?"

My lips tighten, and I think about it. "We don't know anything for sure yet. It still could be an accidental text."

Garrett makes a low noise, and I agree. I'm not counting on it.

"He knows to be careful," Allie concedes. "But he'll wonder why you're at our house."

"He won't be the only one." Garrett leans back in his chair grinning.

"I'll be discreet." As if I care about town gossip right now. "I can come over after hours and leave before sunrise."

"I should give you both my alarm code just in case." Allie quickly jots down the number.

It takes me two seconds to memorize. "I'll talk to Austin, but we'd better head back to school."

Lunchtime is almost over, and the specter of Rip has overshadowed our big rivalry game in my mind.

Still, we have the pep rallies and all the school spirit events to attend this afternoon. At least Allie is right about it being game day—she'll never be out of my sight.

Sitting on the bus for the short drive to the Crystal Shores stadium, I send a quick text.

> Levi's starting QB tonight. I meant to tell you earlier.

DLS: It's been a day.

> Austin will be back next week.

DLS: It's homecoming. Everyone will be here.

> More eyes on both of you.

DLS: That gave me a shiver.

> More eyes that love you.

DLS: Thank you ☺

I think about what I sent. I think about how she's become so much a part of my family these last few years. My siblings do love her—and Austin, too.

I love her and Austin.

Staring at the phone in my hands, I acknowledge the truth right in front of me like a brand, an undeniable fact.

I love Allie.

I love her, and this is where everything changes.

Levi plays a strong game, but the Dolphins have done their homework. They're ready for both of our quarterbacks, and he's sacked more than once.

Going into the fourth quarter, they're up by seven. The score has gone back and forth each quarter with us scoring out the gate and them hot on our heels.

Garrett joined us for practice in the days leading up to tonight, and our defensive line turned in the best game of the season. Still, it isn't enough to hold back this team.

As strong as we play, we miss our chance at scoring a touchdown. In the final seconds, Rome Allen kicks a field goal, but it's not enough to close the gap in the score.

It's our first loss of the season—and against our biggest rival. Our fans are deflated, and the mood on the bus heading back to Newhope is somber.

My mind and my eyes have been on Allie all night, but I stand, facing the boys as we drive.

"You played a good game tonight. I want you all to be proud of yourselves." I look at where Austin and Levi share a seat in the back.

Austin's in the middle, his eyes fixed on me as I speak. Levi's looking out the window at the passing lights, and as a former quarterback, I'm sure I can guess how he's feeling.

"It never feels good to lose, but we've had a strong season. We've got four games to go, and we're still in the running for the playoffs." I look from face to face. "Defense, that was your best game of the year. Let's keep it up, and Levi?"

He doesn't look up from the window.

"Levi?" He finally turns his gaze to me, and I give him a nod. "You played a good game. You'll have another chance to show us what you can do."

He doesn't smile, and I make the decision to let him split the homecoming game with Austin. We're playing the Bears, another tough team, but it'll be on our home turf.

It'll be a high-spirit time with all the festivities and the positive energy. I expect we'll pull out a win.

When we arrive at the school, the boys file off the bus. Austin walks with Levi, Tyreek, and Lucas to the parking lot, and I consider stopping him to let him know I'll be sleeping on his couch tonight.

At the last minute, I decide to wait and talk to him later. In the meantime, I'll get Kimmie settled with her aunt, and I'll check in with Garrett to see if he's heard anything.

Chapter 21

Allie

EDWARD WALKS WITH ME TO THE LIBRARY TO COLLECT MY THINGS before I head home. The rest of the boys are heading down to the beach for a bonfire, but Edward isn't a fan of the loud parties and whatever else they do to burn off energy after the games.

I couldn't believe he wanted to be on the team at all, but Austin told me he wears earplugs on the field.

When they got off the bus, I asked my son to be aware of his surroundings tonight, but I didn't tell him about the text.

Jack's right. It's still possible it could be a text intended for someone else, and I don't want to spoil Austin's senior year by having him paranoid all the time like I am.

I hate that Jack has to worry about me and my poor choices. He has enough on his mind with the loss and George Powell growling in the stands and second-guessing every decision.

Even with Levi starting the game, he isn't satisfied. He's making noise now about how Jack put him in knowing Crystal Shores is our biggest rival. How he spared Austin's record and intentionally made Levi look like the weaker player.

Whereas, I'm sure if they'd pulled out the win, he'd be crowing about how Levi should be starting every time, and how he saved the team in an important game. How he's clearly the stronger player.

My head hurts, and I don't want to think about that man.

"There's a new poem on the graffiti wall." Edward's standing by the sheet, looking up at the couplets.

Taking my bags from behind the circulation desk, I let the positivity of this moment ease the tension in my chest. I'm so happy the students are responding this way.

"I knew they'd like poetry." I smile, going to where he stands. "Show it to me."

"It's here." He points at the four lines written in what looks like a male script.

Your eyes are so beautiful, so blue.

I see them even when I'm alone.

You've woven yourself into my soul.

Losing you now would be losing my home.

As I read the words, my lips part. "I don't recognize this. Is it an original?"

I look at Edward, who simply shrugs. "It's impossible to know."

We stand for a moment, and I reread the poem, thinking how it's more sophisticated than the others.

Most of the "graffiti" are passages from existing works or variations on them. We have a Robert Frost fan, who has copied both "The Road Not Taken" and "Stopping by the Woods on a Snowy Evening."

And miles to go before I sleep.

And miles to go before I sleep.

But this new verse is something different.

"It's really good," I muse. "I can't wait to find out who it is at the end of the contest."

"I'm voting for it." Edward takes one of the Sharpies

hanging on a string and numbers the poem 18, then he puts a slip of paper in the box.

"Thanks for escorting me to the library." We head out, making our way up the hall to the parking lot. "Do you need a ride home?"

"I'm meeting Zane at the restaurant if you'd drop me off there."

I do just that, then I head to my house. It's dark when I pull into the driveway, and my heart beats faster as I survey the dark lawn and surrounding trees.

Jack said he would sleep here tonight, and as much as I tried to say we'd be fine, not to worry about us, I'm glad he is.

Walking to the front door, my breath tightens in my lungs.

"You're safe, Allie," I tell myself as I type in the security code. "The house alarm was armed, and nothing has been touched."

Inside, I quickly shut the door and lock it, arming the system again. I remember the night Garrett walked in with me, and I almost wish he were here to do it now—or someone.

As it is, if anything happens, all I have to do is run out the door and the alarm will go off. Very sensible.

Shaking my head, I go to my bedroom to shower and put away my things.

All my reinforcing thoughts and admonitions don't slow down my movements. I shower quickly, changing into pajama pants and a long-sleeved T-shirt.

Jack's jersey is tucked under my pillow. I only wear it when I'm sure Austin won't see me. I'm not sure how to answer his questions yet.

The nights are growing cooler as we get closer to Halloween, and a shiver sends me to the thermostat in the living room to crank the heat a little higher.

I walk down the hall, and the alarm goes off like a train barreling through the living room. My heart flies to my throat, and I scream.

A man wearing a black hoodie and a baseball cap is at the wall where the control panel is located. His back is to me, but when I scream, he turns.

A series of beeps stops the blaring noise, but my entire body is shaking, and my vision blurs. I think I'm going to faint.

Strong arms surround me, and when I inhale the scent of leather and sandalwood, I start to cry.

"Allie." Jack's hand smooths my hair away from my face, but I can't stop. "Didn't you see my texts? I told you I was on my way here. I didn't know you'd set the alarm."

"I didn't…" A hiccup breaks up my words, "…see your text. I thought… I thought…"

My stomach clenches painfully, and he lifts me off my feet, carrying me to the couch and sitting down with me in his lap. He shushes me, rubbing his hands up and down my arms and kissing the side of my temple.

"I'm so sorry, my beautiful girl. I didn't mean to scare you." His low voice is rich and soothing, and my fingers curl in the soft fabric of his jacket. "I'm here now."

It takes a few moments of breathing to regain control. Shaking my head, I wipe away the tears with the back of my hand. "I'm sorry. I thought… I'm such a mess. I can't believe I screamed like that."

"I should've called. I shouldn't have counted on you seeing a text."

"I just got out of the shower." I'm so embarrassed.

I feel like a complete disaster. Too much work. Too much drama. He's got enough to worry about without adding my trouble to the mix.

His arms surround me like protective bands. It feels so good despite of it all, and slowly, my shaking subsides. I tap the tears out of my eyes.

"I'm sorry I overreacted." Sitting back on the couch, I look up at him sheepishly. "I should've known it was you… or Austin."

"Don't do that. You have every right to be on edge." He

reaches out to cup my chin before leaning forward to pull my lips with his.

It sends warmth through my belly, and I climb onto his lap in a straddle, holding his face and kissing him back.

His tongue sweeps inside, curling with mine, and he grips my ass in his large hands, sliding me forward and back over the length in his gray joggers.

I whimper as orgasm ignites low in my belly. His hands move to my waist, fumbling with the hem of my shirt as I continue to rock my clit back and forth against his growing erection.

Sliding his palms under my shirt, he cups my breasts, lifting and squeezing them. The thin cotton rises over his forearms, and he breaks the kiss, moving his mouth to my hardened nipples. He nibbles and sucks them. It feels amazing, and my head falls back. I moan louder as the friction between us shoots sparks through my inner thighs.

"Your body is so beautiful," he groans, moving from one breast to the other, tasting and savoring me.

My fingers thread in his hair, and I kiss his ear, his temple. "I love the way you love me."

He groans, lifting his face and pulling my mouth to his. We kiss once, twice. Our eyes meet, and his are so deep, so full of unspoken words.

"Stand up." It's a low order, and I'm quick to obey.

I'm ready to do anything he says.

"Pull down your pants."

Again, I do as he says immediately. I start to take off my underwear as well, but his hands catch my wrists.

"Stop." It's just above a growl. "I didn't tell you to take them off."

"I'm sorry," I whisper.

"Take out my cock." Excitement flares in my core, and my eyes go to the hard muscle hidden behind thick cotton.

I start to kneel, but again he stops me. "On your feet."

Chewing my lip, I bend forward, tugging the waist of his

pants lower so his penis rises from the fabric, long and throbbing. I swallow the ache in my throat, and when I look up at him, he's still watching me.

"Straddle me, and put my cock in your pussy."

I climb onto my knees above him, lifting him in my hands. Guiding him to my slippery core. He lifts his hand as well, moving the crotch of my undies to the side.

I put his tip right at my entrance, and his hands grasp my ass again. "Slowly."

Another whimper aches from my throat as I follow his order. Every ridge, every line and vein stretches me, filling me completely.

My eyes lock on his, and they're so dark. His lips part, and he exhales a groan when I sit flush against his body, taking him fully into mine.

"Fuck," he hisses, reaching for the nape of my neck and pulling my mouth to his.

My shirt is still over my bare breasts, and he squeezes my ass as he bites my bottom lip.

"Ride me, beautiful girl. I want to watch your beautiful tits bounce as you come apart on my dick."

"Oh, God," I whimper, lifting up on my knees and watching his eyes fixate on my body.

I'm an exhibitionist, a lap dancer. I roll my hips, arching my back and doing my best to get him off. I twist my hardened nipples, lifting and dropping, feeling like a queen, feeling powerful and free.

"That's it," he whispers. "So beautiful… fuck, you ride me so good."

His voice is low and growly, and his words send flushes of warmth through me. His hand moves from my ass to between my thighs, finding my clit and massaging it forcefully.

"Oh!" I yelp.

I'm already on edge; the orgasm I've been coaxing twists tighter, hotter at the base of my stomach. I rock my hips back and forth, and he massages faster. I'm getting so close, when I feel his other hand slide around to my ass.

My stomach twists as he runs a finger up and down, getting closer, until he slips one into that tight hole. Another yelp, and I start to come. My thighs tighten, and I'm practically jumping on his cock.

He groans, and I feel a second finger slip inside. The ball of tension tightens so hard, I scream when it bursts into sparkling waves of ecstasy.

I grip his shoulders as my muscles jerk me forward. I moan and cry, and he holds me by my ass, moving me faster over his cock. He speaks dirty words, words of desire and darkness as he groans, working out his own orgasm.

I'm fluttering and pulsing, drawing him further into my depths as his mouth latches onto my breast, pulling and sucking my nipple. Then all at once, his back arches. He drives deeper into me, wrapping his arms around my waist and holding me close as he finishes with a shout.

We're so tight, I feel every pulse as he fills me. His body shudders and breaks, and his muscles ripple in my arms. Holding him, I exhale a soft sigh.

This gorgeous man, this fierce protector, is coming apart in my arms. He's all my dreams, my fantasies come to life. We hold each other, and I hum as we drift back to this world, as this small room comes into focus again.

His face is against my chest, and he gathers my hair in his hands, holding it back as he presses warm lips to my neck.

"You're so beautiful, Allie." His mouth rises higher to my ear. "So perfect for me. I'll never let anyone hurt you. You'll always be in my arms. Always."

A smile curls my lips, and I exhale a soft noise of happiness...

Until the sound of a key in the front door lock sends me scrambling.

"Oh, shit!" I hiss, snatching up my pajama pants from the floor and running to my bedroom.

The front door opens just as mine closes, and the low murmur of voices meets my ear, followed by the staccato beeps of the security system code being entered.

Leaning my back against the bedroom door, I do my best to catch my breath.

In the mirror on my armoire, I see the smile covering my face, but I also see the red marks covering my neck and chest. Love bites, swollen lips, sweaty cheeks…

Another flush of warmth floods my veins. It's the warmth of love melting away all my fear. I close my eyes and replay his words in my mind.

I'll never let anyone hurt you. You'll always be in my arms. Always.

Jack said he would explain what's happening to Austin, and I'm in no shape to go out there. Still, pressing my lips together, I put my hand on the doorknob, carefully opening it so I don't make a sound.

"We didn't want to worry you." I catch the end of Jack's explanation for his presence on my couch. "Garrett's got his guys keeping an eye on things."

"You think he'd try to hurt me?" My chest aches at Austin's question.

I'd give anything for his dad to be a better man.

"No," Jack answers quickly. "I don't know what that would accomplish, and he doesn't have a history of that sort of thing."

It's quiet a moment, and if I weren't scared I'd be caught, I'd peek to see what's happening.

"You think he'd try to hurt Mom." It's not a question, and the shock in Austin's voice hits me hard.

My hand covers my mouth, and I inhale slowly. Jack doesn't answer, and I don't know if he's trying to find the right words or if he nodded in assent.

"I won't let anything happen to either of you." His tone is final. "You hear me?"

Rustling in the room makes me want to see what they're doing.

Finally, my son answers. "You always look out for us."

"I always will." More sounds of movement, and I hear what sounds like someone patting another person's back.

I carefully close the door as they're saying goodnight. We've never had a man looking out for us, a husband, a father. Curling under my covers I hug my knees feeling more secure than I ever have in my life.

Chapter 22

Jack

Cooters & Shooters is filled with pumpkins and ghosts, cobwebs and massive black spiders. Purple-caped witches on broomsticks are flattened against trees, and my youngest brother Hendrix is taking his two-year-old daughter Haddy out of her carseat.

"We're here at last!" Raven cries, jogging up to give me a hug. "It's so good to see you. I can't believe it's been four months. Is everybody inside?"

"Yep. They're all waiting for you." I return my sister-in-law's hug. "You're just in time. Dylan is waiting for you to help her with tonight's Dare dish."

Raven snorts a laugh, leaning forward as she steps past me to the restaurant. "I heard about this… Figs and barley?"

Shaking my head, I hold up both hands in surrender. "I'm staying out of it. She's pouty enough with Craig and Allie teasing her all the time."

To be fair, my little sister has been whipping up some seriously gnarly recipes lately.

"Hey, bro!" Hendrix straightens, holding his dark-haired little mini-me.

Her eyes are bright blue just like his, and it's pretty incredible how much Haddy looks like he did as a baby.

"Hey." I step forward to give him a hug, slapping his back.

"You're looking good." He nods, cocking an eyebrow. "Looking pretty relaxed. Hell, I'd say you're glowing. What's your secret? Could it start with an *A* and end with an *ie?*"

"That does it." I start to grab him by the neck when Haddy claps her hands and squeals.

"Take it easy, man, I'm holding an infant!"

"She's two, and you'd better remember who's in charge around here."

"Where is Allie? In the kitchen?" He's teasing, but it does make me smile.

Hell, I'm smiling a lot these days. After two nights sleeping on Allie's couch, she got a text from an old friend back home that Rip had been spotted at a bar in New Orleans.

Garrett confirmed he had a check-in with his parole officer, and we were able to relax a bit. I sleep better in my own bed, but I do miss waking up on Allie's couch with her curled up at my feet.

Possession, protection, satisfaction… all the emotions twined in my stomach at the sight of her there, staying close to me, trusting me.

If it were Kimmie, I'd carry her back to her bed. Instead, I wrapped a blanket around her and kissed her soft cheek before slipping out with the sunrise.

Talking to Austin wasn't easy. Allie didn't want to derail his entire senior year, but as the eldest son myself, and knowing how much he cares about her, I knew he could handle the truth.

He wasn't happy, but I think he knows I'll keep an eye on them. Still, I was glad to tell him things were back to normal for now.

Our big homecoming game is tomorrow night, and with my family all rolling into town, it feels like the holidays have arrived.

The summer heat has broken, and the sights and smells of fall are all around us. Everyone's buzzy and excited.

I follow Hendrix into the restaurant, and at once we're approached by Sadie and two of her cheerleader friends selling tickets to the Halloween festival and hay maze. They're dressed up like those witches in *Hocus Pocus*, complete with wigs and makeup.

"Don't miss the grand opening tomorrow night!" Sadie gives me two tickets. "Some of the guys are dressing up as Michael Myers and Freddy Krueger and Jigsaw. It's going to be *so fun!*"

Hendrix grimaces. "Yeah, I'll watch Haddy while y'all do all that."

"You're not scared of high schoolers, are you?" I can't help teasing him.

"No, but I don't like people jumping out at me. I tend to get punchy."

My lips pucker, and I nod at the girls. "He has a point. Be sure to tell the guys not to get too close. You never know how people will react when they're scared. We don't want anybody getting hurt."

"Yes, sir, Coach!" She does a little salute before skipping off to the next customers entering the restaurant.

"Hendrix!" Liv dashes forward to hug my brother. "Look who's here, Gigi—it's Haddy!"

She's holding her daughter, and the two little girls start to squeal as soon as they see each other. They wiggle to get down, and as soon as they do, they take off running—with their parents right behind them.

"Don't forget the playground," I call as they cross the room.

After having four wild little boys, that playground was a feature our Mom insisted the restaurant have. She wanted an enclosed area so she could sit down and finish one meal without having to jump up every minute.

Hendrix swoops up his toddler, and they head out the screen door in the middle of the back wall facing the bay. I continue on to the kitchen where Garrett and Logan have joined the Thursday night crew.

Female voices laugh, and the conversations are lively and animated.

"Back away from the workstation, Dylan." Raven points the sharp knife at her. "We are *not* putting orange marmalade in the chile de arbol."

"I thought it would be interesting," Dylan argues. "Chefs combine sweet and spicy all the time, and it works really well!"

"Your taste buds are wack right now, Pepper Spice." Allie moves her hands in a sweeping gesture. "Go hang out with Logan and enjoy your pregnancy. Let Raven do this."

Dylan crosses her arms as she walks over to stand with her husband.

"It's okay, babe." Logan leans down to wrap his arms around her shoulders. "I love all your pepper-free dishes."

"It's so wrong." My sister leans her back against his chest, and he holds her.

My lips twist with a half smile, and I think about the day I'll be able to do the same with Allie.

She's standing beside Raven, chopping onions and mincing garlic. Her hair is swept up in that messy bun, and the laughter in her eyes, the easy smile on her lips helps my shoulders relax.

Her glasses have been swapped out for protective goggles, and they're both wearing plastic gloves to keep the hot pepper oil off their skin.

Garrett and Craig are putting together a playlist, both wearing their blond wigs, and Kimmie is right in the middle, dancing around with Apricot in her arms.

Affection unfurls in my chest. This is my family.

"Hey, bro, you guarding the door?" Garrett motions for me to join them, and I walk over to stand beside Zane, who's hanging around the edges quietly like he always does.

"Just making sure nothing's on fire back here." My eyes meet Allie's, and her lips press into a smile.

A cute flush of pink tints her cheeks, and she's fucking adorable. I wonder if she's thinking the same thing as I am. *You belong here. This is your home. I love you…*

"The only thing on fire is this dish!" Raven calls, and I grin at how she also fits right in with this wild crowd. "You ready with the warning, Al?"

Allie pulls off her plastic gloves and goes to the sink to wash her hands. "Ready!"

"Let's do this."

We head out to the waiting crowd, and Dylan introduces Raven as her sister-in-law and partner in pepper-loving crime. Allie reads off her script about how to eat tonight's dish, and with that, the party begins.

"Ring of Fire" is Craig's first spicy song of the night, and as always I hang back, arms crossed as I watch the celebration. From there, the music devolves to Halloween-themed tunes. Purple and orange twinkle lights are strung throughout the dining hall and wrap around the columns in the center of the room.

I spot Kimmie near the booth where Miss Gina always sits, holding hands with her little cousins and jumping up and down to "Ghostbusters." Haddy is more interested in Apricot, but Gigi is ready to dance.

"Who ya gonna call?" The female voice behind me puts my body on alert.

Turning, I look down at Allie standing in front of me with her arms folded behind her back. She lifts her chin and her breasts rise higher, and I'm ready to ditch this party.

"I can handle a ghost."

"Would you say, you ain't afraid-a no ghost?" She tilts her sassy head to the side, batting her blue eyes.

"I'd probably use better English, but yes." Reaching for her hand, I pull her closer. "How are you feeling about old ghosts?"

Her lips tighten, and her gaze slides to the side. "I kind of miss having my handsome protector sleeping at my house."

"I'm not too far." The music changes to the "Monster Mash," and the kids squeal. Leaning down, I speak in Allie's ear. "Will you go with me to the fundraiser tomorrow?"

She nods, stretching higher to reply in my ear. "Liv said we're all meeting here to walk over as a group. But I'll walk with you."

Her hand is on my chest, and her body presses lightly against mine. I hold her waist, doing my best to cool the heat in my blood. "I won't make you wait long."

"Then it's a date."

"Yes, it is."

"Are you going to dress up?"

My brow furrows, and I study her expression. She's serious. "I didn't get that memo. Are you?"

"Mm-hmm." Taking out her phone, she taps a few times and shows me the screen. "I found this cute little Regency gown that isn't too much work to get into. Or out of."

Heat centers low in my belly as I study the soft gray dress. It has some sort of white ruffle around the neckline, and the straight skirt has a slit up the side to reveal white, thigh-high stockings.

"I like it." Tightening my jaw, I think about what might go with it. It's not a lot of notice. "I'll find something."

"It doesn't have to be complicated." She blinks up at me, almost apologetic. "Dylan and Logan are going as peppers. Liv is wearing one of her old dance costumes, and Garrett is wearing his football jersey."

"If it still fits him."

She leans closer. "I have your jersey, but you're not getting it back."

Taking her hand, I hold it in mine a moment, knowing I have an audience everywhere I go. "I gave it to you to keep."

Giving her hand a squeeze, I release her, walking over to

where Kimmie is twirling around and kicking her leg. Apricot has somehow managed to escape, and Rachel is monitoring the girls and Miss Gina.

"What is Gigi doing now?" The old lady asks.

"Garrett's trying to dance with her, and she's trying to get down."

"She's very independent." Miss G chuckles. "I love having a little namesake running around doing all the things I would do."

"You do a lot," Rachel quips.

Stopping at my little girl, I tap her shoulder. "Bedtime."

"Daddy," she whines, her little shoulders dropping. "The party's still going!"

"Not for long, and you have school tomorrow. Then we have the fair tomorrow night."

A frown twists her little features as she thinks. Then she immediately nods and takes my hand. "I can't wait for the fair! I'm going to do the maze and the pumpkin patch and dress up and eat candy…"

Her hand is in mine as she continues listing, and I glance back at Allie dancing with Raven now. Her costume is hot, and I have an idea for how I might match it. It's going to be a night to remember.

Our homecoming game is a shut-out.

Austin came out strong, throwing three back-to-back touchdown passes. It was hard to take him out, but I promised to let Levi share the spotlight.

I don't usually pay much attention to the Homecoming court, but when Austin was announced as king during halftime, we all stepped out to cheer for him.

Allie was crying, and if things were different, I'd go to her and pull her into my arms. Instead, Dylan and Liv crowded around her, hugging and clapping.

Sadie was named homecoming queen, and when she kissed Austin's cheek, he looked down at the ground as if he were embarrassed. I looked over to see Allie's eyes on me from the clutch of my sisters.

I gave her a little smile, and she pressed her fingers to her lips, blowing me a kiss. I looked down, rubbing my cheek as if I felt it, and when I cut my eyes up at her, her nose wrinkled with her laugh.

For the second half of the game, Levi didn't disappoint. He didn't complete any touchdown passes, but he ran thirty-five yards for a thrilling first-down.

Another near-sack resulted in a toss that Tyreek ran in for the score. We even let Edward kick the extra point, making the final score 29-0.

After shaking hands with the other coach, and giving a short congratulatory speech to the boys, I cut out to make my Halloween costume contact.

I lucked out with a friend who does community theater in Mobile, and he was able to hook me up with a long velvet jacket, tan breeches, and tall leather boots.

The boots are a little too big, but I can make them work as I pull into the parking lot at Cooters & Shooters. The lights are all on, and Kimmie is already here with Dylan.

She danced her little heart out on the sidelines with the drill team, and when Austin was announced homecoming king, she screamed so loud, I could hear her from the door of the locker room.

It's silly, but my stomach tightens when I stop outside the door of the restaurant. Looking down at my outfit, there's no going back from what it says. Especially when I pair it with what Allie's wearing.

"Are you coming in or not?" The door flies open, and Zane stands inside dressed in full cowboy gear.

"Well, don't you look fancy!" Rachel is beside him in a red gingham dress that pushes up her chest. Her hair is in two ponytails, and she looks like something off that old country music show *Hee-Haw*.

"Daddy, you look like Prince Phillip!" Kimmie runs to me.

"Is that the one who was married to Queen Elizabeth?" I bend down to pick up my little jumping bean.

Liv helped her dress up as a member of the drill team, so she's in a glittery bodysuit with thick tights and tap shoes. Her hair is slicked back in a bun with sparkles all over it, and her lips are red.

"No, Daddy!" She rolls her brown eyes. "He goes with Princess Aurora!"

Allie sees me from across the room, and her eyes widen. I have to clear my throat, because she's stunning.

Her dress is relatively simple, long and straight with a light gray top layer almost like a coat. A wide pink ribbon is wrapped like a belt just under her breasts, giving them a mouthwatering boost, and her hair is gathered to the side so that it falls in a way that draws my eyes downward to them.

"Have I got the hottest big brother or what?" Dylan walks over in her long red pepper getup and tugs on the lapels of my light-blue velvet coat. "You almost look like you belong with someone. I wonder who it could be?" Her amber eyes roll around like she's thinking, and I huff a laugh. "Oh, I know! It's our very own Jane Austen-Allie!"

"Bruh, that's one fancy getup." Logan walks up in a round, green costume I can only assume is supposed to be a bell pepper. "Where's your horse?"

"Left it down at Gloria's," I quip, holding back a laugh. "Where's your…"

"Don't say it." Logan holds up a hand. "Your sister is having a hard time these days with all the… tasting."

"You're a good man." I pat his arm, turning to look for my partner.

"Looking for someone?" Garrett's jersey stretches across his stomach. "It's about time you got on the bandwagon."

I arch an eyebrow. "It's about time you got on the treadmill."

He slaps his stomach. "I'm loving life."

"When did you ever stop?"

"I had a few years."

"Looking mighty elegant, Coach." Hendrix walks over with Haddy on his arm.

She's in a pink jumpsuit with little wings all around her face. "What's this?"

"Axolotl costume. Raven's sister made it. We're doing this whole ocean thing." He's dressed as a pirate, and Raven's in a mermaid costume. "Glad you're making it official with Allie. We've been wanting this for a long time, in case you didn't know."

Glancing down, I lean a little closer. "I wouldn't call it official just yet."

Hendrix cuts his eyes. "If you're worried she might not be into you, I'm pretty sure she is. Even if you're as slow as molasses in January."

"Stop hassling him! Jack, you two look amazing." Raven has Allie by the hand, dragging her across the room to where I'm standing. "You're like something out of a romance novel."

"Oh, I get it now!" Dylan cries. "It's because Allie's a librarian. Wow, that took longer than it should have."

My sister's brow falls, and Liv puts a hand on her shoulder. "It's called pregnancy brain for a reason."

"Not that again." Dylan sighs, shaking her head and walking back to where Logan is waiting for her.

"Try to have a sense of humor about it." Rachel pats her arm affectionately. "It'll all be a funny memory in just a few more months."

"Are you saying she doesn't have a sense of humor?" Hendrix's voice goes loud. "She's got Logan dressed up like a Fruit of the Loom character."

Garrett has his phone out, snapping photos. "This will definitely be a funny memory for years."

"Laugh all you want. I'm doing it for my lady." Logan leans down to kiss Dylan's red-painted cheek.

Zane adjusts his cowboy hat. "Are we ready, partners?"

The group moves in the direction of the doors, and Garrett scoops Gigi off her feet. She's dressed as a football, and as soon as he lifts her into his arms, she begins to fuss and struggle.

He only laughs, tossing her into the air and catching her, which turns her fussing into squeals of laughter. "Let's get out of here."

I turn to Allie, who's standing beside me, and when I smile, her cheeks flush a pretty shade of pink.

"You look really good." Her voice is quiet.

"So do you." My voice is equally low, and I'd love to pull her into my arms and kiss her. Instead, I lift an elbow. "May I escort you to the fair?"

Lifting her chin she smiles, putting a white-gloved hand on my arm. "Yes, please, kind sir."

"Sir…" I nod. "I like that."

"Me, too," she whispers.

Chapter 23

Allie

Jack Bradford looks like every Regency romance hero I've fallen in love with since the days I was in middle school, sneaking Julia Quinn novels in the library.

He's so tall, and he's always had a proud bearing. His hair is messy, which is how it would look after he'd galloped in on his trusty steed. He's wearing a white shirt with a collar that laces, and I'd love to see his ass in those cotton breeches.

"How did you do it?" I look up at him, and he smiles, letting his eyes run over my body in a way that lifts the small hairs on my upper arms.

"An old friend who does theater. He helped me put it together." His eyes go to the front of his coat, which he opens. "Apparently it's not exactly right since I don't have a waistcoat."

"You won't get any complaints here." I hold his arm, gazing up at him. "You're perfect."

He stops, touching my cheek lightly with his finger. "You're perfect."

"Let's do the maze first!" Raven calls, skipping alongside

Hendrix. "I'm dying to see which characters they have running around inside."

My throat tightens, but I don't want to be the only one to confess I'm a little nervous about the whole thing.

I lean into Jack's shoulder and whisper, "I wish they had a non-character option."

He laughs, and that dimple in his cheek almost makes me swoon. "Don't worry. I won't let them get too close."

"I'll watch the babies." Hendrix holds up a hand, guiding his wife over to Garrett and taking Gigi from his brother.

"All right, Chicken Little," Garrett teases. "We'll meet you at the petting zoo."

"I'm not a baby!" Kimmie cries when Dylan tries to lead her to her uncle. "I'm almost eight years old—I can go in the hay maze, too!"

My lips twist, and Jack squeezes my hand. "Be right back."

I wait as he walks over to take a knee beside his sparkly little girl. "What if I promise to bring you back tomorrow and walk through it when the sun is out?" His voice is so gentle and sweet with her.

"It won't be the same, Daddy! Tonight they have lights and music, and they're doing that smoky thing, and everybody's screaming."

"I know, but they'll do fun things tomorrow, too." He puts a hand on her waist. "Remember that time we watched *The Nightmare Before Christmas*, and you couldn't sleep?"

"That was last year, Daddy." She rolls her eyes, and her inner teenager is coming out strong.

"I sure could use some help with Gigi and Haddy." Hendrix walks over, talking loudly. "I wish there was someone they liked as much as me to help me take them through the pumpkin patch."

Jack glances up at him, then back to his daughter. "Uncle Hen sure could use your help."

Just then a girl comes running out of the hay maze crying,

and her friends gather around her doing their best not to laugh. She's shaking and dabbing away tears, and Kimmie's eyes widen as big as saucers.

She puts her hand on her dad's shoulder. "I should probably help Uncle Hen. Gigi is a lot of work, and he's not around her as much as me."

"That's my girl." Jack pulls her in for a hug.

"You sure are helping me out, KJ." Hendrix holds out his hand, and she takes it, glancing back at the crying girl. "We'll get some caramel corn and maybe an ICEE and some cotton candy."

Jack watches them go a minute before turning to face me again. "I hope she doesn't get sick."

I can't help a laugh. He's so good with her.

"Who's ready to scream?" Garrett yells, and Liv grabs his shoulders, hopping on his back.

"I expect you to keep me safe," she laughs, hugging him close as he holds her legs.

"Nobody's getting close to my lady."

Jack captures my hand in his, pulling it into the crook of his arm. "Mine either."

Reaching up, I hold his bicep with my other hand, warmth pulsing with every heartbeat. "Am I your lady?"

"You know it."

Dylan grabs Logan and heads to the entrance, tickets in hand. Zane and Rachel are right behind them, followed by Garrett carrying Liv on his back.

Eerie music plays over tinny speakers, and every now and then a scream will echo from somewhere deep in the maze, stopping my heart.

Lining the entrance are baby dolls painted white in white dresses with blood spattered all over them, and white-painted masks peer at us from between the bales.

"That's creepy," I mutter, hugging closer to Jack's side.

Bright lights shine down from tall poles scattered around

the maze, and the walls are illuminated with purple and orange twinkle lights or Halloween-store monsters and witches.

We line up to hand over our tickets, and I jump when an automated hand swings out from behind a sheet.

"You're not scared, are you?" He grins down at me, and it's so sexy.

I wonder how crowded it is in this maze. I wonder if every dark corner contains a teenager waiting to scare us or if we might actually have a chance to sneak away and make out.

I'm scared and excited and horny as a teenager when a girl lets out a scream behind me, making me scream and jump in front of Jack.

"Stop doing that, Levi!" she snaps, and I peek around to see it's Sadie dressed up in a pink dress with a poofy skirt along with her homecoming crown and a wand.

"Cut it out, Levi." Austin stands beside her, pinching his lips to hide his grin.

He and Levi are both wearing pirate costumes. Austin has a fake mustache drawn on his upper lip, but Levi is painted up like Jack Sparrow.

"Sorry, Queenie. I slipped." He holds up both hands, doing a little wobble, a flirty gleam in his eyes.

My brows furrow, but Austin doesn't seem to be bothered by his friend's behavior.

"I hope they fortified those hay bales." Edward looks up at the top of the maze. "Some of them are leaning inward."

"Hi, guys!" I take a step away from Jack.

"Oh, Ms. Allie… And Coach Jack?" Sadie clasps her hands, gushing. "You two look amazing! You're like something out of a romance novel."

"Thanks, Sadie." I look down at my dress, doing my best to be casual around Coach Jack in front of the kids. "I thought it would be fun for the library. You know."

"I like your boots." Austin nods at Jack's footwear. "They're better than mine."

"Are we in the same timeline?" Sadie's friend pushes past Austin. She's wearing a sexy pirate-wench costume. "Could we take Coach Jack prisoner and make Ms. Allie walk the plank?"

The way she laughs and leans forward in Jack's direction gives major *Lolita* vibes, and I'm ready to jerk her ponytail when Jack puts his hand on her shoulder, all but stiff-arming her away from him.

"No," he answers flatly.

"Actually, pirates were active during the late seventeenth century," Edward explains logically, distracting us from the potentially awkward moment. "The Golden Age of Piracy was almost two hundred years before the Regency Era."

"What's your costume, Edward?" Levi does another wobble-point. "The Walking Wikipedia?"

My eyes narrow, and I'm not sure I like Levi's attitude. Then I remember his dad.

Edward is nonplussed. "I'm the Theory of Relativity."

We all stare at him. He's wearing jeans and a black T-shirt.

"What does that mean?" Austin finally asks.

"It depends on where you're standing."

Again, crickets. Until Jack huffs a laugh. "Good one, Eddie."

"I'm confused." Sadie frowns up at Edward. "Why does it matter where I stand?"

"Are y'all coming?" Zane yells to us from the entrance to the maze.

"Don't ask him to explain his costume." Rachel cups a hand beside her mouth. "You'll be there twenty minutes, and you still won't understand it."

Edward frowns. "It's not that difficult. Space-time tells matter how to move. Matter tells space-time how to curve, so it depends on where you stand."

"Space-time?" Levi walks over to Sadie and Austin, wrapping his arm around Sadie's shoulders. "You should've come as Dr. Spock. You already sound like him."

"*Mr.* Spock was not a doctor." Edward follows after them.

"Allie?" A voice walking up on my left stops me. "Is that you?"

I turn to see Ronnie Freeman dressed as either a hobbit or one of *Snow White*'s dwarves.

"Ron, hi! Yep, it's me." I smile, hesitating while he catches up to us.

"My goodness, you just get prettier and prettier." He shakes his head.

I feel Jack step closer, and this time, I'm way less flustered by his possessiveness. I almost giggle. It's utterly thrilling.

"That is the sweetest compliment. Thank you, Ron." I reach over and put my hand on Jack's forearm.

Ronnie's eyes flicker to my gesture, and he straightens so fast he takes a step back. "Oh, well, I understand now why you turned me down for dinner." He nods, looking up at Jack. "A fella can't get too bent out of shape when the lady prefers Coach Jack." Then he chuckles, looking even more like a Disney character. "I can't say I blame ya."

"Ronnie." I tilt my head to the side, feeling a little sympathetic. He's not wrong. "You're a real dear."

"Take it easy, Freeman." Jack does not share my sympathy. He puts his hand over mine, leading me to the entrance of the maze.

Cutting my eyes up at him, I love his sullen expression. It's so Mr. Darcy. "Oh, come on. You can't be threatened by Ronnie Freeman. It's just too silly."

He turns and looks down at me with those thrillingly stern blue eyes. "I don't like any man trying to take you away from me."

Stepping closer, I hug his arm to my stomach and rise onto my toes. "You never have to worry about that happening."

His expression relaxes a bit, and the corner of his mouth even tilts up with a smile. "Let's catch up with the group."

We go to where Rachel is talking softly to Edward at the entrance to the maze. "Are you sure you want to do this? It has strobe lights and loud music, and in some places actors jump out and yell at you."

Edward's lip curls, and Jack gives him a nudge. "I think you'll find the singularity in the petting zoo with Hendrix."

Rachel's brother frowns at him, thinking a minute. Then he seems to understand.

"Kim?" he asks.

Jack nods. "You got it."

"Good one."

He walks away in the direction of the petting zoo, and Rachel and I both turn to Jack with our lips parted.

Rachel is the first to ask. "Are you saying you actually understood all that?"

"More like how is Kimmie the singularity?" I add.

"She's very small, and she has no interest in the laws of science."

Rachel blinks at her brother-in-law, and I slide my hand into the crook of his arm. "I never knew you were such a nerd."

"We're going to have to hustle to catch up with the others." Zane walks up to slide his arm around Rachel's waist, glancing down at her breasts. "Not that I'm complaining."

"Y'all go on ahead. We'll catch up." Jack takes my hand again, and warmth slips through my veins.

"Oh, come *on!*" Rachel grabs my hand, pulling me. "There's plenty of time to make out at scary movie night. Anyway, the kids will see you if you do it here."

My eyes widen at Jack's, and he grins, making me heat up even more. Rachel almost pulls me out of his grip, but he holds my hand tightly, never letting me go.

"What the hell took y'all so long?" Garrett booms as we meet up with them around the first turn. "We've got to stay together in here—this thing is hard!"

"That's what she said!" Liv cries from where she's still on his back.

Dylan snorts a laugh. "Did Allie sneak some purple drink into the maze?"

"Not me!" I hold up a hand. "I'm a rule-following librarian."

"That's not what I heard." Liv wiggles her eyebrows, and I tilt my head coyly.

"Garrett!" Dylan quips. "You sneaked a flask, didn't you?"

"How dare you?" Garrett's tone is mock-offense. "I'm the sheriff in this town, little lady… er, pepper."

"Whatever, let's go!" Logan pulls his wife's hand, and the two peppers march ahead of us into the darkness.

My skin prickles as we pass a television with the scene of Jack Nicholson frozen at the end of *The Shining* on it.

"I hate hay mazes," I mutter, wishing I could snuggle with Jack again.

The music grows louder, and ghostly howls float through the air. We pass a sheet strung over an entrance that reads *You'll never get out alive* in brownish-red paint.

"They really went all out," Zane chuckles.

I'm just calming down when Rachel lets out a scream so loud it makes Liv scream, and I grab Jack's arm and jump behind him.

Then Rachel explodes with laughter. "I thought that corn stalk was a person!"

"RACHEL!" Dylan yells. "I almost peed my pants!"

"You're not *that* pregnant, Dee." Liv groans, and we continue walking.

The path is wide, but the way the overhead lights are arranged creates shadowy patches and pitch-black corners.

We walk until the path opens to another straight line. Looking left to right, we're trying to decide which way to go when a low-pitched growl comes running up behind us.

All the girls scream and everyone moves fast. I reach for Jack, but warmth swirls at my side.

The growling and hissing of an animal is close by my ear,

and my heart jumps to my throat. I scream, running as hard as I can from the monster, but it doesn't seem to matter.

I'm breathless, pumping my legs, but I can't get away from him. The growls are right on my heels, gaining on me fast. I take another quick turn to try and lose him.

My heart thunders in my chest, and a high-pitched witch cackle erupts from the corner where I've just stopped to catch my breath.

Another scream, and I try to run back the way I came, but I'm confused when I reach what I thought was our starting point.

Two possible routes come together from the left and the right, and I can't remember which way I came.

Turning my head and my body quickly, I look all around, but I don't see Jack or Dylan or any of our group. I decide to stand still and listen for their voices.

Creeping closer to the hay wall, I pinch my nose to quiet my breathing. Voices are all around, and I'm certain I hear Rachel's laughter from what sounds like a hay wall over.

Jumping back, I put both hands on the wall, looking up at the purple twinkle lights hanging from the top of the maze.

"Rachel?" I yell as loud as I can. "Where are you?"

The music is too loud, but I keep my hand on the prickly bale as I walk in the direction I came, looking up and straining my ears for more voices.

My breath is tight in my chest, and I don't like this at all. I don't like being alone, and I hate hay mazes.

"Allie?" Jack's deep voice echoes from what seems like just ahead, and my heart jumps.

"Jack?" My yell is a panicked cry, and I pull up my skirt to run in the direction of his voice. "I'm here! Jack?"

I'm shouting when a gorilla jumps out with a loud roar from a dark corner, and I scream.

I know it's only a guy dressed up in a costume, but it's so sudden and unexpected, I turn and run away in the opposite direction.

His breath huffs loudly from inside the mask, and I run harder, turning and turning to get away from him. It's my worst nightmare happening. It's that part in *The Shining* where evil Jack is chasing the little boy.

I run as hard as I can, but I can't breathe. And even though I'm running so fast, I can't seem to get away from the sound of this gorilla-man chasing me.

Every time I stop, I hear the swish of feet in the hay, the Darth-Vadar scraping of his breath in the mask as he chases me. Grabbing my skirt higher, I force myself to keep going.

I take another turn and another, and suddenly, I'm face to face with a dead end.

"No!" I scream, ready to collapse.

I'm shaking all over. Tears are in my eyes, and I try to go back the way I came. But the person in the gorilla costume is there, blocking the only way out.

He tilts his head to the side, like he's trying to understand something he's never seen before. It's dark, but I can see his white-blue eyes through the holes in the mask. They're eerily fixed on me.

I know it's all an act, but I don't like it. I don't like it at all.

Still, I have to get control. *It's just a kid, Allie. It's just a game.*

But all the fear I've been holding back since that first alert that Rip was out of prison is breaking loose and crashing down on my head.

"D-do I know you?" I try to calm my shaking voice, to dry the tears on my cheeks with my gloved hands as I force a smile. "Are you one of my students?"

The person shakes his head no, slowly like the monster in the *Halloween* movie, and I hiccup a breath.

"I know it's fun to scare people, but I really need to get back to my friends, to Coach Jack." I hold my hand out, doing my best to maintain distance as I try to circle around him to the only exit. "They're all looking for me."

The gorilla doesn't speak, and he doesn't move. He only stands, watching me.

"I'm going to pass you now." I'm as close as I want to get, and my words are for me as much as for him. "You're not supposed to touch us, remember? Those are the rules."

His eyes narrow, almost as if he's grinning at me. "You know me better than that, Allie."

Ice filters through my veins. Yes, I'd know that scratchy voice anywhere. It hasn't changed in eight years.

"Rip?" His name slips out on a cracked whisper. "What are you doing here?"

"I told you I'd be back." He spreads his arms wide. "Here's Johnny!"

"No!" I grab my dress again, breaking into a run, doing my best to dodge him as I try to get out of this dead end.

"Nope!" He grabs me around the waist, lifting me off my feet with ease. "You're not going anywhere. Not without me."

His arm is tight around me, pinning my arms to my sides so I can't escape.

"You can't do this." I struggle against him. "You're not supposed to leave the state!"

"Don't fight me, Allie." His voice is s sing-song like something I've heard in a scary movie. "This'll be so much easier if you don't fight me."

I lean my head back, opening my mouth to scream as hard as I can when my nose and mouth are covered hard with a soft cloth. I'm breathing fast, and it only takes two inhales for everything to go dark.

Chapter 24

Jack

"**S**OMETHING'S WRONG." I'M STANDING AT THE END OF THE HAY maze with my hands on my hips.

I'm pacing, and we've been out for ten minutes with no sign of Allie.

"I'm going back in there." I start for the door when Garrett catches me around the shoulders, stopping me.

"Hang on, bro." His voice is soothing. "You'll go in there, then Allie will come out, then we'll have to go in to look for you… It's a vicious cycle."

"Does she have her phone?" Dylan skips up to where we're standing. "We've all been texting. Try calling her!"

Garrett and I exchange a glance.

"Bruh." Zane shakes his head. "This is no time to act like y'all aren't calling and texting each other constantly."

I don't even argue. My phone is in my hand so fast, and I tap the name *DLS*. Pacing, I hold the phone to my ear. We actually don't call each other at all, but we do text quite a lot.

Still, she should answer sooner than this. It rings again and again, and my blue eyes rise to Garrett's.

"Did she silence her phone?" Garrett suggests.

"How the fuck should I know?" It's practically a shout as I stride back into the maze exit with both of my brothers at my side.

We reach the first break, and I look left to right. *Fuck.* "Which way?"

Garrett's jaw is tight, and he looks side to side. "We just did this. You'd think we'd know which way to go."

"It all looks the same," Zane muses. "That's the point."

I'm so frustrated, I'm about to yell. I know how nervous she was about doing this. It isn't only that it reminds her of *The Shining*, it's Rip. It's how he texted that he sees her, and the fact he went missing two days ago doing God knows what.

New Orleans is less than three hours from Newhope. He could easily get here in a day—in an afternoon.

Now *I'm* on fucking edge.

"We've got to find her, Garrett." Pressure builds behind my temples, and I'm about to lose it. "You've got to make them turn on the lights and find her now."

He inhales deeply. "That's going to kill the whole event. If she's just lost, and we turn on the emergency lights…"

"Garrett…" My voice is a notch below a shout, when a red-faced hobbit jogs up to us.

"Dang." Ronnie Freeman bends at the waist, putting his hands on his knees as he tries to catch his breath. "That is one tough maze."

"Yeah, good work." I don't have time for him.

I'm starting for the front of the maze to fucking get the lights turned on myself when Ronnie yells to me.

"Coach, wait!" I hesitate, looking over my shoulder as he heaves himself up and starts to jog to me again. "Are you looking for Ms. Allie?"

I close the distance between us fast, grabbing him by both shoulders. "What do you know?"

"Is she missing?" His brown eyes widen, and my nostrils flare. He immediately continues. "I saw her with this gorilla guy.

For a minute, I thought it was a sketch, because she's so pretty. Like he was Donkey Kong and she was Pauline?"

"Ronnie…" It's a low growl.

"He had her over his shoulder. Then he looked side to side and just busted right through the corn wall! It wasn't too far from where I came out just now. I thought it was funny. He didn't even follow the path—Hey, where are you going? Need my help?"

Ronnie yells after me, but I'm running as fast as I can in the direction he just came from.

My breath burns in my lungs. My heartbeat is a roar in my ears.

A little ways back, I hear Garrett's loud voice booming. "Light it up!"

All at once, the entire maze is as bright as a baseball field. A ripple of voices flows through the space, confusion, complaints, curiosity.

I round a corner, skidding to a stop in front of a large hole split through the corn stalks, leading straight to a dark parking lot.

Stepping through, I look all around, but it's completely deserted. I return to the maze to call Garrett when a group of kids surrounds me.

"What's going on, Coach?" Sadie is holding Austin's hand. "Did somebody get hurt?"

My stomach churns when I meet Austin's worried eyes. I'm tweaking with anger and adrenaline, but I don't want to scare him.

"Coach?" Austin frowns, looking up at me. "What's wrong?"

Garrett jogs up to where we're standing. "Did you find her?"

Austin's eyes snap from him to me, and he drops Sadie's hand, stepping closer to the hole in the maze wall. Reaching out, I put my hand on his shoulder.

"Ronnie Freeman saw a guy in a gorilla suit with your mom. We don't know for sure, but we think it was—"

"We didn't have anybody in a gorilla costume," Sadie's pirate-wench friend tells us. "Coach Stef has the list of volunteers, but they were all the movie guys—Michael, Jigsaw, Freddy, Pennywise… no animals."

"But we asked everyone who came to wear a costume." Sadie's voice is worried. "We thought it would be fun for Halloween."

"It was my dad." Austin's eyes hold mine. "He took her."

"We don't know for sure…" I swallow the knot in my throat, but I'm sure he can tell by the look on my face it's what I think as well.

"Let's go." Garrett puts his hand on Austin's arm. "If he's got your mom, we're going to get her back. Trust me. He's not getting away with this."

Hesitating, I look down the row to where costumed attendees are drifting to the exit, confused expressions on their faces.

"Someone should double-check the maze and the area around it." My muscles are tight. "Just to be sure she's not…"

I stop short of saying she might be lying on the ground injured and alone in the dark. I can't even think it for the rage it sparks in my body. I want to tear this maze to the ground to be sure she's not huddled in a corner or worse.

"That right there tells us everything we need to know." Garrett nods at the place where someone clearly forced his way out. "We can't let him get away."

Zane steps up beside me. "Logan and I will double-check every inch of this maze. We'll walk the perimeter and report back. Go with Garrett. Austin needs you."

Our eyes meet, and I give him a nod before we take off with my brother for his truck.

"I sent out an APB for highway patrol to be on the lookout for a car with Louisiana plates possibly headed south on I-10." Garrett is behind his desk in his office in town. "I'll include her driver's license so they'll have something to go on if they stop him."

Austin and I are across from him, but I can't sit down. I'm pacing the small office, needing to get in my truck and go after them. Anything besides sitting here wasting time.

"There's so many different ways to get from here to New Orleans," I muse, looking at the map of the state on his wall.

"If that's even where he's going," Garrett says absently, his brow furrowing. "This is weird."

"What?" I walk around his desk to see his computer screen. Austin's right beside me.

"Searching vehicle records, it says Allie rented a car yesterday." Garrett points at the screen. "She picked it up this morning in Daphne."

Shaking my head, I try to think. "She never said anything about renting a car. Did she say something to you, Austin?"

His arms are crossed, and he frowns as he shakes his head. "This is the first I've heard of it."

"A blue Chevy Malibu, license number..." Garrett is typing again. "I need to update my APB if there's still time."

"Why would she rent a car?" Austin blinks up at me.

"Was she putting yours in the shop?"

"If she was, she didn't tell me."

"It doesn't make any sense." Garrett frowns.

"Maybe he made her." I start for the door, done standing around here waiting. "Or maybe it's something else entirely. We'll ask her when we find her. At least now we know what we're looking for. Let's go, Garrett."

My brother stands, adjusting his belt. "I can't cross state lines in my official capacity as sheriff. If he really did kidnap her and take her out of state, it becomes FBI business."

"Then you're off-duty. Take me to my house so I can change."

The three of us head out into the night, and while Garrett drives, I text Dylan.

Our best guess is he's taking her back to Nola. Garrett got a lead on a blue Malibu... we've got his last known address.

> Dylan: I'll take care of Kimmie. Y'all just
> bring back our Allie 🖤

> I won't come home without her.

When we get to my house, I run straight to my bedroom, stripping off the velvet coat and fancy shirt. I step out of the boots and nearly rip off the tight pants in my haste.

I grab my jeans and a long-sleeved black tee, dressing as fast as humanly possible. I step into my cowboy boots and pause, reaching up on the highest shelf in the back of my closet. I take down a black leather pouch and enter the combination on the lock. Then I take out my Colt .45, checking to be sure it's loaded.

"I didn't know you had a gun." Austin is at my bedroom door, watching.

Tightening my jaw, I nod. "It's for emergencies. Otherwise, it's locked up and hidden."

"Ready?" Garrett walks up, and I put the revolver in the back of my jeans.

"I'll take my truck." The three of us return to the living room. "It's possible he'll avoid the interstate if he thinks we're looking for them."

"You want to take Highway 26 to the causeway?" Garrett passes a hand over his chin. "That'll add two hours to the trip."

"You take I-10." I look down at my phone vibrating in my hand. It's Zane, and I quickly accept the call. "What's up?"

His voice is low. "We found her phone in the maze."

A chill slices through my veins, and I step back. It takes me a minute to catch my breath.

"What?" Garrett grabs my shoulder.

"Zane found her phone." It's a rough reply, and I clear my throat, returning to the call. "I'm putting you on speaker so Garrett can hear you. Any clues?"

"I don't know her passcode," Zane continues. "The only missed call is from you, and she has some text alerts from the girls—all from about the time we got separated in the maze."

"That's good, I guess," Garrett says, looking up at me. "It gives us a hint of the time when she dropped it."

Austin's arms circle over his chest, and I hand the phone to Garrett when I see his expression crumple.

He sniffs hard, putting a hand over his eyes to hide his tears.

"Whoa, come here." I pull him into a hug, wrapping my arms over his.

His body shudders, and my heart aches. Looking up, I fight my own tears.

I know how important it is for him to see me in control. I have to be sure we're going to get the outcome we want, that we're going to find her.

Garrett takes the call off speaker to finish. "We're headed to West Riverside. I found a record on a rental car, so we have at least something to look for."

He walks into the guest room, and Austin takes a second to get himself together. I pat his back and release him.

"I know you and Mom are together." He looks down, wiping a hand over his nose. "I mean, it was pretty obvious tonight with the costumes and the holding hands and all."

It's true, and I'm done hiding. "We were planning to talk to you about it."

"It's okay, I get it, especially after all the stuff Levi's dad was saying. I just wanted you to know it's good. She seems really happy…" His voice breaks off, and I grip his shoulder.

"Look at me. Your mom's going to be okay. Garrett and I will bring her home. Hear me?"

He nods, shoving the dampness off his cheeks. "I'm going with you."

"No." *End of discussion.* "Allie would never forgive me if I brought you with me."

"That's not true. She trusts anything you do."

"That's why you're staying here. I'm not having you get hurt." He starts to argue, but I hold up a hand. "Stay with Dylan.

Help her take care of Kimmie for me. I'll text you as soon as I know something."

His jaw tightens, and I pull him in for a hug. "I love your mom."

My voice is rough. He's the first person I've said it to, and pain twists in my chest at how true it is. I picture Allie's pretty eyes looking up at me with so much trust. I can't think of her being alone in a dangerous situation.

Stepping back, I hold his gaze. "I'm bringing her home."

He relents, dropping his chin. "Okay."

With another pat, I look to my brother. He hands me my phone, and we're out the door.

Chapter 25

Allie

M Y TONGUE IS STUCK TO THE ROOF OF MY MOUTH WHEN I WAKE up, and my vision is blurry. I'm still in my Halloween costume, but I'm belted into the passenger's side of a sedan that's racing down a dark highway.

Country music plays on the radio, and cigarette smoke filters to my nose. I have to blink a few times to clear the haze from my eyes.

My wrists sting like the skin is being torn, and when I shift in my seat, I realize they're zip-tied together.

Then it all comes rushing back—me running away, being chased by a gorilla, and when I look to my left, my chest sinks.

Rip is driving.

His hand is propped on the wheel, and the wind ruffles his graying, light-brown mullet from a crack in the window.

Birth control. This is why I make sure the kids know all about it and how to use it. I wouldn't trade my precious son for anything in the world, but I'd sure trade being tied to this loser forever.

He takes a pull off a cigarette and glances over at me. "Morning, sunshine—or should I say evening?"

I should be afraid. I should be crying and terrified that I've been kidnapped by my ex-con ex-husband, who is now driving like a bat out of hell to God knows where in the middle of the night.

Instead, my dread morphs into anger.

Peeling my dry lips apart, my voice is as rough as sandpaper. "What the fuck have you done?"

"Whoa…" He has the nerve to give me a sly smile. "That's not the sweet Allie I remember. And you look so pretty in that dress, with your hair all pulled up like that. It reminds me of a hot summer day in south Louisiana. You'd be walking around the house in short shorts and one of my white undershirts with no bra." He whistles through his teeth. "You always were a sexy little thing. My New Orleans lady."

"I'm your New Orleans nothing." My voice cracks as I try to fight. "You can stick those memories up your ass. You're going to jail for this."

"Now, don't sell yourself short, darlin. You are not nothing." He grins, and the streetlight reflects off the gold cap on his right canine. "Remember that time you nursed me back to health? You only do something like that when it's true love."

"Or true terror," I snap.

Yes, I remember *very* well the night he was shot in the stomach during a drug deal gone wrong. I was sure he was going to bleed to death, and he wouldn't let me take him to the hospital. He knew he'd be arrested for possession, and this time it was enough to send him away for a long, long time.

Instead, he made me bring him back to our little shotgun house hidden away on the back streets of Uptown by the bend in the river.

"You took care of me," he opines, conjuring a fantasy far different from what really happened. "You changed my bandages and kept watch over me until I was back on my feet."

"You nearly died twice. Then you got an infection."

I shudder remembering how scared I was that he'd die on me. *What would I do then?*

I was sure I'd go to jail for being his accomplice, even though I wasn't involved at all in any of his crimes.

I only found out the hard way that my husband was a *real* criminal and not just a bad boy with tattoos who rode a motorcycle and cut hair for a living.

When he didn't die, the first thing I did was go online to figure out a way to divorce his ass and get as far away from New Orleans as possible.

"We were a regular Bonnie and Clyde." He's still going.

"I never signed up to be your Bonnie." I throw cold water on that fantasy. "Bonnie and Clyde ended up dead, you idiot."

It took all my creative skills to hide his behavior from Austin, who was too young to understand why strange people would show up in the middle of the night.

"You're still my girl, Allie. I never would've signed those divorce papers if you hadn't got me drunk." He has the nerve to sound hurt. "Why'd you do that?"

"To get away from you." My voice is coming back with force. "To get Austin away from you. To give him a chance at a good life."

"Well, it broke my heart."

"It did *not*," I snap. "You only care because if I'd still been your wife, they wouldn't have been able to make me testify against you in federal court."

He doesn't answer right away, and I know I'm right. Selfish bastard.

Then all of a sudden, he rears back and slams his fist against the dash with a roar that makes me jump in my seat. My wrists are still bound, and I swallow the fear in my throat.

As long as we were together, Rip never hit me or Austin. He'd get angry at times and break shit, but he never hurt us. If it got really bad, he'd smoke a blunt or take a pill—or both, and zone out for the rest of the night.

But he's been at Angola for seven years. I don't know what he's like now.

"That's why you're going back with me." He glares, and a different light is in his eyes, a desperate gleam. It chills my blood. "You're going to tell that judge your testimony was false. They forced you to say all those things, and I'm innocent."

"You think a judge is going to believe a word I say when you've broke parole, kidnapped me, and dragged me across state lines to change my story?" Shaking my head, I lean back on the seat. "They'll spot that lie a mile away."

He drops his speed, and we've reached the turn to cross the causeway over Lake Pontchartrain. We're sitting at a red light, and it's the first time I've seen him in some light.

He's lost weight. His features are sharper, and the muscles in his arms are more pronounced. His jaw is tight, and his thin lips tremble as he takes another pull off his cigarette.

It's not a tremble of fear. It's more a tremble of tension, of someone who's right on the edge. It can't be withdrawals, as I'm pretty sure he didn't have drugs in jail.

"I'm not going back there." He exhales a growl as he says the words.

"How are you not going back to jail after this? You'll be lucky if they don't bring the FBI in on your ass."

He snatches my upper arm so hard, a yelp slips from my lips. "They're not bringing in anybody because you're not going to say I kidnapped you. You came to me on your own."

His white-blue eyes fire with anger, and I catch my breath. I'm not so sure he won't hurt me this time.

Thankfully, the light turns green, and the car behind us honks their horn. His eyes flicker to the rearview mirror, and he releases me.

"Fuck you, motherfucker!" he yells, sticking his arm out the window and flipping the bird.

They lean on the horn, and he pulls his arm in, taking the left to get on the long bridge that connects Mandeville to New Orleans. I shift in my seat, and he throws his cigarette out and rolls up the window.

"You're going to tell them you came to me because you were worried about me." He speaks as if he's making up my story on the spot. "You felt bad, and you wanted to make it right."

"How did I come to you?" My tone is cynical. "Tell me how I did that when my car is in Newhope."

"This is your car." He motions to the Malibu, and I frown.

"This isn't my car."

"I rented it in your name in Daphne."

My back straightens, and I struggle to scoot around in my chair. "How the hell did you do that without my permission?"

"You never changed your name." He looks at me like I'm the dumb one. "Your name is still Allie Sinclair, and I still have our marriage license."

My jaw drops, and I have no words. It never occurred to me he could possibly do something like this, but we are in Small-town, USA, where everybody trusts everybody.

It doesn't hurt that this asshole can be a charming moth-erfucker when he puts his mind to it. Who knows what all he could get away with?

"I have to say, not changing your name feels like a not-so-subtle hint you still want to be my wife."

That does it.

"I do *not* want to be your wife. I wouldn't be your wife if you paid me a million dollars. Hell, I wouldn't be your wife for a billion dollars. I didn't change my name because of Austin."

"Methinks she doth protest too much." He smirks, rolling his eyes.

I'm so angry my face is hot. "I didn't change it so Austin and I would have the same last name. If I could change his last name, I would."

I'd change it to a name like Bradford. I'd change it to the

name of the best man I know. My throat thickens, and I inhale a shaky breath.

Thinking of Jack is the one thing that could bring me to tears, and I can't break down. The last thing I want to do is show any sign of weakness.

"I've been watching my boy play football." He pulls out another cigarette and taps it against the back of his hand before slipping it between his lips. "It's how I found you."

"Wha…" My chest quivers at the thought. "Have you been coming to the games?"

"Nah, they got the highlight reels on TV." He lights the cigarette, taking a deep inhale before blowing the smoke in the direction of that crack in the window. "He sure is talented. He must take after his old man."

He is nothing like you, I don't say out loud. No point poking this unpredictable bear.

"Once you clear my name, I plan to be at all his games."

"That's a switch." I look out the window at the dark waters. "You never cared about being a father to him before."

"That's not how you felt when we got married."

"I married you because I was young and stupid. I thought I had to make it work. Now I know better. Now I know what a real father looks like."

"Like that coach you're fucking?"

"That coach I'm fucking is ten billion times a better father than you." My eyes flash, and I snap. "You're never going anywhere near Austin. You'll never drag him down to your level, because I'll never clear your name."

His hand shoots out, and he grabs my face in a grip that makes my eyes water. "I told you, I'm not going back there."

He shoves me so hard, my head bounces off the glass window, and I see stars. Pain radiates through my skull, but dread filters through my veins when he pulls out a gun.

"They'll have to kill me first."

"Don't do anything stupid, Rip." My voice is quiet now,

careful. "Just let me out, and you can go anywhere. Keep driving. Go to Mexico and hide out. They'll never find you there, and you can live like a king."

"*You* don't do anything stupid," he snarls. "You'd better start getting your story straight, or it'll be the last thing you do."

We're quiet, and I shrink down in my seat. Up to now, it was just a kidnapping. Up to now, I didn't know what to expect. Now I'm afraid.

Now somebody might die.

"I've heard there's some really nice places in Mexico." We've arrived at our old shotgun house near the river.

At night the trains go by, laying on the horn as they pass street after street. During the day, the barges float by overhead, taller than the streets below, the waters of the Mississippi River held up by the levees.

Rip replaced the zip ties with nylon rope. I guess he decided it wouldn't look like I came to him out of the goodness of my heart if I have ugly purple bruises around both my wrists. That might indicate force.

"You could live on the beach," I continue, doing my best to redirect his thinking away from a gun fight. "You could start doing hair again. You were really good at it."

It's how I met him. He was punk rock, cool and edgy. Skinny in a ripped white tee with tattoos and a gold-toothed smile, and I thought he was the most fascinating man I'd ever met.

"You liked having my hands in your hair, didn't you baby?" He looks up from where he's packing a bag to give me a smug grin.

"I couldn't believe you weren't gay," I quip.

"That's a stereotype." He throws a pair of socks into the duffel.

"Stereotypes exist for a reason." I'm in a chair at our table, and I shift away from him to look at the dark window. "I so naive, thought I was in love. Now I know what real love looks like. It's kind and generous…"

"If some man's being generous to you, he wants in your pants."

"If a man's being kind and generous, you'd be surprised how far that goes toward a woman *wanting* to sleep with him."

He walks over to where I'm perched, his boots thumping on the hardwood floors. "You never had a problem in that department, did you, Allie-girl?"

"What are you doing with that bag?" I nod in the direction of the bed.

"We're going to Jackson to meet up with Donnie. He's got a lawyer who's going to get me a meeting with the judge."

"Donnie's a two-bit hood." I lift my chin. "How much is he charging you for that favor?"

Rip's eyes narrow, and he pinches my chin between his thumb and forefinger. "You used to be sweet. I don't like this new attitude."

"Hell, I wonder why my attitude changed." I hold his gaze. "It couldn't be because I was chased through a maze, knocked out, kidnapped, and now I'm tied to a chair. That would be a silly response."

"If I thought you'd help me on your own, I wouldn't have to do any of this."

"You realize how crazy that sounds? You're not that far gone, are you?"

He blows a breath through his lips and clomps across the room to the bed. "We've got to find something for you to wear. You can't go looking like… Miss Priss or whoever."

"Jane Austen."

"Who's that?" He frowns at me, and I shake my head. "Maybe Donnie can find something."

"So we're going to Jackson tonight?" My chest tightens.

I've been holding onto the hope that Garrett knows where I am, since Rip had to register his address with his parole officer. They'll never look for me in Jackson, Louisiana. It's 100 miles north of here, and I have no connection to the place.

"We'll sleep here tonight and get on the road in the morning. Donnie's not expecting us until around noon."

I exhale a quiet breath while holding my expression steady. I don't want to appear too relieved and make him suspicious.

"Am I sleeping in this chair all night?" Annoyance helps.

"No way, baby." He grins, walking over to me. "You're sleeping in the bed tonight with me."

I jerk back. "No."

He chuckles, sliding his hand down my cheek, but I turn away. It gets me a scoff, and he roughly pulls me out of the chair.

"Don't shit your pants, I'm not going to do that." He walks me to the bathroom, hesitating as he looks into my eyes. "I'm going to untie you so you can take care of your business and get ready for bed. If you pull any shit like trying to run or whatever, I will tie you up, and you'll never get this chance again. Understand?"

My jaw tightens, and I nod, watching as he loosens the rope. My mind is racing as I try to think. I'm familiar with this little house. The bathroom window is a tiny square, too small for me to fit through, and even if I could, the house is on stilts. It's a long drop to the ground.

The rope falls away, and I exhale a sigh as I rub my aching wrists. As much as he tried to act like it wouldn't leave a mark, my wrists have ugly red lines from the zip ties followed by the ropes.

"On second thought, I'm standing here while you do whatever. It's nothing I haven't seen before."

"I have no intention of disrobing in front of you."

"Okay, fancy."

"Do you have a toothbrush?"

"Use mine."

My lip curls, and I decide I'd rather use my finger. I don't want any of his fluids near any part of me.

He stands in the doorway watching as I do my best to use the bathroom without showing my body.

I splash water on my face, not worrying about my smeared mascara. I make a show of putting a dollop of toothpaste on my finger and using it to clean my mouth.

When I'm finally done, I turn to face him. "That'll do for now."

His lips purse with a frown, and he huffs a laugh. "Fine. Let's go to bed." I follow him to the double bed, and he takes out the rope again. "Lie down on your side."

Inhaling a breath, I fight against the feeling of despair trying to crash down on me. I don't trust this man. I haven't known who he is for so long. For so long in our marriage, I lived in terror, never knowing what might show up on our doorstep or whether they would be armed.

Now I have no choice but to do as he says.

Holding my skirt around my knees, I lie on my side. He makes a noose with the rope, dropping it over my wrist and tying it behind the metal bed frame. It's too far for me to reach, and my arm is already growing numb.

Squeezing my eyes, I hold back the tears. I swallow the fear and focus on Austin. I think about my son, and I think about Jack. I think about surviving. I think about the first thing I'm going to do when I get out of here.

I'm going to put my arms around him and hold him so tight… then I'm going to change my damn name.

Chapter 26

Jack

MY KNUCKLES ACHE FROM GRIPPING THE STEERING WHEEL. I'M taking a route that goes through every small town along the 98 corridor.

It's slow going, made even slower because of the trick or treaters and parties and general Friday-night traffic. I'd much rather be taking the fastest route along the interstate, but what if that's what Rip expects? What if he's going this way to see if we show up at his place ahead of him?

He's not dumb, and it makes sense. It's also killing me every time I stop at a long traffic signal in the middle of nowhere with no cars around.

I've just crossed into Mississippi when Garrett calls me. Tapping the screen, I put him on speaker.

"Have you heard anything?" My shoulders tense, and I squint into the darkness, hoping. "I'm at the address in West Riverside. A blue Malibu with Alabama plates is parked on the street."

"That's it." I quickly exit 59, taking the first highway that will bring me all the way to I-10. "I'm coming as fast as I can get there."

"I'm going to park up the road and wait. It doesn't look like they're going anywhere tonight."

"Stay put. I'm at least an hour away."

"Drive safe."

We disconnect, and I put the pedal down as I chew my lip. Maybe Rip isn't so bright after all. That thought worries me more than the idea he might be watching us. If he's stupid, he'll be sloppy.

If he's sloppy, someone could get hurt, and I don't want that someone to be Allie. Hell, I don't want it to be any of us.

My chest is tight, and I press harder on the accelerator. I need to get there now. Protection is what I do. I protect my family, and Allie is my family now.

I grip the steering wheel tighter and reach over to flick on the radio. Anything to make this drive pass faster.

After what feels like an eternity, but is actually only an hour, I'm finally at Tchoupitoulas, winding around to the address I typed into my phone. Garrett texted me his location, and I turn a block early, circling around until I see his gray truck on the side of the road.

I pull up behind him and get out as quietly as possible. My boots crunch on the light gravel, and I scan the houses as I walk up to where he's parked.

The light from a television screen flickers in the window across the street. The other houses are dark. I tap on his passenger's side door, and the lock clicks allowing me to hop into the cab.

"I tried calling NOPD, but they don't have any cause to come out here." He exhales impatiently, sitting forward. "He hasn't broken parole. He checked in with his officer, and he hasn't left the state."

"As far as they know."

Garrett's brows pinch, and he looks down. "That car right

there is all the proof we need, but it's not that easy. It was rented in Allie's name, they share a kid. From where they stand, she could've come here of her own accord."

"What are you telling me?" My jaw is tight, and I don't give a fuck what the NOPD thinks.

"They said they'd send a cruiser to do a check-in first thing in the morning."

"That's not going to help us tonight."

My brother's head turns slowly, and when our eyes meet, I see the resolve in his expression. "We're on our own. I can't arrest him. I have no jurisdiction here."

I sit straighter in the seat. "We need a plan. We can't just walk up to the door and ask him to hand her over."

"We need our brothers." Garrett's voice is tight. "If all five of us walked up to that door, it might intimidate him into doing the right thing."

"It might." I rub my hand over my chin, thinking. "Or it might make him panic and do something stupid."

I've never met Allie's ex, but from what I've heard, he's a loose cannon.

"You think he's armed?" Garrett's blue eyes meet mine, and no matter how many years have passed, how much growing up we've done, he's still my little brother.

"Definitely. And I don't want you or Allie or any of us getting shot."

Adrenaline tweaks in my muscles, and I can't allow my thoughts to go down that path. I've lost too many people I love in my life. I'm not losing any more.

Garrett punches my arm. "Come on. Let's case the joint."

We climb out of the truck, closing the doors as quietly as possible. Garrett digs around in the second row of his truck, pulling out black jackets and tossing one to me. My gun is in the back of my jeans, but I'm not taking it out yet.

Nothing turns up the heat like bringing out a piece. If we

can keep the temperature down, we might get out of this without anyone getting hurt.

A narrow ditch separates the small yard from the road, and we hop across it, doing our best to stay low, near the shrubs lining the property. It's almost midnight, and I only hope the neighbors aren't watching.

Streetlights provide some illumination, but for the most part, everything is dark shadows. The moon isn't full, which helps, and we jog through the damp grass to the side of the house.

It's completely dark and quiet. It's on stilts, which puts the windows chin-high on me. Garrett's a few inches taller, and he leans forward to peek through the glass. Just as fast he jerks away, pressing his back to the wall beside me.

Lifting his hand, he puts a finger to his lips before pointing to the back of the house. I crouch, moving as quietly as possible to the rear.

When we round the corner, he puts a hand on my shoulder, and we lower to a squat. "He's awake in there."

"How do you know?"

"I saw the light from his cigarette. He's sitting up smoking. Watching."

My throat aches. "Did he see you?"

"I don't know." Garrett looks over his shoulder at the way we came. "Maybe."

My heart ticks faster, and I'm ready to confront this asshole. "Could you see Allie?"

He shakes his head. "I saw that cherry and jerked back as fast as I could."

We freeze at the creak of a screen door opening. It's right above us, where a short landing leads to a flight of five concrete steps down to the narrow strip of weeds constituting a backyard.

Garrett pushes my shoulder, and we roll around the corner away from the light.

"I know you're there." Rip's voice is about what I expect.

He sounds like a con artist.

He sounds like a voice I remember well from my childhood, when I was the only one old enough to understand. Jayden Wells would sit on our porch swing with my parents, talking about all the things they were going to do together when they opened the restaurant.

I remember their smiles, the hope in my mother's eyes as they made plans. I remember him talking a big game…

Before he double-crossed them and stole all our money.

"You're not takin' her," that asshole continues. "She's going to help me get out of this, and if you try and stop us, I'll put a bullet in you and a bullet in her."

My lungs are tight with anger, and my hand is on the gun in the back of my jeans. Garrett grips my shoulder, stopping me from storming around there and shooting him right in his fucking face.

"Now get on back to where you came from," he continues. "You got no business messing with what's mine."

"Mine…" It's a low growl from my burning throat.

"Rip Sinclair?" Garrett's voice is loud and authoritative. "This is the sheriff in Newhope. I know you broke parole, and I know you kidnapped Allie. You're only digging a deeper hole with all this. Now you hand her over to us, and we'll take her home and leave you be. You still have a chance to turn things around. It's your choice."

My brow furrows, and I glare at my brother. He doesn't have a chance at anything. This motherfucker isn't going to stop until he gets what he wants, and apparently he's delusional enough to think that somehow includes Allie.

I shake my head, but Garrett holds up a hand to wait.

Leaning closer, he speaks directly in my ear. "I'm trying to get her out of there. We'll deal with him once we know she's safe."

Clenching my teeth, I concede. He has a point. The last thing we want is a shootout with Allie caught in the crossfire.

"You're not law enforcement," Rip snarls. "You'd be swarming this place if you were. You're that fucking coach who's fucking my wife."

I start for him again, but again, Garrett grabs me around the waist, holding me back.

"It's your last chance, Sinclair," he shouts. "We're just here for the girl. Now give her to us, and we'll be on our way."

My breath is coming in heaves, and it's taking all of Garrett's strength to hold me in place.

"Fuck you, asshole." Rip spits over the rail. "You want her? Come get her."

"With pleasure," I growl, pushing my brother aside.

Storming around the corner, I rip the gun from the back of my jeans, holding it straight out in both hands. Garrett jogs to catch up with me, and the minute we clear the side of the house, two staccato pops echo from the back door.

A splintering noise blasts near my head where one bullet hits the wooden structure behind us.

The other is a solid thump that sends my brother jerking back, knocking him off his feet beside me.

Garrett goes down with a groan.

"God dammit." I duck to the side behind an old motorcycle leaning against the shack of a garage. "You okay, bro?"

My brother is on the ground on his back not moving, and my chest is on fire. Rip has disappeared into the black interior of the house, and I know I can't charge up there without risking getting shot as well.

Garrett lets out another low groan, and I stretch out, grabbing the front of his black jacket.

He strains, pushing with his heels, and I pull him with all my strength to the side of the small building. Shoving the gun in the back of my jeans again, I grab him by the lapels and lean him against the wall.

"Fuck," Garrett groans. "He knocked the wind out of me."

"Are you hurt?" I pull the jacket away to see a black spot on the front of his gray T-shirt at the top of his chest.

He lifts a large hand, gripping the front of my shirt. "Get in there and get that guy. Now."

I check his pulse, and it's elevated, but he seems like he'll be okay for a little longer. "Stay with me, bro."

Looking all around, I grab the lid off a metal trash can in the alley and use it like a shield as I dash to the side of the house again. Another staccato pop, and the wood on the corner of the house splinters as I pass.

I'm breathing hard, and Garrett's right. We should have brought all our brothers with us. It's too late for that now. Now I've got to deal with this asshole on my own.

Garrett makes a soft groan, and I see him lift his hand to his chest. Another staccato pop, and the wood blasts to bits on the side of the small garage.

That's four bullets. I don't know what type of weapon he's using, but it's possible he only has two rounds left. *Could we get that lucky?*

More like, would he be that stupid? Only one way to find out.

Dashing forward, I toss the trash can lid onto the back landing, and another shot rings out in that direction. That's when I hear a soft whimper, a female sound, and my vision tunnels. *Allie.*

She's in there, and I've got to get her out.

Banking everything on the hope that he only has one bullet left, I charge up the back steps yelling at the top of my lungs. Holding the gun in both my hands, I aim high, firing three shots at the ceiling as I run through the screen door.

I don't know if he might be using Allie as a shield, and I don't want to hurt her accidentally.

My hope is to startle him into running. My hope is wrong.

Another pop rings out, and it's a bite to my shoulder. I drop to the floor in the darkness, holding completely still and listening.

Across the room, I hear Rip moving, but a whimper followed by a soft thump to my left tells me Allie is close. I crawl quickly, circling my hands over the floor in the darkness, trying to find her.

It's so dark, but I make out the edge of a bed. Crawling faster, I feel soft cotton. It's a skirt, and my forehead is tight. My chest aches like a heart attack until my fingers finally make contact with her warm skin.

Another muffled cry, and I lunge to where she's crouching in the corner beside the bed.

"Allie," I whisper, feeling all around.

She's still crying, and I don't know if her mouth is taped. Her arm is raised behind her in a way that seems unnatural. Sliding my hands up, I feel a rope around her wrist, and another burst of rage fires in my chest.

Heavy footsteps pound the wood floors, and I don't have time to untie her.

"Stay down," I order, moving away and gripping my gun in both hands again.

He's storming right to us, and I don't care if he's out of bullets. Lifting my weapon, I see a slight variation in the darkness as his shadowy figure emerges.

I don't hesitate.

Pulling the trigger, I hold the gun as it discharges repeatedly. He falls to the floor with a loud crash, and after three shots, my gun jams.

"Fuck!" A roar breaks from my chest.

He makes a noise like a laugh, and I charge across the floor, falling to my knees where he lies and gripping him by the front of the shirt as I slam my fist into his face again and again.

My body is tight. Rage is pushing me, driving me. I see Allie cowering and afraid. I see Austin's face crumple as he cries. I see myself driving in the night, not knowing if she's alive or dead.

Pulling back, I hit him harder until my fist is slick with his blood. I want to kill him with my bare hands. He gurgles, and someone massive grabs my arm on the back swing.

"Jack!" A voice I know holds me. "It's over, Jack. Stop. He's done. He can't do any more."

It's Garrett. He's holding me around both arms, but even my massive offensive lineman little brother can't contain my rage. Rip makes another noise, and I try to hit him again.

Every exhale is a feral animal noise, but Garret has me tight.

"It's okay, brother." He holds on. "You can stop now. It's over."

Chapter 27

Allie

THE HUM OF INSECTS RISES FROM THE GROUND, GROWING LOUDER as it reaches the air, and the metal chains holding the back porch swing squeak softly as it moves gently, back and forth. On the light pink horizon, the sun is a neon-yellow ball sliced into perfect quarters by thin lavender clouds. The water is periwinkle blue with shades of purple haze drifting above it.

I watch a flock of seagulls fly into the pale orange sky, fluttering their wings and dipping their beaks in the rippling waters.

It's a cool Sunday morning. My feet are up, and I'm wrapped in a crocheted blanket holding a mug of coffee. Jack's strong arms surround me, and I rest my head against his chest as he twirls a lock of my hair between his fingers.

I hold his hand. His knuckles are swollen and scarred from where he tried to kill my ex with them. I couldn't love him more if I tried.

Lifting my chin, I look up at him. His blue eyes are on the water. His cheeks are dusted in dark brown scruff, and the rising sun bathes his skin in attractive yellow light.

The set of his jaw is as focused as always, determined, daring.

He's my hero. He saved me, and now I'm here in his house after sleeping in his bed all night safe in his arms.

"How's the wound?" My voice is soft, not wanting to disturb the serenity of this moment.

He blinks down at me, his eyes sliding over my face, from my forehead down my nose to my lips. His expression softens, and he leans forward inhaling the top of my head.

"I'll be fine." His voice shimmers in my veins. "How's your shoulder?"

"Good." I tuck my chin, nestling into his arms again. "It's all good now."

Everything happened with Rip so quickly, my head's still spinning. I read once that most criminals are not masterminds, and after everything that happened these last few days, I'm convinced it's true.

The only excuse I can make for my idiot ex is he never expected I'd be best friends with the younger sister of a sheriff who had access to all his information and knew exactly where he lived.

He counted on me being the same dumb girl who fell for his charming lies all those years ago in New Orleans. He thought he could bully me into helping him, but even if it hadn't been for Garrett and Jack, I'd never have helped him.

The worst part is my friends being hurt.

Garret was wearing a Kevlar vest, which protected him from being killed. He was winded by the shot, and he said he'll have a nasty bruise. But he wasn't critically injured.

Jack caught a bullet to the shoulder. It went straight through, which the urgent care doctor said was a good thing. It didn't hit any major nerves, and he should have a full recovery.

I still blink back tears when I see the bandages and his swollen, damaged knuckles.

My shoulder was strained from jumping out of bed with my hand tied to the frame, but it's the least of my concerns.

We got back after midnight, after spending the day at the

hospital and giving reports to the police department. Garrett stayed behind to be sure everything went smoothly.

Jack didn't kill Rip Sinclair. He claims to be sorry he didn't, but I'm glad he doesn't have that hanging over his head.

Even if it would've been self-defense, even if Rip broke parole, crossed state lines, illegally rented a car in my name, and kidnapped me, I don't want Jack bearing the guilt of taking a life. Even a bad one.

"Were you able to sleep last night?" Jack's voice is gentle, and he rubs the damaged hand I love up and down my arm.

"I slept like a baby." I smile, thinking about curling into his arms in the middle of his large bed. "Better than a baby, since babies don't actually sleep very soundly."

"They sure look cute doing it. Like you."

A laugh huffs through my nose, and I hold his arm. "Speaking of babies, I need to see my big baby."

I texted Austin as soon as I was safe, and we were on our way to urgent care. I had to use Jack's phone, since I'd lost mine in the maze.

Then I FaceTimed with him when I was sure Rip was headed back to prison. I was glad I could tell him we were safe. I could tell him his dad was going away once and for all.

But even seeing his face wasn't enough. I need to hold him, look into his eyes, and be sure he's okay. What happened was traumatic enough, and for so long, it was just Austin and me.

"Dylan said they're making a big breakfast at the restaurant this morning. Everyone's anxious to see you're not hurt."

"Even though you assured them I wasn't?" I look up at him again, and a little smile curls those serious lips.

He leans down and presses them to mine, and I reach up to thread my fingers in the back of his hair. Our mouths open, and our tongues slide together, and I could stay here forever.

Until my stomach growls.

We both laugh, and our teeth clink together. "I'd better get you fed. You haven't had a decent meal since Friday."

"I guess breakfast at McDonald's doesn't count?"

"It does not." His voice is a teasing scold.

He holds my arm as I unwind from the blanket and stand. My lips tighten when I study his arm in a sling.

"I need to talk to Liv anyway." Reaching down, I take his coffee mug. "I'm going to get her to help me change my name ASAP. I never dreamed Rip could pull a stunt like that, and it's never going to happen again."

Jack catches my waist, stopping me before I can go to the kitchen. "Maybe I can help you with that."

My brow furrows, and I hesitate. "Help me with what?"

He carefully removes the sling then takes the coffee cups out of my hands and puts them on the side table. Holding both of my hands in his, he pulls me between his legs while he's still sitting.

"For so long, I tried to bury myself in work and pretend like this wasn't happening between us. I tried to deny my feelings and tell myself you didn't think of me that way…"

My heart beats faster, and energy surges in my stomach. "Jack…"

"I'm not denying it any more." His blue eyes hold mine, and I'm drawn to him like a flower to the sun. "I'm not pretending anymore. I want you standing beside me, and I don't care who knows or what they say. You're mine, Allie, and if you're changing your name, you're changing it to Bradford."

Tears fall onto both my cheeks when I blink. "What are you saying?"

I know what he's saying, but I have to hear him speak the words.

"All the way, on that long drive in the dark, when every mile was an eternity, and I didn't know if you were okay, if you were scared, if he was hurting you. Turning it over and over in my mind, all I could think about were the things we never did… I knew when you were in my arms again, it was for keeps." He looks down at my hands, studying my fingers, specifically my left ones. "Come with me."

He stands abruptly, leading me through the screen door into his large house. We pass through the kitchen into the living room, down the long hall to his master suite.

We're moving quickly, and my heart is racing. My eyes are fixed on his broad shoulders, and I can't stop the smile aching in my cheeks.

"Where are we going?" My voice is high, anticipating what I know is coming.

A little fish is in my stomach… Hell, a whole school of fish is in my stomach flipping and going crazy. When we reach the bed he stops, turning and catching my shoulders.

"Wait here."

I wait as he disappears into the long closet. He drops down, and I hear the sound of boxes moving. A series of short beeps is followed by the sound of a metal door opening. Leaning forward on my toes, I peer at him holding a box and taking something out.

He turns, and I step back quickly, looking around like I wasn't peeking.

"I've had this a long time." His brow furrows as he studies it. "It wasn't with me in Texas, so I never gave it to Kimmie's mom. It wasn't meant for her."

A delicate ring is in his hand, and my stomach dips as a deep exhale pushes down. I can't fight the tears flooding my eyes.

"Oh, Jack…" Clasping my hands together, I lift them to my nose. "Is that—?"

His blue eyes meet mine, and he's so serious. "It was my mother's ring." His voice is quiet. "Dad gave it to me after she died. He told me to save it for the woman I wanted to spend the rest of my life with."

I hiccup, and a quiet whimper slips from my throat. I cover my mouth with my right hand as he takes my left one in both of his.

"I love you, Allie." He looks up at me, and tears blur my vision. "I want you to marry me. I want you to be my wife and live in this house and help me take care of Kimmie and let me be there for you and Austin."

"I love the way you love my son. You're a better dad to him than he's ever had."

"He's a great kid." He smiles, blinking up at me. "He reminds me a lot of myself."

"And I love Kimmie, too." I'm talking fast. "She's so funny and sweet and fierce. I hope she might love me, too."

My hands are shaking, and my mind won't slow down. I can't believe this is happening. I've dreamed of this so many times. I pictured how it might happen, but I never, ever expected his mother's ring.

"She already loves you." His voice is warm. "But what about me?"

"What?" My brows furrow. "What do you mean?"

"How do you feel about me?"

His tone has an unexpected touch of vulnerability, and emotion flashes from my stomach to my chest to my flushed cheeks.

"Seriously?" A laugh bursts through my lips, and I reach up to put my hands on his neck. "I've loved you for so long, Jack Bradford! I've dreamed about you every night, and every time we'd walk down that aisle, I'd imagine what it would be like if it were really us and not your brother or your sister getting married. What if you were my man, looking at me that way, with so much love in your eyes?"

His brow lowers, and he leans down to kiss my lips before straightening. "It is me now, asking you, Allie Sinclair—"

"LaSalle," I quickly correct. "My maiden name is LaSalle."

His full lips press into a smile, and he nods. "Will you marry me, Allie LaSalle? Will you walk down the aisle for real this time and promise to be my wife forever?"

I'm nodding before I say the words. "Yes! Yes yes yes yes yes…" I hiccup another breath as the tears spill onto my cheeks, as he slides the ring along the third finger of my left hand.

Until it hits my knuckle and won't go any further.

"Oh…" My lips purse, and I try to make it fit. "So much for Cinderella. I think my fingers are too big."

"Don't worry." He drops it in the black velvet pouch where it was stored. "I know a guy."

A twinkle is in his pretty, pretty eyes. It's the lightest I've ever seen him, and he wraps his good arm around my waist, pulling me closer to his chest.

"Another guy?" I tease.

"Yeah." He kisses my nose. "I'll have it resized, and I can do this right, in front of everybody."

My lip pokes out in a pout. "Does this mean we're not engaged?"

"No," he answers fast. "It means, I'm coming back with a ring, but we're engaged. You already said yes."

"You bet your ass I did." My palms flatten against his chest as my pout gives way to a big-assed teary smile. "You proposed to me, Jack Bradford, and there's no way in hell I'm letting you take it back."

"No way I ever would." Large hands cup my cheeks. "You belong to me."

He covers my mouth with his, parting my lips and claiming my tongue. Claiming me like he always has, even when it was only in my dreams.

"I've made a special breakfast for the heroes." Dylan walks out with a tray on her shoulder holding plates of what look like omelettes and hash browns.

"I feel like I should be helping." Instead, for the first time at Cooters & Shooters, I'm sitting at the table at Jack's side with his arm around my shoulders and my hand in my son's.

As soon as I walked in and saw Austin, we rushed together for a long, tearful hug. My sweet son squeezed me so tight, then he stood me back, looking all over to be sure I was okay. I couldn't stop the tears as I reassured him we were safe. It was over.

"Wait." Hendrix holds up a hand. "Did you cook this?"

"Don't worry, I was right there with her the whole time." Craig walks out, also carrying a tray laden with plates.

"Rude." Dylan pokes her tongue out at her brother. "Craig made sure I only used the same boring ingredients we always use."

"I was also there supervising." Raven is behind them with another tray. "We really have a big group when we're all together."

"I hope you made enough for one more!" Garrett's loud voice echoes from the doorway, and he walks in holding a squirmy Gigi, with Liv on his arm.

The minute Haddy sees her little cousin, she starts fussing and reaching from where she sits on Hendrix's leg at the table.

I smile watching them all, and my stomach keeps squeezing with all the emotions swirling inside me. I'm here. Rip is gone.

Most of all, I'm going to be a Bradford.

I squeeze Austin's hand. He is, too.

"We've got our special Eggs Florentine," Craig explains, putting a plate in front of me. "Which I know happens to be Allie's favorite."

"How did you know that?" I grin, looking up at him.

"I pay attention." He arches an eyebrow, glancing at Jack's hand on my leg. "I'm also thinking my boyfriend might be getting a call soon about planning another wedding."

Austin inhales sharply, leaning into my ear. "Did he finally ask you?"

I blink at him, confused. "How did you…"

"We talked about it."

My lips part, and as hard as I try, I can't keep the smile off my face. "Is that okay?" I whisper back.

A smile breaks across his face, and he nods. "Definitely."

I shrug at Craig, playing it coy. "You never know what the future holds!"

"Uh-huh…" Craig bumps me with his hip as he puts a plate

holding a light-yellow roll filled with tomato, bell pepper, red pepper, black olives, spinach, and feta cheese. "One loaded Mediterranean omelette for Coach Jack."

I've made so many of these working in the kitchen, and they are delicious. I also happen to know it's Jack's favorite.

"Thanks, Craig." Jack's low voice tickles my stomach, and I want to lean over and kiss his cheek.

Kimmie walks up between us, climbing onto his lap instead. "Daddy's a hero." A wobble is in her voice, and she puts her arms around his neck. "He rescued Miss Allie, but it hurt his hands and shoulder."

Jack puts his fork down to hug his little girl. "I'm okay, baby. Did you just wake up?"

She nods, and he holds her a few seconds, until she slides down into his lap, keeping her small hand on his neck.

He kisses the top of her head, picking up his fork again, and I melt a little more. "You want some breakfast?"

She shakes her head. "Aunt Deedee is making penny cakes."

I've also made many, many of those little quarter-sized pancakes for her in my summers working here.

"Do you need some help?" Dylan stops at his chair, nodding at her niece.

"Nah, I'm good."

It's true. He's an amazing coach, an incredible lover, my hero… and a sweet, sweet dad. My bestie wraps her arms around me, giving me a hug, and I squeeze her back.

"I like what I'm seeing here," she whispers in my ear.

I give her arms another squeeze, whispering back. "Me too."

"You feeling okay, bro?" Garrett slides into the chair beside Jack then reaches for a plate holding an omelette. "You're not looking too bad, considering I had to pull you off that guy."

"He's lucky you were there." Jack nods, and Liv stops behind me, wrapping her arms around my shoulders gently.

"Feeling okay, Bookish Spice?" She tilts her strawberry-blonde head to the side to meet my eyes.

"A lot better than I was two nights ago." I give her a squeeze as well.

"The drill team organized a vigil in the park. They had candles and everybody prayed all night and everything."

"Oh!" My eyes widen, and an ache hits my throat. "That is so…"

My voice catches, and Jack's warm hand slides across my back.

Shaking my head, I swallow the ache. "I'll be glad to see them tomorrow. We'll hug it out."

Liv smiles, kissing the side of my head before patting Jack's good shoulder. "Good work, Coach."

He doesn't reply as she sits beside Garrett. I lean my elbow on the table, smiling up at him, and when his blue eyes flicker to mine, my stomach squeezes.

"I hate we missed our Halloween movie night," Raven complains from where she sits beside Hendrix. "But I'm really, really glad you're safe and you're home."

"Yeah, we're pretty good at taking out the trash." Garrett points at Craig, who holds out his fist for a bump.

Dylan sits on Logan's knee at the head of the table, sliding her hand over her growing midsection. Rachel tilts her head to the side, smiling at me from where she's perched beside Zane with Edward at her side.

As much as my early decisions try to get in my head and make me ashamed, knowing this is where I landed helps me forgive my younger self.

I was brave enough to take the chance coming here, even if I didn't know where I'd land or how it would work out, and it turned out to be the best decision of my life.

Chapter 28

Jack

"LET ME SEE SOME HUSTLE," I SHOUT AS THE BOYS LINE UP ON THE field with Austin in the starting quarterback position.

My shoulder is stiff, and I have to keep it in this damn sling for another week. At least my knuckles have somewhat returned to normal. The swelling is down, but the cuts and broken skin are still healing.

I don't have time to worry about it. State championships are around the corner, and our first playoff game is on Friday.

Glancing to the right, I see the girls on the sidelines practicing their moves. Allie is with them, and she's so pretty with her hair up and those glasses on her nose again. She's wearing that short skirt I like, and every now and then, she'll catch me looking and give me a little wave.

It's a hit of adrenaline right in my chest, and I'm ready to put my ring on her finger today. I'm just waiting for the jeweler to finish resizing it.

"Levi's been showing up these last few games, Coach." George Powell is at it again.

He's on the sideline in my ear, and I do my best to stay cool with the man.

I don't like the way he rides his son. Levi's a good kid, but I see how he's starting to act out, and I've seen this scenario before. It means he's getting too much pressure at home.

"He's playing well." My tone is noncommittal.

"I heard about what happened with the librarian." George shakes his head, looking down and feigning sympathy. "That was too bad."

"It was dangerous and potentially life-threatening." I level my eyes on him, wondering where he's going this time.

"You handled it, though." He nods, seeming to sense the change in my mood.

He'd better watch it. My patience is gone when it comes to my girl.

Allie wants to keep things as normal as possible for Austin's senior year, or I'd have her staying at my house full-time. I can't be with her as much as I want with Kimmie still so young, but I take comfort in knowing Rip Sinclair is solidly behind bars and her son is in the house with her at night.

"The playoffs are no time for sympathy points," George continues. "It's time for the best players to take the lead."

I turn to face him. "How about *you* take a seat, and let me do my job."

Logan strolls up just in time.

"How's it going, George?" My brother-in-law steps between me and the man who's about to meet the business end of my fist, injuries be damned. "We've got things under control here, so you can join the other parents in the stands."

He huffs out a growl, muttering more choice words about the upcoming game, but I return my focus to the boys.

"D-line has really come together." Logan is back at my side, watching them play. "Offense has been strong from Day 1, but no one's getting through that line now."

"Garrett's a natural." I watch with pride as Austin completes a thirty-yard pass for Tyreek to run in for the score.

The stands break into cheers and applause, and the cheerleaders and drill team do kicks and chants as the boys gather in a huddle to congratulate them.

"Aus-tin! Aus-tin!" The girls yell from the sidelines, and my eyes meet Allie's.

I love to see her smile.

I can't clap with my arm in a sling, but that ought to shut Powell's mouth. "I'm glad he's our sheriff, though."

Logan exhales a chuckle. "I couldn't agree more. Who knew Garrett Bradford would make such a kick-ass officer?"

My frown twists, and I can't deny it anymore. "I probably always knew. He was a peacekeeper in school."

"He's a good guy." Logan glances at me. "You are, too, Coach. I'm really proud of how you took care of that asshole and rescued Allie."

I nod. Rescuing Allie goes without question.

"When are you planning to pop the question?" He gives me a nudge. "Or has it already happened?"

"Just waiting for the ring to be sized."

"All right." His voice rises, and he claps. "Let me know what I can do to help."

I hadn't thought of this before, but it gives me an idea. "I will."

We sail through the first playoff game against a team out of Montgomery. I put Levi in as starting quarterback, but by the second quarter, he's been sacked twice. My brow furrows, and I watch as he takes too long to decide what to do.

George is in the stands yelling until his face is tomato-red, and I don't have a choice. I send Austin in to cinch the win.

It's the same thing at the next game, and the next. Weeks are passing, and we're making our way up the bracket to the state championship in Birmingham.

We have one week to go, and the boys, the parents, hell, the whole town is vibrating with excitement. Signs are in front of every business, and the school is decorated with posters and cup fences.

Back at my place, we're putting the final coat of paint on the bookcase for Allie.

Austin has done most of the work with just a bit of guidance on using the jigsaw and making sure the brackets are level so the shelves sit evenly.

"What do you think about these flowers?" He frowns at the pink stencils at the top corners near the curved wooden trim. "Do they look cheap? Should I paint over them?"

A slash of white paint is across the side of his cheek where he probably scratched his face, and he studies his handiwork.

It's a sturdy, wide piece of furniture, painted white with pink and green stenciled hearts and flowers around the top corners and down the sides.

Even when I've been away, he's come over early and spent time working on it. I think about Allie seeing it at Christmas, and I can already picture the tears in her eyes. She's so sweetly sentimental, and her son means the world to her.

"Don't paint over them." I rest my hands on my hips. "You've done a really good job with this. Your mom's going to see how much work you've put into it, and I think it's going to touch her heart."

His shoulders drop, and he puts the paintbrush on the pan.

I expected my words to make him happy, but he seems just the opposite. He's been playing so well in the games, far outperforming Levi.

Still, the championship game is only a week away.

We'll be loading up and heading to Birmingham Friday

morning, and I remember how I used to feel those years play-ing professional ball when we'd be headed to the Big Game.

"Nervous about Friday?" I straighten, glad I'm finally out of the sling and getting back to normal.

"Nah, I'm ready." He sits heavily on the bench outside my workroom, and I walk over to where he's leaning forward, his forearms propped on his knees.

I put a hand on his shoulder. "Is this about your mom and me?"

He shakes his head. "I told you, I'm glad you're finally mak-ing it official. You make her really happy."

The only other thing I can think of is Rip.

He and I haven't talked much about his dad or my chang-ing role in his life. I'm pretty sure how Allie feels about it, but I've never said as much to Austin.

"I hope one day you might think of me as your dad." I didn't expect to feel so vulnerable saying this. "I know I'm *not* your dad, but still, I—"

"You're a way better dad than that guy ever was." Austin's hazel eyes cut up to mine, and I nod, feeling a little better about the situation.

"Okay." I press my lips into a smile. "In that case, maybe I can help with whatever's bothering you?"

His lips purse, and his expression is a mixture of frustration and impatience. Finally, he pushes off his knees, walking roughly in the direction of the door.

"Never mind," he grumbles. "You wouldn't understand."

My brows shoot up. I've known Austin since he was a skinny middle-schooler, and this is the first time he's ever hit me with that teenager shit. It's more what I'm preparing to get from Kimmie.

"Hang on a second." I walk over to where he's facing the wall of hand tools. "Can you at least give me a ballpark idea of what it is before you write me off?"

His eyes roll to the ceiling, and his shoulders fall. "It's about girls—something *you've* never had to worry about."

I slide my hand over my mouth to hide a grin. "You think I've never had to worry about girls?"

"No." He hits the word hard.

I shake my head. "You might be surprised." I reach out to give him a nudge. "Try me."

Hazel eyes meet mine, and I do my best to appear reassuring. Finally, he exhales roughly, looking down at the ground.

"I have no game."

"What? You're a great player—"

"Off the field. I have no game." His voice rises, and he starts talking faster. "Levi talks to girls. He's really good at getting them to talk back to him, go out with him, do stuff…"

He trails off, and I don't have to ask what he means by *stuff.* "Okay?"

"I don't know how. I never know what to say. I stand around laughing like an idiot, watching him collect them like they're freakin flowers. Like it's the easiest thing in the world to pick them up."

I put my hands in my back pockets again, turning to look out at the scrub pines surrounding my house.

I was prepared for the dad talk, even the bad dad talk. I had no idea he was going to hit me with this.

"That's what I thought," he grumbles, waving me away. "You've never had this problem. You always know how to talk to girls, or *women.* They swarm around you like flies to… candy."

"Thanks." I lift my chin, glad he didn't say *shit.* "But it's not true, actually. I had an awkward stage."

"I don't believe it."

"Everybody does. It's not the end of the world." Walking over to the bench, I take a seat. "Come sit and talk to me."

He hesitates a little longer at the door before relenting and walking over to join me.

"You were holding hands with Sadie Duck at the Halloween maze. What about that?"

"She doesn't like me." He looks at his tennis shoes. "She just wants to be with a star player. She talks to me a little while, then she talks to Levi. I might be doing better than him on the field, but off the field, he's got me beat."

"Now, hang on." I put a hand on his arm. "She was holding *your* hand, not Levi's."

"Yeah, but Levi knows what to do." He cuts his eyes up at me, then he looks at his shoes again. "Levi knows how to get from talking to kissing to…"

Leaning back, I try to remember if I ever had this conversation with my brothers.

Zane didn't need it. He read all the time, and hell, he probably knew before I did. Garrett seemed to be born knowing how to charm the pants off anyone and everyone. I was gone when Hendrix was this age, so I assume one of them talked to him.

"If you're talking about sex, I think you need to wait until you're older."

"You sound like Mom," he grumbles. "She's always telling me to wait, and then she's always making sure I know how to use a condom."

My lips tighten, and I swallow a laugh. It sounds just like my passionate girl, and I wonder what Allie's doing right now. I'd like to do some *stuff* with her…

Clearing my throat, I refocus. "If you want to have a girlfriend, it's the same as making friends with anyone else." He squints up at me, and I continue. "When you meet a girl you like, ask her questions. Then listen to what she says. Really listen. Pay attention to what she likes and see if you can do it for her. Some girls like flowers, others like to go to movies. Maybe Sadie likes music. Ask her favorite song. Make her a playlist around it."

He goes from frowning to relieved, and when he looks up at me again, his face is actually brighter. "Those are really good ideas."

"Yeah." I feel pretty proud of myself. "Start with flowers, and maybe you'll get a kiss. But don't maul her… And don't have sex."

I figure Allie would appreciate the backup.

He snorts through his nose, leaning back on the bench. "Right."

"Aus-tin! Aus-tin! Aus-tin!" Kimmie marches into the room pumping her fist over her head. "I'm a cheerleader."

She climbs onto the bench, getting behind him. She leans her stomach against his back, pumping her arms over his head. "Aus-tin! Aus-tin!"

He doesn't even seem to notice. "Thanks, Coach."

"Need a ride home?"

"Nah, I don't mind walking. It's not that far." He stands, and Kimmie is still on his back with her arms around his neck.

She scoots higher, and he holds her legs. "We're like Uncle Grizz and Auntie Liv!"

"I'll let you know how it goes." His expression is lighter.

"Here, let me help you." I reach forward to take my daughter off his back. "Good luck."

"Bye, Aussie!" Kimmie waves as he passes through the door.

He lifts a hand on his way out. "Bye, Peanut."

"Austin's going to marry me." She sticks her little chin out, smiling as she watches him go.

"Speaking of that…" I walk over to sit on the bench again, putting her on my knee. "What do you think it means to get married?"

"It's what the princes and princesses do." Her brown eyes are wide, and she's very serious. "The prince takes the princess's hand, and they get in a royal coach, and the birds fly all around, and everybody waves, and they drive to his castle where they live happily ever after."

It's not too far away from what really happens.

"Actually, when you marry someone, it means you love them so much, you want to spend the rest of your life with them.

You make them part of your family, and you become part of theirs." She looks up at me, nodding, and I smile, sliding my hand over her little head. "How would you feel if I asked Miss Allie to marry me?"

She blinks several times, tilting her head to the side. "Would Miss Allie and Aussie come to live with us and would we all be happily ever after?"

"Miss Allie would." I put my hand on her shoulder. "Austin's going to college. He wants to play football, and he'll have his own house wherever he decides to go."

A smile lifts her cheeks. "Just like you, Daddy!"

"Pretty much." I rub her back. "And Uncle Zane and Garrett and Hendrix."

"I like Miss Allie. She says I'm her best helper, and she thinks I've got the legs to be a cheerleader."

My chin pulls back, and I huff a laugh. "She does?"

"I told her I'd be a good cheerleader because I've got the legs for it, and she said I'd be the best cheerleader."

"Gotcha." Standing, I take her hand as we walk to the house. "So you think it would be okay if I marry her?"

"Would she be my mommy?"

A dry ache twists my throat. These conversations are not going how I expect today. "Would you like her to be?"

Her little lips twist, and her nose wrinkles so much like Dylan's as she breaks into a smile. "I think that would be okay! You always smile when Miss Allie's around."

"I do?"

"Uh-huh." She points at my face. "Just like that. I think you should ask her to marry you."

I pull her in for a hug. "I think I will."

Chapter 29

Allie

W E'VE MADE IT TO THURSDAY, AND TOMORROW WE'LL LOAD ONTO buses to make the long drive to Birmingham for the state championship game.

The city is buzzing. The drill team and cheerleaders have put spirit posters all over town and painted big signs for the school. Cups are in all the fences spelling out *Victory* and *Go Captains*. Everyone's excited, but I'm antsy and restless.

It's been a month since the Halloween incident, since Jack asked me to marry him, and I said yes a hundred times. I've said yes every day since, and he's given me little kisses in the hall.

Sometimes he'll slip his hand under my skirt, and we'll sneak into the single-serve faculty bathroom for a quick make-out session… or more, depending on the time of day.

It's risky as hell and equally hot. But it's not enough.

Jack's been recovering and slammed with playoffs and talking to the senior boys about colleges and scholarships.

The ring is ready.

He told me when he picked it up, but he won't let me see it. He said he has something special in mind, and now I'm walking around waiting for balloons to fall from the ceiling or glitter guns to explode out of a closet.

I do not expect a box wrapped in brown paper to appear on my desk in the library after lunch. It doesn't say who it's from, but I have an idea. *Open in private* is handwritten across the top.

It's been burning a hole in my imagination as each new group of students files into the library all afternoon.

"There's another new poem." Edward points at the graffiti wall. "Based on the subject matter and the rhyme scheme, I think it's the same author as Number 18."

"Where?" I walk over to where he's standing, gazing up at the sheet. "Show me."

Mouths, fingers, hands, eyes.

I live to collect your sighs.

The time is moving so slowly, yet we're so close.

To when you'll crash into me, and we'll be home.

I frown, reaching up to touch my fingertips to the words. "That's really good."

"I'm numbering it 18-B and voting for it, too."

I watch as he grabs a Sharpie and puts the number beside it on the wall, then writes the number on a small sheet of paper and drops it into the wooden box where we've been collecting votes all semester.

I read the words again, wondering who it could be, before I turn and walk to my desk again. "I've got to step out to the restroom. Would you just keep an eye on things? I won't be long."

"Sure." He sits down, taking out a textbook.

I take the box, hiding it inside my cardigan. I can't take the suspense anymore, and the day is almost over. We have one more hour before the final bell rings.

Glancing around like I'm committing a crime, I slip into the single teacher's restroom and lock the door. I sit on the closed toilet lid, ripping the paper away to find an elegant, black cardboard box beneath.

Carefully opening it, my breath catches when I see a large,

sparkling pink jewel. It catches the light, and my lips part with a gasp. I lift the card inside to read the note, handwritten in the same script as on the outside of the box.

Wear this tonight with that skirt. No underwear.

My stomach tingles, and I gently pull the sparkling pink top to reveal a black silicone cone, smaller than my palm. A small tube of lubricant is also in the box.

Ever since our first time together, I've been getting everything waxed down below, and I've never been more thankful to be completely bare.

Chewing my bottom lip, I look around the small room as if someone can see me in here. Then I quickly stand, shoving the small toy in my pocket.

"You're doing better. Just follow the recipe." Craig stands beside Dylan in plastic goggles, gloves, and even a bandana tied over his nose and mouth.

"I thought we were voting on my worst pregnancy dish." My bestie cuts her eyes up at him.

I stand on the periphery, my heart thumping hard against my chest. I wasn't sure what the instruction *tonight* meant, so as soon as I got to the restaurant, I slipped into the bathroom and inserted the plug.

It was so small, I didn't think I'd even feel it, but I was wrong. Now I'm tingling and wet, swallowing hard every time I move or walk. My nipples are hard little points, and sitting is out of the question.

"Don't you think so?" Dylan is looking at me, waiting.

I have no idea what she's talking about. I blink at her, trying to figure out what to say, when she bursts out laughing. "You are so out of it tonight! Are you worried about the game?"

"Ah... yeah!" I smile brightly. "It's a big night for Austin."

"He's going to be great." Craig walks over and puts a hand on my shoulder. "He's been on fire all season, and these last few games he's looked like a pro."

"I don't understand why I can't go to Bethlehem to see Aussie play!" Kimmie's voice makes me jump, and the top of my head tightens.

"Birmingham." Jack's low voice sends a tingle between my thighs, and my lips part so I can breathe. "You have school, and Ms. Plum needs help with Gina."

"But I have to cheer for Aussie," Kimmie whines.

Jack walks into the room, his daughter's pouty head resting on his shoulder. "Is Liv's mom here yet?" He speaks low to Dylan.

"She's coming right after her DnD game at the Senior Center."

"I'll keep an eye out for her." He hesitates, and I'm about to die inside if he leaves, when he stops, and our eyes meet. "Hey, girl."

I swallow air, fire racing to my cheeks. I manage to push out a *Hey*, but it's soft and nervous. My stomach is in knots thinking about what's coming.

Kimmie is spending the night with Ms. Plum, since all of us are going to the game tomorrow.

I know where I'll be tonight.

"Looks like it's time!" Craig lifts the tray of spicy food off the counter.

I haven't even been paying attention to what they made. My brain has been on my butt all evening.

"I'll do the announcement, since you look like you're in space," Dylan teases. "Can you at least help hand out the ice cream cups?"

"Of course!" I blink quickly, doing my best to act normal.

"Garrett's cueing up the mix tonight." Craig is still wearing all his protective gear. "No telling what he'll play."

I follow them from the kitchen, carrying the plastic bin of ice cream cups, and the place erupts into "Fireball" by Pitbull.

Craig nods in approval, and when we all get to the table, the volume slowly lowers for Dylan to read the warning. My eyes scan the room, and I see Jack talking to Liv's mom at the back table, where they all hang out with Miss Gina.

The old lady's smiling, talking to Kimmie, and Jack's daughter seems placated by whatever she's saying. I'm chewing my lip when he turns, and my chest ignites when his blue eyes land on mine.

His chin lifts, and he walks to the door. It's like a summons as I watch him leave, and I survey the line.

"I think they can get their own at this point," I lean into Dylan's ear. "I've got to run an errand."

My friend's eyes narrow, and she glances over to where Kimmie is holding hands and dancing with our dear, blind friend, and Jack is nowhere to be found.

Her amber eyes slide up to me, and she grins. "Have fun."

She has no idea how much fun I'm about to have. For that matter, neither do I, and I'm a mess of nerves and anticipation.

Turning quickly, I start for the kitchen, taking out my phone and sending my son a quick text. He won't be home until later, and he usually goes straight to his room. But just in case, I don't want him to worry.

It's a short drive to my house, which is right down the way from Jack's. I took the plug out at Cooters & Shooters and gave it a quick wash. There was no way I could drive home with it inserted.

Already, I can tell a difference, and air rises in my chest. My phone buzzes, and my car reads the text aloud.

Sir: Park at my place and come inside.

Turning the wheel, I do as he says, parking beside his truck. When I get out, I pause, looking around quickly before bending my knees to reinsert the small cone quickly.

The large room is lit by only a few small lamps when I

enter, and I'm not sure what to do. I start to kneel when I hear his voice.

"Come here." It's a low order, and heat flushes from my breasts to my neck.

I walk to where he's sitting in that leather armchair, blue eyes level on mine. My stomach twists tighter with every step, and I'm so on edge.

I stop in front of him, waiting for his next order.

A predatory gleam is in his eye. "Let me see it."

My lips part as I turn my back and lean forward so the bottom of my skirt rises higher on my thighs. I place my palms on the sides of my legs, sliding them up until the hem is over my lower back.

A soft hiss comes from Jack's lips, and I exhale a whimper when his large hand slips between my thighs. His palm moves higher on my skin until the side of his fingers makes contact with my clit.

I exhale another moan, and he slides his fingers all the way to my core. "You're dripping. Does this mean you like it?"

Nodding, I answer quickly. "Yes."

Both hands grip my ass, and I cry out when he dips two fingers into my pussy. "Go to the table, lean forward on your stomach, and hold onto the edge."

My knees wobble as I do what he says, walking to the sturdy wooden table in the kitchen and leaning down to rest my stomach on the wood. I reach over my head with both hands, hooking my fingers on the edge. Cool air drifts around my private parts as I wait.

"Don't let go." Another low order.

The sound of rustling and the slide of a zipper sends me higher. I brace for his invasion. Instead, large hands cup my rear, spreading me apart as his tongue penetrates my body.

"Oh!" I gasp as he slides it forward, circling it over my clit, firmly and repeatedly.

He growls low, vibrating my body as he eats me. I'm so on

edge, my thighs start to tremble, and my orgasm twists irresistibly tight in my lower pelvis. I hold onto the edge of the table, whimpering with each pass of his expert tongue.

All at once he stops and stands, spreading me apart again, and I feel his finger trace the edge of the pink jewel, moving it inside me. I feel his tip nudging at my entrance, and he leans forward, speaking low in my ear.

"I'm going to fuck you hard." Another whimper escapes on a breath as he continues. "And you're going to love it."

He drives his cock in all the way to the hilt with one firm thrust, and the sensation is overwhelming. The plug dips, and I don't know why it feels so good. I don't understand.

He groans, pulling back and driving in again as he speaks. "This is for all the times you teased me at school, walking around in that short, fuck-me skirt, with those red lips. Looking like you knew how I ached to touch you, but I couldn't." Another hard thrust, and my eyes squeeze as wetness slips onto my inner thighs. "Bending over on the field with this sexy ass in the air like you wanted to make me hard in front of the team…"

He moves faster, thrusting deeper, shifting the cone inside me with every drive. I'm gasping, panting, as the pressure grows tighter. I'm on my toes, lifting my ass, begging for more.

"That's right," he growls. "You love it because it's true."

He slaps my ass hard, and I scream. He does it again, and I moan. He moves faster, and my vision blackens. The top of my head burns, and I'm lost in sensation. I've never felt this way in my life, and all at once, I'm struck by divine lightning.

My entire body shakes. I think I'm screaming.

His strong forearm goes around my chest, and he lifts my stomach off the table, my back to his chest. He's still fucking me, and I'm still coming.

Stars explode behind my eyes. His hand moves between my thighs, where he circles fiercely, massaging my clit, and I erupt again, shaking and crying.

"That's right, take my cock." Flattening his fingers, he slaps my pussy repeatedly, until it smacks of wetness, until my knees buckle, and I reach back to hold his arms to stay upright. "Fuck, you love this, don't you?"

Nodding, I gasp for breath, a trembling plea. "Yes... yes..."

I'm on a different plane, my core is throbbing, and I only know if he stops, I'll fly into a million pieces. His hand moves from my shoulder to my breast, kneading and pinching my tingling nipples, one then the other.

Then with a shout, he comes. His muscles tremble, and I feel him pulsing, holding, again and again before he starts to slow.

I'm still gone, riding out the intensity, wondering if I'll still be able to function normally. If I'll even be able to walk after this.

He gives two more thrusts before guiding us forward and bracing a strong hand on the tabletop.

I melt onto my stomach, boneless and humming, trembling with the aftershocks of the most intense orgasm I've ever had in my life.

He's still deep inside me, pulsing occasionally. The front of his thighs press against the back of mine, and he softly traces my ass with his fingertips until his fingers find the jewel. With a slow, gentle pull, he removes it, setting it to the side, then he massages my ass.

"You were so good tonight." His voice is low, soothing, and he lifts me off my feet. "You were perfect."

He carries me to the large bathroom in his master suite, and he holds me on his lap as water fills the tub. My cheek is against his chest, and my hand is on his shoulder. I'm sleepy and happy and blissed out and my limbs feel like jelly.

"Getting through Dare Night was so hard." I lift my chin to meet his eyes, wrinkling my nose. "That thing made me really horny."

He grins, kissing my lips. Then his expression turns more serious. He cups my jaw in his fingers and kisses me slowly, opening my mouth and sliding his tongue inside. I reach up to hold his cheek, following the lead of his movements with mine.

He pulls my top lip with his mouth, then does it again, swiping his tongue along mine. My nipples tingle and point, and I'm so in love with him.

"All I could think about when I saw you was your pretty little ass and whether you had it in."

"I did…" I lean forward, grinning like we're sharing a secret. "I wasn't sure if you'd drag me into the pantry and want to see it."

"You'd have done it." He grins, kissing the top of my eyebrow.

"I hoped you would."

He never lets me go, swinging a leg over the side of the copper tub and lowering us both into the swirling warm waters.

"You might be a little sore." He lifts a bar of soap, gently cleaning my backside.

We're stomach to stomach in the warm water, and I slide forward to kiss his lips. "Worth it."

He holds my cheeks and kisses me again. "I love you, Allie. Can you stay with me tonight?"

"I love you, Jack." I kiss him back. "Do you think that's a good idea?"

"I don't give a fuck. We're engaged."

"Secretly." I press my finger to his full lips, which he pokes out to kiss it.

"Not for long."

Blinking up, our eyes meet, and emotion like an aching river spills through my lungs. "I'll text Austin so he doesn't worry."

Chapter 30

Jack

THE STADIUM IN BIRMINGHAM IS LOUD WITH CHEERING AND MUSIC and voices over the loudspeaker.

We're facing off against the Pike Road Pirates, and these guys never lose. Last year they beat the opposing team by forty points, and they were both state championship-level teams.

The boys are antsy in the locker room, bouncing up and down in the tunnel heading to the field. When we run out, the stands erupt into screaming, and when we get to the sidelines, everyone's on their feet and stomping.

I bring Levi into a huddle with Austin. "How are you feeling tonight?"

"Great, Coach!" Austin nods, shifting from foot to foot.

I look at Levi, but his expression is stony. On par with the last few weeks, he's not making eye contact, and he seems a million miles away.

"This team is a beast. We're not going to get away with anything." I put a hand on Levi's shoulder, giving him a little shake until he looks at me. "I want to lead out with you as QB-1. Are you with me?"

His lips tighten, and his chin drops. "I don't know, Coach. I'll try."

Not what I want to hear. "If it's not happening, I'm taking you out."

He nods, not even fighting me, and it's like a punch in my stomach. I feel like I've missed something, but we've been together on the field every afternoon for the past two weeks. His dad acts the same as always, and I can't account for it.

"They're letting us call the toss." I give him another shake. "Go do it."

I hope the honor will boost his enthusiasm. Austin stands beside me watching, and I lean over to him. "Be ready to go in."

He nods, and we lose the toss. Levi runs back to grab his helmet, and I catch him before he runs onto the field. "Give me all you've got out there."

Again, he doesn't give me much, and I glance at Austin. It's going to be a tough game, and it's a big ask for him to play the entire time.

Still, he's young and hungry, and half the town is here. I'm not sure I have a choice.

We're on the sidelines, and Levi takes the snap. Jogging back, he looks all over the field. Tyreek is wide open, and even Rich is waiting to take the ball. He hesitates too long and ends up trying to run, quickly getting planted by the Pirates' defense.

"We're going to have to take him out, Coach." Buddy is at my side, and my jaw tightens.

I hear George in the stands losing his voice from yelling, and I cross my arms. Buddy is usually in the box, but Logan took that spot tonight. I lift my chin, and Garrett jogs over to where we're standing.

"I've seen this kind of thing in the pros." Garrett stands beside me as they line up to go again. "It's like he's already retired. His heart's not in it."

"Did something happen?" I look over at Buddy, who simply shrugs.

It's fourth and twenty, and Rome runs out to try for a field goal. My shoulders are tense, and Garrett leans in so only I can hear. "Edward's gotten more reliable than Rome."

"I know." My jaw is tense, and my throat tightens as the ball wobbles wildly through the kick, bouncing off the upright.

"We can't do this here." Logan's in my earpiece. "Put in our leaders."

Garrett revs up the defensive line as they head onto the field. "Keep us in this!"

I pull Austin close. "You're playing the rest of the game."

He nods, eyes serious. "Okay."

Then I walk over to where Edward is quietly talking to himself several paces behind the team under the shelter of an awning. I wave, and he reaches up to take out an earplug.

"You're taking over as kicker."

His expression doesn't change. He simply nods, putting the plug back in his ear and returning to whatever mantra he uses to block out the chaos.

Defense holds them, but one of our players gets hit hard. He's on his back on the field for several minutes, and Garrett is with him, hand on his shoulder, helping him stand and limp off the field.

My jaw tightens. Another of our best players is out of the game. We can't lose anymore.

We finish out the half with no points on the board, and when we run to the locker room, I know I've got to get their spirits up. Allie meets my eyes as I pass the girls preparing to do the halftime show.

Her pretty eyes are worried, but I give her a wink. It was so good to hold her all night, and right now, thinking of her pretty face relaxed and content as she slept in my arms goes a long way to break the punishing tension of this night.

The boys all take a knee in the locker room, and I look over their young faces. "You've all worked hard to get here tonight. You've sacrificed and pushed yourself for the last five months, and we're here, at the state championship, about to do something this team has never done. Are you with me all the way?"

All but Levi yell enthusiastically, and I reach out to high-five and clasp the hands of those around me. "Defense, you're making me proud. Offense, let's bring it home."

Stepping back, I let Garrett take over working his magic, and when it's time to head back to the field, satisfaction is a calm in my chest.

It's going to happen, and that's not all…

The second half is a shutout. Austin, Tyreek, and Rich are a well-oiled machine. They move the ball down the field, completing passes, catching the tosses, and stiff-arming the cornerback.

At one point, Austin is caged, and I'm afraid he's going to take the sack, when miraculously, the Pirates' defensive player slips. Austin hops over him like a hurdler, and when his feet hit the turf, he runs like I've never seen all season for a forty-yard touchdown.

Both the cheer and drill teams are screaming, and Allie is surrounded by Rachel, Liv, and Dylan, who are screaming and crying. I shake my head and laugh, looking down at the turf.

I know the headline tomorrow will be something about my rare show of emotion, and I don't give a shit. Austin's having the time of his life, and I wouldn't have it any other way.

The Pirates manage one touchdown, but in the last seconds of the game, I tap Edward to run out and kick a field goal. Lucas usually holds the ball for the punt, but I let Austin take it this time. It's their last time on the field together, and they're like brothers.

Rachel's hands are clasped in front of her lips, and Allie has her arms around her friend's waist and her head on her shoulder. It's a family affair.

The ball sails cleanly through the uprights, and a cannon fires. Confetti rains red and white all around us, and I jog onto the field to shake the other coach's hand. Turning to face the stands, I count the number of scouts there, and I know Austin will be fielding offers as soon as we roll back into town.

We're on the field when they hand out the massive plaques with the engraving of the state and the year on them. *State Champions* is emblazoned in blue, and I hold it up as the boys gather around yelling and holding it over their heads.

We'll find out players of the year later, but I expect Austin will be among the names listed, if not taking the top prize.

The guys fall back, and my mind is on Allie. We're through the locker rooms, and I'm making my way to the waiting buses when I hear shouts. My throat tightens, and I look around, not wanting to find what I think is happening.

Sure enough, George Powell has Levi against the wall, and he's in the boy's face.

"You think you'll get an offer now?" The man has him by the jersey, holding him against the wall. "Huh? You think you're going to a top school playing like that?"

"I don't care!" Levi yells back. "I don't want to go to a top school. I don't want any of it."

The man rears back, fist clenched, and he's about to punch Levi in the face, when I hustle forward, grabbing his upper arm.

"Stop!" I shout.

The older Powell jerks, trying to get his arm from my grip, but I'm not letting go. "Get off me, Bradford. This isn't your business."

"It *is* my business." I meet his angry eyes head-on. "This won't fix it."

He jerks against my hold, snarling. "You let this happen. You've been thinking with your dick all season."

"That's enough." Garrett jogs up to where we're struggling with Logan right behind him. "You okay, bro?"

"Let's get to the bus, Levi." Zane's tone brings a much-needed calm.

He holds out a hand to the boy leaning against the

cinder-block wall, heaving a breath. Levi nods, pushing forward to follow Zane to the bus, and I loosen my grip on his father.

I think the situation is diffused, but dammit, George grabs Levi by the shoulder and shoves him to the ground, pointing in his face. "Don't come home."

I'm about to take off after the man when the boy beats me to it. He's on his feet, running after his dad and giving him a two-handed shove.

The man falls forward against the fence, his head bouncing back off the links as his son yells, "I'm never coming back. I'm done with you. With all of this."

His voice is shredded, and he takes off. Logan holds up a hand. "Let me handle it."

Garrett and I exchange a look, and I know if anyone understands the special trauma of a punishing father, it's Logan. I'm angry and aching, and I don't even bother to check on George Powell.

One of the team trainers is with him, and I keep walking. I've got a busload of boys waiting for me, and something special planned for the beautiful woman I love.

Chapter 31

Allie

COOTERS & SHOOTERS IS ALL LIT UP.

A banner hangs on the back wall reading *Congratulations, Captains*, and tonight is the big celebration. It's the first time in Jack's tenure as coach at Newhope High that they've brought home the state championship trophy.

It's the first of many, everyone's saying.

Everyone was asleep on the bus by the time we rolled back into town near 2 a.m. The news of the showdown with Levi's dad flew through the group like wildfire, and all the way home, I texted with Jack to be sure he was okay.

I know how much he cares about the boys, and especially when the parents are too much, his protectiveness runs high.

It's so hot. It's one of my favorite things about him.

I'm sorry about Levi's dad. You okay? I know you hate that.

Sir: Logan's got him. He'll spend the night with them, and we'll figure it out tomorrow.

Wish you could get me tonight

Sir: As pretty as you are in my bed, get your sleep tonight. I expect to see you at the celebration tomorrow.

I'll be up front in your jersey.

Sir: Perfect.

Now we're here, and I'm in my white pleated skirt with his baby blue and red Number 17 Mustangs jersey on. I don't give a shit what people think or say.

Really, because Jack said we don't.

I'd still be in the closet if he weren't so adamant our sneaking-around days are over. Although, it was kind of sexy being his dirty little secret.

Now I'll be his dirty little wife.

"You ladies did such a good job with that drill team." Miss Gina walks up, holding Rachel's hand. "It was thrilling to hear the band at every game and know the girls were doing their high kicks. Just like when Liv was captain."

"Miss Gina, you are too much." Liv skips over to give her a hug. "You never saw me once."

"Your energy was electric," the old blind lady argues. "I remember how the stadium would get so excited when you'd lead the team onto the field. It was just like when Dylan would dance in the Nutcracker."

"You were always front and center." Dylan skips over to hug her surrogate grandmother. "And when it ended, you'd be on your feet clapping."

"You're really showing!" Miss Gina runs her hand over my bestie's middle. "How far along are you now?"

"I'm at twenty weeks. Can you believe that?"

"Halfway there!" Miss G's blue eyes lift to the ceiling in delight. "Do you know what you're having?"

Dylan's eyes light, and I can tell she does. Rachel, Liv, and I all lean forward at the same time.

"Y'all!" Dylan laughs, looking at all four of us hanging on the edge. "I had my last ultrasound Wednesday."

"You know!" Rachel bounces on her toes.

Liv's lips twist with a frown. "Are y'all going to do one of those gender-reveal parties?"

"What a face!" Dylan gives her sister-in-law a playful shove. "What if I did?"

"Just don't set anything on fire. Or put your eye out."

"Good lord, Liv!" Rachel laughs, shaking her head. "I think they're fun! We could make balloons that have pink or blue smoke inside them or make a cake where the middle is all blue or pink…"

"Just tell us!" I hold Dylan's arm. "We won't tell anybody, and you can do whatever you want for a reveal."

"Logan would murder me." Dylan laughs. "I already told him we weren't telling anybody we were pregnant until the second trimester, and everybody knew in like a day."

"That's because your Dare dishes tasted like…" I shake my head, making a foul face.

"Mean!" Dylan gives me a shove.

"I'm sorry, babe. It's simply the truth."

"Whatever. All I know is, I'm not telling you tonight." Dylan lifts her chin. "Tonight has already been called."

"For the football team?" Liv's face crinkles. "We're way more interested in a new Bradford."

"Then you should be very happy!" Dylan laughs, giving a side-eye that makes my stomach jump.

The music cranks up, and Garrett is in the front of the room dancing with the team. They're hyped and happy. Austin has his arm around Edward's neck, and Rachel's brother is not smiling. He's doing his best with his earplugs firmly in place, but I see his occasional wince.

"I hope they don't take too long with all of this." I lean closer to Rachel, speaking in her ear. "Edward looks really uncomfortable."

"He wanted to be on the team." She shrugs, shaking her head like there's nothing she can do.

The boys start chanting Jack's name, and Logan and Zane shove him onto the stage. Even Buddy Outlaw is smiling and clapping, his nephew Lucas right beside him, no doubt thinking about next year, when he'll be starting quarterback.

"Yeah, I see you." Jack smiles attractively, clapping hands with the cheering boys as their shouting and the music dies down. "I'm really proud of you guys. You played hard all season, and we've come a long way."

He looks around the room, making eye contact with every member of the team, and I can't help the pride swelling in my chest. They all hang on his every word, and he takes his role so seriously. He's so good with them.

"We did it, and every single one of you was a part of this." He holds up the trophy, and cheers and whistles rip through the room. "This is for us, and the town will always remember this year. Hopefully, as the start of many more to come."

More cheers and shouts. The boys hug and high-five, and Jack leans into the mic. "I'd like to do one more thing if you don't mind." The celebration dies down again, and his blue eyes land on mine. "Allie LaSalle, would you join me up here, please?"

"What?" A knot twists in my throat, and my eyes widen.

Everyone starts to clap, and more whistles cut through the noise. Hands guide me to the stage, and I look up to see Austin at my side smiling so big it makes my breath hiccup.

"Say yes," he whispers, helping me climb onto the stage beside Jack.

"Winning state champs isn't the only big thing to happen this year." He looks out at the room, that grin still on his lips. "I made a big decision of my own as well."

"Jack…" My voice is high, and he takes my hand, lifting it to his lips.

"I thought this would be a surprise," he quips. "But the only surprise was me finding out how many of you already knew it was coming—or were asking when I'd finally do it."

A ripple of laughter is followed by the sound of gasps and squeals as Coach Jack Bradford lowers to one knee in front of me.

"Oh my gosh…" My nose is hot, and I cover my mouth with my right hand.

He's holding my left with that ring poised on my third finger. "Allie, will you make me the happiest man in the world…" His warm eyes hold mine, and when I blink, tears fall onto my cheeks. "And let the town off the hook?"

Laughter flows through the group, and I glance out to see all four of my girls right up front hugging each other, eyes shining with tears.

Lifting my chin, I nod quickly. "Yes! Again, yes yes yes yes yes…"

He rises, cupping my face in both hands, looking deeply into my eyes in a way that steals the breath from my lungs. Then he covers my lips with his, giving me one swipe of his tongue before cutting it short and pulling me into his side in a hug.

"Now it's time for a party!" Garrett shouts, and a roar of cheers goes up.

He lifts his hand to start the music when a snarly voice interrupts our celebration.

"Well, this explains everything." George Powell shoves front and center on the floor in front of the stage, weaving slightly as the crowd parts around him. "I called it from the first day! You people don't have the balls to say what's happening here, but I do."

Levi pushes through the group, shouting, "Dad, stop! Don't do this!"

He grabs his father's arm in an attempt to pull him away, but the man turns on him, hitting Levi with a backhand that sends him to the floor.

"No!" I yell from the stage as Austin and Tyreek rush to their friend.

Jack makes a move, but Logan intercepts him, grabbing the man around the upper arms and pulling him back.

"I've got him—enjoy your night." Logan frowns up at us. "It's time for you to get out."

He starts to muscle George to the door, but the man breaks free from Logan's hold. He squares around to face his son, shouting.

"I gave you everything!" the man yells. "Sacrificed everything! I took you everywhere you needed to go. You had the best of the best, the talent, the drive. You were supposed to be everything I'm not."

"I don't want to be you!" Levi shouts back, his cheek blazing red from the strike. "I don't want to play football! I want to stay here!"

"And be nothing?"

Levi blinks fast, shaking his head as he looks at the man. "And be a dad! Sadie's pregnant."

The room falls silent. My hand tightens in Jack's, and my eyes fly to Austin, who's standing behind his friend.

His expression is shocked, and he takes a step back. My heart aches, and I want to go to him, but George isn't done.

"So?" he snaps. "What does that have to do with you?"

Levi's eyes flash. "It's mine."

"Says who?" his father cries. "That little slut? How do you know it's not the golden boy's? She's been sleeping with the whole team!"

"I have not!" Sadie's wobbly voice cries from somewhere in the crowd.

I scan the room until I find her standing in a clutch of her friends. Her face is red and splotchy, and her eyes are wide. Her cousin Oliver goes to stand beside her, putting his hand on her back.

Levi lunges at his dad, but Garrett catches him around the waist. "Take it easy," he murmurs.

"She's not a slut!" Levi yells. "The baby's mine, and I'm going to stay here with her. I'm going to be the best dad—nothing like you. I hate you!"

George's eyes narrow, and he huffs air through his thick lips. "Real mature, Levi. And how will you pay for this baby with no job, no education…"

"He's got a job," Garrett interrupts. "He's working in animal control."

Levi frowns up at him.

"Animal control?" the elder Powell scoffs.

"He'll start there, and he can work his way up to being one of my deputies." Garrett looks at Levi. "If you want. We can talk about it."

"Sure…" Levi's voice is hoarse. "Okay."

"I'm done." George flings his arm in the direction of his son. "You want to hate me? Just remember when you're my age, I tried to give you something better."

The man storms out of the restaurant leaving silence in his wake. Jack and I are still holding onto each other, and the entire room is stunned.

Lifting my chin, I look up at Jack. "Did I say yes?"

He exhales a grin, nodding as he pulls my head to his lips. Sadie has made her way through the crowd to stand beside Levi, and the team and Logan and Dylan close around them.

They're going to be okay. It's going to be hard, and I don't know if they'll make it. They're two sparrows in a hurricane, but they have a village here. I've seen how the town rallies around its own in times of trouble.

I don't know what the future holds, but they have as good a chance as any of us.

Chapter 32

Jack

CHRISTMAS COMES FAST ON THE HEELS OF THE STATE CHAMPIONSHIP game and all the fallout at the celebration event.

Our engagement was almost completely overshadowed by what happened with Levi and Sadie and his dad, although, to be fair, we were already old news.

I soon discovered everyone was waiting for me to pop the question and wondering why I was taking so long. I have to wonder the same thing every day now, especially with Allie slowly moving into our house.

On the nights when she joins us at bedtime, Kimmie requests Allie's favorite children's book *The Eevil Weevil* by Stephen Cosgrove. Allie has voices for all the parts, which delights my daughter to no end.

"Weevil," Allie reads in a bossy little-bug voice, and Kimmie jumps in to say the next part with her. "Why are you so *evil*?"

Then they laugh and hug, and damn, it's so fucking perfect. I never knew how much I wanted my daughter to have a mom in her life until now, and Allie is so good at it.

Austin sleeps at Allie's house, although the two of them stay over for Christmas Eve night. We huddle around the tree drinking spiced cider—or spiked eggnog for the adults—and watch old Christmas movies until Kimmie falls asleep on Austin, and I start to doze.

The next morning, when we exchange gifts, as I expected, Allie bursts into tears when her son unveils the bookcase he spent all semester making for her.

"You did this all by yourself?" Her teary voice cracks as she traces trembling fingers over the delicate stencils. "It's beautiful!"

Austin smiles as if he's embarrassed, and my chest tightens. Even if I know they're happy tears, it still twists my stomach to see Allie cry.

Austin wasn't as upset as I thought he'd be about the situation with Levi and Sadie. He was disappointed. He saw his mother's point about using protection. But he seemed to be as angry with his friend as he was with his supposed girlfriend.

I met him cleaning out his locker and took a minute to check on him.

"She said she loved me, but she was horny." He frowned, and I could hear the anger in his tone. "I just can't believe Levi did me like that. He could've told me instead of making me look like a dumbass… Sorry, Coach."

"It's okay." I sat on the bench beside him, resting my forearms on my thighs to mirror his posture. I thought about what my dad said to me all those years ago, when I didn't understand how his friend could betray him. "Sometimes in life we trust the wrong people. Sometimes our friends let us down. The best thing you can do is dust yourself off, accept it was their choice, and move on. In the end it's their loss, not yours."

His lips pressed into a frown, and I didn't know if I helped much.

I pulled him in for a side-hug, reminding him of the truth. "You've got a big life ahead of you. Try and focus on that and let these little distractions go."

Football season is so intense, when it ends, it's like the start of summer vacation. Only, it's December, and we have five months left in the school year.

They pass quickly with the number of seniors we have this year. I spend the semester helping them meet with college scouts, giving them advice, talking to nervous parents.

Austin is heavily recruited, but he ultimately stays with his original decision to go to Tennessee. Allie is happy, and she even starts investigating places to stay when we go for visits.

The passing weeks also bring us closer to our wedding date in June. Having her here is so right, so seamless, I honestly don't want to wait, but I know she's savoring these final days with her son.

Her bookcase is in my bedroom now, and she has it filled with her favorite spicy romance novels. Their colorful spines light up my otherwise brown-and-navy space. Occasionally, she reads aloud to me, which usually ends in us trying out the positions—when we're sure Kimmie's asleep and the door is locked.

Wife: How is it already May? I blame Clint and all this additional wedding planning. He's distracting me.

Are you getting cold feet?

Wife: No! Austin's at the table going through his graduation packet, and I'm doing my best not to cry.

I know how to make you smile

Wife: Don't tempt me.

Exhaling a chuckle, I lean back in my bed, studying her face on my phone.

Allie is perfect for me.

I'd given up on finding someone who would want the same things as I do, but she's not only curious, she's eager to try new things. It somehow makes me more protective of her. She's so precious to me. I want to give her everything. I never want her to be sad.

I'll plan something special for our honeymoon and when we drop him off at college.

Wife: Don't even say it! I can't think about that day.

He's going to have the best time.

Wife: I know. I'm just going to miss him so much.

We'll go to see him every weekend.

Wife: He'd hate that! 😏 But I love that you suggested it. You take such good care of me.

I love you.

Wife: I love you more.

I'm ready to have you home permanently.

Wife: Soon. I wish Austin was going to prom 😔 I don't want to be mad at Sadie, but I am. She kind of broke his heart.

Only a little bit. I'll talk to him.

Wife: You're the best dad.

Warmth spreads through my chest, and I remember our conversation all those months ago in the garage.

It gives me an idea.

Chapter 33

Allie

"As if May couldn't be any busier, I added a poetry contest." I grumble, sitting at the desk with Edward double-counting the votes. "We should've ended this at Christmas."

"I thought that was the original plan." Edward is backing up my count.

"I'm glad you didn't." Sadie blinks up at me, smiling nervously.

She started as a library aide in January, and I'm doing my best to accept what Jack said and not be mad at her for hooking up with Austin's friend.

According to Jack, Austin was more hurt by Levi's betrayal than Sadie's, and being a pregnant teenager won't be easy for them. Still, it's not easy.

At least she seems to know what she did, and she tiptoes around me.

"We got some really great additions after Christmas." Her voice is quiet. "I've put together the list of authors, but we still have some unaccounted for."

"Who's Number 18?" Edward leans over to look at her list. "They got my vote—and almost everyone else's."

Sadie ducks her head, flipping pages and running her finger down her list. "Nobody's claimed it."

"If they didn't claim it, we'll have to move to the next person on the list." I close the folder, going behind my desk to get the prizes out of my drawer.

Edward frowns, examining the yellow steno pad. "It's a long drop to second."

The lunch bell rings, and students start pouring in through the double doors. Morning announcements said we'd name the winners at lunch, and everyone's excited for all the events of the last weeks of school.

Seniors are in their final week, and the halls are decorated with posters made by the junior class, naming the class favorites and assorted scholastic and sports accomplishments.

Austin was named *Sports Illustrated*'s high school player of the year, which came with a nice scholarship, not that he needed it after getting a full ride to Tennessee. Jack said it would help with books and incidentals.

Every time I see his poster, my chest squeezes, and I fight back tears.

I'm just coming around the desk when I notice Sadie's cheeks flush. I look up to see Austin walking through the doors, sharing a laugh with Tyreek and Lucas Outlaw.

He's carrying a stack of red Solo cups, and he walks right up to the short bookshelf where Edward is marking our first-, second-, and third-place winners.

Edward doesn't even look up as my son begins stacking the cups in a pyramid design, but I frown, walking over to see what the heck he's up to.

"Hey, babe," I start. "What're you—"

Then he reaches back with a snap, and Lucas steps forward quickly to hand him a folded poster, which he opens to reveal a large message reading, *Don't let me go SOLO to the prom.*

He's standing across the bookshelf from Edward, who still hasn't looked up, but he has caught the attention of the rest of the kids in the library who fall silent except for the occasional noise of muffled laughter.

Austin finally gives up on his friend looking and clears his throat loudly. Edward still doesn't look, so I give him a nudge.

"I'm just making sure I have the correct numbers," he says, and I nod in the direction of my waiting son.

Still frowning, he looks at Austin, who immediately begins speaking. "Edward Wells, will you go with me to the prom?"

More snorts and hushed laughter as the entire library waits to see what will happen next.

Edward blinks several times, reading the poster then studying the pyramid of red Solo cups on the bookshelf beside him.

He hasn't stopped frowning when he says, "You're asking me to the prom?"

"Yes, please." Austin's eyes dance, but he's holding a straight face.

Edward's back straightens. "Well… you're objectively handsome, and you're arguably the best football player on the team." He nods at the sign and visual aid. "Your prom-posal is unexpected and daring, which I admire. However, you should know I'm not a homosexual."

A laugh bursts through my son's nose, and he covers his mouth with his hand, clearing his throat. "Since you put it that way, I'm not either, but that doesn't matter."

"I'm not a senior."

"I am."

Edward's upper lip curls. "Do you want me to wear a dress?"

"No!" Austin almost laughs again, but instead he steps forward to put a hand on Edward's shoulder. "You're my best friend. Let's go and have some fun with the rest of the class. Okay?"

Rachel's brother hesitates a moment. Then he almost seems pleased, nodding. "I'll bring my earplugs."

"I'll pick you up at seven. Wear a tux."

The library bursts into applause, and a few kids whistle. I put my hand over my mouth as I smile, shaking my head.

Austin walks around to lean on the short bookcase beside his best friend, and I couldn't be more proud.

"Look at this one!" Rachel has her phone out, swiping through her pictures of Austin and Edward posing in front of a large oak tree in front of her house.

Austin is on his knee, and Edward is staring at him confused.

"Those boys crack me up." Raven laughs, swiping through Rachel's pictures, showing us one where Austin pins a boutonniere on Edward's lapel. "I hate we're missing all the fun stuff. We've got to move back to Newhope before all the kids are grown."

"You're here for the big things." I put my arm around her shoulders, giving her a cup of purple drink. "Like my wedding… my kidnapping…"

"Gah!" Raven cries, waving her hand. "Don't even say that! I'm so glad you're okay, and that creep is behind bars for good."

"I'll drink to that." Liv holds up her cup, and I grab a cup as well.

We've made it all the way to June. Graduation was last weekend, and tomorrow, all my dreams will come true.

After months of planning—which I pretty much completely turned over to Craig's wedding-planner boyfriend Clint—I'll walk down the aisle and marry Jack Bradford, the man of my dreams.

With everything that's happened since Christmas, I don't even know what all I said yes to, but after three weddings and a birthday party, Clint has proven he has impeccable taste.

The ceremony will be held in the park overlooking the bay down by the pier. We'll say "I do" under an arch covered in pink bougainvillea, with bouquets of white lilies and neon-pink azaleas.

Jack and I agreed since it's a second wedding for both of us, we want to keep it small—family and close friends only. Still, he's a minor celebrity, so we expect some spectators to be on hand.

I found a beautiful dress at one of the boutique stores in town. It's a knee-length cream-colored silk with spaghetti straps and tiers of chiffon on the top and over the skirt. I'll wear my glasses, my hair up, and paint my lips red as a sexy inside joke.

And tonight, we're having our usual bachelorette party—complete with purple drink, or virgin purple drink for Dylan—this time in my honor.

"They were so handsome." I take out my phone to show the pictures we took at my place with Jack and Kimmie. "I can't get over how grown they looked in tuxedos!"

Kimmie watched the whole thing with amazement, holding my hand tightly. She only cried a little bit about not being able to go, but we took her for ice cream to make it up to her.

"They look hot." Liv leans forward to look at my phone. "I bet all the girls were tripping over their heels to dance with them."

"I can confirm they were." Dylan walks out of the kitchen holding her very pregnant stomach with one hand and a tray of toast points in the other. "They looked like models, and Austin had a blast. I couldn't tell how Edward felt."

"You feeling okay, Dee?" I take the tray from her, putting it on the bar.

Her nose wrinkles. "I've just had this heartburn all day."

She attempts a smile, but she still looks uncomfortable.

I pass her a cup of virgin purple drink. "One more week!"

"I like Austin's attitude." Liv lifts her chin as I refill her cup. "He shook that Sadie nonsense right off and had a fun senior year."

"He's shaken off a lot this year." My mood dims slightly. "Jack has helped so much."

"Who ever thought Edward would go to the prom?" Rachel's voice goes high, and she taps the tears off her cheeks with her fingertips. "Austin's the best kid. He included Eddie in everything from the very beginning. Then he called him his best friend…"

"He's pretty great." I pass her a napkin to dry her eyes and a cup of purple drink. "I don't know what I'm going to do next year without him."

"You'll be making whoopee with my big brother!" Dylan cries, holding up her cup. "And it's about damn time."

We all cheers, and Dylan squats awkwardly to dig in her bag. "It's time for our bachelorette round of Marry-Fuck-Kill, and have I got some options lined up for tonight. You guys are going to have the hardest time sorting… sorting… Oh!" Her eyes go wide, and she drops her bag and all of the pens on the floor. "Oh, no!"

A loud whooshing noise is followed by what sounds like water spilling all over the floor.

"What's happening?" Rachel comes running back from where she went to touch up her makeup. "Dylan, oh my god! Did you pee?"

"Rachel, call Logan!" Liv and I both rush forward to grab Dylan's arms. "Tell him to get to the hospital. Dylan's water just broke!"

"Oh no, oh no!" Rachel runs in place tapping her phone as Liv and I do our best to help Dylan to the door.

"This way!" Raven holds the doors open, waving.

"No, this isn't happening!" Dylan cries, then all of a sudden she stops, pulling her arms to her sides.

"What's wrong?" I bend forward to look at her.

Her face is red and horribly scrunched, and she lets out a piercing yell as she holds her stomach.

"Oh, God!" she cries. "It hurts so bad!"

I exchange a worried look with Raven and Liv, and I hear Rachel behind us.

"Yes, right now! We're taking her to the hospital. Meet us there!"

"Liv, it hurts so bad," Dylan cries, leaning her head on her sister-in-law's shoulder.

"You've got this." Liv's voice is calm. "What's our mantra?"

"I forgot." We start walking slowly through the doors and into the parking lot.

"My Rover's closest!" Raven rushes ahead to unlock her car.

"Say it with me, Dylan." Liv holds her arm as we walk. "Soften… Settle… Relax."

Dylan stops again, almost squatting as she screams. "It's not working! I can't do this!"

"Yes, you can!" I hold her hand. "We've all done it, and so can you. We've got to get to the hospital, now. Come on, Dee."

Her brow furrows, and she nods quickly. Raven has driven the car closer, and we help her into the passenger seat. Liv and I jump in the back fast, and Raven throws rocks getting out of the parking lot.

"We left Rachel!" Dylan cries.

"She has a car," Liv answers. "She'll meet us there. Now say it with me, Soften… Settle…"

"Relax," Dylan says, doing her best to breathe through the pain.

Raven and I exchange a glance. I don't know about this hypnobirthing, but Liv swears by it.

Another deep breath, and Dylan's face squeezes right as she yells over Raven's GPS.

Raven's eyes are panicked. "Where do I go?"

"I probably should've driven," Liv muses. "Take a right here."

Raven flies around the corner, and the hospital comes into view. "Oh, thank God… Almost there!"

"Nooo!" Dylan cries. "Why are they coming so fast?"

"Don't have that baby in the car!" Raven's eyes are wide, and she wheels into the parking lot, bouncing all of us over the curb.

I hold Dylan over the back of her seat, and we zoom into the circle drive in front of the emergency department doors.

A man steps forward to stop us. "Ma'am, you can't park in the ambulance drop-off…"

"I'm not parking!" Raven jumps out, running around to the passenger's side. "Help us!"

Dylan lets out another yell. "It's coming out!"

"Shit!" I'm out of the car, opening her door as fast as our other two friends join us. "Hold it in just a few more minutes!"

"I can't hold it in!"

A male nurse joins us with a wheelchair, and as soon as Dylan sits, he flies with her down the hall to the maternity wing.

"I'll take care of the paperwork!" Raven waves to us. "Y'all go!"

Logan bursts through the door as we're about to run. "Where is she?"

His expression is wild, and behind him are Garrett and Craig in hot pants and tank tops. They're also wearing blond wigs, bright pink lipstick, and mascara on their worried eyes.

Jack and Hendrix rush in next. "Zane's picking up Rachel, and Clint's on his way."

"We just got here." I reach out for Jack's hand, and he pulls me to him.

"You okay?" His brow is furrowed.

"We made it." I fall into his chest, laughing. "Holy shit, that was intense."

"Talk about intense," Garrett teases. "We were just about to give your fiancé the lap dance of his life."

"Remind me to thank my little sister later," Jack mutters in my ear.

"I'll thank her when I'm sure Clint isn't going to have a total meltdown."

"Don't worry, baby." Craig takes my hand as we walk down the long hall to maternity. "He's already making phone calls."

Three hours later, we're all cramped in the waiting area of

the maternity wing. Logan and Liv are in the birthing room; the rest of us are pacing, waiting for news.

Clint has his phone out, and he's been texting since he arrived. "I'm able to move everything to the afternoon, but is that what you want to do?"

My smile is more of a grimace, and I blink up at him. "We can't get married without Dylan."

He nods, looking down again. "The wedding is small enough that we can hold off for a few days. The caterer is working with us, and the florist has all the arrangements in the refrigerator. How long does this usually take?"

"I'm not sure." My hand is clasped in Jack's.

"It's going to be okay." His calm voice goes a long way toward soothing my nerves.

"He's here!" Liv walks into the room, smiling brightly. "The doctor couldn't believe how fast he came for a first-timer. Dylan was a pro. She pushed him out so fast, and they're both smiling and well!"

Garrett stands, putting his arm around his wife. "Will they let us back there?"

"She's already asking for her family."

We all start to move, and I catch Clint's arm. "Two days."

Chapter 34

Jack

Two days later

THE BAY IS SHROUDED IN A SMOOTH, GRAY MIST, AND I SIT ON MY swing alone, sipping coffee and watching the pelicans glide low over the water.

Kimmie spent the night at Allie's last night, and Austin is here with me.

My arms ache to hold my bride, but my stomach is tight with anticipation. Pulling out my phone, I send her a quick text.

I'm glad we planned a morning wedding. How long do we have to stay at the reception?

Wife: A few hours at least.

A few?

Wife: We should at least stay for two. Clint worked so hard, and everyone will be there.

Smiling at my phone, I tuck the device into my pocket and lean back to sip my coffee.

We decided to postpone our honeymoon trip until Austin leaves for college. My wife doesn't want to miss any time with her son, and I don't mind taking the pressure off.

Everyone has offered to help us with Kimmie, but I don't want my little peanut to feel like her life is changing or I've forgotten her—not that it seems possible.

Kimmie has never had a problem inserting herself into situations, especially when it concerns her family.

The door opens, and I hear shuffling in the kitchen. Austin digs in the refrigerator, taking out a neon-green Mountain Dew before walking out to the back porch.

"Nervous?" He squints an eye at me, and I grin.

His hair is a snarled mess on his head, and he's only wearing jogging pants. He's a big kid, right on the verge of being a man, but in this moment, he still seems like that middle schooler so determined to be on my team.

"Not a bit." I push to standing. "I'm ready to make you two official Bradfords."

He smiles, taking a sip of his drink. "Me too."

A breeze drifts from the water, and it's still early enough in June to be cool in the morning. I look over the crowd of people we know and love so well. Craig escorts Thomas and his wife to the row we've reserved for family.

He's followed by Edward walking Miss Gina. They repeat the process for Aunt Thelma and Liv's mom, and Gloria and Sandra sit behind them in reserved seats.

Buddy and the boys from the team are scattered throughout the crowd, and I even see Levi and a very pregnant Sadie sitting with her cousins Oliver and Salina.

After the Christmas blow-up, George moved back to Florida and Levi moved into our old family home with Logan and Dylan. Now that high school is over, he started working with Garrett, and the two of them have a little apartment outside of town.

Sadie's talking about getting her teaching degree online, and she has family here. Maybe they'll be okay.

A familiar classical song begins, and I turn my attention to my siblings, stepping out to walk down the aisle like we've done so many times in recent years.

The guys are all in gray suits, and the girls are in knee-length, ocean-blue dresses with different style tops, strapless, one-shoulder, or skinny straps.

Zane and Rachel are first, followed by Garrett and Liv. They part with a kiss in the middle before going to each side of the flowered arch.

Hendrix gives me a wink as he walks Raven down the aisle, and Logan holds Dylan's waist as she carries their newborn son on her chest, eliciting coos from the ladies sitting on the aisles.

Clint hangs back doing his best to guide Gina and Haddy as they make their way to the front, dropping petals for the bride. I frown when I don't see my daughter with them, wondering what might have happened.

Liv's mom helps Clint guide them to the side, and we almost lose Gina when she spots a lady walking a dog along the wide path leading to the park. A soft laugh ripples through the group, but we all grow serious when the music changes.

The bridal march begins, and everyone stands. I'm in the center of the aisle, so I can see when Austin steps from behind the last row of guests with his mother on his arm.

My throat tightens, and I fight to swallow when she steps out like a dream in sand-colored chiffon. Her hand is in the crook of Austin's arm, and Kimmie is at her side, holding her hand.

I place my palm over the ache in my stomach as my eyes drink in the sight of the three most important people in a crowd of very important people.

Allie's red lips break into a big, beautiful smile, despite the tears on her cheeks. I can't take my eyes off her face, her pretty brown hair swept up in a neat twist and those glasses perched on her nose.

It's only a few paces until we're together. Kimmie puts her little hand in mine, guiding it to Allie's, and I reach down to give her a squeeze. Rachel holds out a hand, and my daughter goes to stand by her aunt.

Pastor Rick from Thomas's church steps up to ask, "Who gives this woman to this man?"

"I do," Austin says with confidence, smiling at me.

Stepping forward, I pull him into a hug, doing my best to blink away the mist in my own eyes.

"Thanks, buddy," I whisper in his ear.

He nods, sniffing sharply and wiping a hand over his nose. He steps over beside Zane, who gives him a pat on the back.

Allie's hands are in mine, and her pretty blue eyes are clear and sparkling when she looks up at me. I want to cup her cheeks in my hands and kiss her, but I know we have to say our vows.

The pastor leads us through the traditional promises to love, honor, and protect as long as we both shall live, and it's like I'm hearing the words fresh, for the first time. I say them with all my heart.

When we're done, and it's time to exchange rings, I watch as she slides the gold band onto my third finger.

"With this ring, I thee wed." I love the sound of her voice, so clear and confident.

I hold her hand in mine, studying the delicate gold band as I slide it onto her finger. It fits perfectly beside my mother's engagement ring.

"You've woven yourself into my soul," I quietly speak, almost as if I'm telling her a secret. "I live to collect your sighs. It's finally time to come home, my love, my wife."

When I lift my eyes, hers are wide with surprise. "It was you!" She steps forward, grasping the front of my coat. "You wrote the poems."

Lifting my hand, I slide a tendril off her cheek. "I wrote them for you."

"You may now kiss the bride." The pastor leans in, grinning. "I figured I'd better say it before you did it without me."

We both huff a laugh, and I lean down to seal my lips over hers. I pull her lips, giving her the briefest taste for propriety. Then we turn to face the crowd as we're pronounced Mr. and Mrs. Jack Bradford.

The small group breaks into applause and cheers, and the music changes to the wedding march. Allie's hand is in my arm, and Kimmie skips over to hold Austin's hand as we lead the wedding party out.

Joy burns strong in my chest. It's an emotion I've gotten to know well in these last nine months. When we pass the last row, I pull Allie to the side, looking down into her beautiful face.

"This is the best day of my life." I slide my thumbs over her cheeks, smoothing the fresh tears away. "I don't remember a time I've been this happy."

"Oh, Jack." She blinks up at me, reaching for my cheeks.

"I've loved you for so long, I didn't think I could love you more. I was wrong."

I kiss her again, barely holding back from devouring her. When I lift my head, I see the heat in her eyes as well.

"One hour." I lead her to the waiting limo.

Cooters & Shooters is closed for our wedding reception, but with all the people wc know, it might as well be open.

Craig is playing his usual mix of songs, and everyone is dancing and drinking champagne. Clint arranged for a buffet-style catered lunch, but I'm not hungry.

Allie is in my arms, and all I want to do is take her away, strip that gown off her body, and cover her in kisses. Her hands are on my shoulders, and she gazes up at me in a way that makes me feel like the only man on Earth.

The song ends, and we drift over to where my siblings are gathered around Dylan and the baby. Rachel is at her shoulder, tracing her finger along his dark hairline.

"The doctor said you set a record for first-timers—thirty-five minutes!" Liv is wrapped in Garrett's arms.

Dylan looks up from where she hasn't stopped gazing at her tiny son. "I confess, I was sneaking hot peppers all day before the bachelorette."

"She smoked him out." Logan stands over both of them, gazing down like he won the Big Game all over again.

"I just can't believe you named him after *Top Gun*," Garrett groans.

"I like it!" Raven pushes back. "Maverick Murphy sounds like a star!"

"A legendary wide receiver." Logan lifts his chin, grinning proudly.

"A legendary golfer!" Dylan corrects him.

Austin and Edward walk up to where we're standing, and I notice Kimmie following them. Her arms are crossed, and a pouty expression is on her face.

"You won the poetry contest by a long shot." Edward frowns, looking up at me. "Why didn't you claim them? It's unexpected, like William Carlos Williams."

"My brother, the poet." Garrett stands, looping an arm around my shoulders. "Who knew?"

I shrug. "I just started playing around with words when I was alone, after I put Kimmie to bed."

"That's so sweet." Dylan tilts her head, smiling up at me. "It's a little sad, but I love it."

"I love them so much." Allie slides her hand into my arm.

I look into her pretty face. "They were dreams of you."

"Damn, Jack." Liv laughs, pushing my arm. "Who knew you were such a romantic?"

"Speaking of dreams…" Garrett's voice has an edge. "Here comes a nightmare."

I look over my shoulder to see what he's frowning at, and at the sight of the woman standing in the doorway, the tone of the group changes.

Zane steps up beside me, his voice low. "What the hell is she doing here?"

"What's happening?" Dylan looks around. "Oh."

"What the fuck, Danielle?" Hendrix is the first to speak, and I don't even scold him for swearing.

Raven pulls his arm, but it's basically what we're all thinking.

Allie's fingers tighten on my arm, and I cover her hand with mine, giving her a reassuring squeeze. This woman doesn't bother me.

"Danielle?" I walk over to where she's standing. "What are you doing here?"

"Jack…" She blinks rapidly, seeming nervous.

Her blonde hair is big and wavy, and she's wearing light-blue jeans and a matching denim vest over a long-sleeved, white shirt.

"We were just passing through town, and I couldn't believe it." She looks up and around the space. "The famous Cooters & Shooters. I had to stop the bus."

"Okay." I'm not convinced, but I'll accept her explanation.

"Sorry, it looks like I caught you at a bad time." She gives me a wink.

My lip curls.

I feel absolutely nothing at all toward this woman—other than wishing she'd get back in her tour bus and keep driving.

"Actually, you caught me at a very good time." I straighten. "You caught me at the best time of my life, not counting the day Kimmie was born."

My daughter chooses this particular moment to march up to me. I assume whatever she was pouting about has finally boiled over.

"Daddy…" She grabs my hand in both of hers. "You have to stop being married to Miss Allie right now."

Danielle's eyes flicker to the seven-year-old spitfire with the bouncing brunette curls. "Is this?"

I take a knee beside my little girl. "What's wrong, baby?"

"Edward says I can't marry Austin anymore because you married Miss Allie." Her face is scrunched up like she might cry. "But I have to marry Aussie! He's my handsome prince, and he makes me pancakes on Friday because it's T-G-I-F!"

I've been ignoring her crush on Allie's son for obvious reasons—she's seven, and I figured she'd eventually outgrow it. "Kimmie, Austin's about to leave for college."

"So?" Her voice goes high.

Danielle smiles as she watches us, and I wonder if she ever regrets giving up all her rights to this perfect little miracle she somehow helped me create.

I wonder if she realizes what she walked away from without even looking back.

Her loss.

"It's okay, little lady." As if she possesses some maternal

instinct, she leans down to put her fingers lightly on Kimmie's shoulder.

"No, it's not," Kimmie snaps. "I love Aussie. He takes care of me, and he's the best quarterback like my daddy, and I'm going to marry him."

Danielle nods like she knows anything. "Take it from me, there are plenty of fish in the sea. Don't fall for the first one to make you breakfast."

I'm about to say something when Kimmie crosses her arms, frowning up at Danielle.

"Who are you?" she demands.

"I'm ahh…" Danielle's eyes flicker to mine briefly. "I'm a friend of your dad's."

"I know all my daddy's friends."

"Okay…" Danielle nods. "You're very pretty."

Kimmie's eyes narrow, and she's a handful. She's also smart as a whip. "Thank you."

Allie walks up at this point, reaching for Kimmie's hand. "Come on, baby." My wife's voice is a soothing balm to my insides. "We can talk about it, okay?"

Kimmie's little lips pout, and she shakes her head. "It's not okay, Miss Allie."

"I know," Allie concedes. "I'm going to miss him, too."

"Is this the new wife?" Danielle smiles, holding out her hand.

"Yes, I am." Allie lifts her chin, looking straight into my ex's eyes and ignoring her hand.

"Congratulations. You've got a good man here."

I'm not sure where this is coming from, but Allie's tone is sharp.

"Yes, I do. He's the *best* man. He's an incredible dad, and… well, he's pretty incredible in *every* way, if you know what I mean."

Danielle's brows rise, and I can't help a smug grin.

"Speaking of every way…" She turns to me, lowering her voice. "I ah, I wanted to apologize. I said some things when we were together, and well… I'm sorry. I was harsh and ignorant, and I guess… I'm just saying, I'm more open now."

My eyes narrow. "That door is closed."

She blinks up at me as if she'll say more, but Allie steps between us, adding, "And locked. Now you'd better get going."

Danielle exhales a laugh, looking down. "Well, anyway, I apologize." Looking over at my daughter, she smiles. "Kimmie, good luck with Austin, and Jack, I'll be seeing you."

"No, you won't." Allie takes a step closer. "You're all done here, understand?"

Reaching out, I catch my feisty wife's wrist. "Have a nice life, Danielle. I hope you find whatever it is you're looking for."

She lifts her chin. "You, too."

"I have." My tone is final.

She holds up both hands. "Okay, then. That's all I wanted to say."

She nods at my siblings, who are all giving varying degrees of death glares. Turning on her booted heel, she struts to the doors and out of our lives forever.

"Damn, Allie!" Raven cries when the doors close. "Remind me never to get on your bad side."

Allie holds my arm, grinning at her friends. Kimmie is still at her side pouting, and Dylan holds out a hand.

"Come here, KJ." Kimmie marches over to my sister, who puts a hand on her waist. "Daddy and Miss Allie need a little not-so-quiet time tonight…" I cut her a look, and she continues, grinning up at me from where she's nursing her baby boy. "You're going to stay with Uncle Logan and me, and we're going to talk about this Austin situation, okay?"

Kimmie nods forcefully, and Allie mouths a *Thank you* to her. Dylan waves her away, mouthing back *I got this.* Considering my little sister has been Kimmie's backup mom since I came back to Newhope carrying a six-month-old, I trust her.

I pull Allie to my chest. "Is it honeymoon time yet?"

Her lips press into a smile, and she tilts her head. "We've got to cut the cake."

My head falls back with a groan, which makes her laugh. I actually feel surprisingly lighter myself. Danielle's unexpected appearance has left me feeling intensely grateful I got out of that situation without any lingering ties.

Walking over to my daughter, I lift her off her feet, giving her a firm hug. "I love you, Peanut."

She relents, putting her arms around my neck. "I love you, Daddy."

"I love you, too." Allie puts her hand on my little girl's back.

Kimmie's head pops up, and she reaches for Allie. "I love you, too, Miss Allie. You make Daddy smile."

"Oh… okay?" Allie blinks fast, and I can tell she's fighting tears.

She puts my daughter on her feet, and I hold her hand. I'm so ready to sneak out, but Clint is some kind of psychic mindreader. He holds up a large knife with a chiffon ribbon around the handle.

"Cake!" Kimmie jumps up and down. "I want cake!"

She takes off at top speed to where Craig's boyfriend is waiting, and I put my arm around my wife. "After cake."

The orgasm twists tighter in my stomach, and a bead of sweat slides down my cheek as I fight the urge to come. Allie is on my lap, her back to my chest. A red satin blindfold covers her eyes, and her wrists are bound with a matching satin bow behind her back.

It forces her back to arch, and her sexy tits bounce as she rides my cock faster. She's so fucking hot. Her juicy apple scent is driving me wild.

Her nipples are little points, deep red from the time I spent sucking them. Salt is on my tongue from all the places I've licked, bit, and kissed her, and she emits moans and whimpers with every rock of her hips.

"You're so fucking sexy," I groan, and her breath comes in trembling gasps. "Take my cock, my beautiful wife."

My hand goes between her thighs, and I hold the bullet vibrator to her clit once more.

With a scream, she erupts into sensual shudders, gasping and jerking on my lap, her pussy pulling my erection. I release with a groan, letting her pull me over the edge with her as she goes.

Closing my eyes, I ride out the tidal wave of pleasure, shooting through my body with every pulse.

Allie's trembling, leaning forward, and I slip the satin off her wrists. I reach up to take the blindfold off her eyes, then I wrap her in my arms, easing us down into the soft linen sheets.

Hours later, we're sexy and sated. I'm holding my wife in my arms and we're sharing a glass of champagne from the oversized gift basket that was waiting in the refrigerator when we arrived.

"Maybe we could go skinny-dipping after while." Allie taps my glass with hers. "Miss Gina's pool is heated."

"I'd rather go skinny-fucking." I take a sip of wine, and she snorts a laugh, putting her hand over her nose.

It makes me smile. Everything she does is adorable.

"You almost made me spit-take."

"Just being honest."

She scoots around to lean her back into my side, and I slide my hand over her waist and stomach, wondering how she'd feel about having another baby with me.

"You never told me Danielle was a famous country singer."

My brow lowers, and I set my glass to the side. "I didn't know."

"How did you feel about seeing her?" She turns her head, glancing up at me.

I press my lips to her head, inhaling green apple. "I felt like the luckiest man in the world."

That makes her laugh softly, and my chest expands with warmth. I take her glass and put it on the nightstand, turning her to face me.

"I *am* the luckiest man in the world." Our eyes meet, and she blinks up at me. "I have my daughter, my family, a job I love… And now I have you."

Her full lips spread into a happy smile, and she reaches up to trace her finger along my jaw. "I love you, husband."

"I love you, my dirty little wife." She lifts her chin with a laugh, and I bend down to kiss her neck. "My sexy librarian…" Another kiss. "My beautiful lady…" Lifting my head, I catch her eyes again. "The mother of my baby?"

Her eyes light, and she grins adorably. "You never know what the future holds."

"Perhaps another Bradford?"

"Tell me a poem."

Epilogue

Allie

Two years later

"Say hey to your big brother, Knoxey!" I hold my six week old son in my lap, positioning him to see Austin on the iPad.

"Hey, little Knox!" Austin waves at the screen. "You're a big boy today!"

His dark-haired baby brother wobbles his head and blows bubbles at the screen. Kimmie walks through, and I nod at her.

"Want to say hey to Austin?"

"Oh, hey, Austin." She waves briefly before lowering to her knees to hold her little brother's finger and kiss his teeny nose.

Austin grins. "Hey, Peanut."

She doesn't respond, and my eyebrow arches. I'm not sure what Dylan told her after the wedding, but she hasn't said a word about marrying Austin or Jack and me ever since.

It's like the matter is closed—even if we never miss a Tennessee game, and we all have orange Number 17 jerseys.

"My dream team is Texas." My son resumes our conversation

about his post-graduate plans. "They've shown the most interest, and Jack knows everybody there."

"I like it." I smile warmly at my son, who's quickly turning into a man. "It's not as far as some of the offers you've told me about."

"It's no Buffalo," he groans. "I don't think I could deal with that level of cold. It was bad enough when we played in Minnesota for that exhibition game."

"It's nothing like we're used to down here."

"You can say that again."

Knox starts to fuss, and I lift him onto my shoulder. "I'd better go. I miss you, honey."

"Love you, Mom."

We disconnect, and I shift my little boy around under my shirt to give him lunch. Leaning back in the swing, I look out at the water rippling on the shore.

An autumn breeze blows through the screens, and I look down at the leather-bound notebook I bought for my husband to record his thoughts, his short poems.

They're so beautiful, and at times my heart aches at his words about his father, his parents, his family's loss.

Then he'll follow up with his love for me, his siblings, his daughter, his new son…

Light, hope, life, and all the dreams I ever had.

Bound in this little fist, this beautiful hand, this home.

"Can I hold Knoxey now?" Kimmie sits on the swing beside me, and I lift her little brother onto her shoulder.

"He just had lunch, so he needs to burp. Remember how I showed you?" She smiles, nodding, and it's hard to believe she's already nine.

She was so little for so long, a bossy, hilarious mini-Dylan. Now she's approaching double digits, she's quieter, and occasionally, I'll see her and her best friend Maggie looking at pictures of boys playing football on her aunt's iPad.

Maverick is in his terrible twos, and he shows zero interest in golf, no matter how many sets of toy clubs Dylan buys him. He doesn't seem much interested in football either, for that matter, so who knows. Maybe he'll surprise us all.

Gina and Haddy start kindergarten next year, which blows my mind, and Edward will be a senior in high school.

He's also the starting kicker for the Captains, and Jack said with his talent and consistency, he'll probably get offers from several schools.

Rachel starts to cry every time she talks about it, but Zane only laughs and pulls her in for a hug. She's also pregnant with their first baby. She said she wanted to wait until Edward was settled to start another family, and he's almost there.

I think about our little brood as Kimmie and I swing slowly. Then Knox lets out a burp so loud, we both exchange wide-eyed looks… then we burst out laughing.

"Good grief, Knoxey!" I pat his little back. "How much air did you swallow?"

"He really enjoyed his lunch." Kimmie stands, holding her little brother, and I smile as I watch her carry him into the house.

She's at the perfect age for a baby sibling. Everything he does is infinitely fascinating to her—except poopy diapers, which she commiserates about with Uncle Hen.

Jack meets her at the door, leaning down to kiss his baby boy's head and muss his daughter's hair, which makes her squeal. I rest my head on my hand, blinking up at him.

When my husband's pretty blue eyes land on mine, he smiles. "Feeling sentimental?"

He sits beside me, and I scoot closer to him, loving his strong arms that surround me.

"I was thinking about second chances."

"How so?"

"For so long I felt like a failure because Austin didn't have a good dad. I felt like it was my fault." Jack's brow lowers, and I lift my hand to touch his lips. "Then you came into my life and changed everything. Now I have a second chance with Knox."

His lips poke out to kiss my fingers, and he takes my hand in his. "You're not a failure. You're brave and strong, and when things went wrong, you didn't just fix them, you made them better. You make everything better."

Shaking my head, I huff a laugh. "I don't know about that."

"You saved poetry." He taps his book in my hands. "You saved Dare Night by making it a game. You saved Austin by bringing him here… And you saved me from a lonely life."

I smile up at him. "I was always attracted to bad boys, but you're so patient and good with the kids. You take care of everyone. I'm finally making good choices, choosing a nice man."

"I'm not nice." His eyebrow arches, and heat surges in my core.

Reaching up, I pull his face to mine. "You're a bad boy in the best way. You won me the first day I saw you."

"You won me with that first Mediterranean omelette."

I can't stop a laugh. "They say it's the way to a man's heart."

"You've always had my heart." His hand slides over my cheek, and he covers my lips with a devouring, toe-curling, blister of a kiss.

It's a win I wouldn't have any other way.

Thank you for reading *The Way We Win*!
Be sure to download your **Free Bonus Scene** HERE.

And get ready for the New Bradfords series,
kicking off with *Pinch*…

Hayden "Haddy" Bradford is not falling for Gavin Knight, hockey star and her cousin Maverick's best friend. She's known his arrogant ass since he jilted her best friend in college, and she won't be swayed by his player good looks or the fact he caught her when she fell off the team's parade float (*She was not buzzed on her aunt's purple drink!*).

It's a spicy, funny, enemies to lovers, second-chance romance available in ebook, paperback, and on audio!

Keep turning for a short preview…

Learn about all of my books at TiaLouise.com/Books!

Pinch

Chapter 1

Haddy

"Who says you can't be a beauty queen *and* a scientist?" My best friend, roommate, and cousin Gigi Bradford slides the clippers over the curly coat of a tall goldendoodle secured in a large, empty tub.

As soon as the envelope appeared in our mailbox, I snatched it and ran to her small grooming studio in our converted she-shed behind the house.

I didn't want to open it alone, which is silly. It's just a check in an amount that will cover my entire tuition, room, and board for my next semester of graduate school. Still, my fingers tremble as I carefully rip open the large envelope.

A letter with gold embossed "Congratulations" across the top is the first thing to greet me. Then a check printed on green paper slips into my lap.

"It's kind of… embarrassing." My voice lowers as I recall Dr. Warwick's expression when I told him why I wouldn't be returning as his graduate assistant in the fall.

"Why are you embarrassed?" I watch the shiny, ginger

dog-curls fall to the floor of the tub as Gigi continues. "It's simple genetics."

"Don't say it…"

"You're just like your mother."

"You said it." I fall back against the porcelain-tiled countertop.

My cousin pauses, cutting her green eyes at me. "Stop being a drama queen. Your mom is a meteorologist, which is why you love atmospheric science, and your grandmother was Miss Georgia World. You're a natural for the International Princess Scholarship Woman. It's in your blood."

"So you're saying I'm well-bred?"

"Yes, you are… yes, you are…" Gina puckers her lips as she rubs both hands on the happy Goldendoodle's face. "Those silly scientists should understand. It's in your DNA."

She's talking baby-talk to a dog, and I should accept that as a dog breeder, groomer, trainer, even a judge at championship dog shows, it's exactly how she views the world.

I have a pedigree. My family wins pageants—which also have ridiculous names.

"It's dumb." I frown at the large check. "For a program that awards millions in scholarships every year, I don't understand why they have to have the word *princess* in the title. It's demeaning. They should just call it International Scholarship Woman."

"But they give you a crown?" She tilts her head, glancing up at me.

"Yes."

"And you wear it at events along with an evening gown and a sash."

I exhale a heavy sigh. I can't argue. They're the commitments that come with the title.

"Some women like to be princesses." Gina straightens, picking up a pair of sharp scissors.

"My professors are so confused." I fold the check and slip it into my pocket. It's too big for mobile deposit, so I'll have to make a special trip to the bank. "Calling me a princess only makes it weird."

Gigi pushes a lock of strawberry blonde hair behind her ear and leans closer to trim the dog's whiskers. "Your dad is the one who should be confused. He has plenty of money to cover all your bills. You don't have to keep doing this."

"No." I shake my head determinedly. "I have to pay my own way. If I keep taking money from them, I'll always be a nepo-baby. No one will ever take me seriously."

Gigi cuts her green eyes at me. "I'm pretty sure your mom married Uncle Hen because of that independent streak. She understands you better than you think."

My lips twist and I look at the woman smiling back at me from the cover of the pageant brochure. Unlike my sleek, straight dark hair, hers is wavy and blonde. It's perfectly coiffed, and she's wearing a white, strapless dress with a red and white striped sash that reads *International Princess Woman*.

"Whatever." I shake it all away. "Winning this means I'll be able to finish my labs without having to worry about money. I'll happily pivot, hold, and wave all day for that privilege."

"And ride on the *Welcome Back* float in the parade tomorrow." The screen door slams as our cousin and third roommate Maverick Murphy enters the room. "We're rolling out at 10 a.m. sharp."

Gigi puts the scissors aside and unhooks the dog's leash. "We're just happy to be your ladies in waiting. Aren't we, Haze?"

"Somebody named a dog *Haze*?" Mav's dark brows furrow. "He's not even purple."

"*Her* name is Some Like it Hot Hazel, but I call her Haze for short."

"What the fuck?" Mav goes to the cabinet and opens the door, digging around. "What dog is going to come to *Some Like it Hot Hazel*? Here, Some Like it Hot Hazel!" He pretends to call the dog, who doesn't even move. "Dog breeders are weird."

"What are you looking for in my supplies?" Gigi lifts the large dog out of the grooming pen.

"I need to borrow your good tweezers." He takes out the stainless-steel implements. "I've got something stuck in my blade."

"Maverick, no." Gigi reaches over his shoulder in an attempt to grab the tool. "I can't afford to have you break those. They cost two hundred dollars!"

"I can afford to replace them." He dodges her arms.

Gigi is five-eight like me, but Mav is six-two and wiley. I shake my head at them wrestling like we used to do as kids as I head for the door.

"I've got to finish grading papers. See y'all in the morning."

"Wave pretty," Maverick calls after me, and I wave my middle finger over my head. "Isn't she classy? I'm so proud."

Mav recently moved to the West Coast to join the LA Champions hockey team, much to his mother's chagrin. After years of doing her best to guide him into the "safe sport" of golf our aunt literally cried when her only boy turned into the best hockey player in the southern region.

He was heavily recruited all over the country and only chose LA because we're here.

Gigi and I share an adorable two-story bungalow with four bedrooms and two bathrooms in the best part of Los Feliz. We weren't looking for a roommate, but with the cost of everything these days, we were glad to have another person to split expenses.

He was more than happy to move in with us, especially since we all basically grew up like siblings. Say what he wants, Mav's a total family guy.

"I'll bring the purple drink!" Gigi shouts after me, and I snort a laugh.

Purple drink is a New Orleans concoction made of purple Kool-Aid and everclear. It's been in our family for special occasions since before we were born, so of course, we ran off with the recipe as soon as we turned twenty-one.

"Purple drink before ten in the morning?" I turn, pushing the door open with my back.

"Our mammas raised us right!" she replies.

If we're going to have a purple drink Saturday, I definitely have to lock up in my bedroom tonight. I'll possibly be out for two days, and these finals won't grade themselves.

"Why is it so cold?" I'm standing at the back of the line of cars with Maverick's coat around my shoulders. "September is supposed to be one of the best times to visit LA!"

"Talk to your mom," Gina quips.

"She'll just blame global warming."

Maverick shoves a red Solo cup into my hand. "Drink more purple drink. It'll warm you up."

"Hold it a second." I smooth my dark hair behind before placing the crown on my head. "Help me pin this, Geeg."

"Hold Haze's leash." She passes the sparkling strap to me before taking the hair pins.

Under Mav's bright purple coat I'm wearing a sequined white dress with black accents to match the Champions' jerseys. My *International Princess Woman* sash is in place, and a helper is holding an oversized bouquet of white and black roses for me to hold.

"Where do you get black roses?" Gina squints at the bouquet. "Will you be able to hold those and the safety bar?"

"Of course." I take the Solo cup from Mav. "This isn't my first rodeo."

Or pageant parade.

"Hurry up—it's almost time." He nods at my cup.

I take a big gulp, pulling my chin back as I swallow. "How

much everclear did you put in this, Gigi? You're not supposed to taste it."

"Maverick made it. I had a doggy emergency last night."

My shoulders drop, and my blue eyes meet Mav's. He gives me a maniacal grin as he nods, sticking out his tongue. "Extra strength, baby!"

He takes another big gulp, and my stomach drops.

I'm about to fuss at him about how as a representative of the International Princess Woman Scholarship Program, I can't be drunk on a float, when a lady on a bull horn announces all riders take their place.

I'm already feeling the effects of too much grain alcohol when I take my first step up the short flight of stairs to the platform that will carry us through the crowd of fans lining the streets.

"Why didn't you warn me?" I hiss as I stow Mav's jacket behind the decorated podium I'll hold as I wave. "What's a doggy emergency anyway?"

Gigi arranges my skirt then positions Hazel and her own show dog, a white standard Poodle she calls Spanky—short for Spank My Bottom.

"One of the breeders had a breakdown… it might have been related to her messy divorce." Gigi makes a worried face. "We're fostering a dog for the next few weeks."

Before I can argue that *we said no more fostering dogs*, the attendant shoves the massive bouquet of roses in my arms.

"Hold these over your shoulder…" He proceeds to push my hair behind my back. "Then hold this strap around your wrist."

"I need something sturdier than a strap." I'm still speaking as the guy walks to the edge and hops off the float. "Wait—I'm in three-inch heels!"

Not to mention I've had two cups of extra-strength purple drink.

The guy doesn't look back as he mixes in with the rest of the organizers preparing to roll.

Gigi steps closer. "Grab my arm if you get wobbly."

"And throw these flowers everywhere. They're heavy!" For a reason called *purple drink* and the lingering, horrifying memory of dog vomit from our last foster pet, I want to sit down right here and cross my arms. "Who is this foster dog, anyway?"

"Oh, she's the cutest little thing!" Gigi's eyes take on a dreamy light. "She's a little teacup poodle named Princess Petunia. You'll love her. She's practically made to be your pet!"

"I don't need a pet." Again, *purple drink*. "Where is she?"

"She's at the house." Gigi's eyes narrow. "Are you okay? You're swaying and we haven't started moving yet."

She's right. I didn't eat breakfast, and it feels like the float is already rolling.

"Hey, ladies…" Maverick waves at us from where he stands at the side of the float. "I want y'all to meet my new teammate. He's going to be staying at the house a few days while he finds his own place."

"Maverick!" Gigi's voice is loud and cross. "We didn't discuss this!"

"You're one to talk." I'm still cross. "Worried Miss Priss Petunia will have to give up her bed?"

Our cousin waves at a big guy with shaggy, golden-brown hair, then he holds out a red Solo cup as the new guy hustles up to give him a bro-hug.

"That's my man!" Maverick is still yelling, pointing at the guy whose back is turned.

The lady is on the bullhorn again, telling us all to take our places. Shaking the buzz away, I roll my shoulders back as I adjust my posture. The float takes a sharp lurch forward, and I wobble on my heels, jerking hard on the strap.

"Whoa…" It's a low yell, and Gina grabs my hand.

"Are you okay?"

"Yo, Queenie! Princess!" Mav is still yelling, and now his arm is looped around the new teammate's shoulders. "I present to you the famous Gavin Knight!"

The tall fellow lifts his square chin. Hazel eyes blink up to mine, and when they clash, cold water surges through my bloodstream. It's quickly followed by fire.

He's standing there, all six-foot-three, broad shoulders, rounded biceps, square jaw with that dimple right in the middle of his cheek. Full lips part over straight white teeth, and my stomach dips.

I'm frozen as my mind tumbles back over college in North Carolina, Chapel Hill, my roommate Karen crying her eyes out on the sofa because the man she loved, the man she left her small-town Georgia home to follow to college was sleeping with every girl in the Tri-Delta sorority house.

I don't know when he changed his name to Gavin, but *Lane Knight* is the most notorious playboy I've ever met. He has the body of a god and the heart of a villain.

"No!" My voice is sharp, and I release the strap, taking a step in the direction of my cousin.

I guess purple drink makes me think I'm going to do something to stop this right here in the middle of a parade in my dress, crown, and full pageant regalia.

"Not Lane Knight!" The float starts to move, and the words morph into a scream as white and black roses fly into the air.

Spanky lunges forward, dragging Gina with him, as if he'll rescue me from falling.

Nothing is going to stop me as I fly through the air—nothing except the rock-hard chest of the world's biggest asshole, who I vowed to my college roommate I'd never speak to again.

With an *oof!* I land, Cinderella-style in his arms.

He has the nerve to catch me.

"Well hello, Hayden." The man I knew as Lane dips his chin, grinning down at me like the player he is. "Nice of you to drop in. I hear we're going to be roommates."

Pinch is available in print, ebook, and audiobook.

Books by
TIA LOUISE

ROMANCE IN KINDLE UNLIMITED

THE NEW BRADFORDS
*Pinch, 2024**
*Cage, 2025**
*Flow, 2025**
*Zone, 2025**
*Caught, 2025**
(*Available in Audiobook.)

THE BRADFORD BOYS
*The Way We Touch, 2024**
*The Way We Play, 2024**
*The Way We Score, 2025**
*The Way We Collide, 2025**
*The Way We Win, 2025**
(*Available on Audiobook.)

THE BE STILL SERIES
*A Little Taste, 2023**
*A Little Twist, 2023**
*A Little Luck, 2023**
*A Little Naughty, 2024**
(*Available on Audiobook.)

THE HAMILTOWN HEAT SERIES
*Fearless, 2022**
*Filthy, 2022**
For Your Eyes Only, 2022
*Forbidden, 2023**
(*Available on Audiobook.)

THE TAKING CHANCES SERIES
*This Much is True**
*Twist of Fate**
*Trouble**
(*Available on Audiobook.)

FIGHT FOR LOVE SERIES
*Wait for Me**
*Boss of Me**
*Here with Me**
*Reckless Kiss**
(*Available on Audiobook.)

BELIEVE IN LOVE SERIES
Make You Mine
*Make Me Yours**
*Stay**
(*Available on Audiobook.)

SOUTHERN HEAT SERIES
When We Touch
When We Kiss

THE ONE TO HOLD SERIES

One to Hold (#1 - Derek & Melissa)★

One to Keep (#2 - Patrick & Elaine)★

One to Protect (#3 - Derek & Melissa)★

One to Love (#4 - Kenny & Slayde)

One to Leave (#5 - Stuart & Mariska)

One to Save (#6 - Derek & Melissa)★

One to Chase (#7 - Marcus & Amy)★

One to Take (#8 - Stuart & Mariska)

(*Available on Audiobook.)

THE DIRTY PLAYERS SERIES

PRINCE (#1)★

PLAYER (#2)★

DEALER (#3)

THIEF (#4)

(*Available on Audiobook.)

THE BRIGHT LIGHTS SERIES

Under the Lights (#1)

Under the Stars (#2)

Hit Girl (#3)

COLLABORATIONS

The Last Guy★

The Right Stud

Tangled Up

Save Me

(*Available on Audiobook.)

PARANORMAL ROMANCES

One Immortal (vampires)

One Insatiable (shifters)

GET THREE FREE STORIES!
Sign up for my New Release newsletter and never miss a sale
or new release by me!
Sign up now!

Acknowledgments

Ending a series is always so emotional. So many of you have been with me since the first book, The Way We Touch, came out in June 2024. Now, writing The End on Jack & Allie's story a year later, I have so many people to thank…

Always, always massive thanks to my husband "Mr. TL" for all the things he does, from encouragement to brainstorming to reading the first draft to support when I'm doubting everything… I love you!

My amazing PA Kat is never allowed to leave me ever… even if she's my daughter and she claims to want to go to graduate school. She'll have to do it while working for me.

The team who produces my covers and all the fun supporting art, illustrator Laura Moore (@LCMdesignss) and Kari March (cover design); Wander Aguiar (model photographer) and Lori Jackson (cover design). You always make my vision come to life, and I love you all!

Jen DeJong is my rock, cheering me on as I write, Leticia Teixeira is my guide when I'm stuck and my eyes when I miss things, and a BIG welcome and HUGE thanks to Patti Rapozo for being my football pro!

Huge thanks to my *incredible* betas, Maria Black, Corinne Akers, Amy Reierson, Courtney Anderson, Jennifer Christy, Heather Heaton, Michelle Mastandrea, and Diane Holtrey. I ADORE you!

Thanks to Jaime Ryter for your eagle-eyed edits and to the super talented Stacey Blake for making my paperbacks gorgeous.

Thanks to my dear Starfish, to my Mermaids, and to my Veeps for keeping me sane and organized and helping me spread the word and all the incredible BookTokers, Bookstagrammers, and book lovers, who I've come to think of as friends.

Last but not least, to my readers everywhere—**thank you** for allowing me do what I do.

Always winning,

❤*Tia*

About the Author

Tia Louise is the *USA Today* and #4 Amazon bestselling author of (*primarily*) small-town, single-parent, second-chance, and military romances set at or near the beach.

From Readers' Choice awards, to *USA Today* "Happily Ever After" nods, to winning Favorite Erotica Author and the "Lady Boner Award" (*lol!*), nothing makes her happier than communicating with fellow Mermaids (*fans*) and creating romances that are smart, sassy, and *very sexy*.

A former journalist and displaced beach bum, Louise lives in the Midwest with her trophy husband, two young-adult geniuses, and one clumsy "grand-cat."

Sign up for her newsletter and never miss a new release or sale—and get a free story collection!

Signed Copies of all books online at:
https://geni.us/SignedPBs

Connect with Tia:
TiaLouise.com
Instagram—@AuthorTLouise
TikTok—@TheTiaLouise

www.ingramcontent.com/pod-product-compliance
Lightning Source LLC
Chambersburg PA
CBHW021017310726
48969CB00006B/1438